Resounding Praise for *New*

DENNIS LEHANE and

SACRED

"... ...e whodunit ghetto as a
... ...lent. . . . When it comes
... ...ere he wants them, Mr.
Lehane offers a bravura demonstration of how it's done."
New York Times

"[With] *Darkness, Take My Hand*, Dennis Lehane proved
that he was second to none as a crime novelist. *Sacred*
further burnishes his reputation. . . . Pitch-perfect dia-
logue, arresting characters and splendid writing."
Orlando Sentinel

"Dennis Lehane is one of the strongest voices in contem-
porary detective fiction."
Seattle Times

"The heir apparent to Robert Parker in Boston detective
fiction. . . . *Sacred*, the third [Kenzie and Gennaro] adven-
ture, is as witty and evil as the previous two. . . . Gripping;
it'll keep you reading."
Dallas Morning News

"Lehane [has an] uncanny knack for getting inside his
characters' heads and hearts in a way that few storytellers
can."
Denver Rocky Mountain News

"Dennis Lehane is the heir apparent. You read his stuff
and think he's got the great ones—Chandler, MacDon-
ald, Parker—watching over hi...
But his voice is an original."
Michael Co...

SACRED

Also by Dennis Lehane

A Drink Before the War
Darkness, Take My Hand
Gone, Baby, Gone
Prayers for Rain
Mystic River
Shutter Island
Coronado: Stories
The Given Day
Moonlight Mile
Live by Night
The Drop
World Gone By
Since We Fell

DENNIS LEHANE

SACRED

WILLIAM MORROW
An Imprint of HarperCollins*Publishers*

SACRED. Copyright © 1997 by Dennis Lehane. All rights reserved. Printed in the United States of America. No part of this book may be used or reproduced in any manner whatsoever without written permission except in the case of brief quotations embodied in critical articles and reviews. For information address HarperCollins Publishers, 195 Broadway, New York, NY 10007.

HarperCollins books may be purchased for educational, business, or sales promotional use. For information please email the Special Markets Department at SPsales@harpercollins.com.

First Avon Books paperback printing: June 1998
First HarperTorch paperback printing: December 2000
First Harper paperback printing: May 2008
First Harper premium paperback printing: August 2010
First William Morrow paperback printing: May 2013
Second William Morrow paperback printing: August 2021

Library of Congress Cataloging-in-Publication Data has been applied for.

ISBN 978-0-06-308377-6

21 22 23 24 25   ov/LSC   10 9 8 7 6 5 4 3 2 1

For Sheila

ACKNOWLEDGMENTS

My deepest gratitude to Claire Wachtel and Ann Rittenberg for finding the book within the manuscript, and not letting up on me until I found it, too.

What little I know about field-stripping a semiautomatic handgun, I learned from Jack and Gary Schmock of Jack's Guns and Ammo in Quincy, Massachusetts.

What I couldn't remember about the St. Pete/Tampa area, the Sunshine Skyway Bridge, and specific points of Florida law was filled in by Mal and Dawn Ellenburg. Any remaining mistakes are mine.

And thanks, as always, to those who read the early versions and gave me honest feedback: Chris, Gerry, Sheila, Reva Mae, and Sterling.

Do not give dogs what is sacred;
do not throw your pearls to pigs.
If you do, they may trample them underfoot,
and then turn and tear you to pieces.

—MATTHEW 7:6

PART ONE

GRIEF RELEASE

1

A piece of advice: If you ever follow someone in my neighborhood, don't wear pink.

The first day Angie and I picked up the little round guy on our tail, he wore a pink shirt under a gray suit and a black topcoat. The suit was double-breasted, Italian, and too nice for my part of town by several hundred dollars. The topcoat was cashmere. People in my neighborhood could afford cashmere, I suppose, but usually they spend so much on the duct tape that keeps their tail pipes attached to their '82 Chevys, that they don't have much left over for anything but that trip to Aruba.

The second day, the little round guy replaced the pink shirt with a more subdued white, lost the cashmere and the Italian suit, but still stuck out like Michael Jackson in a day care center by wearing a hat. Nobody in my neighborhood—or any of Boston's inner-city neighborhoods that I know of—wears anything on their head but a baseball cap or the occasional tweed Scally. And our friend, the Weeble, as we'd come to call him, wore a bowler.

3

A fine-looking bowler, don't get me wrong, but a bowler just the same.

"He could be an alien," Angie said.

I looked out the window of the Avenue Coffee Shop. The Weeble's head jerked and then he bent to fiddle with his shoelaces.

"An alien," I said. "From where exactly? France?"

She frowned at me and lathered cream cheese over a bagel so strong with onions my eyes watered just looking at it. "No, stupid. From the future. Didn't you ever see that old *Star Trek* where Kirk and Spock ended up on earth in the thirties and were hopelessly out of step?"

"I hate *Star Trek*."

"But you're familiar with the concept."

I nodded, then yawned. The Weeble studied a telephone pole as if he'd never seen one before. Maybe Angie was right.

"How can you not like *Star Trek*?" Angie said.

"Easy. I watch it, it annoys me, I turn it off."

"Even *Next Generation*?"

"What's that?" I said.

"When you were born," she said, "I bet your father held you up to your mother and said, 'Look, hon, you just gave birth to a beautiful crabby old man.'"

"What's your point?" I said.

The third day, we decided to have a little fun. When we got up in the morning and left my house, Angie went north and I went south.

And the Weeble followed her.

But Lurch followed me.

I'd never seen Lurch before, and it's possible I never would have if the Weeble hadn't given me reason to look for him.

Before we left the house, I'd dug through a box of summer stuff and found a pair of sunglasses I use when the weather's nice enough to ride my bicycle. The glasses had a small mirror attached to the left side of the frame that could be swung up and out so that you could see behind you. Not quite as cool as the equipment Q gave Bond, but it would do, and I didn't have to flirt with Ms. Moneypenny to get it.

An eye in the back of my head, and I bet I was the first kid on my block to have one, too.

I saw Lurch when I stopped abruptly at the entrance of Patty's Pantry for my morning cup of coffee. I stared at the door as if it held a menu and swung the mirror out and rotated my head until I noticed the guy who looked like a mortician on the other side of the avenue by Pat Jay's Pharmacy. He stood with his arms crossed over his sparrow's chest, watching the back of my head openly. Furrows were cut like rivers in his sunken cheeks, and a widow's peak began halfway up his forehead.

In Patty's, I swung the mirror back against the frame and ordered my coffee.

"You go blind all a sudden, Patrick?"

I looked up at Johnny Deegan as he poured cream into my coffee. "What?"

"The sunglasses," he said. "I mean, it's, what, middle of March and no one's seen the sun since Thanksgiving. You go blind, or you just trying to look hipper'n shit?"

"Just trying to look hipper'n shit, Johnny."

He slid my coffee across the counter, took my money.

"It ain't working," he said.

Out on the avenue, I stared through my sunglasses at Lurch as he brushed some lint off his knee then bent to tie his shoelaces just like the Weeble had the day before.

I took off my sunglasses, thinking of Johnny Deegan. Bond was cool, sure, but he never had to walk into Patty's Pantry. Hell, just try and order a vodka martini in this neighborhood. Shaken or stirred, your ass was going out a window.

I crossed the avenue as Lurch concentrated on his shoelace.

"Hi," I said.

He straightened, looked around as if someone had called his name from down the block.

"Hi," I said again and offered my hand.

He looked at it, looked down the avenue again.

"Wow," I said, "you can't tail someone for shit but at least your social skills are honed to the quick."

His head turned as slowly as the earth on its axis until his dark pebble eyes met mine. He had to look down to do it, too, the shadow of his skeletal head puddling down my face and spreading across my shoulders. And I'm not a short guy.

"Are we acquainted, sir?" His voice sounded as if it were due back at the coffin any moment.

"Sure, we're acquainted," I said. "You're Lurch." I looked up and down the avenue. "Where's Cousin It, Lurch?"

"You're not nearly as amusing as you think you are, sir."

I held up my coffee cup. "Wait till I've had some caffeine, Lurch. I'm a certified bust-out fifteen minutes from now."

He smiled down at me and the furrows in his cheeks turned to canyons. "You should be less predictable, Mr. Kenzie."

"How so, Lurch?"

A crane swung a cement post into the small of my back and something with sharp tiny teeth bit into the skin over the right side of my neck and Lurch lurched past my field of vision as the sidewalk lifted off itself and rolled toward my ear.

"Love the sunglasses, Mr. Kenzie," the Weeble said as his rubbery face floated past me. "They're a real nice touch."

"Very high-tech," Lurch said.

And someone laughed and someone else started a car engine, and I felt very stupid.

Q would have been appalled.

"My head hurts," Angie said.

She sat beside me on a black leather couch, and her hands were bound behind her back, too.

"How about you, Mr. Kenzie?" a voice asked. "How's your head?"

"Shaken," I said. "Not stirred."

I turned my head in the direction of the voice, and my eyes met only a hard yellow light fringed by a soft brown. I blinked, felt the room slide a bit.

"Sorry about the narcotics," the voice said. "If there had been any other way . . ."

"No regrets, sir," a voice I recognized as Lurch's said. "There was no other way."

"Julian, please give Ms. Gennaro and Mr. Kenzie some aspirin." The voice sighed behind the hard yellow light. "And untie them, please."

"If they move?" The Weeble's voice.

"See that they don't, Mr. Clifton."

"Yes, sir. I'd be happy to."

"My name is Trevor Stone," the man behind the light said. "Does that mean anything to you?"

I rubbed at the red marks on my wrists.

Angie rubbed hers, sucked a few gulps of oxygen from what I assumed was Trevor Stone's study.

"I asked you a question."

I looked into the yellow light. "Yes, you did. Very good for you." I turned to Angie. "How you doing?"

"My wrists hurt and so does my head."

"Otherwise?"

"I'm generally in a foul mood."

I looked back into the light. "We're in a foul mood."

"I'd assume so."

"Fuck you," I said.

"Witty," Trevor Stone said from behind the soft light and the Weeble and Lurch chuckled softly.

"Witty," the Weeble repeated.

"Mr. Kenzie, Ms. Gennaro," Trevor Stone said, "I can promise you that I don't want to hurt you. I will, I suppose, but I don't want to. I need your help."

"Oh, well." I stood up on wobbly legs, felt Angie rise beside me.

"If one of your morons could drive us home," Angie said.

I gripped her hand as my legs swayed back against the couch and the room tilted to the right just a bit too much. Lurch pressed his index finger into my chest so lightly I barely felt it, and Angie and I fell back into the couch.

Another five minutes, I told my legs, and we'll try it again.

"Mr. Kenzie," Trevor Stone said, "you can keep trying to get up from that couch and we can keep knocking you back down with a feather for at least another, oh, thirty minutes by my estimate. So, relax."

"Kidnapping," Angie said. "Forced incarceration. Are you familiar with those terms, Mr. Stone?"

"I am."

"Good. You understand that they're both federal crimes, carrying pretty stiff penalties?"

"Mmm," Trevor Stone said. "Ms. Gennaro, Mr. Kenzie, how acquainted are you with your own mortality?"

"We've had a few brushes," Angie said.

"I'm aware of them," he said.

Angie raised her eyebrows at me. I raised mine back.

"But those were brushes, as you said. Quick glimpses, here and gone. You're both alive now, both young, both with reasonable expectations that you'll be here on this Earth thirty or forty years from now. The world—its laws, its mores and customs, its mandatory sentences for federal crimes—holds sway

over you. I, however, don't have that problem anymore."

"He's a ghost," I whispered, and Angie elbowed me
in the ribs.

"Quite right, Mr. Kenzie," he said. "Quite right."

The yellow light swung away from my eyes, and I
blinked into the black space that replaced it. A pin-
point of white in the center of the black pirouetted
into several larger circles of orange and expanded
past my field of vision like tracers. Then my vision
cleared, and I was looking at Trevor Stone.

The top half of his face seemed to have been
carved from blond oak—cliffs of eyebrows cutting
shadows over hard green eyes, an aquiline nose, and
pronounced cheekbones, flesh the color of pearl.

The lower half, however, had caved in on itself. His
jaw had crumbled on both sides; the bones seemed
to have melted somewhere into his mouth. His chin,
worn to a nub, pointed straight down at the floor
within the casing of a rubbery flap of skin, and his
mouth had lost all shape whatsoever; it floated within
the mess of his lower face like an amoeba, the lips
seared white.

He could have been anywhere from forty to seventy years old.

Tan bandages covered his throat in patches, wet
like welts. As he stood from behind his massive desk,
he leaned on a mahogany walking stick with a gold
dragon's head handgrip. His gray, glen plaid trousers
billowed around his thin legs, but his blue cotton
shirt and black linen jacket clung to his massive chest
and shoulders as if they'd been born there. The hand

gripping the cane looked capable of crushing golf balls to dust with a single squeeze.

He planted his feet and shook against the cane as he stared down at us.

"Take a good look," Trevor Stone said, "and then let me tell you something about loss."

2

"Last year," Trevor Stone said, "my wife was driving back from a party at the Somerset Club on Beacon Hill. You're familiar with it?"

"We throw all our functions there," Angie said.

"Yes, well anyway, her car broke down. I was just leaving my office downtown when she called, and I picked her up. Funny."

"What?" I said.

He blinked. "I was just remembering how little we'd done that. Driven together. It was the sort of thing that had become a casualty of my commitment to work. Something as simple as sitting side by side in a car for twenty minutes, and we were lucky if we did it six times in a year."

"What happened?" Angie said.

He cleared his throat. "Coming off the Tobin Bridge, a car tried to run us off the road. A carjacking, I believe it's called. I had just bought my car—a Jaguar XKE—and I wasn't about to give it up to a pack of thugs who thought wanting something was the same thing as being entitled to it. So . . ."

12

He stared out a window for a moment, lost, I can only assume, in the crunching of metals and revving of engines, the smell of the air that night.

"My car flipped onto the driver's side. My wife, Inez, couldn't stop screaming. I didn't know it then, but she'd shattered her spine. The carjackers were angry because I'd destroyed the car they presumably thought of as theirs already. They shot Inez to death as I tried to remain conscious. They kept firing into the car, and three bullets found my body. Oddly, none caused critical damage, though one lodged in my jaw. These three men then spent some time trying to light the car on fire, but they never thought to puncture the gas tank. After a time, they grew bored, and left. And I lay there with three bullets in my body and several broken bones and my wife dead beside me."

We'd left the study and Lurch and the Weeble behind and had made our way unsteadily into Trevor Stone's rec room or gentleman's parlor or whatever one called a room the size of a jet hangar with both a billiard and snooker table, cherrywood backing to the dart board, a poker table, and a small putting green in one corner. A mahogany bar ran up the east side of the room with enough glasses hanging overhead to get the Kennedys through a month of partying.

Trevor Stone poured two fingers of single-malt into his glass, tilted the bottle toward my glass, then Angie's, and both of us refused.

"The men—boys, actually—who committed the crime were tried rather quickly and convicted and recently began serving life without possibility of parole at Norfolk, and that's as close to justice as there is, I guess. My daughter and I buried Inez, and that should have been it except for the grief."

"But," Angie said.

"While the doctors were removing the bullet from my jaw, they found the first sign of cancer. And as they probed deeper they found it in my lymph nodes. They expect to find it in my small and large intestines next. Soon after that, I'm sure, they'll run out of things to cut."

"How long?" I said.

"Six months. That's their opinion. My body tells me five. Either way, I've seen my last autumn."

He swiveled his chair and looked out the window at the sea again. I followed his gaze, noted the curve of a rocky inlet across the bay. The inlet forked and thrust out into something that resembled lobster claws, and I looked back to its middle until I found a lighthouse I recognized. Trevor Stone's house sat on a bluff in the midst of Marblehead Neck, a jagged finger of landscape off Boston's North Shore where the asking price for a house was slightly less than that for most towns.

"Grief," he said, "is carnivorous. It feeds whether you're awake or not, whether you fight it or you don't. Much like cancer. And one morning you wake up and all those other emotions—joy, envy, greed, even love—are swallowed by it. And you're alone with grief, naked to it. And it owns you."

The ice cubes in his glass rattled, and he looked down at them.

"It doesn't have to," Angie said.

He turned and smiled at her with his amoeba mouth. His white lips shook with tremors against the decayed flesh and pulverized bone of his jaw, and the smile disappeared.

"You're acquainted with grief," he said softly. "I know. You lost your husband. Five months ago, was it?"

"Ex-husband," she said, her eyes on the floor. "Yes."

I reached for her hand, but she shook her head, placed her hand on her lap.

"I read all the newspaper accounts," he said. "I even read that terrible 'true crime' paperback. You two battled evil. And won."

"It was a draw," I said and cleared my throat. "Trust me on that."

"Maybe," he said, his hard green eyes finding my own. "Maybe for the two of you, it was a draw. But think of how many future victims you saved from those monsters."

"Mr. Stone," Angie said, "with all due respect, please don't talk to us about this."

"Why not?"

She raised her head. "Because you don't know anything about it, so it makes you sound like a moron."

His fingers caressed the head of his cane lightly before he leaned forward and touched her knee with his other hand. "You're right. Forgive me."

Eventually she smiled at him in a way I'd never seen her smile at anyone since Phil's death. As if she and Trevor Stone were old friends, as if they'd both lived in places where light and kindness can't reach.

"I'm alone," Angie had told me a month ago.

"No, you're not."

She lay on a mattress and box spring we'd thrown down in my living room. Her own bed, and most of her belongings, were still back in her house on Howes Street because she wasn't capable of entering the place where Gerry Glynn had shot her and Evandro Arujo had bled to death on the kitchen floor.

"You're not alone," I said, my arms wrapped around her from behind.

"Yes, I am. And all your holding and all your love can't change that right now."

Angie said, "Mr. Stone—"

"Trevor."

"Mr. Stone," she said, "I sympathize with your grief. I do. But you kidnapped us. You—"

"It's not my grief," he said. "No, no. Not my grief I was referring to."

"Then whose?" I said.

"My daughter's. Desiree."

Desiree.

He said her name like it was the refrain of a prayer.

His study, when well lighted again, was a shrine to her.

Where before I'd seen only shadows, I now faced

photos and paintings of a woman in nearly every stage of life—from baby snapshots to grade school, high school yearbook photos, college graduation. Aged and clearly mishandled Polaroids took up space in new teakwood frames. A casual photo of her and a woman who was quite obviously her mother looked to have been taken at a backyard barbecue as both women stood over a gas grill, paper plates in hand, neither looking at the camera. It was an inconsequential moment in time, fuzzy around the edges, taken without consideration of the sun being off to the women's left and thereby casting a dark shadow against the photographer's lens. The kind of photo you'd be forgiven if you chose not to incorporate it into an album. But in Trevor Stone's study, framed in sterling silver and perched on a slim ivory pedestal, it seemed deified.

Desiree Stone was a beautiful woman. Her mother, I saw from several photos, had probably been Latin, and her daughter had inherited her thick, honey-colored hair, the graceful lines of her jaw and neck, a sharp bone structure and thin nose, skin that seemed perpetually under the glow of sunset. From her father, Desiree had been bequeathed eyes the color of jade and full, fiercely determined lips. You noticed the symmetry of genetic influence most in a single photograph on Trevor Stone's desk. Desiree stood between mother and father, wearing the purple cap and gown of her graduation, the main campus of Wellesley College framed behind her, her arms around her parents' necks, pulling their faces close to hers. All three were smiling, robust with riches and health it seemed, and the delicate beauty of the mother and prodigious aura of power in the father seemed to meet and meld in the face of the daughter.

"Two months before the accident," Trevor Stone said and picked up the photo for a moment. He looked at it, and the lower half of his ruined face spasmed into what I assumed was a smile. He placed it back on the desk, looked at us as we took the seats in front of him. "Do either of you know a private detective by the name of Jay Becker?"

"We know Jay," I said.

"Works for Hamlyn and Kohl Investigations," Angie said.

"Correct. Your opinion of him?"

"Professionally?"

Trevor Stone shrugged.

"He's very good at his job," Angie said. "Hamlyn and Kohl only hire the best."

He nodded. "I understand they offered to buy the two of you out a few years ago if you'd come to work for them."

"Where do you get this stuff?" I said.

"It's true, isn't it?"

I nodded.

"And it was a rather handsome offer from, what I understand. Why did you refuse?"

"Mr. Stone," Angie said, "in case you haven't noticed, we're not the power suits and boardroom type."

"But Jay Becker is?"

I nodded. "He did a few years with the FBI before he decided he liked the money in the private sector more. He likes good restaurants, nice clothes, nice condo, that sort of thing. He looks good in a suit."

"And as you said, he's a good investigator."

"Very," Angie said. "He's the one who helped blow the whistle on Boston Federal Bank and their mob ties."

"Yes, I know. Who do you think hired him?"

"You," I said.

"And several other prominent businessmen who lost some money when the real estate market crashed and the S and L crises began in '88."

"So if you used him before, why're you asking us for a character reference?"

"Because, Mr. Kenzie, I recently retained Mr. Becker, and Hamlyn and Kohl as well, to find my daughter."

"Find?" Angie said. "How long has she been missing?"

"Four weeks," he said. "Thirty-two days to be exact."

"And did Jay find her?" I said.

"I don't know," he said. "Because now Mr. Becker is missing as well."

In the city this morning, it had been cold but reasonable with not much of a wind, the mercury hovering in the low thirties. Weather that made you aware of it, but not enough to make you hate it.

On Trevor Stone's back lawn, however, the wind screamed off the Atlantic and the whitecaps churned, and the cold hit my face like pellets. I turned the collar of my leather jacket up against the ocean breeze, and Angie dug her hands deep into her pockets and hunched over, but Trevor Stone leaned into the wind. He'd added only a light gray raincoat to his wardrobe before leading us out here, and it flapped open around his body as he faced the ocean, seemed to dare the cold to infiltrate him.

"Hamlyn and Kohl has returned my retainer and dropped my case," he said.

"What's their cause?"

"They won't say."

"That's unethical," I said.

"What are my options?"

"Civil court," I said. "You'd take them to the cleaners."

He turned from the sea and looked at us until we understood.

Angie said, "Any legal recourse is useless."

He nodded. "Because I'll be dead before anything gets to trial." He turned into the wind again and spoke with his back to us, his words carried on the stiff breeze. "I used to be a powerful man, unaccustomed to disrespect, unaccustomed to fear. Now I'm impotent. Everyone knows I'm dying. Everyone knows I have no time to fight them. Everyone, I'm sure, is laughing."

I crossed the lawn and stood beside him. The grass dropped away just past his feet and revealed a bluff of craggy black stones, their surfaces shining like polished ebony against the raging surf below.

"So why us?" I said.

"I've asked around," he said. "Everyone I've talked to says you both have the two qualities I need."

"Which qualities?" Angie said.

"You're honest."

"Insofar—"

"—as that goes in a corrupt world, yes, Mr. Kenzie. But you're honest to those who earn your trust. And I intend to."

"Kidnapping us probably wasn't the best way to go about it."

He shrugged. "I'm a desperate man with a ticking clock inside me. You've shut down your office and refuse to take cases or even meet with potential clients."

"True," I said.

"I've called both your home and office several times in the last week. You don't answer your phone and you don't have an answering machine."

"I have one," I said. "It's just disconnected at the moment."

"I've sent letters."

"He doesn't open his mail unless it's a bill," Angie said.

He nodded, as if this were common in some circles. "So I had to take desperate measures to ensure you'd hear me out. If you refuse my case, I'm prepared to pay you twenty thousand dollars just for your time here today and your inconvenience."

"Twenty thousand," Angie said. "Dollars."

"Yes. Money means nothing to me anymore and I have no heirs if I don't find Desiree. Besides, once you check up on me, you'll find that twenty thousand dollars is negligible in comparison to my total worth. So, if you wish, go back inside my study and take the money from the upper-right-hand desk drawer and go back to your lives."

"And if we stay," Angie said, "what do you want us to do?"

"Find my daughter. I've accepted the possibility that she's dead. I'm aware of the likelihood of that, in fact. But I won't die wondering. I have to know what happened to her."

"You've contacted the police," I said.

"And they've paid me lip service." He nodded. "But they see a young woman, beset with grief, who decided to go off on a jaunt and get herself together."

"And you're sure that's not the case."

"I know my daughter, Mr. Kenzie."

He pivoted on his cane and began walking back across the lawn toward the house. We followed and I could see our reflections in the large panes of glass fronting his study—the decaying man who stiffened his back to the wind as his raincoat flapped around him and his cane searched for purchase on the frozen lawn; on his left, a small, beautiful woman with dark hair blowing across her cheeks and the ravages of loss in her face; and on his right, a man in his early thirties wearing a baseball cap, leather jacket, and jeans, a slightly confused expression on his face as he looked at the two proud, but damaged people beside him.

As we reached the patio, Angie held the door open for Trevor Stone and said, "Mr. Stone, you said you'd heard we had the two qualities you were looking for most."

"Yes."

"One was honesty. What's the other?"

"I heard you were relentless," he said as he stepped into his study. "Utterly relentless."

3

"Fifty," Angie said as we rode the subway from Wonderland Station toward downtown.

"I know," I said.

"Fifty thousand bucks," she said. "I thought twenty was insane enough, but now we're carrying fifty thousand dollars, Patrick."

I looked around the subway car at the mangy pair of winos about ten feet away, the huddled pack of gangbangers considering the emergency pull switch in the corner of the car, the lunatic with the buzz-cut blond hair and thousand-yard stare gripping the hand strap beside me.

"Say it a little louder, Ange. I'm not sure the G-boys down back heard you."

"Whoops." She leaned into me. "Fifty thousand dollars," she whispered.

"Yes," I whispered back as the train bucked around a curve with a metal screech and the fluorescents overhead sputtered off, then on, then off, then on again.

Lurch, or Julian Archerson as we'd come to know him, had been prepared to drive us all the way home, but once we hit the stand-still traffic on Route 1A, after sitting in an earlier automotive thicket on Route 129 for forty-five minutes, we had him drop us as close to a subway station as possible and walked to Wonderland Station.

So now we stood with the other sardines as the decrepit car heaved its way through the maze of tunnels and the lights went on and off and we carried fifty thousand of Trevor Stone's dollars on our persons. Angie had the check for thirty thousand tucked in the inside pocket of her letterman's jacket, and I had the twenty thousand in cash stuffed between my stomach and belt buckle.

"You'll need cash if you're going to start immediately," Trevor Stone had said. "Spare no expense. This is just operating money. Call if you need more."

"Operating" money. I had no idea if Desiree Stone was alive or not, but if she was, she'd have to have found a pretty remote section of Borneo or Tangier before I blew through fifty grand in order to find her.

"Jay Becker," Angie said and whistled.

"Yeah," I said. "No kidding."

"When's the last time you saw him?"

"Six weeks ago or so," I said and shrugged. "We don't keep tabs on each other."

"I haven't seen him since the Big Dick awards."

The lunatic on my right raised his eyebrows and looked at me.

I shrugged. "You can dress 'em up nice, you know? But you can't take 'em out."

He nodded, then went back to staring at his reflection in the dark subway window as if it pissed him off.

The Big Dick award was actually the Boston Investigators Association's Gold Standard Award for
Excellence in Detecting. But everyone I knew in the
field called it the Big Dick award.

Jay Becker won the Big Dick this year as he had
last year and back in '89 as well, and for a while rumors abounded in the private detective community that he was going to open an office of his own,
break away from Hamlyn and Kohl. I knew Jay well,
though, and I wasn't surprised when the rumors
proved false.

It wasn't that Jay would have starved on his own.
On the contrary, he was easily the best-known PI
in Boston. He was good-looking, smart as hell, and
could have charged retainers in the mid five figures
if he chose. Several of Hamlyn and Kohl's wealthiest
clients would have happily crossed the street if Jay
had opened his doors there. The problem was, those
clients could have offered Jay all the money in New
England, and he still couldn't have taken their cases.
Every investigator who signed a contract with Hamlyn and Kohl also signed a promissory note to the
effect that should the investigator leave Hamlyn and
Kohl, he agreed to wait three years before accepting
any case from a client with whom he'd worked at
Hamlyn and Kohl. Three years in this business
might as well be a decade.

So Hamlyn and Kohl had a pretty good hold on
him. If any investigator was good enough and respected enough, however, to jump ship from Everett
Hamlyn and Adam Kohl and make a profit, Jay
Becker was. But Jay was also shitty with money, as

bad as anyone I've ever known. As soon as he got it, he spent it—on clothes, cars, women, leather sectionals, what have you. Hamlyn and Kohl paid his overhead, paid for his office space, provided and protected his stock options, his 401(k), his portfolio of municipal funds. They daddied him, basically, and Jay Becker needed a daddy.

In Massachusetts, aspiring private investigators must perform twenty-five hundred hours of investigatory work with a licensed private investigator before getting their licenses themselves. Jay only had to do one thousand hours because of his FBI experience, and he did his with Everett Hamlyn. Angie did hers with me. I did mine with Jay Becker.

It was a recruiting technique of Hamlyn and Kohl to pick an aspiring private eye who they believed showed promise and provide that hungry wannabe with a seasoned investigator to show him the ropes, get him his twenty-five hundred hours, and, of course, open his eyes to the gilded world of Hamlyn and Kohl. Every one I know who got his license this way then went to work for Hamlyn and Kohl. Well, everyone except me.

Which didn't sit well with Everett Hamlyn, Adam Kohl, or their attorneys. There were grumblings for a while there that usually reached me on cotton-bond stationery bearing the letterhead of Hamlyn and Kohl's attorneys, or occasionally on the stationery of Hamlyn and Kohl themselves. But I'd never signed anything or given them even a verbal indication that I planned to join their firm, and when my own attorney, Cheswick Hartman, noted this on his stationery (which was a very attractive mauve linen bond), the grumbling ceased appearing in my mailbox. And somehow I built an agency whose success exceeded even my own expectations by working for a clientele that could rarely afford Hamlyn and Kohl.

But recently, shell-shocked I suppose by our exposure to the raging psychosis of Evandro Arujo, Gerry Glynn, and Alec Hardiman—an exposure that cost Angie's ex-husband, Phil, his life—we'd closed the agency. We hadn't been doing much of note since, unless you count talking in circles, watching old movies, and drinking too much as doing something.

I'm not sure how long it would have lasted—maybe another month, maybe until our livers divorced us by citing cruel and unusual punishment—but then Angie looked at Trevor Stone with a kinship she'd shown toward no one in three months and actually smiled without affectation, and I knew we'd take his case, even if he was so impolite as to kidnap and drug us. And the fifty grand, let's admit it, went a long way toward helping us overlook Trevor's initial bad form.

Find Desiree Stone.

Simple objective. How simple the execution of that objective would be remained to be seen. To find her, I was pretty sure we'd have to find Jay Becker or at least follow his tracks. Jay, my mentor, and the man who'd given me my professional maxim:

"No one," he told me once near the end of my apprenticeship, "and I mean, no one, can stay hidden if the right person is looking for him."

"What about the Nazis who escaped to South America after the war? No one found Josef Mengele until he'd died peacefully and free."

And Jay gave me a look I'd become accustomed to during our three months together. It was what I called his "G-man look," the look of a man who'd done his time in the darkest corridors of government, a man who knew where bodies were buried and which papers had been shredded and why, who understood the machinations of true power better than most of us ever would.

"You don't think people knew where Mengele was? Are you kidding me?" He leaned over our table in the Bay Tower Room, tucked his tie against his waist even though our plates and table crumbs had been cleared, impeccable as always. "Patrick, let me assure you of something, Mengele had three huge advantages over most people who try to disappear."

"And they were?"

"One," he said and his index finger rose, "Mengele had money. Millions initially. But millionaires can be found. So, two"—his middle finger joined the index—"he had information—on other Nazis, on fortunes buried under Berlin, on all sorts of medical discoveries he'd made using Jews as guinea pigs—and this information went to several different governments, including our own, who were supposedly looking for him."

He raised his eyebrows and sat back smiling.

"And the third reason?"

"Ah, yes. Reason number three, and the most important—Josef Mengele never had me looking for him. Because nobody can hide from Jay Becker. And now that I've trained you, D'Artagnan, my young Gascon, nobody can hide from Patrick Kenzie, either."

"Thank you, Athos."

He made a flourish with his hand and tipped his head.

Jay Becker. No one alive ever had more style.

Jay, I thought as the subway car broke from the tunnel into the waxy green light of Downtown Crossing, I hope you were right. Because here I come. Hide-and-seek, ready or not.

Back at my apartment, I stashed the twenty grand in the space behind the kitchen baseboard where I stow my backup guns. Angie and I dusted off the dining room table and spread out what we'd accumulated since this morning. Four photographs of Desiree Stone were fanned out in the center, followed by the daily progress reports Trevor had received from Jay until he disappeared thirteen days ago.

"Why did you wait so long to contact another investigator?" I'd asked Trevor Stone.

"Adam Kohl assured me he'd put another man on it, but I think he was stalling. A week later, they dropped me as a client. I spent five days looking into every private investigator in the city who had an honest reputation, and eventually settled on the two of you."

In the dining room, I considered calling Hamlyn and Kohl, asking Everett Hamlyn for his side of the story, but I had the feeling they'd stonewall me. You drop a client of Trevor Stone's stature, you're not going to be advertising it or gossiping about it to a fellow competitor in the trade.

Angie slid Jay's reports in front of her and I looked through the notes we'd each taken in Trevor's study.

"In the month after her mother died," Trevor told us after we came in off the lawn, "Desiree suffered two separate traumas, either of which would have devastated a girl on their own. First, I was diagnosed with terminal cancer and then a boy she'd dated in college died."

"How?" Angie said.

"He drowned. Accidentally. But Desiree, you see, had been, well, insulated most of her life by her mother and me. Her entire existence up until her mother's death had been charmed, untouched by even minor tragedy. She always considered herself strong. Probably because she was headstrong and stubborn like me and she confused that with the kind of mettle one develops under extreme opposition. So, you understand, she was never tested. And then with her mother dead and her father lying in intensive care, I could see that she was determined to bear up. And I think she would have. But then came the cancer revelation followed almost immediately by the death of a former suitor. Boom. Boom. Boom."

According to Trevor, Desiree began to disintegrate under the weight of the three tragedies. She became an insomniac, suffered drastic weight loss, and rarely spoke as much as a full sentence on any given day.

Her father urged her to seek counseling, but she broke each of the four appointments he made for her. Instead, as Lurch, the Weeble, and a few friends informed him, she was sighted spending most of her days downtown. She'd drive the white Saab Turbo her parents had given her as a graduation present to a garage on Boylston Street and spend her days walking the downtown and Back Bay greens of the Emerald Necklace, the seven-mile park system that surrounds the city. She once walked as far as a stretch of the Fens behind the Museum of Fine Arts, but usually, Lurch informed Trevor, she preferred the leafy mall that cuts through the center of Commonwealth Avenue and the Public Garden that abuts it.

It was in the Garden, she told Trevor, that she met a man who, she claimed, finally provided some of the solace and grace she'd been searching for throughout the late summer and early autumn. The man, seven or eight years older than her, was named Sean Price, and he too had been rocked by tragedy. His wife and five-year-old daughter, he told Desiree, had died the previous year when a faulty air conditioning unit in their Concord home had leaked carbon monoxide into the house while Sean was out of town on business.

Sean Price found them the next night, Desiree told Trevor, when he returned home from his trip.

"That's a long time," I said, looking up from my notes.

Angie raised her head from Jay Becker's reports. "What's that?"

"In my notes, I have it that Desiree told Trevor that Sean Price discovered his wife and child almost twenty-four hours after they died."

She reached across the table, took her own notes

from where they lay by my elbow, leafed through them. "Yup. That's what Trevor said."

"Seems a long time," I said. "A young woman—a businessman's wife and probably upscale if they were living in Concord—she and her five-year-old daughter aren't seen for twenty-four hours and nobody notices?"

"Neighbors are less and less friendly and less and less interested in their fellow neighbors these days."

I frowned. "But, okay, maybe in the inner city or the lower-middle-class burbs. But this happened in Concord. Land of Victorians and carriage houses and the Old North Bridge. Main Street, lily-white, upper-class America. Sean Price's child is five years old. She doesn't have day care? Or kindergarten or dance classes or something? His wife doesn't go to aerobics or have a job or a lunch date with another upper-middle-class young wife?"

"It bugs you."

"A bit. It doesn't feel right."

She leaned back in her chair. "We in the trade call that feeling a 'hunch.'"

I bent over my notes, pen in hand. "How do you spell that? With an 'h,' right?"

"No, a 'p' for pinhead." She tapped her pen against her notes, smiled at me. "Check out Sean Price," she said as she scribbled the same words on the upper margin of her notes. "And death by carbon monoxide poisoning in Concord circa 1995 through '96."

"And the dead boyfriend. What was his name?"

She flipped a page. "Anthony Lisardo."

"Right."

She grimaced at the photos of Desiree. "A lot of people dying around this girl."

"Yeah."

She lifted one of the photos and her face softened. "God, she is gorgeous. But it makes sense, her finding comfort in another survivor of loss." She looked over at me. "You know?"

I held her eyes, searched them for a clear glimpse of the battery and hurt that lay somewhere behind them, the fear of caring enough to be battered again. But all I saw were the remnants of recognition and empathy that had appeared when she looked at Desiree's photograph, the same remnants she'd borne after looking into the eyes of Desiree's father.

"Yeah," I said. "I know."

"But someone could prey on that," she said, looking back into Desiree's face again.

"How so?"

"If you wanted to reach a person who was near catatonic with grief, but didn't necessarily want to reach them for benevolent motives, how would you go about it?"

"If I was cynically manipulative?"

"Yes."

"I'd form a bond based on shared loss."

"By pretending to have suffered severe loss yourself, perhaps?"

I nodded. "That'd be just the tack to take."

"I think we definitely need to find out more about Sean Price." Her eyes glistened with burgeoning excitement.

"What's in Jay's reports about him?"

"Well, let's see. Nothing we don't know already."

She began to riffle the pages, then stopped suddenly, looked up at me, her face beaming.

"What?" I said, feeling a smile growing on my
face, her excitement infectious.

"It's cool," she said.

"What?"

She lifted a page, motioned at the mess of paper
on the table. "This. All this. We're back in the chase,
Patrick."

"Yeah, it is." And until that moment I hadn't realized how much I'd missed it—untangling the tangles,
sniffing for the scent, taking the first step toward
demystifying what had previously been unknowable
and unapproachable.

But I felt my grin fade for a moment, because it
was this very excitement, this addiction to uncovering things that sometimes would be better left covered, which had brought me face-to-face with the
howling pestilence and moral rot of Gerry Glynn's
psyche.

This same addiction had put a bullet in Angie's
body, given me scars on my face and nerve damage
to one hand, and left me holding Angie's ex-husband
Phil in my arms while he died, gasping and afraid.

"You're going to be okay," I'd told him.

"I know," he said. And died.

And that's what all this searching and uncovering
and chasing could lead to again—the icy knowledge
that we probably weren't okay, any of us. Our hearts
and minds were covered because they were fragile,
but they were also covered because what often fes-
tered in them was bleaker and more depraved than
others could bear to look upon.

"Hey," Angie said, still smiling, but less certainly, "what's wrong?"

I've always loved her smile.

"Nothing," I said. "You're right. This is cool."

"Damn straight," she said and we high-fived across the table. "We're back in business. Criminals beware."

"They're shaking in their boots," I assured her.

4

HAMLYN & KOHL WORLDWIDE INVESTIGATIONS

THE JOHN HANCOCK TOWER, 33RD FLOOR

150 CLARENDON STREET

BOSTON, MA 02116

Operative's Report

to: Mr. Trevor Stone

fr: Mr. Jay Becker, Investigator

re: The disappearance of Ms. Desiree Stone

February 16, 1997

First day of investigation into the disappearance of Desiree Stone, last seen leaving her residence, 1468 Oak Bluff Drive, Marblehead, at 11 A.M., EST, February 12.

This investigator interviewed Mr. Pietro Leone, cashier of a parking garage at 500 Boylston Street, Boston, which led to the discovery of Ms. Stone's white 1995 Saab Turbo on Level P2 of said garage. Ticket stub found in the glove compartment of car revealed it had arrived at garage at exactly 11:51 A.M., February 12. Search of the car and the premises nearest to it yielded no suggestion of foul play. Doors were locked, alarm was engaged.

Contacted Julian Archerson (Mr. Stone's valet), who agreed to pick up Ms. Stone's car from the premises using her spare set of keys and bring it back to the above-mentioned residence for further investigation. This investigator paid Mr. Leone five and a half days' parking fee of $124.00 (USD) and left garage. [See receipt attached to enclosed daily expenditure sheet.]

This investigator proceeded to canvass the Emerald Necklace park system from the Boston Common, through the Public Garden, Commonwealth Avenue Mall, and ending in The Fens at Avenue Louis Pasteur. By showing park patrons several photographs of Ms. Stone, this investigator found three individuals who claimed to have seen her at some time during the previous six months:

> 1. *Daniel Mahew, 23, Student, Berklee College of Music.* Sighted Ms. Stone on at least four occasions seated on a bench in Comm. Ave. Mall between Massachusetts Avenue and Charlesgate East. Dates are approximate, but sightings occurred during third week of August, second week of September, second week of October, first week of November. Mr. Mahew's interest in Ms. Stone was of the romantic nature, but met distinct lack of interest from Ms. Stone. When Mr. Mahew attempted to engage her in conversation, Ms. Stone walked away on two occasions, ignored him on a third, and ended their fourth encounter, according to Mr. Mahew, by spraying his eyes with either Mace or pepper spray.

Mr. Mahew stated that on each occasion Ms. Stone was unequivocally alone.

2. *Agnes Pascher, 44, Transient.* Ms. Pascher's testimony is questionable as this investigator noted physical evidence of both alcohol and drug (heroin) abuse about her person. Ms. Pascher claims to have seen Ms. Stone on two occasions—both in September (approximate)—in the Boston Common. Ms. Stone, according to Ms. Pascher, sat on the grass by the entrance at the corner of Beacon and Charles Streets, feeding squirrels with handfuls of sunflower seeds. Ms. Pascher, who had no contact with Ms. Stone, called her the "squirrel girl."

3. *Herbert Costanza, 34, Sanitation Engineer, Boston Parks & Recreation Department.* Mr. Costanza on numerous occasions from mid-August through early November observed Ms. Stone, whom he dubbed "the sad, pretty girl," sitting under a tree in the northwest corner of the Public Garden. His contact with her was limited to "polite hellos," which she rarely responded to. Mr. Costanza believed Ms. Stone to be a poet, though he never witnessed her writing anything.

Note that the last of these sightings occurred in early November. Ms. Stone claimed to have met a man she identified as Sean Price in early November as well.

Computer search of statewide NYNEX telephone listings for Sean or S. Price yielded 124 matches. State DMV listings for Sean Price reduced the number to 19 matches within the target age (25–35). Since Ms. Stone's sole physical description of Sean Price mentioned only his general age and race (Caucasian), the number was further reduced to 6 matches upon cross-referencing for ethnicity.

This investigator will begin contacting and interviewing the six remaining Sean Prices tomorrow.

Respectfully,
Jay Becker
Investigator

cc: Mr. Hamlyn, Mr. Kohl, Mr. Keegan, Ms. Tarnover.

Angie looked up from the reports and rubbed her eyes. We sat side by side, reading the pages together.

"Christ," she said, "he is one thorough guy."

"He's Jay," I said. "A model for all of us."

She nudged me. "Say it—he's your hero."

"Hero?" I said. "He's my God. Jay Becker could find Hoffa without breaking a sweat."

She patted his report pages. "Yet he seems to be having trouble finding either Desiree Stone or Sean Price."

"Have faith," I said and turned a page.

Jay's rundown of the six Sean Prices had taken three days and yielded a big goose egg. One was a recent parolee who'd been in prison until late December of 1995. Another was a paraplegic and shut-in. A third was a research chemist for Genzyme Corporation who'd been consulting on a project at UCLA throughout the autumn. Sean Edward Price of Charlestown was a marginally employed roofer and full-time racist. When Jay asked him if he'd recently been to either the Public Garden or the

Boston Common, he responded, "With the fruits and the liberals and the fucking mud races asking for handouts so's they can buy themselves some crack? They should throw a fence around the whole downtown and nuke it from space, pal."

Sean Robert Price of Braintree was a chubby, bald salesman for a textile company who took one look at Desiree Stone's photograph and said, "If a woman who looked like that glanced in my direction I'd have a cardiac on the spot." Since he covered the South Shore and the upper Cape in his job, it would have been impossible for him to make trips into Boston without being noticed. His attendance record, his boss assured Jay, was flawless.

Sean Armstrong Price of Dover was an investment consultant for Shearson Lehman. He ducked Jay for three days and Jay's daily reports began to show an inkling of excitement until he finally caught up with Price while Price entertained clients at Grill 23. Jay pulled a chair up to the table and asked Price why he'd been avoiding him. On the spot, Price (who mistook Jay for an SEC investigator) admitted to a fraudulent scheme in which he advised clients to buy blocks of stock in floundering companies that Price himself had already invested in through a dummy corporation. This, Jay discovered, had been going on for years, and during October and early November, Sean Armstrong Price had made several trips—to the Cayman Islands, Lower Antilles, and Zurich to bury money he never should have had.

Two days later, Jay noted, one of the clients Price had been entertaining reported him to actual SEC investigators and he was arrested at his office on

Federal Street. Reading between the lines of the rest of the data Jay gathered on Price, you could tell he thought Price was too dumb, too transparently slick, and too obsessed with finance to ever dupe or form a connection with Desiree.

Outside of that minor success, however, Jay was getting nowhere, and five days into his reports his frustration began to show. Desiree's few close friends had lost contact with her after her mother's death. She and her father had rarely spoken, nor had she confided in Lurch or the Weeble. With the exception of the macing of Daniel Mahew, she'd been remarkably unobtrusive during her trips downtown. If she hadn't been so beautiful, Jay noted once, she probably wouldn't have been noticed at all.

Since her disappearance, she'd used none of her credit cards, written no checks; her trust fund, various stocks, and certificates of deposit remained untouched. A check of her private phone line records revealed that she had made no calls between July and the date of her disappearance.

"No phone calls," Jay had underlined in red in his report of February 20.

Jay was not the type to underline, ever, and I could tell that he had moved beyond the point of frustration and injury to his professional pride and toward the point of obsession. "It's as if," he wrote on February 22 "this beautiful woman never existed."

Noting the unprofessional nature of this entry, Trevor Stone had contacted Everett Hamlyn and on the morning of the twenty-third, Jay Becker was called to an emergency meeting with Hamlyn, Adam

Kohl, and Trevor Stone at Trevor's home. Trevor included a transcript with Jay's reports:

HAMLYN: We need to discuss the nature of this report.

BECKER: I was tired.

KOHL: Modifiers such as "beautiful"? In a document you know will circulate throughout the firm? Where is your head, Mr. Becker?

BECKER: Again, I was tired. Mr. Stone, I apologize.

STONE: I'm concerned that you're losing your professional distance, Mr. Becker.

HAMLYN: With all due respect, Mr. Stone, it is my opinion that my operative has already lost his distance.

KOHL: Without question.

BECKER: You're pulling me off the case?

HAMLYN: If Mr. Stone agrees with our recommendation.

BECKER: Mr. Stone?

STONE: Convince me why I shouldn't, Mr. Becker. This is my daughter's life we're talking about.

BECKER: Mr. Stone, I admit I've become frustrated by the lack of any physical evidence to either your daughter's disappearance or this Sean Price she claimed to have met. And that frustration has caused some disorientation. And, yes, what you've told me about your daughter, what I've heard from witnesses, and undoubtedly her physical beauty has helped to create a sentimental attachment to her which is not conducive to a professionally detached investigation. All true. But I'm close. I'll find her.

STONE: When?

BECKER: Soon. Very soon.

HAMLYN: Mr. Stone, I urge you to allow us to employ another operative on this case as chief investigator.

STONE: I'll give you three days, Mr. Becker.

KOHL: Mr. Stone!

STONE: Three days to come up with tangible proof of my daughter's whereabouts.

BECKER: Thank you, sir. Thank you. Thank you very much.

"This is bad," I said.

"What?" Angie lit a cigarette.

"Never mind everything else in the transcript, look at Jay's last line. He's being obsequious, almost sycophantic."

"He's thanking Stone for saving his job."

I shook my head. "That's not Jay. Jay's too proud. You get a single 'thanks' out of the guy, you probably just saved him from a burning car. He's not a 'thank you' type of guy. He's way too cocky. And the Jay I know would have been ripshit they even considered taking him off the case."

"But he's losing it here. I mean, look at his last few entries before they called that meeting."

I stood up, paced back and forth along the dining room table. "Jay can find anyone."

"So you've said."

"But in a week oh this case, he'd found nothing. No Desiree. No Sean Price."

"Maybe he was looking in the wrong places."

I leaned over the table, worked the kinks out of

my neck, and looked down at Desiree Stone. In one photo, she was sitting on a porch swing in Marblehead, laughing, her bright green eyes staring directly into the lens. Her rich honey hair was in tangles and she wore a raggedy sweater and torn jeans, her feet bare, dazzling white teeth exposed.

Her eyes drew you in, no question, but it was more than that that kept you fixated on her. She had what I'm sure a Hollywood casting director would call "presence." Frozen in time, she still radiated an aura of health, of vigor, of effortless sensuality, an odd mixture of vulnerability and poise, of appetite and innocence.

"You're right," I said.

"How's that?" Angie said.

"She is gorgeous."

"No kidding. I'd kill to look that good in an old sweater and torn jeans. Christ, her hair looks like she hadn't brushed it in a week and she's still perfect."

I grimaced at her. "You give her a good run in the beautiful department, Ange."

"Oh, please." She stubbed out her cigarette, joined me over the photo. "I'm pretty. Okay. Some men might even say beautiful."

"Or gorgeous. Or knockout, drop-dead, volup—"

"Right," she said. "Fine. Some men. I'll give you that. Some men. But not all men. Plenty would say I'm not their type, I'm too Italian-looking, too petite, too whatever or not enough of whatever else."

"For the sake of debate," I said, "okay. I'll go along with you."

"But this one," she said and tapped Desiree's

forehead with her index finger, "there's not a straight man alive who wouldn't find her attractive."

"She is something," I said.

"Something?" she said. "Patrick, she's flawless."

Two days after the emergency meeting in Trevor Stone's house, Jay Becker did something that would have proven he'd gone off the deep end if it hadn't proven instead to be a stroke of genius.

He became Desiree Stone.

He stopped shaving, allowed his hair and appearance to become disheveled, and stopped eating. Dressed in an expensive, but rumpled suit, he retraced Desiree's steps around the Emerald Necklace. This time, however, he didn't do it as an investigator; he did it as she had.

He sat on the same bench in the Commonwealth Avenue mall, on the same stretch of grass in the Common, under the same tree in the Public Garden. As he noted in his reports, he initially hoped that someone—maybe Sean Price—would contact him, act on a perception that Jay was vulnerable, laid waste by loss. But when that didn't happen, he instead tried to adopt what he assumed was Desiree's mind-set in the weeks before she disappeared. He soaked in the sights she'd seen, heard the sounds she'd heard, waited and prayed, as she probably had, for contact, for an end to grief, for a human connection found and forged in loss.

"Grief," Jay wrote in his report of that day. "I kept coming back to her grief. What could console it? What could manipulate it? What could touch it?"

Alone, for the most part, in the wintery parks, as a light snow misted across his field of vision, Jay almost didn't see what had been in front of his face and rattling through his subconscious since he'd taken this case nine days before.

Grief, he kept thinking. Grief.

And he saw it from his bench on Commonwealth Avenue. He saw it from the corner of grass in the Common. He saw it from under the tree in the Public Garden.

Grief.

Not the emotion, but the small gold nameplate.

GRIEF RELEASE, INC., it said.

There was the gold nameplate on the facade of the headquarters directly across from his bench on Commonwealth Avenue, another on the door of the Grief Release Therapeutic Center on Beacon Street. And the business offices of Grief Release, Inc., were located a block away, in a red brick mansion on Arlington Street.

Grief Release, Inc. When it dawned on him, Jay Becker must have laughed his ass off.

Two days later, after reporting to Trevor Stone and Hamlyn and Kohl that he'd found enough evidence to suggest Desiree Stone had visited Grief Release, Inc., and that there was enough that was fishy about the organization to warrant it, Jay went undercover.

He entered the offices of Grief Release and asked to speak with a counselor. He then told the counselor how he'd been a UN relief worker in Rwanda and then Bosnia (a cover friends of Adam Kohl in the UN would back up) and that he was suffering a complete collapse of moral, psychological, and emotional strength.

That night he attended an "intensive seminar" for acute sufferers of grief. Jay told Everett Hamlyn in a tape-recorded conversation during the early hours of February 27 that Grief Release categorized its clients as suffering from six levels of grief: Level One (Malaise); Level Two (Desolate); Level Three (Serious, with Hostility or Emotional Estrangements); Level Four (Severe); Level Five (Acute); and Level Six (Watershed).

Jay explained that "watershed" meant a client had reached the point at which he would either implode or find his state of grace and acceptance.

To ascertain whether a Level Five was in danger of reaching Level Six, Grief Release encouraged Level Fives to enroll in a Release Retreat. As luck would have it, Jay said, the next Release Retreat left Boston for Nantucket the next day, February 28.

After a phone call to Trevor Stone, Hamlyn and Kohl authorized an expenditure for two thousand dollars and Jay left for the Release Retreat.

"She's been here," Jay told Everett Hamlyn during their phone call. "Desiree. She's been in the Grief Release headquarters on Comm. Ave."

"How do you know?"

"There's a bulletin board in the function room. All sorts of Polaroids on it—you know, Thanksgiving party, aren't-we-all-perfectly-fucking-sane-now party, shit like that. She's in one of them, at the back of a group of people. I've got her, Everett. I can feel it."

"Be careful, Jay," Everett Hamlyn said.

And Jay was. On the first day of March, he returned from Nantucket unharmed. He called Trevor

Stone and told him he'd just arrived back in Boston
and would be dropping by the house in Marblehead
in an hour with an update.

"You've found her?" Trevor said.

"She's alive."

"You're sure."

"I told you, Mr. Stone," Jay said with some of his
old cockiness, "no one disappears from Jay Becker.
No one."

"Where are you? I'll send a car."

Jay laughed. "Don't worry about it. I'm twenty
miles away. I'll be there in no time."

And somewhere in those twenty miles, Jay, too,
disappeared.

5

"Fin de siècle," Ginny Regan said.

"Fin de siècle," I said. "Yes."

"It bothers you?" she asked.

"Of course," I said. "Doesn't it bother you?"

Ginny Regan was the receptionist at the business offices of Grief Release, Inc., and she seemed a little confused. I didn't blame her. I don't think she knew the difference between fin de siècle and a Popsicle, and if I hadn't consulted a thesaurus before coming over here, I wouldn't have, either. As it was, I was still making this shit up on the fly and I was starting to confuse myself. Chico Marx, I kept thinking, Chico Marx. Where would Chico take a conversation like this?

"Well," Ginny said, "I'm not sure."

"Not sure?" I thumped her desktop with the palm of my hand. "How can you not be sure? I mean, you talk about fin de siècle and you're talking about some pretty serious shit. The end of the millennium, utter chaos, nuclear Armageddon, roaches the size of Range Rovers."

Ginny looked at me nervously as a man in a drab brown suit shrugged his way into a topcoat in the office behind her and approached the small gate that, along with Ginny's desk, separated the lobby from the main office.

"Yes," Ginny said. "Of course. It's very serious. But I was—"

"The writing's on the wall, Ginny. This society's coming apart at the seams. Look at the evidence—Oklahoma City, the World Trade Center bombings, David Hasselhoff. It's all there."

" 'Night, Ginny," the man in the topcoat said as he pushed the gate open by Ginny's desk.

"Uh, 'night, Fred," Ginny said.

Fred glanced at me.

I smiled. " 'Night, Fred."

"Uh, yes," Fred said. "Well then." And he left.

I glanced at the clock on the wall over Ginny's shoulder: 5:22 P.M. All the office staffers, as far as I could see, had gone home by now. All except for Ginny, anyway. Poor Ginny.

I scratched the back of my neck several times, my "all-clear" signal for Angie, and locked Ginny in my benign, beatific, benevolent, lunatic stare.

"It's hard to get up in the morning anymore," I said. "Very hard."

"You're depressed!" Ginny said gratefully, as if she finally understood that which had been just beyond her grasp.

"Grief-stricken, Ginny. Grief-stricken."

When I said her name, she flinched, then smiled. "Grief-stricken about, uh, fin-de-sickles?"

"Fin de siècle," I corrected her. "Yes. Very much

so. I mean, I don't agree with his methods, mind you, but maybe Ted Kaczynski was right."

"Ted," she said.

"Kaczynski," I said.

"Kaczynski."

"The Unabomber," I said.

"The Unabomber," she said slowly.

I smiled at her.

"Oh!" she said suddenly. "The Unabomber!" Her eyes cleared and she seemed excited and freed of a great weight suddenly. "I get it."

"You do?" I leaned forward.

Her eyes clouded over in confusion again. "No, I don't."

"Oh." I sat back.

In the rear corner of the office, over Ginny's right shoulder, a window rose. The cold, I thought suddenly. She'll feel the cold air on her back.

I leaned into her desk. "Modern critical response to the best of popular culture confuses me, Ginny."

She flinched, then smiled. It seemed to be her way. "It does."

"Utterly," I said. "And that confusion leads to anger and that anger leads to depression and that depression"—my voice rose and thundered as Angie slid over the windowsill and Ginny's eyes widened to the size of Frisbees as she watched me, her left hand slipping into her desk drawer—"leads to grief! Real grief, don't kid yourself, about the decay of art and critical acumen and the end of the millennium and accompanying sense of fin de siècle."

Angie's gloved hand closed the window behind her.

"Mr. . . ." Girtny said.

"Doohan," I said. "Deforest Doohan."

"Mr. Doohan," she said. "Yes. I'm not sure if grief is the correct word for your troubles."

"And Björk," I said. "Explain Björk."

"Well, I can't," she said. "But I'm sure Manny can."

"Manny?" I said as the door behind me opened.

"Yes, Manny," Ginny said with the hint of a self-satisfied smile. "Manny is one of our counselors."

"You have a counselor," I said, "named Manny?"

"Hello, Mr. Doohan," Manny said and came around in front of me with his hand outstretched.

Manny, I ascertained by craning my neck to look up, was huge. Manny was humongous. Manny, I have to tell you, wasn't a person. He was an industrial complex with feet.

"Hi, Manny," I said as my hand disappeared into one of the catcher's mitts attached to his wrists.

"Hi yourself, Mr. Doohan. What seems to be the problem?"

"Grief," I said.

"Lotta that going around," Manny said. And smiled.

Manny and I walked cautiously along the icy sidewalks and streets as we cut around the Public Garden toward the Grief Release Therapeutic Center on Beacon Street. Manny kindly explained that I'd made the common, understandable mistake of walking into the business offices of Grief Release when obviously I was seeking help of a more therapeutic nature.

"Obviously," I agreed.

"So what's bothering you, Mr. Doohan?" Manny had the softest voice for a man his size. It was calm, earnest, the voice of a kind uncle.

"Well, I don't know, Manny," I said as we waited for a break in the rush hour traffic at the corner of Beacon and Arlington. "I've become saddened lately by the state of it all. The world, you know. America."

Manny touched the back of my elbow and led me into a momentary lull in the traffic. His hand was firm, strong, and he walked with the strides of a man who'd never known fear or hesitation. When we reached the other side of Beacon, he dropped his hand from my elbow, and we headed east into the stiff breeze.

"What do you do for work, Mr. Doohan?"

"Advertising," I said.

"Ah," he said. "Ah, yes. A member of the mass media conglomerate."

"If you say so, Manny."

As we neared the Therapeutic Center, I noticed a familiar group of kids in their late teens wearing identical white shirts and sharply pressed olive trousers. They were all male, all with neatly clipped hair, and all wore similar leather bomber jackets.

"Have you received the Message?" one of them asked an older couple ahead of us. He thrust a piece of paper at the woman, but she swiveled past him with a practiced sidestep that left his hand holding the paper to empty space.

"Messengers," I said to Manny.

"Yes," Manny said with a sigh. "This is one of their preferred corners for some reason."

The "Messengers" were what Bostonians called

these earnest youth who stepped suddenly out from crowds and thrust literature at your chest. Usually male, sometimes female, they wore the white and olive uniform and the short hair, and their eyes were usually kind and innocent with just a touch of a fever in the irises.

They were members of the Church of Truth and Revelation and unfailingly polite. All they wanted was for you to take a few minutes and listen to their "message," which I think had to do with the coming apocalypse or rapture or whatever happened when the Four Horsemen descended from the heavens and galloped down Tremont Street and hell opened up beneath the earth to swallow the sinners or those who'd ignored the Message, which I think was the same thing.

These particular kids worked this corner hard, dancing around people and threading themselves through the weary crowd of pedestrians heading home from a day's work.

"Won't you receive the Message while there's still time?" one desperately asked a man who took the piece of paper and kept walking, balling it in his fist as he went.

But Manny and I, it seemed, were invisible. Not one kid came near us as we approached the doorway of the Therapeutic Center. In fact, they moved away from us in a sudden wave.

I looked at Manny. "You know these kids?"

He shook his massive head. "No, Mr. Doohan."

"They seem to know you, Manny."

"Probably recognize me from being around here so often."

"Sure," I said.

As he opened the door and stepped aside so I'd enter first, one of the kids glanced at him. The kid was about seventeen, with a light freckling of acne across his cheeks. He was bowlegged and so thin I was sure the next strong gust of winter would cast him into the street. His glance at Manny lasted about a quarter of a second, but it was telling enough.

This kid had seen Manny before, no question, and he was afraid of him.

6

"Hello!"

"Hello!"

"Hello!"

"Good to see you!"

Four people were coming out as Manny and I entered. And God, were they happy people. Three women and a man, their faces glazed with joy, their eyes bright and clear, their bodies damn near rippling with vigor.

"Staffers?" I said.

"Hmm?" Manny said.

"Those four," I said. "Staffers?"

"And clients," Manny said.

"You mean some were staffers, some were clients?"

"Yes," Manny said. Obtuse bastard, our Manny.

"They don't seem terribly grief-stricken."

"We aim to cure, Mr. Doohan. I'd say your assessment is a selling point of our operation, wouldn't you?"

We passed through the foyer and climbed the

right side of a butterfly staircase that seemed to take up most of the first floor. The steps were carpeted and a chandelier the size of a Cadillac hung down between the wings of the staircase.

Must be a lot of grief going around to pay for this place. No wonder everyone seemed so happy. Grief, it seemed, was definitely a growth industry.

At the top of the stairs, Manny pulled back two great oaken doors and we stepped onto a parquet floor that seemed to run for a mile or so. The room had probably been a ballroom once. The ceiling was two stories up, painted a bright blue with gold etchings of angels and creatures of myth floating side by side. Several more Cadillac chandeliers shared space with the angels. The walls bore heavy burgundy brocades and Roman tapestries. Couches and settees and the odd desk or two occupied the floor where once Boston's staunchest Victorians, I was sure, had danced and gossiped.

"Some building," I said.

"It sure is," Manny said as several brightly grief-stricken people looked up from their couches at us.

I had to assume some were clients and some were counselors, but I couldn't tell which, and I had a feeling ol' Manny wouldn't do much to help me differentiate.

"Everyone," Manny said as we passed through the maze of couches, "this is Deforest."

"Hello, Deforest!" twenty voices cried in unison.

"Hi," I managed and started looking around for their pods.

"Deforest is suffering a bit of late-twentieth-century malaise," Manny said, leading me farther back into the room. "Something we all know about."

Several voices cried, "Yes. Oh yes," like we were at a Pentecostal revival meeting and the gospel singers were due on the floor any minute.

Manny led me to a desk in the rear corner and motioned for me to sit in an armchair across from it. The armchair was so plush I had a feeling I'd drown in it, but I took a seat anyway and Manny grew another foot as I sank and he took a high-backed chair behind the desk.

"So, Deforest," Manny said, pulling a blank notepad from his desk drawer and tossing it on top, "how can we help you?"

"I'm not sure you can."

He leaned back in his chair, opened his arms wide, and smiled. "Try me."

I shrugged. "Maybe it was a dumb idea. I just was walking past the building, I saw the sign . . ." Another shrug.

"And you felt a tug."

"A what?"

"A tug." He leaned forward again. "You feel displaced, am I right?"

"A little," I said and looked at my shoes.

"Maybe a little, maybe a lot. We'll see. But displaced. And then you're out walking, carrying that weight in your chest that you've been carrying so long you barely notice it anymore. And you see this sign. Grief Release. And you feel it tug you. Because that's what you'd like. A release. From your confusion. Your loneliness. Your displacement." He raised an eyebrow. "Sound about right?"

I cleared my throat, skipped my glance across his steady gaze as if I were too embarrassed to meet his eyes. "Maybe."

"No 'maybe,'" he said. "Yes. You're in pain, Deforest. And we can help you."

"Can you?" I said, working the slightest crack into my voice. "Can you?" I said again.

"We can. If"—he held up a finger—"you trust us."

"Trust isn't easy," I said.

"I agree. But trust is going to have to be the foundation of our relationship if it's going to work. You have to trust me." He clapped his chest. "And I have to trust you. In that way, we can work toward a connection."

"What sort of connection?"

"A human one." His kind voice had grown even softer. "The only kind that matters. That's what grief stems from, what pain stems from, Deforest—a lack of connection with other human beings. You've mislaid your trust in the past, had your faith in people broken, shattered even. You've been betrayed. Lied to. So you've chosen not to trust. And this protects you to some extent, I'm sure. But it also isolates you from the rest of humanity. You are disconnected. You are displaced. And the only way to find your way back to a place, to a connection, is to trust again."

"And you want me to trust you."

He nodded. "You have to take a chance sometime."

"And why should I trust you?"

"Well, I'll earn your trust. Believe me. But it's a two-way street, Deforest."

I narrowed my eyes.

"I need to trust you," he said.

"And how can I prove I'm worthy of your trust, Manny?"

He crossed his hands over his belly. "You can start by telling me why you're carrying a gun."

He was good. My gun was in a holster clipped to the waistband at the small of my back. I'd worn a loose, European-cut suit under a black topcoat as part of my ad exec look, and none of the clothing hugged the gun. Manny was very good.

"Fear," I said, trying to look sheepish.

"Ah! I see." He leaned forward and wrote "fear" on a piece of lined paper on the desk. In the margin above it, he wrote "Deforest Doohan."

"You do?"

His face was noncommittal, flat. "Any specific fear?"

"No," I said. "Just a general sense that the world is a very dangerous place and I feel lost in it sometimes."

He nodded. "Of course. That's a common affliction these days. People often sense that even the smallest things in such a large, modern world are beyond their control. They feel isolated, small, afraid they've become lost in the bowels of a technocracy, an industrialized world that has sprawled well beyond its own capacity to keep its worst impulses in check."

"Something like that," I said.

"As you said, it's a feeling of fin de siècle common to the end of every century."

"Yes."

I hadn't said fin de siècle in Manny's presence.

Which meant the accounting offices were bugged.

I tried to keep that realization from flickering in my eyes, but I must have failed, because Manny's brow darkened and the heat of sudden recognition rose between us.

The plan had been to get Angie inside before the alarm system was engaged. She'd trip it on her way out, of course, but by the time anyone official arrived on the scene, she'd be long gone. That had been the theory, but neither of us considered the possibility of an internal bugging system.

Manny stared at me, his dark eyebrows arched, his lips pursed against the tent he'd made of his hands. He didn't look much like a sweet, big man anymore, nor like a counselor in grief. He looked like one mean motherfucker who shouldn't be messed with.

"Who are you, Mr. Doohan? Really?"

"I'm an advertising executive with deep fears about modern culture."

He removed his hands from his face, looked at them. "Yet, your hands aren't soft," he said. "And a few of your knuckles look like they've been broken over the years. And your face—"

"My face?" I sensed the room going deeply quiet behind me.

Manny glanced at something or someone over my shoulder. "Yes, your face. In the right light, I can see scars along your cheeks under your beard. They look like knife scars, Mr. Doohan. Or maybe from a straight razor?"

"Who are you, Manny?" I said. "You don't seem much like a grief counselor."

"Ah, but this isn't about me." He glanced over my shoulder again, and then the phone on his desk rang. He smiled and picked it up. "Yes?" His left eyebrow arched as he listened and his eyes found mine. "That makes sense," he said into the phone. "He's probably not working alone. Whoever that is inside the offices"—he smiled at me—"hit them hard. Make sure they feel it."

Manny hung up the phone and reached into his desk drawer and I put my foot against the desk and pushed so hard I knocked the chair out from under me and toppled the desk onto Manny's chest.

The guy who'd been behind me making eye contact with Manny came at me from my right, and I sensed him before I saw him. I pivoted to my right, my elbow extended, and hit him so hard in the center of his face that my funny bone shrieked and the fingers of my hand numbed.

Manny pushed back the desk and stood as I stepped around and placed my gun in his ear.

Manny, for his part, was very poised for a guy with an automatic weapon against his head. He didn't look scared. He looked like he'd been through this before. He looked annoyed.

"You're going to use me as a hostage, I suppose?" He chuckled. "I'm a pretty big hostage to lug around, pal. Have you thought that through?"

"Yes, I have."

And I hit him in the temple with the butt of the gun.

Some guys, that's all it would take. Just like in the movies, they'd drop like a sack of dirt and lie on the floor, breathing heavily. But not Manny, and I hadn't expected him to.

When his head jerked back from the hit to the temple, I hit him again where the neck meets the collarbone, and once again in the temple. The last shot was the lucky one, because he'd been raising his massive arms and would have tossed me across the room like a throw pillow if his eyes hadn't rolled back into his head instead. He pitched back into his overturned chair and smashed into the floor with just a bit more noise than a piano dropped from the ceiling would have made.

I spun away from him and pointed my gun at the guy who'd collided with my elbow. He had a runner's ropy build and the trim black hair on the sides of his head was offset by the swath of bare skin on top. He rose off the floor, face bleeding into his cupped hands.

"Hey, you," I said. "Asshole."

He looked at me.

"Put your hands over your head and walk in front of me."

He blinked.

I extended my arm, leveled the gun on him. "Do it."

He locked his fingers together atop his head and started walking with my gun between his shoulder blades. The crowd of shiny, happy people parted in waves as we walked, and they didn't look very happy or shiny as they did. They looked venomous, like asps who'd had their nest upended.

Halfway across the old ballroom, I saw a guy

standing behind a desk, a phone to his ear. I cocked the hammer on my gun and pointed it at him. He dropped the receiver.

"Hang it up," I said.

He did, his hand shaking.

"Step back from the desk."

He did.

The guy in front of me with the broken face called out to the room, "Don't anyone call the police." Then to me, "You're in a lot of trouble."

"What's your name?" I said and dug the pistol into his back.

"Screw you," he said.

"Nice name. Is that Swedish?" I said.

"You're dead."

"Mmm." I reached around him with my free hand and slapped his broken nose lightly with my fingers.

A woman standing frozen to our left said, "Oh, God," and Mr. Screw You gasped and wavered for a moment before he regained his footing.

We reached the double doors and I stopped Screw You by placing my free hand on his shoulder and the muzzle of my pistol under his chin. Then I reached down and pulled his wallet from his back pocket, flipped it open, read the name on his license: John Byrne. I dropped the wallet in the pocket of my top-coat.

"John Byrne," I whispered in his ear, "if there's anyone on the other side of these doors, you get an extra hole added to your face. Understand?"

Sweat and blood dripped off his cheek into the collar of his white shirt. "I got it," he said.

"Good. We're leaving now, John."

I looked back at the happy people. No one had moved. Manny, I guessed, was the only one packing a gun in his desk.

"Anyone comes out that door after us," I said, my voice a little hoarse, "they will die. Okay?"

I got several nervous nods, and then John Byrne pushed the doors open.

I pushed him out, holding on tight, and we stepped out at the top of the staircase.

It was empty.

I turned John Byrne around so he was facing the ballroom. "Close the doors."

He did, and then I turned him around again and we started down the stairs. There are very few places with less room in which to maneuver or fewer places to hide than a butterfly staircase. I kept trying to swallow as my eyes darted left, right, up, down, and back again, but my mouth was dry. Halfway down, I felt John's body tense, and I yanked him back into me, dug the muzzle into his flesh.

"Thinking about flipping me down ahead of you, John?"

"No," he said through gritted teeth. "No."

"Good," I said. "That'd be real dumb."

He went slack in my arm, and I leaned him forward again and we walked down the rest of the staircase. His blood and sweat mixture had found the arm of my topcoat and formed a moist, rusty, stain.

"You ruined my topcoat, John."

He glanced at my arm. "It'll come out."

"It's *blood*. On virgin wool, John."

"A good dry cleaner though, you know . . ."

"I hope so," I said. "Because if it doesn't, I have your wallet. Which means I know where you live. Think about that, John."

We stopped at the door leading to the entrance foyer.

"You thinking about it, John?"

"Yeah."

"There going to be anyone waiting for us outside?"

"I don't know. Cops maybe."

"I don't have a problem with cops," I said. "I'd love to get arrested right now, John. You understand?"

"I guess."

"What I'm concerned about, John, is a bunch of grief-stricken behemoths like Manny waiting out on Beacon Street with more guns than I have."

"What do you want me to say here?" he said. "I don't know what's waiting out there. I'm the one who'll catch the first bullet anyway."

I tapped his chin with my gun. "And the second, John. Remember that."

"Who the hell are you, man?"

"I'm the really scared guy with the fifteen-bullet clip. That's who. What's the deal with this place? Is it a cult?"

"No way," he said. "You can shoot me, but I'm not telling you shit."

"Desiree Stone," I said. "You know her, John?"

"Pull the trigger, man. I ain't talking."

I leaned in close, looked at his profile, at his left eye skittering in the socket.

"Where is she?" I said.

"I don't know what you're talking about."

I didn't have time to question him or beat the answer out of him now. All I had was his wallet, and that would have to be good enough for a second round with John at a future date.

"Let's hope this isn't the last minute of our lives, John," I said and pushed him into the foyer ahead of me.

7

The front door of Grief Release, Inc., was black birch without so much as an eyehole glass in its center. To the right of the door was brick, but to the left were two small rectangles of green glass, thick and fogged over by a combination of icy wind outside and warm air inside.

I pushed John Byrne to his knees by the glass and wiped the glass with my sleeve. It didn't help much; it was like looking out from a sauna through ten sheets of plastic wrap. Beacon Street lay before me like an impressionist painting, foggy forms I took for people moving past in the liquid haze, the white streetlights and yellow gas lamps making everything worse somehow, as if I were staring at a picture that had been overexposed. Across the street, the trees in the Public Garden rose in clumps, indistinguishable from one another. I couldn't be sure if I was seeing things or not, but it seemed that several smaller blue lights flashed repeatedly through the trees. There was no way to know what was out there. But I couldn't stay here any longer. I could hear voices growing louder in the ballroom, and any minute someone would risk opening the door onto the staircase.

Beacon Street, in the early evening just after rush hour, had to be semicrowded. Even if armed clones of Manny waited out front, it wasn't like they'd shoot me in front of witnesses. Then again, I didn't know that for sure. Maybe they were Shiite Muslims, and shooting me was the quickest route to Allah.

"The hell with it," I said and pulled John to his feet. "Let's go."

"Shit," he said.

I took a few deep breaths through my mouth. "Open the door, John."

His hand hovered over the doorknob. Then he dropped it and wiped it on his pant leg.

"Take the other hand off your head, John. Just don't try anything stupid."

He did, then looked at the doorknob again.

Upstairs, something heavy fell to the floor.

"Any time you're ready, John."

"Yeah."

"Tonight, for instance," I said.

"Yeah." He wiped his hand on his pants again.

I sighed and reached around him and yanked open the door myself, dug my gun into his lower back as we came out on the staircase.

And came face-to-face with a cop.

He'd been running past the building when he caught movement out of the corner of his eye. He stopped, pivoted, and looked up at us.

His right hand went to his hip, just over his gun, and he peered up at John Byrne's bloody face.

Up the block at the corner of Arlington, several patrol cars had pulled up in front of the corporate offices of Grief Release, their blue and white lights streaking through the trees in the Garden, bouncing off the red brick buildings just past the *Cheers* bar.

The cop glanced up the block quickly, then back at us. He was a beefy kid, rusty haired and pug-nosed, with the studied glare of a cop or a punk from one of the neighborhoods. The kind of kid some people would take for slow just because he moved that way, and never figure out how wrong they'd been until this kid proved it to them. Painfully.

"Ahm, you two gentlemen have a problem?"

With John's body blocking my own from the cop's view, I slipped my gun into my waistband, closed the suit jacket over it. "No problem, Officer. Just trying to bring my friend to the hospital."

"Yeah, about that," the kid said and took another step toward the stairs. "What happened to your face, sir?"

"I fell down the stairs," John said.

Interesting move, John. All you had to do to get rid of me was tell the truth. But you didn't.

"And broke the fall with your face, sir?"

John chuckled as I buttoned my topcoat over my suit jacket. "Unfortunately," he said.

"Could you step out from behind your friend, sir?"

"Me?" I said.

The kid nodded.

I stepped to John's right.

"And would you both mind coming down to the sidewalk?"

"Uh, sure," we both said in unison.

The kid's name was Officer Largeant, I saw as we got close enough to read his name tag. Someday he'd make sergeant. Sergeant Largeant. I had the feeling that somehow nobody would give him a hard time about it. I bet nobody would give this kid a hard time about much of anything.

He pulled his flashlight from his hip, shined it on the door of Grief Release, read the gold plate.

"You gentlemen work here?"

"I do," John said.

"And you, sir?" Largeant pivoted in my direction and the flashlight shone in my eyes just long enough to hurt.

"I'm an old friend of John's," I said.

"You'd be John?" The flashlight found John's eyes.

"Yes, Officer."

"John . . . ?"

"Byrne."

Largeant nodded.

"I'm kind of in some pain here, Officer. We were going to walk up to Mass General to get my face looked at." Largeant nodded again, looked down at his shoes. I took the moment to pull John Byrne's wallet from my coat pocket.

"Could I see some ID, gentlemen?" Largeant said.

"ID?" John said.

"Officer," I said and put my arm on John's back as if to steady him. "My friend might have a concussion."

"I'd like to see some ID," Largeant said and he smiled to underscore the edge in his voice. "If you'd step away from your friend. Now, sir."

I shoved the wallet into the waistband of John's pants and removed my hand, began searching my pockets. Beside me, John chuckled very softly.

He held the wallet out to Largeant and smiled for my benefit. "Here you are, Officer."

Largeant opened it as a crowd began to gather. They'd been on the perimeter the whole time, but now it was really getting interesting and they closed in from either side of us. A few were the Messengers we'd seen earlier, all wide-eyed and gee-gosh-golly about this example of late-twentieth-century decadence happening right in front of them. Two men getting rousted on Beacon Street, another sure sign of the apocalypse.

Others were office workers or folks who'd been out walking their dogs or having coffee at the Starbucks fifty yards away. Some had come from the perpetual line out in front of Cheers, presumably deciding that they could take out a second mortgage to buy a beer anytime, but this was special.

And then there were a few I didn't like seeing at all. Men, well dressed, coats closed over their waists, eyes like pinpoints bearing down on me. Sprung from the same pods as Manny. They stood on the edges of the crowd, spread out so that they surrounded me whether I headed up toward Arlington, down toward Charles, or across to the Garden. Mean-looking, serious men.

Largeant handed John's wallet back and John gave me another little smile as he placed it in his front pants pocket.

"Now you, sir."

I handed him my wallet and he opened it, shone his flashlight on it. As inconspicuously as possible, John tried to crane his neck around to get a look, but Largeant snapped it shut too quickly.

I caught John's eye and smiled myself. Better luck next time, shithead.

"There you go, Mr. Kenzie," Largeant said and I felt several of my internal organs drop into my stomach. He handed me back the wallet as John Byrne beamed a grin the size of Rhode Island, then mouthed "Kenzie" to himself with a satisfied nod.

I felt like weeping.

And then I looked out on Beacon and saw the one thing that hadn't depressed me in the last five minutes—Angie idling by the Garden in our brown Crown Victoria. The car interior was dark, but I could see the coal of her cigarette every time she brought it to her lips.

"Mr. Kenzie?" a voice said softly.

It was Largeant and he was looking up at me like a puppy and I suddenly felt pure dread because I had a pretty good idea where this was going.

"I'd just like to shake your hand, sir."

"No, no," I said, a sick smile on my face.

"Go on," John said gleefully. "Shake the man's hand!"

"Please, sir. It would be an honor to shake the hand of the man who brought down those skells Arujo and Glynn."

John Byrne raised an eyebrow at me.

I shook Largeant's hand even though I wanted to coldcock the stupid bastard. "My pleasure," I managed.

Largeant was smiling and nodding and rippling all over. "You know who this is?" he said to the crowd.

"No, tell us!"

I turned my head, saw Manny standing on the landing above me, a smile even bigger than John's on his face.

"This," Largeant said, "is Patrick Kenzie, the private detective who helped catch that serial killer Gerry Glynn and his partner. The hero who saved that woman and her baby in Dorchester back in November? You remember?"

And a few people clapped.

But none as loud as Manny and John Byrne.

I resisted the urge to drop my head into my hands and cry.

"Here's my card." Largeant pressed it into my hand. "Any time, you know, you want to hang out or you need help on a case, you just pick up the phone, Mr. Kenzie."

Any time I need help on a case. Right. Thanks.

The crowd was dispersing now that they were reasonably sure no one was going to get shot. All except for the men with the buttoned-up coats and the stony faces—they stepped aside for the other onlookers to leave and kept their eyes on me.

Manny came down the steps to the sidewalk, stood beside me, leaned in close to my ear.

"Hi," he said.

Largeant said, "Well, I guess you have to get your friend to the hospital and I have to get over there." He gestured in the direction of the Arlington Street corner. He clapped my shoulder with his hand. "A real pleasure meeting you, Mr. Kenzie."

"Sure," I said as Manny took a step closer to me.

"G'night." Largeant turned and stepped out onto Beacon, began to cross.

Manny clapped his hand on my shoulder. "A real pleasure meeting you, Mr. Kenzie."

"Officer Largeant," I called, and Manny dropped his hand.

Largeant turned, looked back at me.

"Wait up." I walked to the curb, and two pituitary cases stepped in front of me for a moment. Then one of them glanced over my shoulder, made a face, and then both parted grudgingly. I stepped between them and out onto Beacon.

"Yeah, Mr. Kenzie?" Largeant seemed confused.

"I thought I'd join you, see if any of my buddies are at the scene." I nodded in the direction of Arlington.

"What about your friend, Mr. Kenzie?"

I looked back at Manny and John. They had their heads cocked, waiting for my answer.

"Manny," I called. "You sure you'll take him?"

Manny said, "I—"

"I guess your car is faster than walking. You're right."

"Oh," Largeant said, "he's got a *car*."

"Nice one, too. Ain't that right, Manny?"

"Cherry," Manny said with a tight smile.

"Well," Largeant said.

"Well," I said, "Manny, you best get going. Good luck, John." I waved.

Largeant said, "So, Mr. Kenzie, I've been meaning to ask you about Gerry Glynn. How'd you—"

The Crown Victoria slid up behind us.

"My ride!" I said.

Largeant turned and looked at the car.

"Hey, Officer Largeant," I said, "give me a call sometime. Really, it's been great. Have a good one. Best of luck." I opened the passenger door. "Keep up the good work. Hope everything works out. Bye-bye."

I slid in, shut the door.

"Drive," I said.

"Pushy, pushy," Angie said.

We pulled away from Largeant and Manny and John and the Pods and turned left on Arlington, past the three patrol cars parked in front of Grief Release's corporate offices, their lights bouncing off the windows like ice afire.

Once we were reasonably sure no one had followed us, Angie pulled over behind a bar in Southie.

"So, honey," she said, turning on the seat, "how was your day?"

"Well—"

"Ask me about mine," she said. "Come on. Ask."

"Okay," I said. "How was your day? *Sweetie?*"

"Man," she said, "they were there in five minutes."

"Who? The police?"

"The police." She snorted. "No. Those freaka-zoids with the glandular problems. The ones who were standing around you and the cop and the guy with the busted face."

"Ah," I said. "Them."

"No shit, Patrick, I thought I was dead. I'm in the back office clipping some computer discs, and then, bang, the doors are flying open all over the place, alarms are going sonic on me, and . . . well, it wasn't pretty, partner, lemmee tell ya."

"Computer discs?" I said.

She held up a handful of 3.5 diskettes, bound by a red elastic.

"So," she said, "besides busting some guy's face and almost getting arrested, have you accomplished anything?"

Angie had made her way into the back office just before Manny arrived to take me over to the Thera-peutic Center. She waited there as Ginny shut off the lights, turned off the coffeemaker, pushed chairs neatly into their desks, all the while singing "Foxy Lady."

"By Hendrix?" I said.

"At the top of her lungs," Angie said, "complete with air guitar."

I shuddered at the image. "You should get combat pay."

"Tell me about it."

After Ginny left, Angie went to step out of the rear office and noticed the thin beams of light shafting across the main office. They crisscrossed one another like wires, and rose from the wall at several points, some as low as six inches off the ground, some as high as seven feet.

"Hell of a security system," I said.

"State-of-the-art. So now I'm stuck in the back office."

She started by picking the locks of the file cabinets but found mostly tax forms, job description forms, workmen's-comp forms. She tried the computer on the desk, but couldn't get past the password prompt. She was rifling through the desk when she heard a commotion at the front door. Sensing the jig was up, she used the pry bar she'd used on the window to bust the lock on the file drawer built into the lower right side of the desk. She ripped a gash in the wood, tore the drawer off its rockers, and wrenched it from the desk frame to find the diskettes waiting for her.

"Finesse being the operative word here," I said.

"Hey," she said, "they were coming through the front door like a plane crash. I grabbed what I could and went out the window."

There was a guy waiting out there for her but she popped his head with the pry bar a couple of times and he decided he preferred to sleep in the bushes for a while.

She came out onto Beacon through a small yard in front of a nondescript brownstone, found herself in a stream of Emerson College students heading to a night class. She walked with them as far as Berkeley Street and then retrieved our company car from its illegal parking spot on Marlborough Street.

"Oh, yeah," she told me, "we got a parking ticket."

"Of course, we did," I said. "Of course, we did."

Richie Colgan was so happy to see us he almost broke my foot trying to slam his front door on it.

"Go away," he said.

"Nice bathrobe," I said. "Can we come in?"

"No."

"Please?" Angie said.

Behind him, I could see candles in his living room, a flute glass half-filled with champagne.

"Are you playing some Barry White?" I said.

"Patrick." His teeth were gritted and something akin to a growl rumbled in his throat.

"It is," I said. "That's 'Can't Get Enough of Your Love' coming from your speakers, Rich."

"Leave my doorstep," Richie said.

"Don't sugarcoat it, Rich," Angie said. "If you'd rather we came back . . ."

"Open the door, Richard," his wife, Sherilynn, said.

"Hi, Sheri." Angie waved through the crack in the door.

"Richard," Sherilynn said.

Richie stepped back and we came into his house.

"Richard," I said.

"Blow me," he said.

"I don't think it'd fit, Rich."

He looked down, realized his robe had opened. He closed it and punched me in the kidneys as I passed.

"You prick," I whispered and winced.

Angie and Sherilynn hugged by the kitchen counter.

"Sorry," Angie said.

"Oh, well," Sherilynn said. "Hey, Patrick. How are you?"

"Don't encourage them, Sheri," Richie said.

"I'm good. You look great."

She gave me a little curtsy in her red kimono, and I was, as always, a little taken aback, flustered like a schoolboy. Richie Colgan, arguably the top newspaper columnist in the city, was chunky, his face perpetually hidden behind five o'clock shadow, his ebony skin splotched with too many late nights and caffeine and antiseptic air. But Sherilynn—with her toffee skin and milky gray eyes, the sculpted muscle tone of her slim limbs and the sweet musical lilt of her voice, a remnant of the sandy Jamaican sunsets she'd seen every day until she was ten years old—was one of the most beautiful women I'd ever encountered.

She kissed my cheek and I could smell a lilac fragrance on her skin.

"So," she said, "make it quick."

"Gosh," I said, "am I hungry. You guys have anything in the fridge?"

As I reached for the refrigerator, Richie hit me like a snowplow and carried me down the hall into the dining room.

"What?" I said.

"Just tell me it's important." His hand was an inch from my face. "Just tell me, Patrick."

"Well . . ."

I told him about my night, about Grief Release and Manny and his Pods, about the encounter with Officer Largeant and Angie's B and E of the corporate offices.

"And you say you saw Messengers out front?" he said.

"Yeah. At least six of them."

"Hmm."

"Rich?" I said.

"Give me the diskettes."

"What?"

"That's why you came here, isn't it?"

"I—"

"You're a computer illiterate. Angie, too."

"I'm sorry. Is that bad?"

He held out his hand. "The discs."

"If you could just—"

"Yeah, yeah, yeah." He snapped the diskettes from my hand, tapped them against his knee for a moment. "So, I'm doing you another favor?"

"Well, sorta, yeah," I said. I shifted my feet, looked up at the ceiling.

"Oh, please, Patrick, try the aw-shucks-bawse routine on someone who gives a shit." He tapped my chest with the diskettes. "I help you, I want what's on these."

"How do you mean?"

He shook his head, smiled. "Now, see, you think I'm playing, don't you?"

"No, Rich, I—"

"Just 'cause we went to college together, all that

shit, you think I'm just going to say, 'Patrick's in trouble. Lawsy, I'll do whatever I can.'"

"Rich, I . . ."

He stepped up close to me, hissed. "You know the last time I had a good old romantic, I'm-gonna-have-sex-with-my-wife-and-take-my-time sorta night?"

I stepped back. "No."

"Well, I don't either," he said loudly. He closed his eyes, tightened the belt on his robe. "I don't either," he repeated in his hissed whisper.

"So, I'm leaving," I said.

He stepped in front of me. "Not until we get this straight."

"Okay."

"I find something on these diskettes I can use, I'm using it."

"Right," I said. "As always. As soon as—"

"No," he said. "No 'as soon as.' I'm up to here with that 'as soon as' shit. As soon as you're okay with it? No. *As soon as I can*, Patrick. That's the new rule. I find something on here, I use it as soon as I can. Okay?"

I looked at him and he stared back at me.

"Okay," I said.

"I'm sorry." He held a hand to his ear. "I didn't hear you."

"Okay, Richie."

He nodded. "Good. How soon you need it?"

"Tomorrow morning, the latest."

He nodded. "Fine."

I shook his hand. "You're the best, Rich."

"Yeah, yeah. Get out of my house so I can have sex with my wife."

"Sure."

"Now," he said.

8

"So they know who you are," Angie said as we entered my apartment.

"Yup."

"Which means it's just a matter of hours before they know who I am."

"One would imagine."

"Yet they didn't want you to get arrested."

"Something to gnaw on there, eh?"

She dropped her purse in the living room by the mattress on the floor. "What'd Richie seem to think?"

"He was pretty pissy, but he seemed to perk up when I mentioned the Messengers."

She tossed her jacket on the living room couch, which these days doubled as a chest for her clothing. The jacket landed on a pile of freshly laundered, folded T-shirts and sweaters.

"You think Grief Release is connected to the Church of Truth and Revelation?"

"It wouldn't surprise me."

She nodded. "It wouldn't be the first time a cult or what-have-you had front organizations."

"And this is one powerful cult," I said.

"And we may have angered them."

"We seem to be good at that—-angering people who shouldn't be angered by people as wee and powerless as us."

She smiled around her cigarette as she lit it. "Everyone needs a field of expertise."

I stepped over her bed and pressed the blinking button on my answering machine:

"Hey," Bubba said into the machine, "don't forget tonight. Declan's. Nine o'clock." He hung up.

Angie rolled her eyes. "Bubba's going-away party. I almost forgot."

"Me, too. Think of the trouble we'd be in then."

She shuddered and hugged herself.

Bubba Rogowski was our friend, unfortunately it seemed at times. Other times, it was quite fortunate, because he'd saved our lives more than once. Bubba was so big he'd cast a shadow on Manny, and he was about a hundred times scarier. We'd all grown up together—Angie, Bubba, Phil, and I—but Bubba had never been what you'd call, oh, sane. And whatever minute chance he'd had to become so ended in his late teens when he joined the Marines to escape a prison term and found himself assigned to the American embassy in Beirut the day a suicide bomber drove through the gates and wiped out most of his company.

It was in Lebanon that Bubba made the connections that would create his illegal arms business in the States. Over the last decade he'd begun to branch out into often more lucrative enterprises such as fake IDs and passports, counterfeit money and name-brand appliance replicas, flawlessly bogus credit cards, permits and professional licenses. Bubba could get you a degree from Harvard in four years' less time than it took Harvard to confer it, and he himself proudly displayed his own doctoral certificate from Cornell on the wall of his warehouse loft. In physics, no less. Not bad for a guy who'd dropped out of St. Bartholomew's Parochial in the third grade.

He'd been downsizing his weapons operation for years, but it was that (as well as the disappearance of a few wise guys over the years) for which he was best known. Late last year, he'd been rousted, and the cops found an unregistered Tokarev 9mm taped to his wheel well. There are very few certainties in this life, but in Massachusetts, if you're found with an unregistered firearm on your person, it is certain that you're going to spend a mandatory year in jail.

Bubba's attorney had kept him out of jail as long as he could, but the waiting was over now. Tomorrow night, by nine, Bubba had to report to Plymouth Correctional to serve out his sentence.

He didn't mind particularly; most of his friends were there. The few left on the outside were joining him tonight at Declan's.

Declan's in Upham's Corner sits amid a block of boarded-up storefronts and condemned houses on Stoughton Street directly across from a cemetery. It's a five-minute walk from my house, but it's a walk through the epitome of slow but certain urban decay and rot. The streets around Declan's rise steeply toward Meeting House Hill, but the homes there always seem ready to slide in the other direction, crumble into themselves, and cascade down the hilly streets into the cemetery below, as if death is the only promise with any currency around here anymore.

We found Bubba in the back, shooting pool with Nelson Ferrare and the Twoomey brothers, Danny and Iggy. Not exactly a brain trust, and they seemed to be burning through whatever cells were left by trading shots of grain alcohol.

Nelson was Bubba's sometime partner and knock-about pal. He was a small guy, dark and wiry, with a face that seemed set in a perpetual angry question mark. He rarely spoke, and when he did, he did so softly, as if afraid the wrong ears would hear, and there was something endearing about his shyness around women. But it wasn't always easy feeling endearment toward a guy who'd once bitten off another guy's nose in a barfight. And took it home as a souvenir.

The Twoomey brothers were small-time button men for the Winter Hill Gang in Somerville, supposedly good with guns and driving getaway cars, but if a thought ever entered either of their heads it died from malnourishment. Bubba looked up from the pool table as we came into the back, bounded over to us.

"Hot shit!" he said. "I knew you two wouldn't let me down."

Angie kissed him and slid a pint of vodka into his hand. "Perish the thought, you knucklehead."

Bubba, far more effusive than usual, hugged me so hard I was sure I felt one of my ribs cave in.

"Come on," he said. "Do a shot with me. Hell, do two."

So it was going to be that kind of night.

My recollection of that evening remains a bit hazy. Grain alcohol and vodka and beer will do that to you. But I remember betting on Angie as she ran the table against every guy stupid enough to put his quarters on it. And I remember sitting for a while with Nelson, apologizing profusely for getting his ribs broken four months ago during the height of hysteria in the Gerry Glynn case.

"'S okay," he said. "Really. I met a nurse in the hospital. I think I love her."

"And how does she feel about you?"

"I'm not sure. Something's wrong with her phone, and I think she mighta moved and forgot to tell me."

Later, as Nelson and the Twoomey brothers ate really questionable-looking pizza at the bar, Angie and I sat with Bubba, our three pairs of heels up on the pool table, backs against the wall.

"I'm going to miss all my shows," Bubba said bitterly.

"They have TV in prison," I reminded him.

"Yeah, but they're monopolized by either the brothers or the Aryans. So you're either watching sitcoms on Fox or Chuck Norris movies. Either way, it sucks."

"We can tape your shows for you," I said.

"Yeah?"

"Sure," Angie said.

"It's not a problem? I don't want to put you out."

"No problem," I said.

"Good," he said, reaching into his pocket. "Here's my list."

Angie and I looked at it.

"Tiny Toons?" I said. *"Dr. Quinn, Medicine Woman?"*

He leaned in to me, his huge face an inch from mine. "There's a problem?"

"Nope," I said. "No problem."

"Entertainment Tonight," Angie said. "You want a full year's worth of *Entertainment Tonight?"*

"I like to keep up with the stars," Bubba said and belched loudly.

"You never know when you could run into Michelle Pfeiffer," I said. "If you've been watching *ET*, you might just know the right thing to say."

Bubba nudged Angie, jerked his thumb at me. "See Patrick knows. Patrick understands."

"Men," she said, shaking her head. Then, "No, wait, that doesn't apply to you two."

Bubba belched again, looked at me. "What's her point?"

When the tab finally came, I ripped it out of Bubba's hand. "On us," I said.

"No," he said. "You two haven't worked in four months."

"Until today," Angie said. "Today we got a big job. Big money. So let us pay for you, big boy."

I gave the waitress my credit card (after making sure they knew what one was in this place) and she came back a few minutes later to tell me it had been declined.

Bubba loved that. "Big job," he crowed. "Big money."

"Are you sure?" I said.

The waitress was wide and old with skin as hard and beaten as a Hell's Angel's leather jacket. She said, "You're right. Maybe the first six times I punched your number in, I did it wrong. Lemmee try again."

I took the card from her as Nelson and the Twoomey brothers joined in Bubba's snickering.

"Moneybags," one of the Twoomey nitwits cackled. "Musta maxed out the card buying that jet last week."

"Funny," I said. "Ha," I said.

Angie paid the tab with some of the cash we'd gotten from Trevor Stone that morning and we all stumbled out of the place.

On Stoughton Street, Bubba and Nelson argued over which strip club best fit their refined aesthetic tastes, and the Twoomey brothers tackled each other in a pile of frozen snow, started rabbit-punching each other.

"Which creditor did you piss off this time?" Angie said.

"That's the thing," I said, "I'm sure this is paid off."

"Patrick," she said in a tone my mother used to use. She even wore the same frown.

"You're not going to shake your finger at me and call me by my first, middle, and last name, are you, Ange?"

"Obviously they didn't get the check," she said.

"Hmm," I said because I couldn't think of anything else to say.

"So you guys coming with us?" Bubba said.

"Where?" I asked, just to be polite.

"Mons Honey. In Saugus."

"Yeah," Angie said. "Sure, Bubba. Let me just go break a fifty so I have something to shove in their G-strings."

"Okay." Bubba leaned back on his heels.

"Bubba," I said.

He looked at me, then at Angie, then back at me. "Oh," he said suddenly, throwing back his head, "you were kidding."

"Was I?" Angie said, touching her hand to her chest.

Bubba grabbed her by the waist and scooped her off the ground, hugged her to him one-handed, her heels up by his knees. "I'm going to miss you."

"We'll see you tomorrow," she said. "Now put me down."

"Tomorrow?"

"We agreed to drive you to jail," I reminded him.

"Oh, yeah. Cool."

He dropped Angie and she said, "Maybe you *need* some time away."

"I do." Bubba sighed. "It's hard being the guy who does all the thinking for everybody."

I followed his gaze, watched as Nelson dove on top of the Twoomey brothers and they all slid down the side of the frozen snow pile, punching each other, giggling.

I looked at Bubba. "We all have our crosses to bear," I told him.

Nelson tossed Iggy Twoomey off the snow pile into a parked car and set off the alarm. It screamed into the night air and Nelson said, "Uh-oh," and then he and the brothers burst out in fresh peals of laughter.

"See what I mean?" Bubba said.

I wouldn't find out what had happened with my credit card until the next morning. The automated operator I contacted when we got back to the apartment would only tell me that my credit had been placed on hiatus. When I asked her to explain "hiatus," she ignored me and told me in her computer drone that I could press "one" for more options.

"I don't see that I have many options in hiatus," I told her. Then I reminded myself that "she" was a computer. Then I remembered that I was drunk.

When I got back to the living room, Angie was already asleep. She was on her back. A copy of *The Handmaid's Tale* had slipped down her rib cage and rested in the crook of her arm. I bent over her and removed it and she groaned and turned onto her side, clutched a pillow, and tucked her chin into it.

That's the position I usually found her in when I came out into the living room every morning. She didn't drift to sleep so much as burrow into it, her body curling up so tight and fetal that it barely took up a fourth of the bed. I reached down again and removed a strand of hair from underneath her nose, and she smiled for a moment before burrowing further into the pillow.

When we were sixteen, we made love. Once. The first time for the both of us. At the time, neither of us probably suspected that in the sixteen years that would follow we'd never make love again, but we didn't. She went her way, as they say, and I went mine.

Her way was twelve years of a doomed and abusive marriage to Phil Dimassi. Mine was a five-minute marriage of my own to her sister, Renee, and a succession of one-nighters and quick affairs and a pathology so predictable and male that I would have laughed at it if I hadn't been so busy practicing it.

Four months ago, we'd begun to come back together in her bedroom on Howes Street, and it had been beautiful, achingly so, as if the sole purpose of my life had been to reach that bed, that woman, that moment in time. And then Evandro Arujo and Gerry Glynn had slaughtered a twenty-four-year-old cop on their way through Angie's front door and put a bullet in her abdomen.

She got Evandro back, though, fired three big fuck-yous into his body, left him kneeling on her kitchen floor, trying to touch a piece of his head that wasn't there any longer.

And Phil and I and a cop named Oscar took down Gerry Glynn as Angie lay in ICU. Oscar and I walked away. But not Phil. Not Gerry Glynn, either, but I'm not sure that was much of a consolation prize for Angie.

Human psyches, I knew as I watched her brow furrow and her lips part slightly against the pillow, are so much harder to bandage than human flesh. And thousands of years of study and experience have made it easier to heal the body, but no one has gotten much past square one on the human mind.

When Phil died, his dying swam deep into Angie's mind, happened over and over and over again without stop. Loss and grief and everything that tortured Desiree Stone tortured Angie, too.

And just as Trevor had discovered with his daughter, I looked at Angie and knew there was very little I could do about it until the cycle of pain ran itself down, and melted like the snow.

9

Richie Colgan claims his ancestors are from Nigeria, but I'm not sure I believe him. Given his sense of revenge, I'd be willing to swear he's half Sicilian.

He woke me at seven in the morning by throwing snowballs at my window until the sound reached my dreams and I was yanked from a walk in the French countryside with Emmanuelle Beart and thrown into a muddy foxhole where the enemy was inexplicably catapulting grapefruits into our midst.

I sat up in bed and watched a hunk of wet snow splat into my windowpane. At first, I was happy it wasn't a grapefruit; then my head cleared and I walked over and saw Richie standing below.

The miserable bastard waved to me.

"Grief Release, Incorporated," Richie said as he sat at my kitchen table, "is one interesting organization."

"How interesting?"

"Enough that when I woke my editor up two

hours ago, he agreed to give me two weeks off from my column to research them and a five-day, front-page, lower-right-corner feature series if I come up with what I think I will."

"And what do you think you'll come up with?" Angie said. She glared at him over her cup of coffee, her face puffy and hair hanging in her eyes, not at all happy to greet the day.

"Well . . ." He flipped his steno notebook open on the table. "I've only perused the diskettes you gave me, but, Christ, these people are dirty. Their 'therapy' and its 'levels,' from what I can see, involves a systematic breakdown of the psyche followed by a fast buildup. It's very similar to the American military's concept of break-'em-down-so-you-can-build-'em-back-up approach to soldiers. But the military, to give them their due, is up front about their technique." He rapped his notebook on the table. "These mutants, however, are another story."

"Example," Angie said.

"Well, do you know about the levels—Level One, Two, et cetera?"

I nodded.

"Well, within each of these levels is a set of steps. The names of these steps vary depending on what level you're at, but they're all essentially the same. The object of these steps is 'watershed.'"

"Watershed is Level Six."

"Right," he said. "Watershed is the alleged goal of everything. So, to reach Total Watershed, you have to have a bunch of little watersheds first. Such as, if you're a Level Two—a Desolate, say—you go through a series of therapeutic developments, or 'steps,' by which you reach 'watershed' and are no longer Desolate. Those steps are: Honesty, Nudity—"

"Nudity?" Angie said.

"Yes. Emotional, not physical, though that's accepted. Honesty, Nudity, Exhibition, and Revelation."

"Revelation," I said.

"Yes. The 'watershed' of Level Two."

"What's it called in Level Three?" Angie said.

He checked his notes. "Epiphany. You see? It's the same thing. In Level Four, it's called the Unveiling. In Five, it's Apocalypse. In Six, it's called the Truth."

"How biblical," I said.

"Exactly. Grief Release is selling religion under the pretext of psychology."

"Psychology," Angie said. "Which is, in and of itself, a religion."

"True. But it isn't an organized one."

"The high priests of psychology and psychoanalysis don't pool their tips is what you're saying."

He tapped his coffee mug into my own. "Exactly."

"So," I said, "what's their objective?"

"Grief Release?"

"No, Rich," I said. "Burger King. Who are we talking about?"

He sniffed his coffee. "Is this the extra-caffeine kind?"

"Richie," Angie said. "Please."

"Grief Release's objective, as far as I see it, is to recruit for the Church of Truth and Revelation."

"You've proved their connection?" Angie said.

"Not so as I can print it yet, but, yeah, they're in

bed together. The Church of Truth and Revelation as far as we all know is a Boston church. Correct?"

We nodded.

"So how come their management company is out of Chicago? And their real estate broker? And the law firm which is currently petitioning the IRS for religious tax-exempt status on their behalf?"

"Because they like Chicago?" Angie said.

"Well so does Grief Release," Richie said. "Because those same Chicago firms handle all their interests, too."

"So," I said, "how long to link the two in newsprint?"

He leaned back in his chair, stretched and yawned. "Like I said, at least two weeks. Everything's buried in dummy corporations and blinds. At this point, I can *infer* a connection between Grief Release and the Church of Truth and Revelation, but I can't prove it in black and white. The Church, anyway, is safe."

"But Grief Release?" Angie said.

He smiled. "I can bury them cold."

"How?" I said.

"Remember what I told you about all the steps in each separate level being essentially the same? Well, if you look at it from a benevolent point of view, they've found a technique that works and they just utilize it with different degrees of subtlety depending on the level of grief the particular person is suffering."

"But if you look at it less benevolently."

"As any good newspaperman should . . ."

"Goes without saying . . ."

"Then," Richie said, "these people are first-class grifters. Let's look at the Level Two steps again, bearing in mind that all the other steps in the other levels are the same thing under different names. Step One," he said, "is Honesty. Essentially what it says—you come clean with your primary counselor about who you are, why you're there, what's *really* bugging you. Then you move onto Nudity, which is stripping your entire inner self bare."

"In front of whom?" Angie said.

"Just your primary counselor at this point. Basically all the little embarrassing shit you hid during Step One—you killed a cat as a child, fucked around on your wife, embezzled funds, whatever—it's all supposed to come out during Step Two."

"It's supposed to roll off your tongue," I said. "Just like that?" I snapped my fingers.

He nodded, got up, and refilled his coffee cup. "There's a stratagem the counselors use in which the client disrobes, as it were, in pieces. You start by admitting something basic—your net worth, perhaps. Then the last time you told a lie. Then maybe something you did in the last week which you feel shitty about. And on and on. For twelve hours."

Angie joined him at the coffee maker. "*Twelve hours?*"

He grabbed some cream from the fridge. "More if necessary. I've got documentation on those discs of these 'intensive sessions' lasting nineteen hours."

"Is it illegal?" I said.

"For a cop it is. Think about it," he said and sat

back down across from me. "If a cop in this state interrogates a suspect for one second over twelve hours, he's violated the suspect's civil rights and nothing that suspect says—before or after the twelve-hour point—is admissible in court. And there's a good reason for that."

"Ha!" Angie said.

"Oh, not one you law-and-order types like all that much, but let's face it: If you're being interrogated by a person in a position of authority for more than twelve hours—personally I think ten should be the limit—you'll stop thinking straight. You'll say anything just to end the questions. Hell, just to get some sleep."

"So, Grief Release," Angie said, "is brainwashing clientele?"

"In some cases. In others, they're accumulating vast stores of private knowledge about their clients. Say you're a married guy, wife and two kids, picket fence, but you've just admitted you go to gay bars twice a month and sample the wares. And then the counselor says, 'Good. Excellent nudity. Let's try something easier. I have to trust you, so you have to trust me. What's your bank PIN code?'"

"Wait a second, Rich," I said. "You're saying this is all about getting financial information so they can, what, embezzle from their clients?"

"No," he said. "It's not that simple. They're building dossiers on their clients which include complete physical, emotional, psychological, and financial information. They learn *everything* there is to know about a person."

"And then?"

He smiled. "Then they own them, Patrick. For-ever."

"To what end?" Angie said.

"You name it. Let's go back to our hypothetical client with the wife and kids and covert homosexuality. He moves from nudity to exhibition, which is basically admitting ugly truths in front of a group of other clients and staff. From there, he usually goes on a retreat to property they own in Nantucket. He's been stripped bare, he's a shell, and he hangs out for five days with all these other shells, and they talk, talk, talk—always 'honestly,' laying themselves bare over and over in an environment controlled and protected by Grief Release staff. These are usually pretty fragile, screwed-up people, and now they belong to a community of other fragile, screwed-up people who have as many skeletons in their closets as they do. Our hypothetical guy, he feels a great weight lifted. He feels cleansed. He's not a bad person; he's okay. He's found a family. He's reached Revelation. He came in there because he was feeling desolate. Now he doesn't feel desolate anymore. Case closed. He can go back to his life. Right?"

"Wrong," I said.

He nodded. "Exactly. He needs his new family now. He's told he's made progress, but he can slip anytime. There are other classes to take, other steps to follow, other levels to reach. And, oh, by the way, someone asks him, have you ever read *Listening for the Message*?"

"The bible of the Church of Truth and Revelation," Angie said.

"Bingo. By the time our hypothetical guy realizes he's part of a cult and going deep into hock with dues and tithes and seminar and retreat fees or what have you, it's too late. He tries to leave Grief Release or the Church, he finds he can't. They have his bank records, his PIN, all his secrets."

"You're theorizing here, though," I said. "You don't have hard proof."

"Well, on Grief Release, I do. I have a training manual for counselors which advises them specifically to get financial information from their clients. I can bury them with that manual alone. But the Church? No. I need to match membership rolls."

"Come again?"

He reached into the gym bag by his feet, pulled out a stack of computer paper. "These are the names of everyone who's ever received treatment from Grief Release. If I can get a copy of the membership rolls of the Church and match them, I'm on my way to a Pulitzer."

"You wish," Angie said. She reached for the list, rifled through it until she found the page she wanted. Then she smiled.

"It's there, isn't it?" I said.

She nodded. "In black and white, babe." She turned the sheaf of paper so I could see the name halfway down the page:

Desiree Stone.

Richie unloaded nine inches of hard-copy printout from his bag and left it on the table for us to sift through. Everything he'd found on the discs so far was there. He also returned the discs, having made copies for himself last night.

Angie and I stared at the stack of paper between us, trying to decide where to start, and my phone rang.

"Hello," I said.

"We'd like our discs," someone said.

"I'm sure you would," I said. I dropped the mouthpiece to my chin for a moment, said to Angie, "They'd like their discs."

"Hey, finders keepers," she said.

"Finders keepers," I said into the phone.

"Have any trouble paying for things lately, Mr. Kenzie?"

"Excuse me?"

"You might want to call your bank," the voice said. "I'll give you ten minutes. Make sure the line's clear when I call back."

I hung up and immediately went into my bedroom for my wallet.

"What's wrong?" Angie said.

I shook my head and called Visa, worked my way through the automated operators until I got a person. I gave her my card number, expiration date and zip code.

"Mr. Kenzie?" she said.

"Yes."

"Your card has been revealed to be counterfeit."

"Excuse me."

"It's counterfeit, sir."

"No, it's not. You issued it to me."

She gave me a bored sigh. "No, we didn't. An internal computer search has revealed that your card and number were part of a large-scale infiltration of our accounting data banks three years ago."

"That's not possible," I said. "*You issued it to me.*"

"I'm sure we didn't," she said in a patronizing singsong.

"What the hell does that mean?" I said.

"Our attorneys will be contacting you, Mr. Kenzie. As will the Attorney General's Office, Division of Mail and Computer Fraud. Good day."

She hung up in my ear.

"Patrick?" Angie said.

I shook my head again, dialed my bank.

I grew up poor. Always afraid, terrified actually, of faceless bureaucrats and bill collectors who looked down on me from above and decided my worth based on my bank account, judged my right or lack of right to earn money by how much I'd started out with in the first place. I worked my ass off over the last decade to earn and save and build upon those earnings. I would never be poor, I told myself. Not again.

"Your bank accounts have been frozen," Mr. Pearl at the bank told me.

"Frozen," I said. "Explain frozen."

"The funds have been seized, Mr. Kenzie. By the IRS."

"Court order?" I said.

"Pending," he said.

And I could hear it in his voice—disdain. That's what the poor hear all the time—from bankers, creditors, merchants. Disdain, because the poor are second-rate and stupid and lazy and too morally and spiritually lax to hold on to their money legally and contribute to society. I hadn't heard that tone of disdain in at least seven years, maybe ten, and I wasn't ready for it. I felt immediately reduced.

"Pending," I said.

"That's what I said." His voice was dry, at ease, secure with his station in life. He could have been talking to one of his children.

I can't have the car, Dad?

That's what I said.

"Mr. Pearl," I said.

"Yes, Mr. Kenzie?"

"Are you familiar with the law firm of Hartman and Hale?"

"Of course I am, Mr. Kenzie."

"Good. They'll be contacting you. Soon. And that pending court order better be—"

"Good day, Mr. Kenzie." He hung up.

Angie came around the table, put one hand on my back, the other on my right hand. "Patrick," she said, "you're white as a ghost."

"Jesus," I said. "Jesus Christ."

"It's going to be okay," she said. "They can't do this."

"They're doing it, Ange."

When the phone rang three minutes later, I picked it up on the first ring.

"Money a little tight these days, Mr. Kenzie?"

"Where and when, Manny?"

He chuckled. "Oooh, we sound—how shall I put it—deflated, Mr. Kenzie."

"Where and when?" I said.

"The Prado. You know it?"

"I know it. When?"

"Noon," Manny said. "High noon. Heh-heh."

He hung up.

Everyone was hanging up on me today. And it wasn't even nine.

10

Four years ago, after a particularly lucrative case involving insurance fraud and white-collar extortion, I went to Europe for two weeks. And what struck me most at the time was how many of the small villages I visited—in Ireland and Italy and Spain—resembled Boston's North End.

The North End was where each successive wave of immigrants had left the boat and dropped their bags. So the Jewish and then the Irish and finally the Italians had called this area home and given it the distinctly European character it retains today. The streets are cobblestone, narrow, and curve hard around and over and through each other in a neighborhood so small in physical area that in some cities it would barely constitute a block. But packed in here tight are legions of red and yellow brick rowhouses, former tenements co-opted and restored, and the odd cast-iron or granite warehouse, all fighting for space and getting really weird on top where extra stories were added after "up" became the only option. So clapboard and brick rise up from what were once mansard roofs, and laundry still stretches between opposite fire escapes and wrought-iron patios, and "yard" is an even more alien concept than "parking space."

Somehow, in this, the most cramped of neighborhoods in the most cramped of cities, a gorgeous replica of an Italian village piazza sits behind the Old North Church. Called the Prado, it's also known as the Paul Revere Mall, not only because of its proximity to both the church and Revere's house, but because the Hanover Street entrance is dominated by Dallin's equestrian statue of Revere. In the center of the Prado is a fountain; along the walls that surround it are bronze plaques testifying to the heroics of Revere, Dawes, several revolutionaries, and some lesser-known luminaries of North End lore.

The temperature had risen into the forties when we arrived at noon, entering from the Unity Street side, and dirty snow melted into the cracks in the cobblestone and puddled in the warps of the limestone benchtops. The fresh snowfall that had been expected today had turned into a light drizzle of rain due to the temperature, so the Prado was empty of tourists or North Enders on their lunch breaks.

Only Manny and John Byrne and two other men waited for us by the fountain. The two men I recognized from last night; they'd been standing to my left as John and I dealt with Officer Largeant, and while neither was as big as Manny, they weren't small either.

"This must be the lovely Miss Gennaro," Manny said. He clapped his hands together as we approached.

"A friend of mine has a few nasty welts on his head because of you, ma'am."

"Gee," Angie said, "sorry."

Manny raised his eyebrows at John. "Sarcastic little strumpet, isn't she?"

John turned from the fountain, his nose criss-crossed in white bandages, the flesh around both eyes blue-black and puffy. "Excuse me," he said, and came out from behind Manny and punched me in the face.

He threw himself into it so hard his feet left the ground, but I leaned back with it, took it on my temple after it had lost about half of its velocity. All and all, it was a pretty shitty punch. I've had bee stings that hurt more.

"What else your mother teach you besides boxing, John?"

Manny chuckled and the two big guys snickered.

"Laugh it up," John said and stepped in close. "I'm the guy who owns the paper on your entire life now, Kenzie."

I pushed him back, looked at Manny. "So this is your computer geek, eh, Manny?"

"Well, he's not my muscle, Mr. Kenzie."

I never saw Manny's punch. Something in the center of my brain exploded and my whole face went numb and I was suddenly sitting on my ass on the wet cobblestone.

Manny's buddies loved it. They high-fived and hooted and did little jigs as if they were about to piss their pants.

I swallowed against the vomit surging up through

my alimentary canal and felt the numbness leave my face, replaced by pins and needles, a deep flush of blood rushing up behind my ears, and the sensation that my brain had been replaced by a brick. A hot brick, a brick on fire.

Manny held out his hand and I took it, and he lifted me to my feet.

"Nothing personal, Kenzie," he said. "Next time you raise a hand to me, though, I'll kill you."

I stood on wobbly feet, still swallowing against the vomit, and the fountain seemed to shimmer at me from underwater.

"Good to know," I managed.

I heard a loud rumble and turned my head to my left, watched a garbage truck lumber up Unity Street, its body so wide and the street so narrow that its wheels rolled along the sidewalk. I had a horrendous hangover, a probable concussion, and now I had to listen to a garbage truck clang and wheeze its way down Unity Street, banging trash cans against cement and metal the whole way. Oh, rapture.

Manny put his left arm around me and his right around Angie, guided us to sit beside him around the fountain. John stood over us and glared down at me, and the two steroid cases remained where they were, watching the entrances.

"I liked that shit you pulled with the cop last night," Manny said. "That was good. 'Manny, you *sure* you'll take him to the hospital?'" He chuckled. "Christ. You're very quick on your feet."

"Thanks, Manny. Means so much coming from you."

He turned to Angie. "And you, going right for

those diskettes like you knew where they'd be all along."

"I had no choice."

"How's that?"

"Because I was trapped in the back office by the laser light show you had in the main office."

"Right." He nodded his huge head. "I initially thought you'd been hired by the competition."

"You have competition?" Angie said. "In grief therapy?"

He smiled at her. "But then John told me you were looking for Desiree Stone, and then I discovered you couldn't even get past the computer password, so I realized it was just dumb luck."

"Dumb luck," Angie said.

He patted her knee. "Who has the discs?"

"I do," I said.

He held out his hand.

I placed them on his palm and he tossed them to John. John placed them in an attaché case and snapped it shut.

"What about my bank account, credit cards, all that?" I said.

"Well," Manny said, "I thought of killing you."

"You and these three guys?" Angie laughed.

He looked at her. "That's amusing?"

"Look at your crotch, Manny," I said.

He looked down, saw Angie's gun there, the muzzle a tenth of an inch from Manny's family jewels.

"That," Angie said, "is amusing."

He laughed and she laughed too, holding his eyes, the gun never wavering.

"God," he said, "I like you, Miss Gennaro."

"God," she said, "the feeling definitely ain't mutual, Manny."

He turned his head, looked toward the bronze plaques and the great stone wall across from him. "So, okay, nobody gets killed today. But, Mr. Kenzie, I'm afraid you bought yourself seven years of bad luck. Your credit is gone. Your money is gone. And it isn't coming back. Myself and some associates decided you needed to be taught a lesson in power."

"Obviously I have, or you wouldn't have those discs."

"Ah, but, while the lesson is over, I need to be sure it sinks in. So, no, Mr. Kenzie, you're back to square one. You have my promise we'll leave you alone from this point, but the damage that's been done will remain that way."

On Unity Street, the garbagemen were tossing the metal cans back to the sidewalk from a height of over four feet and a van that had come up behind them was blaring its horn and some old lady was screaming from her window at everyone in Italian. All in all, it wasn't helping my hangover.

"So that's it?" I thought of the ten years of saving, the four credit cards in my wallet I'd never be able to use again, the hundreds upon hundreds of shitty cases—big and small—which I'd labored through. All for nothing. I was poor again.

"That's it." Manny stood up. "Be careful who you fuck with, Kenzie. You know nothing about us, and we know everything about you. That makes us dangerous and you predictable."

"Thanks for the lesson," I said.

He stood over Angie until she looked up at him.

Her gun was still in her hands, but pointing at the ground.

"Maybe until Mr. Kenzie can afford to take you to dinner again, I can pick up some of his slack. What do you say?"

"I'd say pick up a copy of *Penthouse* on your way home, Manny, and say hello to your right hand."

"I'm a lefty." He smiled.

"I don't care," she said and John laughed.

Manny shrugged, and for a moment looked like he was considering a retort, but instead he spun on his heel without another word and walked toward Unity Street. John and the other two men followed. At the entrance, Manny stopped and turned back to us, his massive physique framed by the blue and gray of the idling garbage truck.

"See you around, kids." He waved.

And we waved back.

And Bubba, Nelson, and the Twoomey brothers came out from behind the garbage truck, each brandishing a weapon.

John started to open his mouth, and Nelson hit him dead in the face with a sawed-off hockey stick. Blood spurted from John's broken nose, and he pitched forward and Nelson caught him and hoisted him over his shoulder. The Twoomey brothers came through the entranceway with metal trash cans in their hands. They swung the cans in pinwheels over their shoulders and brought them down on the heads of Manny's steroid cases, pile-drove the men into the cobblestone. I heard a loud crack as one of them shattered his kneecap on the stone, and then both crumpled and curled into the ground like dogs sleeping in the sun.

Manny had frozen. His arms out by his sides, he watched bewildered as the three men around him were knocked out cold in under four seconds.

Bubba stood behind him, a metal trash can lid raised like a gladiator's shield. He tapped Manny on the shoulder and Manny got a sick look on his face.

When he turned around, Bubba's free hand found the back of his head, grabbed it tight, and then the metal lid snapped down four times, each hit sounding like the wet splat of a watermelon dropped from the roof of a row house.

"Manny," Bubba said as Manny sagged toward the ground. Bubba yanked at his hair and Manny's body twisted in his grip, loose and elastic. "Manny," Bubba repeated, "how's it going, pal?"

They tossed Manny and John in the back of the van, then lifted the other two guys and threw them into the back of the garbage truck with the stewed tomotoes and black bananas and empty frozen-food trays.

For one scary moment, Nelson put his hand on the hydraulic line lever at the back of the truck and said, "Can I, Bubba? Can I?"

"Better not," Bubba said. "Might make too much noise."

Nelson nodded, but he looked sad.

They'd stolen the garbage truck from the BFI yard in Brighton this morning. They left it where it was and walked back to the van. Bubba looked up at the windows fronting the street. Nobody was looking out. But, even if they were, this was the North End, home of the Mafia, and one thing people knew around here from birth was no matter what they saw, they didn't see it, Officer.

"Nice getup," I said to Bubba as he climbed into the van.

"Yeah," Angie said, "you look good dressed up as a garbageman."

Bubba said, "That's sanitation engineer to you."

Bubba paced around the third floor of the warehouse he owned, sucking from a vodka bottle, smiling and occasionally looking over at John and Manny, who were tied tight to metal chairs, still unconscious.

The first floor of Bubba's warehouse was gutted; the third was empty now that he'd liquidated his stock-in-trade. The second was his apartment, and it would have been more comfortable, I suppose, but he'd covered everything in quilts in anticipation of his yearlong departure, and besides, the place was mined with explosives. That's right. Mined. Don't ask.

"The little guy's coming to," Iggy Twoomey said. Iggy sat with his brother and Nelson on adjoining piles of old pallets, passing a bottle back and forth. Every now and then, one of them giggled for no apparent reason.

John opened his eyes as Bubba leaped across the floor and landed in front of him, hands on his knees like a sumo wrestler.

For a moment, I thought John would faint.

"Hi," Bubba said.

"Hi," John croaked.

Bubba leaned in close. "Here's the deal, John. Is it John?"

"Yes," John said.

"Okay. Well, John, my friends, Patrick and Angie, they're going to ask you some questions. You understand?"

"I do. But I don't know—"

Bubba put a finger to John's lips. "Sssh. I'm not finished. If you don't answer their questions, John, then my other friends? You see them over there?"

Bubba stepped aside and John got a look at the three head cases sitting back on the pallets in the shadows, swilling booze, waiting for him.

"If you don't answer, Patrick and Angie will leave. And me and my other friends will play this game we like involving you, Manny, and a Phillips-head screwdriver."

"A rusty one," one of the Twoomeys giggled.

John began to convulse, and I don't even think he was aware of it. He looked up at Bubba as if he were looking at the physical reality of a phantom that had haunted his dreams.

Bubba straddled John and brushed his hair back off his forehead. "That's the deal, John. Okay?"

"Okay," John said and nodded several times.

"Okay," Bubba said with a satisfied nod. He patted John's cheeks and climbed off him. Then he stepped over to Manny and tossed some vodka in his face.

Manny woke coughing, bucking at the ropes, spitting at the vodka on his lips.

The first thing he said was "What?"

"Hi, Manny."

Manny looked up at Bubba and for a moment he tried to look fearless, used to this. But Bubba smiled, and Manny sighed, then looked at the ground.

"Manny!" Bubba said. "Glad you could join us. Here's the deal, Manny. John's going to tell Patrick and Angie what they want to know. If I think he's lying, or if you interrupt, I'm going to set you on fire."

"Me?" Manny said.

"You."

"Why not him? I mean, if he's the one who's lying?"

"Because there's more of you to burn, Manny."

Manny bit his upper lip and tears welled in the pockets of his eyes. "Tell them the truth, John."

"Fuck off, Manny."

"Tell them!"

"I'll tell them!" John screamed. "But not because of you. 'Why not burn him?'" he mimicked. "Some friend. If we get out of this, I'm telling everyone you wept like an old woman."

"I did not."

"Did too."

"John," Angie said, "who screwed with Patrick's bank account and credit cards?"

He looked at the floor. "I did."

"How?" I said.

"I work for the IRS," he said.

"So you'll fix it?" Angie said.

"Well," he said, "actually it's a lot easier to wreck than it is to fix."

"John," I said. "Look at me."

He did.

"Fix it."

"I—"

"By tomorrow."

"Tomorrow? I can't do that. It'd take—"

I stood over him. "John, you can make my credit disappear, and that's a very scary thing. But I can make *you* disappear, and that's a little more scary, wouldn't you say?"

He swallowed and his Adam's apple bobbed in his throat for a moment.

"Tomorrow, John. Morning."

"Yeah," he said. "Okay."

"You make other people's credit disappear?" I asked.

"I—"

"Answer him," Bubba said, looking down at his shoes.

"Yes."

"People who try to leave the Church of Truth and Revelation?" Angie said.

Manny said, "Hey, wait a minute."

Bubba said, "Who's got a match?"

"I'll shut up," Manny said. "I'll shut up."

"We know all about Grief Release and the Church," Angie said. "One of the ways you deal with naughty members is to screw with their finances. Correct?"

"Sometimes," John said, his lower lip protruding like a kid caught looking up the girls' dresses in school.

I said, "You have people working in all the good companies, don't you, John—the IRS, police department, banks, the media, where else?"

His shrug was constricted by the ropes. "You name it."

"Nice," I said.

He snorted. "I don't see anyone complaining when Catholics work for those same organizations. Or Jews."

"Or Seventh-Day Adventists," Bubba said.

I looked at him.

"Oh." He held up a hand. "Sorry."

I bent down by John, placed my elbows on his knees, and looked up into his face.

"Okay, John. Here's the important question. And don't even think about lying to me."

"That would be bad," Bubba said.

John glanced nervously at Bubba, then back at me.

"John," I said, "what happened to Desiree Stone?"

11

"Desiree Stone," Angie repeated. "Come on, John. We know she was treated by Grief Release."

John licked his lips, blinked. He hadn't spoken in over a minute and Bubba was getting restless.

"John," I said.

"I know I had a lighter around here somewhere." Bubba looked bewildered for a moment. He patted his pants pockets, then suddenly snapped his fingers. "Left it downstairs. That's what I did with it. Be right back."

John and Manny watched him jog toward the stairs at the end of the loft, the hammering clunk of his combat boots echoing off the beams overhead.

As Bubba disappeared downstairs, I said, "Now you've done it."

John and Manny looked at each other.

"He gets like this," Angie said, "you never know what he'll do. He tends to get, you know, creative."

John's eyes spun in their sockets like saucers. "Don't let him hurt me."

"Not much I can do, if you don't tell us about Desiree."

"I don't know anything about Desiree Stone."

"Sure you do," I said.

"Not like Manny does. Manny was her primary counselor."

Angie and I swiveled our heads slowly, looked at Manny.

Manny shook his head.

Angie smiled and walked over to him. "Manny, Manny, Manny," she said. "The secrets you keep." She tilted his chin until he was looking in her eyes. "'Fess up, muscle boy."

"I have to take this shit from that psychotic, but I ain't taking it from no fucking girl." He spit at her and she leaned back from it.

"My," she said. "You get the feeling Manny spends way too much time at the gym? You do, don't you, Manny? Lifting your little weights and pushing smaller guys off the StairMaster and telling all your steroid buddies about the bimbo you used and abused the night before. That's you, Manny. That's you all over."

"Hey, fuck you."

"No, Manny. Fuck you," she said. "Fuck you and die."

And Bubba came bounding back into the room with an acetylene torch screaming, "Suc-*cess*! Suc-*cess*!"

Manny screamed and bucked against his ropes.

"This is getting good," one of the Twoomey brothers said.

"No!" Manny shrieked. "No! No! No! Desiree

Stone came to the Therapeutic Center on November nineteenth. She, she, she was depressed because, because, because—"

"Slow down, Manny," Angie said. "Slow down."

Manny closed his eyes and took a deep breath, his face drenched in sweat.

Bubba sat on the floor and fondled his acetylene torch.

"Okay, Manny," Angie said. "From the top." She placed a tape recorder on the floor in front of him and turned it on.

"Desiree was depressed because her father had cancer, her mother had just died, and a guy she'd known in college had drowned."

"We know that part," I said.

"So, she came to us and—"

"How'd she come to you?" Angie said. "Did she just walk in off the street?"

"Yes." Manny blinked.

Angie looked at Bubba. "He's lying."

Bubba shook his head slowly and turned on the torch.

"Okay," Manny said. "Okay. She was recruited."

Bubba said, "I turn this on again, I'm using it, Ange. Whether you like it or not."

She nodded.

"Jeff Price," Manny said. "He was the recruiter."

"Jeff?" I said. "I thought his name was Sean."

Manny shook his head. "That was his middle name. He used it as an alias sometimes."

"Tell us about him."

"He was the treatment supervisor at Grief Release and a member of the Church Council."

"Which is?"

"The Church Council is like the board of directors. It's made up of people who've been with the Church since its days in Chicago."

"So, this Jeff Price," Angie said, "where's he now?"

"Gone," John said.

We looked at him. Even Bubba seemed to be getting interested. Maybe he was taking mental notes for the day he'd start his own Church. The Temple Defective.

"Jeff Price stole two million dollars from the Church and disappeared."

"How long ago?" I said.

"Little over six weeks ago," Manny said.

"Which is when Desiree Stone disappeared."

Manny nodded. "They were lovers."

"So you think she's with him?" Angie said.

Manny looked at John. John looked at the floor.

"What?" Angie said.

"I think she's dead," Manny said. "Jeff, you gotta understand, he's—"

"A first-class bastard," John said. "Coldest prick you'll ever meet."

Manny nodded. "He'd trade his mother to the alligators for a pair of fucking shoes, if you know what I mean."

"But Desiree could be with him," Angie said.

"I suppose. But Jeff's traveling light. You know? He knows we're looking for him. And he knows a girl as good-looking as Desiree kind of stands out in a crowd. I'm not saying she might not have left Massachusetts with him, but he would have cut her loose at some point. Probably as soon as she found out about the money he stole. And I don't mean cut her loose like leave her behind at a Denny's or something. He would have buried her deep."

He looked down and his body sagged against the ropes.

"You liked her," Angie said.

He looked up and you could see it in his eyes. "Yeah," he said softly. "Look, I scam people? Yes. Right. I do. But most of these assholes? They come in bitching about malaise or chronic fatigue syndrome, how they'll never get over having wet the bed as a child. I say, fuck 'em. They obviously have too much time and too much money on their hands, and if some of that money can help the Church, all the better." He stared up at Angie with a cold defiance that gradually warmed or weakened into something else. "Desiree Stone wasn't like that. She came to us for help. Her whole fucking world caved in on her in a period of, like, two weeks and she was afraid she was going to crack up. You might not believe this, but the Church could have helped her. I really think that."

Angie shook her head slowly and turned her back to him. "Save us some time, here, Manny. Jeff Price's story about his family getting killed by carbon monoxide poisoning?"

"Bullshit."

I said, "Someone infiltrated Grief Release recently. Someone like us. You know who I'm talking about?"

He was genuinely confused. "No."

"John?"

John shook his head.

"Any leads on Price's whereabouts?" Angie said.

"How do you mean?"

"Come on," I said. "Manny. You can wipe out my credit and bank account, at night, in less than twelve hours, I'd say it'd be pretty hard to hide from you people."

"But that was Price's specialty. He came up with the whole concept of counter-ops."

"Counter-ops," I said.

"Yeah. Get to your opponent before they can get to you. Silence dissent. Do what the CIA does. All the information gathering, the sessions, the PIN test, that was all Price's idea. He started that back in Chicago. If anyone can hide from us, he's the guy."

"There was that time in Tampa," John said.

Manny glared at him.

"I'm not getting burned," John said. "I'm not."

"What time in Tampa?" I said.

"He used a credit card. His own. He must have been drunk," John said. "That's his weakness. He's a drinker. We have a guy, all he does, day in day out, is sit by a computer linked up to all the banks and credit companies Price has accounts with. Three weeks ago, this guy, he's staring at the computer screen one night and it starts making noise. Price used his credit card at a motel in Tampa, the Courtyard Marriott."

"And?"

"And," Manny said, "we had guys there in four hours. But he was gone. We don't even know if it was him. The desk clerk told us it was a chick used the card."

"Desiree maybe," I said.

"No. This chick was blond, had a big scar on her neck. The desk clerk said he was sure she was a hooker. Claimed the card was her daddy's. I think Price probably sold his credit cards or threw them out a window, let the vagrants find them. Just to screw with us."

"Have any been used since?" Angie said.

"No," John said.

"Kind of shoots holes in that theory, Manny."

"She's dead, Mr. Kenzie," Manny said. "I don't want her to be, believe me, but she is."

We grilled them for another thirty minutes, but we didn't come up with anything new. Desiree Stone had met, been manipulated by, and fallen in love with Jeff Price. Price stole $2.3 million that couldn't legally be reported because it was from the slush fund Grief Release and the Church had built out of money bilked from members. At ten A.M., February 12, Price accessed the bank code for the account in the Grand Cayman Islands, wired the money into his personal account at Commonwealth Bank, and withdrew it at eleven-thirty that same morning. He walked out of the bank and disappeared.

Twenty-one minutes later, Desiree Stone parked her car at 500 Boylston Street, nine city blocks from Price's bank. And that was the last anyone ever saw of her, either.

"By the way," I said, thinking of Richie Colgan, "who runs the Church? Who're the moneymen?"

"No one knows," Manny said.

"Please."

He glanced at Bubba. "Really. I'm serious. I'm sure the members of the council know, but not guys like us."

I looked at John.

He nodded. "The head of the Church, in name, is the Reverend Kett, but nobody's actually seen him in the flesh in at least fifteen years."

"Maybe even twenty," Manny said. "We get paid well, though, Kenzie. Real well. So we don't complain, and we don't ask questions."

I looked at Angie. She shrugged.

"We'll need a picture of Price," she said.

"It's on the diskettes," Manny said. "In a file called PFCGR—Personnel Files, Church and Grief Release."

"Anything else you can tell us about Desiree?"

He shook his head and his voice was pained when he spoke. "You don't meet many good people. I mean, good. No one in this room is a good person." He looked around at all of us. "But Desiree was. She would have been good for this world. And now she's probably in a ditch somewhere."

Bubba knocked Manny and John cold again, and then he and Nelson and the Twoomey brothers drove them out to a section of urban waste under the Mystic River Bridge in Charlestown. They waited for them to wake up with their hands bound and their mouths gagged. Then they booted them both out the back of the van, fired a couple of rounds into the ground near their heads until John whimpered and Manny wept. Then they drove off.

* * *

"People surprise you sometimes," Bubba said.

We sat on the hood of the Crown Victoria, parked by the side of the road in front of Plymouth Correctional. From here we could see the inmates' gardens and greenhouse, hear the boisterous sound of men playing basketball in the crisp air on the other side of the wall. But one look at the Cyclone fence stretched, coiled and vicious, around the top of the walls or the silhouettes of guard and rifle in the towers, and you couldn't mistake it for anything but what it was—a place that caged human beings. No matter how you felt about crime and punishment, that fact was always there. And it was an ugly one.

"She could be alive," Bubba said.

"Yeah," I said.

"No, seriously. Like I said, people surprise you. You two told me before those shitheads woke up in my place, she Maced some guy once."

"So?" Angie said.

"So it shows she's strong. You know? I mean, you got a guy sitting beside you and you pull out a can of Mace and shoot it in his eyes? You know what kind of strength that takes? That's a girl with some spine. Maybe she found a way to get away from this guy, this Price shitbird."

"But then she would have called her father. She would have made some sort of attempt at contact."

He shrugged. "Maybe. I don't know. You're the detectives, I'm the moron going to jail for packing a piece."

We leaned back against the car, looked up again

at the granite walls and Cyclone fence, the hard, darkening sky.

"Gotta go," Bubba said.

Angie hugged him tightly and kissed his cheek.

I shook his hand. "You want us to walk you to the door?"

"Nah. Feel like you were my parents on the first day of school."

"The first day of school," I said, "I remember you beat the hell out of Eddie Rourke."

"'Cause he gave me shit about my parents walking me to the door." He winked. "See you in a year."

"Before that," Angie said. "You think we'd forget to visit?"

He shrugged. "Don't forget what I told you. They'll surprise you, people."

We watched him walk up the crushed shell and gravel walkway, his shoulders hunched, hands in his pockets, the stiff breeze rising off the frozen furrows of vegetation in the fields and mussing his hair.

He went through the doors without a look back.

12

"So my daughter's in Tampa," Trevor Stone said.

"Mr. Stone," Angie said, "did you hear what we said?"

He tightened his smoking jacket at his throat, looked at her through bleary eyes. "Yes. Two men believe she's dead."

"Yes," I said.

"Do you?"

"Not necessarily," I said. "But from what we've heard of this Jeff Price, he doesn't seem like the type who'd keep a woman as noticeable as your daughter with him while he tries to lie low. So the Tampa lead . . ."

He opened his mouth to speak, then closed it. His eyes clenched shut and he seemed to be biting back against something acidic. His face was slick with sweat and paler than bleached bone. Yesterday morning, he'd been prepared for us, and he'd used his cane and dressed smartly and presented the figure of a frail but proud and resilient warrior.

Tonight, however, with no time to prepare for

our arrival, he sat in the wheelchair Julian told us he used three quarters of the time now, his mind and body exhausted by cancer and the chemotherapy trying to combat it. His hair stuck out in wispy static tufts from his head and his voice was a thin whisper soaked in gravel.

"It's a lead, however," he said, his eyes still closed, tremulous fist pressed to his mouth. "Maybe that's where Mr. Becker disappeared to also. Hmm?"

"Maybe," I said.

"How soon can you leave?"

"Huh?" Angie said.

He opened his eyes. "For Tampa. Could you be ready first thing in the morning?"

"We'd have to make flight arrangements," I said.

He scowled. "Flight arrangements are unnecessary. Julian can pick you up first thing in the morning and take you to my plane."

"Your plane," Angie said.

"Find my daughter or Mr. Becker or Mr. Price."

"Mr. Stone," Angie said. "It's a long shot."

"Fine." He coughed into his fist, closed his eyes again for a moment. "If she's alive, I want her found. If she's dead, I need to know. And if this Mr. Price is behind her death, will you do something for me?"

"What?" I said.

"Would you be so kind as to kill him?"

The air in his room suddenly felt like ice.

"No," I said.

"You've killed people before," he said.

"Never again," I said as he turned his head toward the window. "Mr. Stone."

He turned his head back, looked at me.

"Never again," I repeated. "Is that understood?"

He closed his eyes, lay his head back against the headrest in his wheelchair, and waved us from the room.

"You see a man who is closer to dust than flesh," Julian said as he held Angie's coat in the marble foyer.

Angie reached for her coat and he motioned for her to turn her back to him. She grimaced, but did so, and Julian slid her coat up her arms and over her back.

"I see a man," he said as he reached into the closet for my jacket, "who towered over other men, who towered over industry and finance and every world he chose to place his foot upon. A man whose foot-falls caused trembling. And respect. Utmost respect."

He held out my jacket and I stepped into it, smelled the clean, cool scent of his cologne. It wasn't a brand I recognized, but somehow I knew it was out of my price range anyway.

"How long have you been with him, Julian?"

"Thirty-five years, Mr. Kenzie."

"And the Weeble?" Angie said.

Julian gave her a thin smile. "That would be Mr. Clifton?"

"Yes."

"He has been with us for twenty years. He was Mrs. Stone's valet and personal secretary. Now he helps me with property upkeep and maintenance, attending to Mr. Stone's business interests when Mr. Stone himself is too tired."

I turned to face him. "What do you think happened to Desiree?"

"I wouldn't know, sir. I only hope it's nothing irreparable. She's a divine child."

"And Mr. Becker?" Angie said.

"How do you mean, Miss?"

"The night he disappeared he was en route to this house. We checked with the police, Mr. Archerson. There were no reports of any disturbances or strange incidents along Route One-A that night. No car accidents or abandoned vehicles. No cab companies which drove a fare to or toward this address at the time in question. No rental cars rented to a Jay Becker that day, and his own car is still parked in his condo parking lot."

"And this leads you to assume?" Julian said.

"We have no assumptions," I said. "Just feelings, Julian."

"Ah." He opened the door for us and the air that flowed into the foyer was arctic. "And those feelings tell you what?"

"They tell us someone's lying," Angie said. "Maybe a lot of someones."

"Food for thought. Yes." Julian tipped his head. "Good evening, Mr. Kenzie, Miss Gennaro. Do drive carefully."

"Up is down," Angie said as we drove over the Tobin Bridge and the lights of the city skyline spread before us.

"What?" I said.

"Up is down. Black is white. North is south."

"Okay," I said slowly. "Do you want to pull over and let me drive?"

She shot me a look. "This case," she said. "I'm

starting to get the feeling everyone's lying and everyone has something to hide."

"Well, what do you want to do about it?"

"I want to stop taking anything at face value. I want to question everything and trust no one."

"Okay."

"And I want to break into Jay Becker's place."

"Now?" I said.

"Right now," she said.

Jay Becker lived in Whittier Place, a high-rise overlooking the Charles River or the Fleet Center depending on the placement of your condo.

Whittier Place is part of the Charles River Apartments, a horrific complex of modern luxury housing built in the seventies along with City Hall, the Hurley and Lindemann Center buildings, and the JFK Building to replace the old West End neighborhood, which several genius city planners decided had to be razed so Boston in the 1970s would look like London in *A Clockwork Orange*.

The West End had looked a lot like the North End, if a bit dustier and dingier in places due to its proximity to the red-light districts of Scollay Square and North Station. The red-light districts are gone now, as is the West End, as are most pedestrians after five o'clock. In the place of a neighborhood, city planners erected a cement complex of squat sprawling erector-set municipal buildings, no function and all form, and the form hideous too, and tall cinderblock apartment complexes that look like nothing so much as an arid, characterless hell.

"If You Lived Here," the clever signs told us as

we looped around Storrow Drive toward the entrance to Whittier Place, "You'd Be Home Now."

"If I lived in this car," Angie said, "wouldn't I be home, too?"

"Or under that bridge."

"Or in the Charles."

"Or in that Dumpster."

We ran with that until we found a parking space, another place we'd call home had we lived there.

"You really hate modern, don't you?" she said as we walked toward Whittier Place and I looked up at it with a scowl on my face.

I shrugged. "I like modern music. Some TV shows are better than they've ever been. That's about it, though."

"There's not a single modern piece of architecture you like?"

"I don't instantaneously want to nuke Hancock Towers or the Heritage when I see them. But Frank Lloyd Wrong and I. M. Pei have never designed a house or building which could compete with even the most basic Victorian."

"You're definitely a Boston boy, Patrick. Through and through."

I nodded as we walked up toward the doors of Whittier Place. "I just want them to leave my Boston alone, Ange. Go to Hartford if they want to build shit like this. Or L.A. Wherever. Just away."

She squeezed my hand, and I looked in her face, saw a smile there.

We entered the visitors' foyer through a set of glass doors, came face-to-face with another set that was locked. To our right was a bank of nameplates.

The nameplates bore three-digit numbers beside them and there was a phone to the left of the entire bank of names. Just as I'd feared. You couldn't even do the old trick of pressing ten buzzers at once and hoping someone would buzz you in. If you used the phone, the person who picked it up could see you through a security camera.

All those darn criminals have made it awful hard on us private detectives.

"It was fun watching you get worked up out there," Angie said. She opened her purse, held it over her head, and dumped the contents on the floor.

"Yeah?" I knelt beside her and we began scooping things back into the purse.

"Yeah. It's been a while since you got worked up over anything."

"You, too," I said.

We looked at one another, and the questions in her eyes probably lived in my own right then:

Who are we these days? What's left in the wake of all the things Gerry Glynn took? How do we get happy again?

"How many sticks of lip balm can one woman have?" I said and went back to the pile on the floor.

"Ten's about right," she said. "Five if you gotta travel light."

A couple approached on the other side of the glass. The man looked like an attorney, sculpted salt-and-pepper hair and red and yellow Gucci tie. The woman looked like an attorney's wife, pinched and suspicious.

"Your play," I said to Angie.

The man pushed open the door and Angie moved

her knee out of the way, a long strand of hair falling out from behind her ear as she did so, swinging down by her cheekbone and framing her eye.

"Excuse me," she said, chuckling softly and holding the guy with her eyes. "Clumsy as always."

He looked down at her and his merciless boardroom eyes picked up her gaiety. "I can't walk across an empty room without tripping, myself."

"Ah," Angie said. "A kindred spirit."

The man smiled like a shy ten-year-old. "Coordinated people beware," he said.

Angie gave it a short, hard laugh, as if his uncommon wit had surprised her. She scooped up her keys. "There they are."

We rose from our knees as the wife moved past me and the man held the door open.

"Be more careful next time," he said with mock sternness.

"I'll try." Angie leaned into the words a bit.

"Lived here long?"

"Come, Walter," the woman said.

"Six months."

"Come, Walter," the woman repeated.

Walter took one last look in Angie's eyes and went.

When the door closed behind them, I said, "Heel, Walter. Roll over, Walter."

"Poor Walter," Angie said as we reached the elevator bank.

"Poor Walter. Please. Could you have been any more breathy by the way?"

"Breathy?"

"'Sex months,'" I said in my best Marilyn Monroe voice.

"I didn't say 'sex.' I said 'six.' And I wasn't that breathy."

"Whatever you say, Norma Jean."

She elbowed me and the elevator doors opened and we rode them up to the twelfth floor.

At Jay's door, Angie said, "You got Bubba's gift?"

Bubba's gift was an alarm decoder. He'd given it to me last Christmas but I hadn't had the chance to try it out yet. It read the sonic pitch of an alarm's call and decoded it in a matter of seconds. The moment a red light appeared in the tiny LED screen of the decoder, you pointed it at the alarm source and pressed a button in the center and the alarm's bleat stopped.

That was the theory anyway.

I'd used Bubba's equipment before and usually it was fine as long as he didn't use the phrase "cutting edge." Cutting edge, in Bubbaspeak, meant it still had a few bugs in the system or hadn't been tested yet. He hadn't used the phrase when he gave me the decoder, but I still wouldn't know if it worked until we got into Jay's place.

I knew from previous visits that Jay also had a silent alarm wired into Porter and Larousse Consultants, a security firm downtown. When the alarm was tripped, you had thirty seconds to call the security firm and give them the password, or Johnny Law was on his way.

On the way over, when I mentioned that to Angie, she said, "Let me worry about that. Trust me."

She picked the two door locks with her kit while I watched the hall, and then she opened the door and we stepped inside. I closed the door behind me, and Jay's first alarm went off.

It was only slightly louder than an air raid siren, and I pointed Bubba's decoder at the blinking box above the kitchen portico, pressed the black button in the center. Then I waited. One-Mississippi, two-Mississippi, three-Mississippi, come on, come on, come on . . . Bubba was pretty close to losing his ride back from prison, and then the red light appeared on the LED and I pressed the black button again and the air raid siren died.

I looked at the small box in my hand. "Wow," I said.

Angie picked up the phone in the living room, pressed a single digit on the speed-dial console, waited a moment, then said, "Shreveport."

I came into the living room.

"You have a nice night, too," she said into the receiver and hung up.

"Shreveport?" I said.

"It's where Jay was born."

"I know that. How did you know it?"

She shrugged, looked around the living room. "I must have heard him mention it over drinks or something."

"And how'd you know it was his code word?"

She gave me another little shrug.

"Over *drinks*?" I said.

"Mmm." She moved past me and headed for the bedroom.

The living room was immaculate. A black leather

L-shaped sectional took up a third with a charcoal smoked-glass coffee table in front of it. On the coffee table lay three neatly stacked issues of *GQ* and four remote controls. One was for the fifty-inch wide-screen TV, another for the VCR, a third for the laser disc machine, and a fourth for the stereo component system.

"Jay," I said, "buy a universal remote for crying out loud."

There were several technical handbooks in the bookcase, a few Le Carré novels, and several by the surrealists Jay loved—Borges, García Márquez, Vargas Llosa, and Cortázar.

I gave the books and then the couch cushions a cursory once-over, found nothing, and moved into the bedroom.

Good private detectives are notoriously minimalist. They've seen firsthand what the random jottings on a piece of paper or the hidden diary can lead to, so they're very rarely pack rats. More than one person has said that my apartment resembles a hotel suite more than a home. And Jay's place, while far more plushly materialistic than my own, was still pretty impersonal.

I stood in the bedroom doorway as Angie lifted the mattresses on the antique sleigh bed, lifted the throw rug by the walnut dresser. The living room had been icy modern, all blacks and charcoals and cobalt-blue postmodern paintings on the walls. The bedroom seemed to be following a more naturalistic motif, the blond hardwood floor polished and gleaming under the small antique replica chandelier. The bedspread was hand-sewn and bright, the desk in the corner a matching walnut to the dresser and bureau.

As Angie moved to the desk, I said, "So when did you and Jay have drinks?"

"I slept with him, Patrick. Okay? Get over it."

"When?"

She shrugged as I came over to the desk behind her. "Last spring or summer. Around there somewhere."

I opened a drawer as she opened its counterpart beside me. "During your 'days of unleashing'?" I said.

She smiled. "Yeah."

"Days of unleashing" had been what Angie called her dating ritual after she separated from Phil—extremely short-term relationships with no attachments, dominated by as casual an approach as was possible to sex in the years since the discovery of AIDS. It was a phase, one she grew bored with far quicker than I had. Her days of unleashing had lasted maybe six months, mine about nine years.

"So how was he?"

She frowned at something in the drawer. "He was good. But he was a moaner. I can't stand guys who moan too loud."

"Me, either," I said.

She laughed. "You find anything?"

I closed the last of the drawers. "Stationery, pens, car insurance policy, nothing."

"Me either."

We checked the guest bedroom, found nothing there, went back to the living room.

"What are we looking for again?" I said.

"A clue."

"What kind of clue?"

"A big one."

"Oh."

I checked behind the paintings. I took the back off the TV. I looked in the laser disc tray, the multiple CD tray, the tape port in the VCR. All were distinctly lacking in the clue department.

"Hey." Angie came back out of the kitchen.

"Find a big clue?" I said.

"I don't know if I'd call it big."

"We're only accepting big clues here today."

She handed me a newspaper clipping. "This was hanging on the fridge."

It was a small item from a back page, dated August 29 of last year:

MOBSTER'S SON DROWNS

Anthony Lisardo, 23, son of reputed Lynn loan shark, Michael "Crazy Davey" Lisardo, died of apparent accidental drowning in the Stoneham Reservoir late Tuesday evening or early Wednesday morning. The younger Lisardo, who police believe may have been intoxicated, entered the grounds illegally through a hole in the fence. The Reservoir, long a popular, though illegal, swimming hole for local youths, is patrolled by two Marshals of the State Park Service, but neither Marshal Edward Brickman or Marshal Francis Merriam noticed Anthony Lisardo enter the grounds or saw him swimming in the reservoir during thirty minute patrols. Due to evidence that Mr. Lisardo was with an unidentified companion, police have left the case open pending the identification of Mr. Lisardo's companion, but Captain Emmett Groning of the Stoneham Police stated: "Foul play has been ruled out in this case, yes. Unequivocally."

The elder Lisardo refused to comment on this case.

"I'd say that's a clue," I said.

"Big or small?"

"Depends whether you measure by width or length."

I got a good dope-slap for that on the way out the door.

13

"Who'd you say you're working for?" Captain Groning said.

"Ahm, we didn't," Angie said.

He leaned back from his computer. "Oh. But just because you're friends with Devin Amronklin and Oscar Lee of BPD Homicide, I'm supposed to help you?"

"We were kinda counting on it," I said.

"Well, until Devin called me, I was kinda counting on getting home to the old lady, fella."

It had been a couple decades, at least, since someone had called me "fella." I wasn't sure how to take it.

Captain Emmett Groning was five foot seven and weighed about three hundred pounds. His jowls were longer and fleshier than any bulldog's I'd ever seen and his second and third chins hung down from the first like scoops of ice cream. I had no idea what the fitness requirements for the Stoneham Police Department were, but I had to assume Groning had been behind a desk for at least a decade. In a reinforced chair.

He chewed a Slim Jim, not eating it really, just sort of rolling it from side to side in his mouth and taking it out occasionally to admire his tooth marks and slick spittle residue. At least I think it was a Slim Jim. I couldn't be sure, because I hadn't seen one in a while—since around the same time I last heard the word "fella."

"We don't want to keep you from . . . the old lady," I said, "but we're sort of pressed for time."

He rolled the Slim Jim across his lower lip, somehow managed to suck on it as he spoke. "Devin said you're the two who settled Gerry Glynn's hash."

"Yes," I said. "His hash was settled by us."

Angie kicked my ankle.

"Well." Captain Groning stared over his desktop at us. "Don't have that kind of thing round here."

"What kind of thing?"

"Your sicko killers, twisted deviants, your cross-dressers and baby rapers. No, sir. We leave that for all you in the Big City."

The Big City was approximately eight miles from Stoneham. This guy seemed to think there was an ocean or two in between.

"Well," Angie said, "that's why I've always wanted to retire here."

It was my turn to kick her.

Groning raised an eyebrow and leaned forward as if to see what we were doing on the other side of his desk. "Yeah, well, like I always say, miss, you could do whole lots worse than this here town, but not whole lots better."

Call the Stoneham Chamber of Commerce, I thought, you got yourselves a town slogan.

"Oh, absolutely," Angie said.

He leaned back in his chair and I waited for it to tip, send him back through the wall into the next office. He pulled the Slim Jim out of his mouth, looked at it, and sucked it back in again. Then he looked at his computer screen.

"Anthony Lisardo of Lynn," he said. "Lynn, Lynn, City of Sin. You ever hear it called that?"

"First time." Angie smiled brightly.

"Oh, sure," Groning said. "That's a hell of a place, ol' Lynn. Wouldn't raise a dog there."

Bet you'd eat one, though.

I chewed my tongue, reminded myself I'd resolved to work on my maturity this year.

"Wouldn't raise a dog," he repeated. "Well. Anthony Lisardo, yeah, had himself a heart attack."

"I thought he drowned."

"He did, fella. He surely did. First, though, he had a heart attack. Our doc didn't think it was so big it would have killed him on its own, him being a young kid and all, but he was in five feet of water when it happened, so that was pretty much all she wrote. All she wrote," he repeated with the same musical lilt he'd used on "wouldn't raise a dog."

"Anybody know what caused the heart attack?"

"Well, sure, fella. Sure someone knows. And that someone is Captain Emmett T. Groning of Stoneham." He leaned back in his chair, left eyebrow cocked, and nodded at us, that Slim Jim rolling along his bottom lip.

If I lived here, I'd never commit a crime. Because to do so would put me in the box with this guy, and five minutes with Captain Emmett T. Groning of

Stoneham, and I'd confess to everything from the Lindbergh baby's killing to Jimmy Hoffa's disappearance just to get locked up in a federal pen, as far away as possible.

"Captain Groning," Angie said, using the same breathy voice she'd used on Poor Walter, "if you could tell us what caused Anthony Lisardo's heart attack, why, I'd be much obliged."

Much obliged. Angela "Daisy Mae" Gennaro.

"*Cocaína,*" he said. "Or yeh-yo as some call it."

I was stuck in Stoneham with a fat guy doing his Al Pacino-as-Tony Montana imitation. Life didn't get much better.

"He snorted cocaine, had a heart attack, and drowned?" I said.

"Didn't snort it. Smoked it, fella."

"So it was crack?" Angie said.

He shook his tiny head and his jowls made a flapping noise. "Your standard cocaine," he said. "Mixed in with tobacco. What's known as an Ecuadoran cigarette."

"Tobacco followed by a hit of coke, followed by tobacco, then coke, tobacco, then coke," I said.

He seemed impressed. "You're familiar with it."

A lot of people who went to college in the early to mid eighties were, but I didn't tell him that. He struck me as the kind of guy who decided whether or not to elect presidents based on whether he believed they'd "inhaled" or not.

"I've heard rumors of it," I said.

"Well, that's what this Lisardo boy smoked. Had himself a groovy high going, man, but that high came a crashing on down in a real bummer way."

"Word," I said.

"What?"

"Def," I said.

"What?"

"Never mind," I said.

Angie's heel ground into my toe and she smiled sweetly at Captain Groning. "What about the witness? The newspaper said Lisardo had a companion."

Groning took his confused eyes off me and looked back at his computer screen. "Kid named Donald Yeager, aged twenty-two. Left the scene in a panic, but called it in about an hour later. We ID'd him from a jacket he left behind, sweated him in the box for a bit, but he didn't do jack. He just went to the reservoir with his buddy, drank some beer, smoked some mary jew wanna, and went for a dip."

"Did he do any coke?"

"Nah. He claimed he didn't know Lisardo was doing it either. Said, 'Tony hated coke.'" Groning clucked his tongue. "I said, 'And coke hated Tony, fella.'"

"Terrific comeback," I said.

He nodded. "Sometimes when me and the boys get going in the box, there's just no stopping us."

Captain Groning and the Boys. Bet they had barbecues and went to church together and sang Hank Williams, Jr., songs together and never met a rubber hose they didn't like.

"So how does Anthony's father feel about his son's death?" Angie asked.

"Crazy Davey?" Captain Groning said. "You see in the paper how they called him a 'mobster'?"

"Yes."

"Every corrupt guinea north of Quincy's a mobster all a sudden, I swear."

"And this particular guinea?" Angie said, her hands locked together into fists.

"Small-time. The papers said 'loan shark,' which is partly true, but mostly he's a chop-shop guy on the Lynnway."

Boston is one of the safest major metropolitan cities in the country. Our murder and assault and rape rates are barely blips on the screen compared with those of Los Angeles or Miami or New York, but we have all those cities beat when it comes to car theft. Boston criminals, for some reason, love to boost cars. I'm not sure why that is, since there's nothing terribly wrong with our public transportation system, but there you go.

And most of these cars end up on the Lynnway, a stretch of Route 1A that cuts over the Mystic River, and is lined from end to end with car dealerships and garages. Most of those dealerships and garages are legitimate, but several aren't. That's why most Bostonians who get their cars stolen shouldn't even bother checking their LoJack satellite-tracking system—it will just beep from a spot in the depths of the Mystic, just off the Lynnway. The tracking system, not the car. The car's in pieces and those pieces are on their way to fifteen different places within half an hour after you parked.

"Crazy Davey isn't pissed about his son's death?" I said.

"I'm sure he is," Captain Groning said. "But there's not much he can do about it. Oh, sure, he gave us all the usual 'My son don't do coke' bullshit, but what else is he going to say? Luckily, the way the mob's all messed up around here these days, and Crazy Davey not even being in the running for a slot, I don't have to care what he thinks."

"So Crazy Davey's small-time?" I said.

"Like a guppy," Captain Groning said.

"Like a guppy," I said to Angie.

And got another kick.

14

The offices of Hamlyn and Kohl Worldwide Investigations occupied the entire thirty-third floor of the John Hancock Tower, I. M. Pei's icy skyscraper of metallic blue glass. The edifice consists of sheets of mirrored glass, each twenty feet high and sixty feet long. Pei designed them so that the surrounding buildings would be captured in the glass with perfect resolution, and as you approach, you can see the light granite and red sandstone of Trinity Church and the imposing limestone of the Copley Plaza Hotel trapped in the smoked-blue of merciless glass. It's not all that unattractive an image, really, and at least the sheets of glass don't have a habit of falling out like they used to.

Everett Hamlyn's office faced the Trinity Church side and you could see clear to Cambridge on a sharp cold night like tonight. Actually, you could see clear to Medford, but I don't know anyone who'd want to look that far.

We sipped Everett Hamlyn's top-shelf brandy and watched him stand by his sheet of glass and stare out at the city laid in a carpet of lights at his feet.

He cut a hell of a figure, Everett did. Ramrod straight, skin so tight to his hard frame that I often thought if a paper cut appeared in the flesh, he'd burst wide open. His gunmetal hair was trimmed tight to the scalp, and I'd never seen so much as a hint of stubble or shadow on his cheeks.

His work ethic was legendary—the one who turned on the lights in the morning and shut them off at night. A man who'd been overheard more than once saying that any man who needed more than four hours of sleep couldn't be trusted, because treachery lay in sloth and a need for luxury and more than four hours' sleep was a luxury. He'd been with the OSS during World War II, just a kid then, but now, more than fifty years later, he still looked better than most men half his age.

Retirement would come for Everett Hamlyn, it was said, the same night death did.

"You know I can't discuss this," he said, his eyes watching our reflections in the glass.

I met his eyes the same way. "Off the record, then. Everett, please."

He smiled softly and raised his glass, took a parsimonious sip of brandy. "You knew you'd find me alone, Patrick. Didn't you?"

"I assumed I would. You can see your light from the street if you know what square to look for."

"Without a partner to protect me if you both decided to double-team me, wear an old man down."

Angie chuckled. "Now, Everett," she said, "please."

He turned from the window, a twinkle in his eyes. "You are as ravishing as ever, Angela."

"Flattery won't deflect our questions," she said, but a blush of rose lit the flesh under her chin for a moment.

"Come on, you ol' smoothie," I said. "Tell me how good I look."

"You look like shit, dear boy. Still cutting your own hair, I see."

I laughed. I'd always liked Everett Hamlyn. Everyone did. The same couldn't be said of his partner, Adam Kohl, but Everett had an effortless ease with people that belied his military past, his stiff bearing and uncompromising sense of right and wrong.

"Mine's all real, though, Everett."

He touched the hard stubble atop his head. "You think I'd pay to have this on my head?"

"Everett," Angie said, "if you'd please tell us why Hamlyn and Kohl dropped Trevor Stone as a client we'll be out of what little hair you have left. I promise."

He made the smallest movement with his head, one that I knew from experience was a negative motion.

"We need some help here," I said. "We're trying to find two people now—Desiree Stone and Jay."

He came around to his chair, seemed to study it before he sat in it. He turned it so that he was facing us directly and placed his arms on his desk.

"Patrick," he said, his voice soft and almost paternal, "do you know why Hamlyn and Kohl offered you a job seven years after you'd turned down our first offer?"

"Envy of our client base?"

"Hardly." He smiled. "Actually, Adam was dead set against it at first."

"I'm not surprised. No love lost there."

"I'm sure of that." He sat back, the brandy snifter warming in his palm. "I convinced Adam that you were both seasoned investigators with an admirable—some would say astonishing—case clearance rate. But that wasn't all there was to it, and, Angela, please don't take any offense at what I'm about to say, because none is intended."

"I'm sure I won't, Everett."

He leaned forward, held my eyes with his own. "I wanted you, Patrick, specifically. You, my boy, because you reminded me of Jay and Jay reminded me of myself at a young age. You both had smarts, you both had energy, but there was more to it than that. What you both had that is so rare these days is passion. You were like little boys. You'd take any job, no matter how small, and treat it like a big job. You see, you loved the *work*, not just the job. You loved everything about it, and it was a joy to come to work those three months the two of you worked together here. Your excitement filled these rooms—your bad jokes, and your sophomoric high jinks, your sense of fun, and your absolute determination to close every case." He leaned back in his chair and sniffed the air above him. "It was a tonic."

"Everett," I said, but stopped there, unsure what else to say.

He held up a hand. "Please. I was like that once, you see. So when I tell you Jay was as close to a son as I've ever had, do you believe me?"

"Yes," I said.

"And if the world were more populated with men like him and myself and even you, Patrick, I think it would be a better place. The raging ego of a proud man, I know, but I'm old, so I'm entitled."

"You don't look it, Everett," Angie said.

"You're a dear child." He smiled at her. He nodded to himself and looked down at his brandy snifter. He carried it with him as he left his chair again, crossed back to the window, and stood looking out at the city. "I believe in honor," he said. "No other human attribute deserves the exaltation honor does. And I've tried to live my life as an honorable man. But it's hard. Because most men aren't honorable. Most people aren't. To most, honor is an antiquated notion at best, a corrosive naïveté at worst." He turned his head and smiled at us, but it was a tired smile. "Honor, I think, is in its twilight. I'm sure it will die with the century."

"Everett," I said, "if you could just—"

He shook his head. "I can't discuss any aspects of Trevor Stone's case or Jay Becker's disappearance with you, Patrick. I simply can't. I can only tell you to remember what I've said about honor and the people without it. And to fend for yourselves with that knowledge." He walked back to his chair and sat in it, turned it halfway back to the window. "Good night," he said.

I looked at Angie and she looked at me and then we both looked at the back of his head. I could see his eyes reflected in the glass again, but they weren't looking at my reflection this time, only his own. He peered at the ghostly image of himself trapped and swimming in the glass and the reflected lights of other buildings and other lives.

We left him sitting in his chair, staring out at the city and himself simultaneously, bathed in the deep blue of the night sky.

At the door, his voice stopped us, and it bore a tone I'd never recognized before. It was still rich with experience and wisdom, still steeped in lore and expensive brandy, but now it carried the barest hint of fear.

"Be careful in Florida," Everett Hamlyn said.

"We never said we were going to Florida," Angie said.

"Be careful," he repeated and leaned back in the chair to sip from his glass of brandy. "Please."

PART TWO

SOUTH OF THE BORDER

15

I'd never been on a private jet before, so I really had nothing to compare it to. I couldn't even make a leap and compare it with being on a private yacht or a private island because I'd never been on one of those, either. About the only "private" thing I owned was my car, a rebuilt '63 Porsche. So . . . being on a private jet was a lot like being in my car. Except the jet was bigger. And faster. And had a bar. And flew.

Lurch and the Weeble picked us up at my apartment in a dark blue limousine, which was also a lot bigger than my car. Actually, it was bigger than my apartment.

From my place, we drove down Columbia Road past several onlookers who were probably wondering who was getting married or which high school was holding a prom in mid-March at nine in the morning. Then we glided through rush hour traffic and the Ted Williams Tunnel to the airport.

Instead of entering the traffic heading toward the main terminals, we looped around and headed toward the southern tip of the airport landmass,

drove past several freight terminals and food pack-
aging warehouses, a convention hotel I'd never even
known was there, and pulled up in front of the General Aviation Headquarters.

Lurch went inside as Angie and I rifled the wet
and dry bar compartments for orange juice and pea-
nuts, stuffed our pockets, and debated whether to
clip two champagne flutes.

Lurch returned, followed by a short guy who
jogged to a brown and yellow minivan with the words
PRECISION AVIATION on the side.

"I want a limousine," I said to Angie.

"Parking in front of your apartment would be a
bitch."

"I wouldn't need my apartment anymore." I leaned
forward, asked the Weeble, "Does this thing have
closets?"

"It has a trunk." He shrugged.

I turned back to Angie. "It has a trunk."

We pulled in behind the van and followed it to
a guard kiosk. Lurch and the van driver got out,
showed their licenses to the guard, and he noted the
numbers on a pad and handed Lurch a pass, which
Lurch placed on the dash when he got back in. The
orange barrier arm in front of the van rose and we
drove past the kiosk onto the tarmac.

The van pulled around a small building and we
followed, and cruised along a path between two run-
ways, with several more spread out around us, the
pale bulbs of their lights glistening in the morning
dew. I saw cargo planes and sleek jets and small white
puddle-jumpers, fuel trucks and two idling ambulances, a parked fire engine, three other limousines.

It was as if we'd entered into a formerly hidden world, which reeked of power and influence and lives so important they couldn't be bothered with normal modes of transport or something so banal as a schedule designed by others. We were in a world where a first-class seat on a commercial airliner was considered second-class, and the true corridors of power lay before us dotted with landing lights.

I guessed which was Trevor Stone's jet before we pulled to a stop in front of it. It stood out even in the company of Cessnas and Lears. It was a white Gulfstream with the thin slanted beak of the Concorde, a body as streamlined as a bullet, wings tucked tight against the hull, a tail the shape of a dorsal fin. A mean-looking machine, a white hawk in holding pattern.

We took our bags from the limousine and another Precision employee took them from our hands and placed them in the luggage compartment by the tail.

I said to Lurch, "What's a jet like this run—about seven million?"

He chuckled.

"He's amused," I said to Angie.

"Busting a gut," she said.

"I believe Mr. Stone paid twenty-six million for this Gulfstream."

He said "this" Gulfstream, as if there were a couple more back in the garage in Marblehead.

"Twenty-six." I nudged Angie. "Bet the salesman was asking twenty-eight, but they talked him down."

On board, we met Captain Jimmy McCann and his copilot, Herb. They were a jolly pair, big smiles and bushy eyebrows raised behind mirrored glasses.

They assured us we were in good hands, don't you worry, haven't crashed one in months, ha ha ha. Pilot humor. The best. Can't get enough of it.

We left them to play with their dials and their torques and think up amusing ways to make us lose bowel control and whimper, and we headed back into the main compartment.

It, too, seemed bigger than my apartment, but maybe I was just star-struck.

There was a bar, a piano, three single beds in the rear. The bathroom had a shower in it. Plush lavender carpeting covered the floor. Six leather seats were spread out along the right and left side and two of them had cherrywood tables riveted to the floor in front of them. Each seat reclined like a Barca-Lounger.

Five of the seats were empty. The sixth was occupied by Graham Clifton, aka the Weeble. I'd never even seen him leave the limousine. He sat facing us, a leather-bound notebook in his lap, a closed fountain pen on top of it.

"Mr. Clifton," I said, "I didn't know you'd be joining us."

"Mr. Stone thought you could use an extra hand down there. I know the Gulf Coast of Florida well."

"We don't usually need extra hands," Angie said and sat down across from him.

He shrugged. "Mr. Stone insisted."

I picked up the phone attached to my seat console. "Well, let's see if we can't change Mr. Stone's mind."

He placed his hand on mine, pushed the phone

back into the console. For such a small man, he was very strong.

"Mr. Stone doesn't change his mind," he said.

I looked into his tiny black eyes, and saw only my reflection blinking back at me.

We landed at Tampa International at one, and I felt the sticky heat in the air even before our wheels touched down on the tarmac without so much as a bump. Captain Jimmy and copilot Herb might have seemed like goofball knuckleheads, and maybe they were in all other aspects of their lives, but by the way they handled that plane during takeoff, landing, and one bit of turbulence over Virginia, I suspected they could land a DC-10 on the tip of a pencil in the middle of a typhoon.

My first impression of Florida after the heat was one of green. Tampa International looked to have erupted from the center of a mangrove forest, and everywhere I looked I saw shades of green—the dark blackish green of the mangrove leaves themselves, the wet gray-green of their trunks, the grassy small hills that bordered the ramps into and out of the airport, the bright teal tramcars that crisscrossed the terminals like something out of *Blade Runner* if it had been directed by Walt Disney.

Then my gaze rose to the sky and found a shade of blue I'd never seen before, so rich and bright against the white coral arches of the expressway that I would have sworn it had been painted there. Pastels, I thought, as we blinked against the light streaming through the windows of the tramcar—I hadn't seen this many assaultive pastels since the nightclub scene in the mid-eighties.

And the humidity. Jesus. I'd gotten a whiff of it as I left the jet, and it was like a hot sponge had punched a hole in my chest and burrowed straight into my lungs. The temperature in Boston had been in the mid-thirties when we left, and that had seemed warm after such a long winter. Here, it had to be eighty, maybe more, and the moist, furry blanket of humidity seemed to kick it up another twenty degrees.

"I've got to quit smoking," Angie said as we arrived at the terminal.

"Or breathing," I said. "One of the two."

Trevor, of course, had a car waiting for us. It was a beige Lexus four-door with Georgia plates and Lurch's southern double for a driver. He was tall and thin and of an age somewhere between fifty and ninety. His name was Mr. Cushing, and I had a feeling he'd never been called by his first name in his life. Even his parents had probably called him Mr. Cushing. He wore a black suit and driver's cap in the broiling white heat, but when he opened the door for Angie and myself, his skin was drier than talc. "Good afternoon, Miss Gennaro, Mr. Kenzie. Welcome to Tampa."

"Afternoon," we said.

He closed the door and we sat in the air conditioning as he walked around and opened the front passenger door for the Weeble. Mr. Cushing took his place behind the wheel and handed three envelopes to the Weeble, who took one and handed two back to us.

"Your hotel keys," Mr. Cushing informed us as he pulled away from the curb. "Miss Gennaro, you are staying in Suite Six-eleven. Mr. Kenzie, you are in Six-twelve. Mr. Kenzie, you'll also find in your envelope a set of keys to a car Mr. Stone has rented on your behalf. It's parked in the hotel parking lot. The parking space number is on the back of the envelope."

The Weeble opened a personal computer the size of a small paperback, pressed a few buttons. "We're staying at the Harbor Island Hotel," he said. "Why don't we all go back and shower and then we'll drive to the Courtyard Marriott where this Jeff Price supposedly stayed?"

I glanced at Angie. "Sounds fine."

The Weeble nodded and his laptop beeped. I leaned forward and saw that he'd called up a map of Tampa on the screen. It morphed into a series of city grids, each growing tighter and tighter until a blinking dot I assumed was the Courtyard Marriott sat in the center of the screen and the lines around it filled with street names.

Any moment I expected to hear a tape-recorded voice tell me what my mission was.

"This tape will self-destruct in three seconds," I said.

"What?" Angie said.

"Never mind."

16

Harbor Island looked to be man-made and relatively new. It grew out of the older section of downtown, and we reached it by crossing a white bridge the length of a small bus. There were restaurants and several boutiques and a yacht basin that glittered gold in the sun. Everything seemed to be following a coral, Caribbean motif, lots of sandblasted whites and ivory stucco and crushed-shell walkways.

As we pulled up to the hotel, a pelican swooped in toward the windshield and both Angie and I ducked, but the freaky-looking bird caught a bit of wind and rode it in a low swoop onto the top of a piling by the dock.

"Friggin' thing was huge," Angie said.

"And awfully brown."

"And very prehistoric-looking."

"I don't like them, either."

"Good," she said. "I didn't want to feel silly."

Mr. Cushing dropped us at the door and the bellmen took our bags and one said, "Right this way, Mr. Kenzie, Ms. Gennaro," even though we hadn't introduced ourselves.

"I'll meet you at your room at three," the Weeble said.

"You bet," I said.

We left him chatting with Mr. Cushing and followed our impossibly tanned bellboy to an elevator and up to our rooms.

The suites were enormous and looked down on Tampa Bay and the three bridges that intersected it, the milky green water sparkling under the sun and all of it so pretty and pristine and placid I wasn't sure how long I could take it before I puked.

Angie came through the door that adjoined the suites and we stepped out onto the balcony and closed the sliding glass door behind us.

She'd changed from basic black city clothes into light-blue jeans and a white mesh tank top, and I tried to keep both my mind and my eyes off the way the tank top hugged her upper body so I could discuss the business at hand.

"How fast do you want to dump the Weeble?" I said.

"Now isn't soon enough." She leaned over the rail and puffed lightly on her cigarette.

"I don't trust the room," I said.

She shook her head. "Or the rental car."

Sunlight streaked through her black hair and lit the chesnut highlights that had been hiding under all that darkness since last summer. Heat flushed her cheeks.

Maybe this place wasn't so bad.

"Why'd Trevor put the pressure on all of a sudden?"

"The Weeble you mean?"

"And Cushing." I waved my arm at the room behind me. "All this shit."

She shrugged. "He's getting frantic about Desiree."

"Maybe."

She turned and leaned back against the railing, the bay framing her, her face tilted to the sun. "Plus, you know how it is with rich guys."

"No," I said. "I don't."

"Well, it's like if you go out on a date with one—"

"Hang on, let me get a pen for this."

She flicked her cigarette ash at me. "They're always trying to impress you with how fast they can get the world to jump at a snap of their fingers, how every wish they think you have can be predicted and accommodated. So you go out and valet people open your car door, doormen open other doors, maître d's pull out your chair, and the rich guy orders your meal for you. This is supposed to make you feel good, but it makes you feel enslaved instead, like you don't have a mind of your own. Or," she said, "a choice in the matter. Trevor probably wants us to feel that every one of his resources is at our disposal."

"But you still don't trust the room or the rental car."

She shook her head. "He's used to power. He's probably not very good at trusting others to do what he'd do on his own if he were healthy. And once Jay went missing . . ."

"He wants to know our every move."

"Exactly."

I said, "I like the guy and all . . ."

"But too bad for him," she agreed.

Mr. Cushing was standing by his Lexus out front when we stopped to look out the window from the mezzanine level. I'd gotten a look at the parking garage on the way in and saw that its exit came out the other side of the hotel and emptied onto a small street of boutiques. From where Cushing stood, he couldn't see the exit or the small bridge that led off the island.

Our rental car was a light blue Dodge Stealth and had been rented from a place called Prestige Imports on Dale Mabry Boulevard. We found the car and drove it out of the lot and off Harbor Island.

Angie navigated from a map on her lap and we turned onto Kennedy Boulevard and then found Dale Mabry and drove north.

"Lotta pawnshops," Angie said, looking out the window.

"And strip malls," I said. "Half of them closed, half of them new."

"Why don't they just reopen the closed ones instead of building new ones?"

"It's a mystery," I said.

The Florida we'd seen until now had been the postcard Florida, it seemed—coral and mangroves and palm trees, glittering water and pelicans. But as we drove Dale Mabry for at least fifteen of the flattest miles I've ever driven, its eight lanes spread out wide and pointing infinitely through waves of rubbery heat at the overturned bowl of blue sky, I wondered if this wasn't the real Florida.

Angie was right about the pawnshops and I was right about the strip malls. There was at least one of each per block. And then there were bars with cleverly subtle names like Hooters and Melons and Cheeks broken up by fast-food drive-through places and even drive-through liquor stores for the drunk on the go. Pocking the landscape within all this were several trailer parks and trailer park dealerships and more used car lots than I'd ever seen on the Lynnway Automile.

Angie tugged at her waist. "Jesus, these jeans are hot."

"Take 'em off then."

She reached over and turned on the air conditioning, hit the switch on the console between our seats and the power windows rolled up.

"How's that?" she said.

"I still like my suggestion better."

"You don't like the Stealth?" Eddie, the rental agent, seemed confused. "Everyone likes the Stealth."

"I'm sure they do," Angie said. "But we're looking for something a little less conspicuous."

"Wow," Eddie said as another rental agent came in off the lot through the sliding glass doors behind him. "Hey, Don, they don't like the Stealth."

Don screwed up his sunburned face and looked at us like we'd just beamed down from Jupiter. "Don't like the Stealth? Everyone likes the Stealth."

"So we've heard," I said. "But it doesn't quite fit our purposes."

"Well what y'all looking for—an Edsel?" Don said.

Eddie loved that one. He slapped his hand on the counter and he and Don made noises I can only describe as hee-hawing.

"What we all are looking for," Angie said, "is something like that green Celica you have in the parking lot."

"The convertible?" Eddie said.

"Sure 'nuff," Angie said.

We took the car as is, even though it needed a wash and gas. We told Don and Eddie we were in a rush, and they seemed even more confused by that than our desire to trade in the Stealth.

"A rush?" Don said, as he checked our driver's license information against that on the original rental agreement Mr. Cushing had filled out.

"Yeah," I said. "It's when you have places to go in a hurry."

Surprisingly, he didn't ask me what "hurry" meant. He just shrugged and tossed me the keys.

We stopped at a restaurant called the Crab Shack to pore over the map and figure out a plan.

"This shrimp is unbelievable," Angie said.

"So's this crab," I said. "Try some."

"Trade."

We did, and her shrimp was indeed succulent.

"And cheap," Angie said.

The place was literally a shack of clapboard and

old piling wood, the tables pocked and scarred, the food served on paper plates, our plastic pitcher of beer poured into waxed paper cups. But the food, better than most seafood I'd ever had in Boston, cost about a fourth of what I was used to paying.

We sat on the back patio, in the shade, overlooking a swamp of sea grass and beige water that ended about fifty yards away at the back of, yep, a strip mall. A white bird with legs as long as Angie's and a neck to match landed on the patio railing and looked down at our food.

"Jesus," Angie said. "What the hell is that?"

"That's an egret," I said. "It's harmless."

"How do you know what it is?"

"*National Geographic*."

"Oh. You're sure it's harmless?"

"Ange," I said.

She shuddered. "So I'm not a nature girl. Sue me."

The egret jumped off the rail and landed by my elbow, its thin head up by my shoulder.

"Christ," Angie said.

I picked up a crab leg and flung it out over the rail and the egret's wing hit my ear as it took off over the rail and dove for the water.

"Great," Angie said. "Now you've encouraged it."

I picked up my plate and cup. "Come on."

We went inside and studied the map as the egret returned and stared at us through the glass. Once we had a pretty good idea where we were going, we folded up the map, and finished our food.

"You think she's alive?" Angie said.

"I don't know," I said.

"And Jay," she said. "You think he came here after her?"

"I don't know."

"Me either. We don't know much, do we?"

I watched as the egret craned its long neck to get a better look at me through the glass.

"No," I said. "But we're quick studies."

17

No one we talked to at the Courtyard Marriott recognized Jeff Price or Desiree from the photos we showed them. They were pretty sure about it, too, if only because the Weeble and Mr. Cushing had shown them the same photographs half an hour before we arrived. The Weeble, smarmy little bastard that he was, had even left a note for us with the Marriott concierge requesting our presence in the Harbor Hotel bar at eight.

We tried a few more hotels in the same area, got nothing but blank stares, and returned to Harbor Island.

"This isn't our town," Angie said as we rode the elevator down from our rooms to the bar.

"Nope."

"And it drives me crazy. It's useless our even being here. We don't know who to talk to, we don't have any contacts, we don't have any friends. All we can do is walk around like idiots showing everyone these stupid photographs. I mean, duh."

"Duh?" I said.

"Duh," she repeated.

"Oh," I said, "*duh*. I get it. For a minute there I thought you were just saying duh."

"Shut up, Patrick." She walked off the elevator and I followed her into the bar.

She was right. We were useless here. The lead was useless. To fly fourteen hundred miles simply because Jeff Price's credit card had been used at a hotel over two weeks ago was moronic.

But the Weeble didn't agree. We found him in the bar, sitting at a window overlooking the bay, an abnormally blue concoction filling the daiquiri glass in front of him. The pink plastic stirrer in his glass was carved at the top into the shape of a flamingo. The table itself was nestled in between two plastic palm trees. The waitresses wore white shirts tied off just below their breasts and black Lycra biking shorts so tight they left no doubt as to the existence (or lack thereof) of a panty line.

Ah, paradise. All that was missing was Julio Iglesias. And I had a feeling he was on his way.

"It's not fruitless," the Weeble said.

"You talking about your drink or this trip?" Angie said.

"Both." He worked his nose around the flamingo and sipped the drink, wiped at the blue mustache left behind with his napkin. "Tomorrow, we'll split up and canvass all the hotels and motels in Tampa."

"And once we run out?"

He reached for the bowl of macadamia nuts in front of him. "We try all the ones in St. Petersburg."

And so it was.

For three days, we canvassed Tampa, then St.

Petersburg. And we discovered that parts of both weren't as clichéd as Harbor Island had led us to believe or as ugly as our drive down Dale Mabry. The Hyde Park section of Tampa and the Old Northeast section of St. Pete were actually quite attractive, with cobblestone streets and old southern houses with wraparound porches and gnarled, ancient banyan trees providing canopies of shade. The beaches in St. Pete, too, if you could ignore all the crotchety blue-hairs and sweaty redneck bikers, were gorgeous.

So we found something to like.

But we didn't find Jeff Price or Desiree or Jay Becker.

And the cost of our paranoia, if that's what it was, was becoming tiring, too. Each night we parked the Celica in a different spot, and each morning we checked it for tracking devices and found none. We never bothered looking for bugs because the car was a convertible and whatever conversations we had in it would be drowned out by the wind, the radio, or a combination of the two.

Still, it felt odd to be so aware of the watchful eyes and ears of others, almost as if we might be trapped in a movie everyone was watching except us.

The third day, Angie went down by the hotel pool to reread everything in our case file and I took the phone out onto the balcony, checked it for bugs, and called Richie Colgan at the city desk of the *Boston Tribune*.

He answered the phone, heard my voice, and put me on hold. Some pal, I swear.

Six stories below, Angie stood by her chaise lounge

and stripped off her gray shorts and white T-shirt to reveal the black bikini underneath.

I tried not to watch. I really did. But I'm weak. And a guy.

"What're you doing?" Richie said.

"You wouldn't believe me if I told you."

"Try me."

"Watching my partner squirt sunblock on her legs."

"Bullshit."

"I wish," I said.

"She know you're watching?"

"You kidding?"

At that moment, Angie turned her head and looked up at the balcony.

"I've just been busted," I said.

"You're dead."

Even from this distance, though, I could see her smile. Her face stayed tilted toward mine for a moment, then she shook her head gently and turned back to the business at hand and rubbed the oil into her calves.

"Christ," I said, "it is way too hot in this state."

"Where are you?"

I told him.

"Well, I got some news," he said.

"Pray tell."

"Grief Release, Incorporated, filed suit against the *Trib*."

I leaned back in my chair. "You published a story already?"

"No," he said. "That's the point. My inquiries,

such as they've been, have been extremely discreet. There's no way they could've known I was onto them."

"But they do."

"Yeah. And they aren't fucking around, either. They're taking us into federal court for invasion of privacy, interstate theft—"

"Interstate?" I said.

"Sure. A lot of their clients don't necessarily live in the Bay State. They got files on those discs for clients from across the Northeast and Midwest. Technically, Angie stole *information* that crossed state lines."

"That's a fine line," I said.

"Of course it is. And they still have to prove I have the discs and a whole lot of other shit, but they must have a judge in their pocket because at ten this morning my publisher got an injunction slapped on him prohibiting the publication of any article on Grief Release which can be directly linked to information found only on those discs."

"Well, then you got them," I said.

"How so?"

"They can't prove what's on those discs if they don't have them. And even if they have everything backed up on a hard drive, they can't prove that what's on the hard drive is necessarily what's on those discs. Right?"

"Exactly. But that's the beauty of the injunction. We can't prove that what we intend to publish *doesn't* come from those discs. Unless we're stupid enough to produce them, of course, in which case they're useless anyway."

"Catch-twenty-two."

"Bingo."

"Still," I said, "this sounds like a smokescreen, Rich. If they can't prove you have the discs or that you even know about them, then sooner or later, some judge is going to say they don't have a legal leg to stand on."

"But we have to find that judge," Richie said. "Which means filing appeals, maybe going to a federal superior court. Which takes time. Meanwhile, I have to run around and independently substantiate everything on those discs by using other sources. They're eating up a clock on us, Patrick. That's what they're doing. And they're succeeding."

"Why?"

"I don't know. And I also don't know how they got onto me so quick. Who'd you tell?"

"No one."

"Bullshit."

"Richie," I said, "I didn't even tell my client."

"Who is your client, by the way?"

"Rich," I said, "come on."

There was a long dead pause on the line.

When he spoke again, his voice was a whisper. "You know what it takes to buy a federal judge?"

"A lot of money."

"A lot of money," he said. "And a lot of power, Patrick. I've been looking into the alleged head of the Church of Truth and Revelation, guy by the name of P. F. Nicholson Kett—"

"No shit? That's his full name?"

"Yeah. Why?"

"Nothing," I said. "Just, what a dorky name."

"Yeah, well, P. F. Nicholson Kett is like a god and

guru and high priest all rolled into one. And no one has seen him in over twenty years. He transmits messages through underlings, supposedly from his yacht off the coast of Florida. And he—"

"Florida," I said.

"Right. Look, I think the guy's bullshit. I think he died a long time ago and he was never much to begin with. He was just the face someone put on the Church."

"And the face behind the face is?"

"I don't know," he said. "But it ain't P. F. Nicholson Kett. The guy was a moron. A former advertising copy editor from Madison, Wisconsin, who used to write porno scripts under an assumed name to make ends meet. The guy could barely spell his own name. But I've seen films and he had charisma. Plus he had that look in his eyes of all fanatics, part fervent belief, part comatose. So someone took this guy with good looks and charisma and propped his ass up to be a little tin god. And that someone, I'm sure of it, is the guy who's suing my ass at the moment."

On his end I heard the sudden eruption of several beeping phone lines.

"Call me later. Gotta run."

"Bye," I said, but he was already gone.

As I came out of the hotel onto the walkway that curled through a garden of palm trees and incongruous Australian pines, I saw Angie sitting on the chaise, her hand over her eyes to block the sun, looking up at a young guy in an orange Speedo so small that comparing it to a loincloth would probably be an insult to loincloths.

Another guy in a blue Speedo sat on the other side of the pool watching the two of them, and I could tell by the smile on his face that Orange Speedo was his pal.

Orange Speedo held a half-full bottle of Corona by his shiny hip, a lime floating in the foam, and as I approached, I heard him say, "You can be friendly, can't you?"

"I can be friendly," Angie said. "I'm just not in the mood right now."

"Well, change your mood. You're in the land of fun 'n' sun, darlin'."

Darlin'. Big mistake.

Angie shifted in her chaise, placed the case file on the ground by the chair. "The land of fun 'n' sun?"

"Yeah!" The guy took a swig of the Corona. "Hey, you should be wearing your sunglasses."

"Why's that?"

"Protect those pretty eyes of yours."

"You like my eyes," she said in a tone I'd heard before. Run, I wanted to scream to the guy. Run, run, run.

He rested the beer on his hip. "Yeah. They're feline."

"Feline?"

"Like a cat's," he said and leaned over her.

"You like cats?"

"Love 'em." He smiled.

"Then you should probably go to a pet store and buy one," she said. "Because I get the feeling that's the only pussy you're going to get tonight." She picked up the case file and opened it on her lap: "Know what I mean?"

I stepped off the path onto the pool patio as Orange Speedo took a step back and cocked his head and his hand tightened around the Corona bottle neck until his knuckles grew red.

"Hard to come up with a comeback to that one, ain't it?" I smiled brightly.

"Hey, partner!" Angie said. "You braved the sun to join me. I'm touched. And you're even wearing *shorts.*"

"Crack the case yet?" I squatted by her chaise.

"Nope. But I'm close. I can feel it."

"Bullshit."

"Okay. You're right." She stuck her tongue out at me.

"You know . . ."

I looked up. It was Orange Speedo and he was shaking in rage, pointing his finger at Angie.

"You're still here?" I said.

"You know," he repeated.

"Yes?" Angie said.

His pectorals pulsed and rippled and he held the beer bottle up by his shoulder. "If you weren't a woman, I'd—"

"Be in surgery about now," I said. "Even as it is, you're pushing it."

Angie pushed herself up on the chaise and looked at him.

He breathed heavily through his nostrils and suddenly spun on his heel and walked back to his buddy. They whispered to each other, then took turns glaring at us.

"You get the feeling my temperament just isn't right for this place?" Angie said.

* * *

We drove over to the Crab Shack for lunch.
Again.

In three days, it had become our home away from
home. Rita, a waitress in her mid-forties who wore a
weathered black cowboy hat, fishnet stockings under cutoff jeans, and smoked cheroots, had become
our first pal in the area. Gene, her boss and the
chief cook at the Crab Shack, was fast becoming our
second. And the egret from the first day—her name
was Sandra, and she was well behaved as long as you
didn't serve her beer.

We sat out on the dock and watched another
late afternoon sky gradually turn deep orange and
smelled the salt off the marsh and the gas too, unfortunately, and a warm breeze fingered its way through
our hair and shook the bells on the pilings and
threatened to toss our case file folder into the milky
water.

At the other end of the dock, four Canadians with
pink lemonade skin and ugly floral shirts scarfed plat-
ters of fried food and talked loudly about what a dangerous state they'd chosen in which to park their RV.

"First those drugs on the beach. Eh?" one of them
said. "Now this poor girl."

The "drugs on the beach" and the "poor girl" had
been all over the local news the last two days.

"Oh, yuh. Oh, yuh," one of the women in the
group clucked. "We might as well be in Miami, and
that is the truth, yuh."

The morning after we arrived, a few members
of a Methodist widows' support group on vacation
from Michigan were walking the beach in Dunedin

when they noticed several small plastic bags littering the shoreline. The bags were small and thick and, as it turned out, filled with heroin. By noon, several more had washed up on beaches in Clearwater and St. Petersburg, and unconfirmed reports even placed some as far north as Homosassa and as far south as Marco Island. The Coast Guard surmised that a storm that had been battering Mexico, Cuba, and the Bahamas may have sunk a ship carrying the heroin, but as yet they hadn't been able to sight the wreckage.

The "poor girl" story had been reported yesterday. An unidentified woman had been shot to death in a Clearwater motel room. The murder weapon was believed to have been a shotgun, the blast fired at pointblank range into the woman's face, making identification difficult. A police spokesman reported that the woman's body had also been "mutilated" but refused to specify how. The woman's age was estimated at anywhere between eighteen and thirty, and Clearwater police were trying to identify her through dental records.

My first thought upon reading about her was, *Shit. Desiree.* But after checking into the section of Clearwater where the body was found and hearing the coded language used on last night's six o'clock news, it became apparent that the victim had probably been a prostitute.

"Sure," one of the Canadians said, "it's like the Wild West down here. That is for sure."

"You are right there, Bob," his wife said and dipped her entire batter-fried grouper finger in a cup of tartar sauce.

It was a strange state, I'd been noticing, but in ways it was growing on me. Well, actually, the Crab Shack was growing on me. I liked Sandra and Rita and Gene and the two signs behind the bar that said, "If You Like the Way They Do Things in New York So Much, Take I-95 North," and "When I Get Old I'm Going to Move to Canada and Drive Real Slow."

I was wearing a tank top and shorts and my normally chalk-white skin had reached a happy shade of beige. Angie wore her black bikini top and a multicolored sarong and her dark hair was twisted and curled and the chestnut highlights were turning almost blond.

I'd enjoyed my time in the sun, but these past three days had been a godsend to her. When she forgot her frustration over the case, or once we'd reached the end of yet another fruitless day, she seemed to stretch and blossom and unwind into the heat, the mangroves, the deep blue sea and salty air. She stopped wearing shoes unless we were actively on the chase for Desiree or Jeff Price, drove to the beach at night to sit on the hood of the car and listen to the waves, even eschewed the bed in her suite at night for the white rope hammock on her balcony.

I met her eyes and she gave me a smile that was part sad knowledge and part intense curiosity.

We sat awhile like that, smiles fading, eyes locked, searching each other's faces for answers to questions that had never been vocalized.

"It's been Phil," she said and reached across the table to take my hand. "It felt like sacrilege for us two to, you know . . ."

I nodded.

Her sandy foot curled up over mine. "I'm sorry if it's been causing you pain."

"Not pain," I said.

She raised an eyebrow.

"Not real pain," I said. "Aches. Here and there. I've been worried."

She brought my hand to her cheek and closed her eyes.

"Thought you two were partners, not lovers," a voice cried.

"That," Angie said, eyes still closed, "would be Rita."

And it was. Rita, in her ten-gallon hat, her fishnet stockings red today, bringing us our plates of crawfish and shrimp and Dungeness crab. Rita loved that we were detectives. Wanted to know how many shoot-outs we'd had, how many car chases we'd been on, how many bad guys we'd killed.

She placed our plates on the table and moved the pitcher of beer off the case file to put our plastic utensils somewhere, and the warm wind picked up the folder and the plastic sporks and tossed them to the deck.

"Oh, dear," she said.

I got up to help her but she was quick. She scooped up the folder and closed it, caught the one stray photo between her thumb and index finger just as it had lifted off the deck and headed over the railing in a gust. She turned to us and smiled, her left leg still up in a half pirouette from when she'd lunged for the photo.

"You missed your calling," Angie said. "Shortstop for the Yankees."

"I had a Yankee," she said, as she looked down at the photo she'd caught. "Wasn't worth shit in the sack, always talking about—"

"Go on, Rita," I said. "Don't be shy."

"Hey," she said, her eyes fixed on the photo. "Hey," she said again.

"What?"

She handed me the folder and the photo and dashed off the dock inside.

I looked at the photo she'd caught.

"What was that all about?" Angie said.

I handed the photo to her.

Rita came running back onto the dock and handed me a newspaper.

It was a copy of the *St. Petersburg Times*, today's edition, and she'd folded it back to page 7.

"Look," she said, breathless. She pointed to an article midway down the page.

The headline read: MAN HELD IN BRADENTON SLAYING.

The man's name was David Fischer and he was being held for questioning in the stabbing death of an unidentified man found in a motel room in Bradenton. Details in the article were sketchy, but that wasn't the point. One look at a photo of David Fischer and I knew why Rita had handed it to me.

"Jesus," Angie said, looking at the photo. "That's Jay Becker."

18

To get to Bradenton, we drove 275 south through St. Petersburg and then rode up onto a monstrous bridge called the Sunshine Skyway, which stretched over the Gulf of Mexico and connected the Tampa/St. Petersburg area with the Sarasota/Bradenton landmass.

The bridge had two spans, which seemed to be modeled after dorsal fins. From a distance, as the sun dipped toward the sea and the sky turned purple, the dorsal fins appeared to have been painted a smoky gold, but as we rode over the bridge itself, we saw that the fins were made up of several yellow beams that converged in ever-smaller triangles. At the base of the beams were lights that when turned on and combined with the setting sun, gave the fins a golden hue.

Christ, they loved their colors down in these parts.

"'. . . the unidentified man,'" Angie read from the paper, "'believed to be in his early thirties, was found facedown on the floor of his room at the Isle of Palms Motel with a fatal knife wound to his abdomen. The suspect, David Fischer, forty-one, was arrested in his room which adjoined the victim's. Police refused to speculate on motive or comment on what led them to arrest Mr. Fischer.'"

Jay was being held in the Bradenton County Jail, according to the paper, pending a bond hearing, which would have been held sometime today.

"What the hell is going on?" Angie said as we drove off the bridge and the purple in the sky deepened.

"Let's ask Jay," I said.

He looked awful.

His dark brown hair was flecked with gray that had never been there before and the bags under his eyes were so puffy I'd have doubted anyone who told me he'd slept this week.

"Well, is that Patrick Kenzie sitting before me or is that Jimmy Buffett?" He gave me a weak smile as he came through the doorway into the visitation area and picked up the phone on the other side of the Plexiglas.

"Barely recognize me, eh."

"You almost look tan. I didn't know such a thing was possible for you pasty Celtic folk."

"Actually," I said, "it's makeup."

"Cash bail is a hundred grand," he said and sat down in his cubicle across from mine, cradled the phone between chin and shoulder long enough to light a cigarette. "In lieu of a million-dollar bond. My bail bondsman's a guy name of Sidney Merriam."

"When'd you start smoking?"

"Recently."

"Most people are quitting at your age, not starting."

He winked. "I'm no slave to fashion."

"A hundred grand," I said.

He nodded and yawned. "Five-fifteen-seven."

"What?" I said.

"Locker twelve."

"Where?" I said.

"Bob Dylan in St. Pete," he said.

"What?"

"Run the clue down, Patrick. You'll find it."

"Bob Dylan in St. Pete," I said.

He looked over his shoulder at a slim, muscular guard with a diamondback's eyes.

"Songs," he said. "Not albums."

"Got it," I said, though I didn't yet. But I trusted him.

"So they sent you," he said with a rueful smile.

"Who else?" I said.

"Yeah. Makes sense." He leaned back in his chair and the harsh fluorescents overhead only accentuated how much weight he'd lost since I'd last seen him two months ago. His face looked like a skull.

He leaned forward. "Get me out of here, buddy."

"I will."

"Tonight. Tomorrow, we'll go to the dog races."

"Yeah?"

"Yeah. I got fifty bucks on a gorgeous greyhound. You know?"

I'm sure I looked confused again, but I said, "Sure."

He smiled, his lips cracked by the sun. "I'm counting on it. Those nice Matisse prints we saw in Washington that time? They're not going to last forever."

It took me thirty seconds of looking into his face before I understood.

"See you soon," I said.

"Tonight, Patrick."

Angie drove back over the bridge as I looked through a street map of St. Petersburg we'd bought at a gas station.

"So he doesn't think his prints will hold up?" Angie said.

"No. He told me once that when he was with the FBI, he made himself up a false identity. I guess it was this David Fischer guy. He has a friend in Latent Prints at Quantico, so his fingerprints are actually on file twice."

"Twice?"

"Yeah. It's not a solution, it's a Band-Aid. The local police send his prints to Quantico, this friend of his has the computer programmed to spit out the Fischer identity. But only for a couple of days. Then the friend, to save his job, will have to call back and say, 'The computer's coming up with something odd. These prints also match a Jay Becker, who used to work for us.' See, Jay always knew if he got in some sort of jam, his only hope was to make bail and skip."

"So we're aiding and abetting bail-jumping."

"Not so as they can prove it in court," I said.

"Is he worth it?"

I looked at her. "Yeah."

We crossed into St. Petersburg and I said, "Name some Dylan songs."

She glanced at the map on my lap. "'Highway Sixty One Revisited.'"

"Nope."

"'Leopard-Skin Pill-Box Hat.'"

I grimaced at her.

"What?" She scowled. "Okay. *Positively Fourth Street.*"

I looked down at the map. "You're a wonder," I said.

She held up an imaginary tape recorder. "Could you say that into the mike, please?"

Fourth Street in St. Petersburg ran from one end of the city to the other. At least twenty miles. With a lot of lockers in between.

But only one Greyhound station.

We pulled in the parking lot and Angie sat in the car while I went inside, found locker twelve, and dialed the combination on the lock. It popped open on the first try and I pulled out a leather gym bag. I hefted it, but it wasn't terribly heavy. It could have been filled with clothes for all I knew, and I decided to wait until I was back in the car before I checked. I closed the locker and walked back out of the terminal, got in the car.

Angie pulled onto Fourth Street and we drove through what appeared to be a slum, lots of people lounging on the porches in the heat, waving at flies, kids huddled in groups along the corners, half the streetlights knocked out.

I placed the bag on my lap and unzipped it. I stared inside for a full minute.

"Drive a little faster," I said to Angie.

"Why?"

I showed her the contents of the bag. "Because there's at least two hundred thousand dollars in here."

She stepped on the gas.

19

"Jesus, Angie," Jay said, "last time I saw you, you looked like Chrissie Hynde taking fashion tips from Morticia Addams, and now you look like an island girl."

The jail clerk slid a form over the counter to Jay.

Angie said, "You always knew how to smooth-talk a girl."

Jay signed the form and handed it back. "No shit, though? I didn't know a white woman's skin could get that dark."

The clerk said, "Your personal effects," and emptied a manila envelope onto the counter.

"Careful," Jay said as his watch bounced on the counter. "That's a Piaget."

The clerk snorted. "One watch. *Pi-a-jay.* One money clip, gold. Six hundred seventy-five dollars cash. One key chain. Thirty-eight cents in coins . . ."

As the clerk checked off each of the remaining items and slid them across to Jay, Jay leaned against the wall and yawned. His eyes skipped from Angie's face to her legs, rose back up over her cutoff jeans and ripped sweatshirt with the sleeves shorn off at the elbows.

She said, "Would you like me to pivot so you could ogle the back?"

He shrugged. "Been in prison, ma'am, you'll have to excuse me."

She shook her head and looked at the floor, hid her smile in the hair that fell around her face.

It was odd to watch them occupy similar space, knowing what I did now about their past together. Jay always wore a certain wolfish look around beautiful women, but rather than take offense, most women found it innocuous and a bit charming if only because Jay was so blatant and boyish about it. But there was more to the look tonight. Jay's face held a melancholia I'd never seen before, an aura of bone-deep fatigue and resignation as he glanced at my partner.

She seemed to notice it, too, and a curious curl formed in her lips.

"You okay?" she said.

Jay pushed himself off the wall. "Me? Fine."

"Mr. Merriam," the clerk said to Jay's bail bondsman, "you'll have to cosign here and here."

Mr. Merriam was a middle-aged man in an off-white three-piece suit who tried to give off the air of the genteel southern gentleman, even though I picked up traces of New Jersey in his accent.

"Be mah pleasure," he said, and Jay rolled his eyes. They signed the papers and Jay scooped up the last of his rings and his wrinkled silk tie, placed the rings in his pocket and the tie loosely under the collar of his white shirt.

We walked out of the station and stood in the parking lot to wait for a cop to bring Jay's car around front.

"They let you drive here?" Angie said.

Jay sucked the wet night air into his nostrils. "They're very courteous down these parts. After they questioned me at the motel, this old cop with a real polite way about him asked me if I'd mind following him down to the station for a few questions. He even said, 'If ya'll got the time, we sure would 'preciate it, yes sir,' but he wasn't really asking if you know what I mean."

Merriam stuck a card in Jay's hand. "Sir, if you ever require mah services again, why it would—"

"Sure." Jay snapped the card from his hand and looked off at the soft blue circles that pulsed around the yellow streetlights fringing the parking lot.

Merriam shook my hand, then Angie's, then walked with the stilted steps of the constipated or the practicing drunk to his Karmann Ghia convertible with the dented passenger door. The car stalled once on its way out of the parking lot, and Mr. Merriam kept his head down as if mortified before he got it going again and pulled out onto the main road.

Jay said, "If you guys hadn't shown up, I would have had to send *that* guy to the Greyhound station. You believe it?"

"If you jump bail," Angie said, "won't that poor guy get ruined financially?"

He lit a cigarette, looked down at her. "Don't worry, Ange, I got everything figured out."

"That's why we're bailing you out of jail, Jay."

He looked at her, then at me, and laughed. It was a short, hard sound, more bark than anything. "Jesus, Patrick, she give you this much shit on a regular basis?"

"You're looking rough, Jay. Bad as I've ever seen you."

He stretched his arms out, cracked the muscles between his shoulder blades. "Yeah, well, I get me a shower and a good night's sleep, I'll be good as new."

"We have to go somewhere and talk first," I said.

He nodded. "You didn't come fourteen hundred miles just to work on your tans, marvelous as they are. And they are marvelous." He turned and looked at Angie's body openly, his eyebrows raised. "I mean, my God, Ange, I gotta tell you again, your skin, I mean, it's the color of a coffee-regular at Dunkin' Donuts for Chrissakes. Makes me want to—"

"Jay," she said, "will you just quit it? Give it a fucking rest, for crying out loud."

He blinked and leaned back on his heels. "Okay," he said with a sudden coldness. "No, when you're right, you're right. And you're right, Angela. You are right."

She looked at me and I shrugged.

"Right is right," he said. "Right is definitely right."

A black Mitsubishi 3000 GT pulled up with two young cops in it. They were laughing as they approached, and the tires smelled like they'd just had some rubber burned off.

"Nice car," the driver said as he got out by Jay.

"You like it?" Jay said. "It handle well?"

The cop giggled as he looked at his partner. "Handled just fine, buddy."

"Good. Steering wasn't too tight when you were doing your doughnuts?"

"Come on," Angie said to Jay, "get in the car."

"Steering was just fine," the cop said.

His partner stood by me at the open passenger door. "Axles felt a little wobbly, though, Bo."

"That's true," Bo said, still blocking Jay from entering the car. "I'd get a mechanic take a look at your U-joints."

"Sound advice," Jay said.

The cop smiled and stepped out of Jay's way. "You drive her careful, Mr. Fischer."

"Remember," his partner said, "a car is not a toy."

They both laughed at that one and walked up the steps into the station.

I didn't like the look in Jay's eyes, or his whole demeanor since he'd been released. He seemed paradoxically lost and determined, adrift and focused, but it was an angry, spiteful focus.

I hopped in the passenger seat. "I'll ride with you."

He leaned in. "I'd really prefer if you didn't."

"Why?" I said. "We're going to the same place. Right, Jay? To talk?"

He pursed his lips and exhaled loudly through his nostrils, looked at me with a burned-out gaze. "Yeah," he said eventually. "Sure. Why not?"

He got in and started the car as Angie walked over to the Celica.

"Buckle up," he said.

I did, and he slammed the gearshift into first and hailed the gas, dropping into second a split second later with his wrist flexed for another quick push into third. We cleared the small ramp leading out of the parking lot, and Jay shifted into fourth while the wheels were still in the air.

He took us to an all-night diner in downtown Bradenton. The streets around it were deserted, devoid of even the memory of human life, it seemed, as if a neutron bomb had hit an hour before we arrived. Blank, dark window squares in the few skyscrapers and squat municipal buildings around the diner stared down at us.

There were a few people in the diner, night owls by the look of them—a trio of truck drivers at the counter flirting with the waitress; a lone security guard with a patch for something called Palmetto Optics on his shoulder reading a newspaper with a pot of coffee for companionship; two nurses with wrinkled uniforms and low, tired voices two booths over from our own.

We ordered two coffees and Jay ordered a beer. For a minute we all studied our menus. When the waitress returned with our drinks, we each ordered a sandwich, though none of us sounded particularly enthusiastic about it.

Jay placed an unlit cigarette in his mouth and stared out the window as a clap of thunder ripped a hole in the sky and it began to rain. It wasn't a light rain or one that grew heavy gradually. One moment the street was dry and pale orange under the street-lights, and the next, it disappeared behind a wall of water. Puddles formed in seconds and boiled on the sidewalk, and the raindrops hammered the tin roof of the diner so loudly it seemed the heavens had dumped several truckloads of dimes.

"Who'd Trevor send down here with you?" Jay said.

"Graham Clifton," I said. "There's another guy, too. Cushing."

"They know about you coming to get me out of jail?"

I shook my head. "We've been shaking their tails since we arrived."

"Why?"

"I don't like them."

He nodded. "The papers release the identity of the guy I supposedly killed?"

"Not that we know of."

Angie leaned across the table and lit his cigarette. "Who was it?"

Jay puffed on the cigarette, but didn't withdraw it from his mouth. "Jeff Price." He glanced at his reflection in the window as the rain poured down the pane in rivulets and turned his features to rubber, melted his cheekbones.

"Jeff Price," I said. "Former treatment supervisor for Grief Release. That Jeff Price?"

He took the cigarette from his mouth, tapped the ash into the black plastic ashtray. "You've done your homework, D'Artagnan."

"Did you kill him?" Angie asked.

He sipped his beer and looked across the table at us, his head cocked to the right, his eyes swimming from side to side. He took another drag off his cigarette and his eyes left us and followed the smoke as it pirouetted from the ash and floated over Angie's shoulder.

"Yeah, I killed him."

"Why?" I said.

"He was a bad man," he said. "A bad, bad man."

"There are lots of bad men out there," Angie said. "Bad women, too."

"True," he said. "Very true. Jeff Price, though? That fucker deserved a lot slower death than I gave him. I guarantee you that." He took a good-sized slug from his beer. "He had to pay. Had to."

"Pay for what?" Angie said.

He raised the beer bottle to his mouth, and his lips trembled around it. When he placed the bottle back on the table, his hand was as tremulous as his lips.

"Pay for what, Jay?" Angie repeated.

Jay gazed out the window again as the rain continued to clatter against the roof and boil and snap in the puddles. The dark hollows under his eyes reddened.

"Jeff Price killed Desiree Stone," he said and a single tear fell from his eyelid and rolled down his cheek.

For a moment, I felt a deep ache bore through the center of my chest and leak into my stomach.

"When?" I said.

"Two days ago." He wiped his cheek with the back of his hand.

"Wait," Angie said. "She was with Price all this time, and he just decided to kill her two days ago?"

He shook his head. "She wasn't with Price the entire time. She ditched him three weeks ago. The last two weeks," he said softly, "she was with me."

"With you?"

Jay nodded and sucked at the air, blinked back the tears in his eyes.

The waitress brought our food but we barely looked at it.

"*With* you?" Angie said. "As in . . . ?"

Jay gave her a bitter smile. "Yes. *With* me. As in, Desiree and I were falling in love, I guess." He chuckled but it only half left his mouth; the other half seemed to strangle in the back of his throat. "Hilarious, ain't it? I come down here hired to kill her and I end up falling for her."

"Whoa," I said. " 'Hired to kill her'?"

He nodded.

"By whom?"

He looked at me like I was retarded. "Who do you think?"

"I don't know, Jay. That's why I'm asking."

"Who hired you?" he said.

"Trevor Stone."

He looked at us until we got it.

"Jesus Christ," Angie said and hit the table with her fist so loudly the three truck drivers turned in their seats to look at us.

"Glad I could bring you both up to speed," Jay said.

20

For the next few minutes, none of us spoke. We sat in our booth as the rain spewed against the windows and the wind bent the row of royal palms along the boulevard, and we ate our sandwiches.

Nothing, I thought as I chewed my sandwich without really tasting it, was as it seemed just fifteen minutes ago. Angie had been right the other night—black was white, up was down.

Desiree was dead. Jeff Price was dead. Trevor Stone had hired Jay not just to find his daughter, but to kill her.

Trevor Stone. Jesus Christ.

We had taken this case for two reasons—greed and empathy. The first was not an honorable motive. But fifty thousand dollars is a lot of money, particularly when you haven't worked in several months and your chosen profession isn't known for its workmen's comp bennies.

But it was still greed. And if you accept a job because you're greedy, you can't really bitch too much when your employer turns out to be a liar. The pot calling the kettle black and all that . . .

However, greed wasn't our only motivation. We'd taken this case because Angie had looked at Trevor Stone with sudden recognition—the recognition of one griever upon meeting another. She'd cared about his grief. I had, too. And any lingering doubts I'd had disappeared when Trevor Stone showed us the shrine he'd erected to his lost daughter.

But it hadn't been a shrine. Had it?

He hadn't surrounded himself with photos of Desiree because he needed to believe she was alive. He'd filled his room with his daughter's face so his blood could feed off his hate.

Once again, my perspective of prior events was reshaping, transmogrifying, reinventing itself until I felt increasingly stupid for ever trusting my initial instincts.

This case, I swear.

"Anthony Lisardo," I said to Jay eventually.

He chewed his sandwich. "What about him?"

"What happened to him?"

"Trevor had him whacked."

"How?"

"Laced a pack of cigarettes with coke, gave it to Lisardo's friend—what was his name, Donald Yeager—and Yeager left the pack in Lisardo's car the night they went to the reservoir."

"What," Angie said, "the coke was laced with strychnine or something?"

Jay shook his head. "Lisardo had an allergic reaction to coke. He'd collapsed once at a college party when he was dating Desiree. That was his first heart attack. And that was the first and only time he was stupid enough to try coke. Trevor knew about it, laced the cigarettes, the rest is history."

"Why?"

"Why'd Trevor kill Lisardo?"

"Yeah."

He shrugged. "Man had a problem sharing his daughter with anyone, if you know what I mean."

"But then he hired you to kill her?" Angie said.

"Yup."

"Again," Angie said. "Why?"

"I don't know." He looked down at the table.

"You don't *know*?" Angie said.

His eyes widened. "I don't know. What's so—"

"Didn't she tell you, Jay? I mean, you were 'with' her these past few weeks. Didn't she have some idea why her own father would want her, oh I dunno, dead?"

His voice was hard and loud. "If she did, Ange, she didn't want to talk about it, and now she's sort of beyond the point where she can."

"And I'm sorry about that," Angie said. "But I have to have a little more sense of Trevor's motives to believe he'd want to kill his own daughter."

"The fuck do I know?" Jay hissed. "Because he's crazy. He's whacked and the cancer's in his brain. I don't know. But he wanted her dead." He crumpled an unlit cigarette in his palm. "And now she is. Whether by his hand or not, she's gone. And he's going to pay."

"Jay," I said softly, "back up. To the beginning.

You went on that Grief Release retreat to Nantucket, and then you disappeared. What happened in the interim?"

He kept his glare on Angie for another few seconds, then let it drop. He looked at me.

I raised my eyebrows up and down a couple of times.

He smiled and it was his old smile, his old self for a moment. He looked around the diner, gave one of the nurses a sheepish grin, then looked back at us.

"Gather round, children." He rubbed crumbs off his hands and leaned back in his chair. "A long time ago, in a galaxy far, far away . . ."

21

The Grief Release retreat for Level Fives was held in a nine-bedroom Tudor on a bluff overlooking Nantucket Sound. The first day, all Level Fives were encouraged to join in a group "purging" session in which they'd try to shed their layers of negative aura (or "malapsia blood poisoning," as Grief Release termed it) by talking in depth about themselves and what had led them there.

In the session, Jay, using the David Fischer alias, immediately identified the first "purger" as a fraud. Lila Cahn was in her early thirties and pretty, with the sinewy body of an aerobics junkie. She claimed to have been the girlfriend of a small-time drug runner in a Mexican town called Catize, just south of Guadalajara. Her boyfriend had ripped off the local consortium of drug lords, who had taken their revenge by kidnapping Lila and her boyfriend off the street in broad daylight. They were dragged by a gang of five men to the basement of a bodega, where her boyfriend was shot once in the back of the head. The five men then raped Lila for six hours, an experience she described in vivid detail to the group. She was allowed to live to serve as a warning to any other *gringas* who might think of coming to Catize and getting mixed up with the wrong element.

Once Lila finished her story, the counselors hugged her and complimented her on her bravery in retelling such a horrific story.

"Only problem was," Jay told us in the diner, "the story was utter horseshit."

In the late 1980s, Jay was part of a joint FBI-DEA task force that went to Mexico in the wake of the murder of Kiki Camarena, a DEA agent. Ostensibly an information-seeking force, the real job of Jay and his fellow agents was to kick ass, take names, and make sure the Mexican drug lords would sooner shoot their own young before they'd entertain the idea of shooting a federal agent again.

"I lived in Catize for three weeks," he said. "There's not a basement in the entire town. The ground's too soft because the town's built over swampland. The boyfriend getting shot in the back of the head? No way. That's an American Mafia hit, not a Mexican one. You rip off a drug lord down there, you die one way and one way only—Colombian necktie. They cut your throat and pull your tongue out through the hole, toss your body from a moving car into the village square. And no Mexican gang rapes an American woman for six hours and lets her live to serve warning to other *gringas*. Warning for what? They wanted to send a warning, they would have cut her into pieces and airmailed her back to the States."

Looking for lies and inconsistencies now, Jay

identified four other alleged Level Fives whose stories didn't hold water. It was, he'd find out as the retreat wore on, standard operating procedure for Grief Release to place these frauds in groups of truly grief-stricken people because internal studies had shown that a client was far likelier to first confide in a "peer" before a counselor.

And what pissed Jay off most was hearing the bullshit stories threaded in with the real ones: a mother who'd lost her infant twins in a fire she escaped; a twenty-five-year-old man with an inoperable brain tumor; a woman whose husband had walked out on her for his nineteen-year-old secretary twenty years after their wedding and six days after the woman lost a breast in a mastectomy.

"These were shattered people," Jay told us, "looking for a lifeline, for hope. And these Grief Release scumbags nodded and cooed and probed for every dirty secret and every piece of financial minutiae just so they could blackmail them later and enslave them to the Church."

When Jay got mad, he usually got even.

By the end of the first night, he noticed Lila glancing at him, giving him shy smiles. The next night, he went to her room, and far from fitting the psychological profile of a woman who'd been gang-raped less than a year ago, Lila was joyfully uninhibited and quite inventive in bed.

"You know the golf-ball-through-the-garden-hose analogy?" Jay asked me.

"Jay," Angie said.

"Oh," he said. "Sorry."

For five torrid hours, Jay and Lila had sex in her

room. During breaks between rounds, she'd probe for information about his past, his current means, his hopes for the future.

"Lila," he whispered in her ear during their final tryst that night, "there are no basements in Catize."

His interrogation of her took two more hours, during which he convinced her that he was a former hit man for the Gambino family in New York who was trying to lie low awhile and figure out Grief Release's angles before he muscled his way in on whatever con they had going here.

Lila, who Jay correctly guessed got turned on by men of danger, was no longer enamored of her position with either Grief Release or the Church. She told Jay the story of her former lover, Jeff Price, who'd heisted over two million dollars from the coffers of Grief Release. After promising to take her with him, Price ditched her and took off with the "Desiree bitch," as Lila called her.

"But, Lila," Jay said, "you know where Price went. Don't you?"

She did, but she wasn't telling.

But then Jay convinced her that if she didn't cough up Price's whereabouts, he'd make sure her fellow Messengers knew she was in on the heist with Price.

"You wouldn't," she said.

"Wanna bet?"

"What do I get if I tell you?" She pouted.

"A flat fifteen percent of whatever I take off Price."

"How do I know you'll pay it?"

"Because if I don't," Jay said, "you'll rat me out."

She chewed on that and eventually she said, "Clearwater."

Jeff Price's hometown, and the place where he planned to turn the two million into ten by going in on a drug deal with old friends who had heroin connections in Thailand.

Jay left the island that morning, but not before giving Lila one final piece of advice:

"You hold your breath until I get back, and you'll have a nice chunk of change. But, Lila? You try and warn Price I'm coming, and I'll do far worse to you than any five Mexicans would have."

"So, I got back from Nantucket and called Trevor."

Trevor, far from what he told us or Hamlyn and Kohl, sent a car for Jay, and the Weeble drove him back to the house in Marblehead.

He commended Jay on his diligent work, toasted him with his fine single-malt, and asked Jay how he felt about Hamlyn and Kohl's attempt to remove him from the case.

"It must be a tremendous ego blow to a man with your skills."

And it had been, Jay admitted. As soon as he found Desiree and returned her safely, he was going out on his own.

"How are you going to do that?" Trevor said. "You're broke."

Jay shook his head. "You're mistaken."

"Am I?" Trevor said. And he explained to Jay exactly what Adam Kohl had been doing with the 401(k)s, municipal funds, and stock options Jay had so blindly entrusted to him. "Your Mr. Kohl invested heavily, and on margin I might add, in stocks I advised him on recently. Unfortunately, those stocks didn't perform as well as expected. And then there's Mr. Kohl's unfortunate and well-documented gambling addiction."

Jay sat stunned as Trevor Stone detailed Adam Kohl's long history of playing fast and loose with the stock and dividends of Hamlyn and Kohl employees.

"In fact," Trevor said, "you won't have to concern yourself with leaving Hamlyn and Kohl because they'll be filing for Chapter Eleven within six weeks."

"You ruined them," Jay said.

"Did I?" Trevor moved his wheelchair over by Jay's chair. "I'm sure I didn't. Your dear Mr. Kohl overextended himself as he's been doing for years. This time, however, he put too many of his eggs into one basket—a basket I advised him on, I admit, but without malice." He placed his hand on Jay's back. "Several of those investments are in your name, Mr. Becker. Seventy-five thousand six hundred forty-four dollars and twelve cents' worth, to be exact."

Trevor stroked the back of Jay's neck with his palm. "So let's talk truthfully, shall we?"

"He had me," Jay told us. "And it wasn't just the debt. I was shell-shocked when I realized that Adam, and maybe Everett, too, had actually betrayed me."

"Did you talk to them?" Angie asked.

He nodded. "I called Everett and he confirmed it. He said he hadn't known it himself. I mean, he'd known Kohl had a gambling problem, but he never thought he'd stoop to wiping out a fifty-three-year-old company in about seven weeks. Kohl had even pilfered the pension fund on Trevor Stone's advice.

Everett was devastated. You know his big thing about honor, Patrick."

I nodded, remembering how Everett had spoken to Angie and me about honor in its twilight, about how hard it was to be an honorable man surrounded by dishonorable ones. How he'd stared at the view out his window as if it were the last time he'd ever see it.

"So," Jay said, "I told Trevor Stone I'd do whatever he wanted. And he gave me two hundred and thirty thousand dollars to kill Jeff Price and Desiree."

"I am more things than you could possibly fathom," Trevor Stone told Jay that night. "I own trading corporations, shipping companies, more real estate than can be assessed in a day. I own judges, policemen, politicians, whole governments in some countries, and now I own you." His hand tightened on Jay's neck. "And if you betray me, I will reach across any oceans you try to put between us, and rip your jugular from your throat and cram it through the hole in your penis."

So Jay went to Florida.

He had no idea what he'd do once he found Desiree or Jeff Price, only that he wouldn't kill anyone in cold blood. He'd done that once for the feds in Mexico, and the memory of the look in the drug lord's eyes just before Jay blew his heart all over his silk shirt had haunted him so completely, he quit the government a month later.

Lila had told him about a hotel in downtown Clearwater, the Ambassador, which Price had often raved about due to the vibrating beds and varied selection of porn movies available through the satellite TVs.

Jay thought it was a long shot, but then Price proved stupider than he'd thought when he walked out the front door two hours after Jay began staking the place out. Jay followed Price all day as he met with his buddies with the Thailand connections, got drunk in a bar in Largo, and took a hooker back to his room.

The next day, while Price was out, Jay broke into his room, but found no evidence of the money or Desiree.

One morning Jay watched Price leave the hotel and was about to give the room another toss when he got the feeling he was being watched.

He turned in his car seat and focused his binoculars, panned down the length of the street until he came face-to-face with another set of binoculars watching him from a car two blocks down.

"That's how I met Desiree," he told us. "Each of us watching the other through binoculars."

He'd been wondering by this time if she'd ever really existed at all. He dreamed about her constantly, stared at her photographs for hours, believed he knew what she smelled like, how her laugh sounded, what her bare legs would feel like pressed against his own. And the more he built her up in his mind, the more she grew into something mythic—the tortured, poetic, tragic beauty who'd sat in Boston parks through the mists and rains of autumn, awaiting deliverance.

And then one day she was standing in front of him.

She didn't drive away when he left his car to approach hers. She didn't pretend it was all a misunderstanding. She watched him come with calm, steady eyes, and when he reached her car, she opened the door and stepped out.

"Are you from the police?" she said.

He shook his head, unable to speak.

She wore a faded T-shirt and jeans, both of which looked like they'd been slept in. Her feet were bare, her sandals on the floor mat of the car, and he found himself worrying that she might cut her feet on the glass or pebbles that littered the city street.

"Are you a private detective, perhaps?"

He nodded.

"A mute private detective?" she said with a small smile.

And he laughed.

22

"My father," Desiree told Jay two days later, once they'd begun to trust each other, "owns people. That's what he lives for. He owns businesses and homes and cars and whatever else you can think of, but what he really lives for is the owning of people."

"I'm starting to figure that out," Jay said.

"He owned my mother. Literally. She was from Guatemala originally. He went down there in the 1950s to oversee construction of a dam his company was financing, and he bought her from her parents for less than a hundred dollars American. She was fourteen years old."

"Nice," Jay said. "Real fucking nice."

Desiree had holed up in an old fisherman's shack on Longboat Key, which she'd rented at exorbitant rates, until she could figure out her options. Jay had been sleeping on the couch, and one night he woke to Desiree screaming from a nightmare, and they both left the house for the cool of the beach at three in the morning, both too rattled to sleep.

She wore only a sweatshirt he'd given her, a threadbare blue thing from his undergraduate days with LSU embossed on the front in white letters that had chipped and flaked over the years. She was broke, he'd discovered, afraid to use her credit cards on the chance her father would notice and send someone else to kill her. Jay sat beside her on the cool white sand as the surf roared white out of a wall of darkness, and he found himself staring at her hands clasped under her thighs, at the point where her toes disappeared in the white sand, at the glow from the moon as it threaded through the tangles in her hair.

And for the first time in his life, Jay Becker fell in love.

Desiree turned her head and met his eyes. "You won't kill me?" she said.

"No. Not a chance."

"And you don't want my money?"

"You don't have any," Jay said, and they both laughed.

"Everyone I care about dies," she said.

"I know," Jay said. "You've had some shitty luck."

She laughed, but it was bitter and fearful. "Or betrays me like Jeff Price."

He touched her thigh just below the hem of the sweatshirt. He waited for her to remove his hand. And when she didn't, he waited for her to close her own over it. He waited for the surf to tell him something, to suddenly know the right thing to say.

"I won't die," he said and cleared his throat. "And I won't betray you. Because if I do betray you"—and he was as sure of this as he'd ever been of anything—"I definitely will die."

And she smiled at him, her teeth the white of ivory in the night.

Then she peeled off the sweatshirt and came to him, brown and beautiful and shaking from fear.

"When I was fourteen," she told Jay that night as she lay beside him, "I looked just like my mother had. And my father noticed."

"And acted upon it?" Jay said.

"What do you think?"

"Trevor give you his speech about grief?" Jay asked us as the waitress brought us two more coffees and another beer. "The one about grief being carnivorous?"

"Yeah," Angie said.

Jay nodded. "Gave me the same speech when he hired me." He held his hands out in front of him on the table, turned them back and forth. "Grief isn't carnivorous," he said. "Grief is my hands."

"Your hands," Angie said.

"I can feel her flesh in them," he said. "Still. And the smells?" He tapped his nose. "Sweet Jesus. The scent of sand on her skin or the salt in the air coming through the screens of that fisherman's shack? Grief, I swear to God, doesn't live in the heart. It lives in the senses. And sometimes, all I want to do is cut off my nose so I can't smell her, hack my fingers off at the joint."

He looked at us, as if suddenly realizing we were there.

"You son of a bitch," Angie said and her voice cracked as tears glistened on her cheekbones.

"Shit," Jay said. "I forgot. Phil. Angie, I'm sorry."

She waved away his hand and wiped her face with a cocktail napkin.

"Angie, really, I—"

She shook her head. "It's just sometimes, I hear his voice and the sound of it is so clear, I'd swear he's sitting beside me. And for the rest of the day, that's all I can hear. Nothing else."

I knew better than to reach for her hand, but she surprised me by suddenly reaching for mine.

I closed my thumb over hers and she leaned into me.

So this, I wanted to say to Jay, is what you felt with Desiree.

It was Jay who came up with the idea to rip off the money Jeff Price had stolen from Grief Release.

Trevor Stone had made his threats, and Jay believed him, but he also knew that Trevor didn't have long to live. With two hundred thousand dollars, Jay and Desiree might not be able to hide deep enough to elude Trevor's grasp for six months.

But with over two million, they could elude him for six years.

Desiree didn't want anything to do with it. Price, she told Jay, had tried to kill her when she found out about the money he'd stolen. She'd only survived by cold-cocking him with a fire extinguisher, then bolting from their hotel room at the Ambassador in such a rush, she'd left behind every piece of clothing she owned.

Jay said, "But, honey, you were casing the hotel again when we met."

"Because I was desperate. And alone. I'm not desperate anymore, Jay. And I'm not alone. And you have two hundred thousand dollars. We can run on that."

"But how far?" Jay said. "He'll find us. It's not just the running that matters. We can run to Guyana. We can run to the Eastern bloc even, but we won't have enough money left over to buy off people so they'll answer questions right when Trevor sends people looking."

"Jay," she said, "he's dying. How many more people can he send? It took you over three weeks to find me, and I left a trail, because I wasn't sure anyone would be coming after me."

"*I* left a trail," he said. "And it'll be a hell of a lot easier for someone to find me and you than it was for me to find just you. I left reports behind, and your father knows I'm in Florida."

"It's all about money," she said, her voice soft, her eyes refusing to meet his. "Fucking money, as if that's all there is in the world. As if it's anything more than paper."

"It is more than paper," Jay said. "It's power. And power moves things and hides things and creates opportunities. And if we don't take down this douche bag, Price, someone else will because he's stupid."

"And dangerous," Desiree said. "He's dangerous. Don't you get that? He's killed people. I'm sure of it."

"So have I," Jay said. "So have I."

* * *

But he couldn't convince her.

"She was twenty-three," he said to us. "You know? A kid. I'd forget that a lot, but she had a kid's way of looking at the world, even after all the shit she'd been through. She kept thinking that somehow everything would just work out, all by itself. The world, she was sure, had a happy ending in it for her somewhere. And she wasn't going to have anything to do with all that money that had caused all this shit in the first place."

So Jay began to tail Price again. But Price never went near the money as far as Jay could tell. He had his meetings with his drug dealer friends, and Jay bugged Price's room and ascertained that they were all concerned about a boat lost at sea off the Bahamian coast.

"That boat that sank the other day?" Angie said. "The one that sent all the heroin up onto the beaches?"

Jay nodded.

So Price was worried now, but he never went near the money as far as Jay could tell.

While Jay was out tailing Price, Desiree would read. The tropics, Jay noticed, had given her a taste for the surrealists and the sensualists he'd always favored himself, and he'd come home to find her lost in Toni Morrison or Borges, García Márquez or Isabelle Allende, the poetry of Neruda. In the fisherman's shack, they'd cook fish Cajun-style and boil shellfish, fill the tiny space with the smell of salt and cayenne pepper, and then they'd make love. After, they'd go outside and sit by the ocean, and she'd tell him stories from whatever she was reading that day, and Jay would feel as if he were rereading the books himself, as if she were the writer, sitting beside him and spinning fantastical yarns into the darkening air. And then they'd make love again.

Until one morning Jay woke to find that his alarm clock had never gone off and Desiree wasn't in bed beside him.

There was a note:

Jay,

I think I know where the money is. It matters to you, so I guess it matters to me. I'm going to get it. I'm scared, but I love you, and I think you're right. We wouldn't be able to hide long without it, would we? If I'm not back by ten a.m., please come get me.
 I love you. Completely.

 Desiree

By the time Jay reached the Ambassador, Price had checked out.

He stood in the parking lot, looking up at the U-shaped balcony that ran along the wall on the second floor, and that's when the Jamaican housekeeper began to scream.

Jay ran up the stairs and saw the woman bent at the waist and screaming outside Price's room. He stepped around her and looked through the open door.

Desiree's corpse sat on the floor between the TV and the minifridge. The first thing Jay noticed was that the fingers and thumbs of both her hands had been severed at the joints.

Blood dripped from what remained of her chin onto Jay's LSU sweatshirt.

Desiree's face was a shattered hole, pulverized by a shotgun blast fired from less than ten feet. Her honey hair, which Jay had shampooed himself the previous night, was matted with blood and speckled with brain tissue.

From far, far away, it seemed to Jay, he heard the sound of screaming. And the hum of several air conditioners, thousands going at once it seemed in this cheap motel, trying to pour cool air into the hellish heat of these cinder block cells, until the sound was like a swarm of bees in his ears.

23

"So, I tracked down Price at a motel just up the street from here." Jay rubbed his eyes with his fists. "I got the room next door to him. Cheap walls. I sat with my head against the wall an entire day listening to him over there in his room. Maybe, I dunno, I was listening for sounds of regret, weeping, anguish, anything. But he just watched TV and drank all day. Then he called for a hooker. Less than forty-eight hours after he shot Desiree in the face and cut off her fingers, the prick orders up a woman like takeout."

Jay lit another cigarette, stared at the flame for a moment.

"After the hooker left, I went over to his room. We had some words and I pushed him around a little bit. I was hoping he'd grab a weapon, and whatta ya know? He did. A six-inch switchblade. Fucking pimp's knife. Good thing he pulled it, though. Made what I did next look like self-defense. Sort of."

Jay turned his worn face toward the window,

looked out as the rain let up just a bit. When he spoke again, his voice was flat and souless:

"I cut a smile through his abdomen from hip to hip, held his chin tight and made him look me in the eyes as his large intestine spilled out onto the floor."

He shrugged. "I think Desiree's memory was owed that."

It was probably seventy-five degrees outside, but the air in the diner felt colder than slate in a mortuary.

"So what are you going to do now, Jay?" Angie said.

He smiled the smile of a ghost. "I'm going back to Boston, and I'm going to open up Trevor Stone, too."

"And then what, spend the rest of your life in jail?"

He looked at me. "I don't care. If the fates so decide, fine. Patrick, you get one shot at love, that's if you're very lucky. Well, I was very lucky. Forty-one years old, I fall in love with a woman nearly half my age for two weeks. And she dies. And, okay, the world's a tough place. You get something good, sooner or later you'll get served up something really bad just to even up the scales." He patted the table-top in a quick drumbeat. "Fine. I accept that. Don't like it, but I accept it. The scales have evened up for me. Now I'm going to even them up for Trevor."

"Jay," Angie said. "It'd be a suicide mission."

He shrugged. "Tough shit. He dies. Besides, you think he hasn't already put a hit out on me? I know

too much. The moment I broke off daily contact
with him from here, I signed my death warrant.
Why do you think he sent Clifton and Cushing
with you guys?" He closed his eyes, sighed audibly.
"Nope. That's it. The fucker eats a bullet."

"He'll be dead in five months."

Another shrug. "Not soon enough for me."

"What about the law?" Angie said. "You can testify he paid you to kill his daughter."

"Good idea, Ange. Case should reach trial maybe
only six or seven months after he's already died." He
dropped several bills on the check. "I'm taking that
old piece of shit out. This week. Slowly and painfully." He smiled. "Any questions?"

Most of Jay's things were still in an efficiency
unit he'd rented when he'd first arrived at the Ukum-
bak Apartments in downtown St. Petersburg. He
was going to swing by, grab his stuff, and hit the
road, planes being too undependable, airports too
easily watched. Without sleep or any other prepara-
tion, he was going to drive twenty-four hours straight
up the eastern seaboard, which would put him in
Marblehead by two-thirty in the morning. There, he
planned to break into Trevor Stone's house and torture the old man to death.

"Hell of a plan," I said as we bolted from the steps
of the diner and ran toward our cars in the pelting
rain.

"You like it? Just something I came up with."

Angie and I, having no other options that we could
conceive of, decided to follow Jay back to Massachusetts. Maybe we could keep discussing it at rest stops

and gas stations, either talk Jay out of it or come up with a more sane solution to his problem. The Celica we'd rented from Elite Motors—the same place Jay had rented his 3000 GT—we'd send back on an Amtrak, have them send the bill to Trevor. Dead or alive, he could afford it.

The Weeble would discover we were gone sooner or later, and fly back home with his laptop and his tiny eyes, and figure out a way to explain to Trevor how he'd lost us. Cushing, I assumed, would climb back into his coffin until he was needed again.

"He's crazy," Angie said as we followed Jay's taillights toward the highway.

"Jay?"

She nodded. "He thinks he fell in love with Desiree in two weeks, but that's bullshit."

"Why?"

"How many people—adult people—do you know who fall in love in two weeks?"

"Doesn't mean it can't happen," I said.

"Maybe. But I think he fell in love with Desiree even before he met her. The beautiful girl who sat alone in the parks, waiting for a savior. It's what all guys want."

"A beautiful girl who sits alone in parks?"

She nodded. "Waiting to be saved."

Up ahead, Jay turned onto a ramp leading onto 275 North, his small red taillights blurring in the rain.

"Possibly true," I said. "Possibly. But whatever the case, if you got involved with someone for a short time, under intense circumstances, and then that person was taken from you, shot in the face—you'd become obsessed, too."

"Granted." She downshifted into neutral as the Celica hit a puddle the size of Peru and the back wheels slid out and to the left for a moment. Angie turned into the skid and the car righted itself as we passed beyond the puddle. She shifted back into fourth, and then quickly into fifth, stepped on the gas, and caught back up with Jay.

"Granted," she repeated. "But he's going to assassinate a virtual cripple, Patrick."

"An evil cripple," I said.

"How do we know that?" she said.

"Because Jay told us and Desiree confirmed it."

"No," she said as the yellow dorsal fins of the Skyway Bridge climbed into the night sky about ten miles ahead. "Desiree didn't confirm it. Jay *said* she did. All we have to go on is what Jay's told us. We can't confirm it with Desiree. She's dead. We can't confirm it with Trevor, because he'd deny it in either case."

"Everett Hamlyn," I said.

She nodded. "I say we call him when we get to Jay's place. From a pay phone out of Jay's earshot. I want to hear it from Everett's mouth that this is all as Jay said it is."

The rain, as it drummed the canvas hood of the Celica, sounded like ice cubes.

"I trust Jay," I said.

"I don't." She looked at me for a moment. "It's nothing personal. But he's a wreck. And I don't trust anyone right now."

"Anyone," I said.

"Except you," she said. "And that goes without saying. Otherwise, everyone is suspect."

I leaned back against the seat and closed my eyes.

Everyone is suspect.

Even Jay.

Hell of a weird world in which fathers give orders to assassinate their daughters and therapeutic organizations offer no real therapy and a man I would have once easily trusted with my life suddenly couldn't be trusted.

Maybe Everett Hamlyn had been right. Maybe honor was in its twilight. Maybe it had always been heading that way. Or worse, maybe it had always been an illusion.

Everyone is suspect. *Everyone is suspect.*

It was starting to become my mantra.

24

The road curved as we broke from a no-man's-land of blacktop and grass and approached Tampa Bay, the water and the land that abutted it so dark behind walls of rain that it was hard to tell where one ended and the other began. Small white shacks, some with signs on their roofs that I couldn't read in the blurry darkness, cropped up on either side and seemed to hover effortlessly in a rainy netherworld without foundation. The Skyway's yellow dorsal fins didn't appear to grow any closer or any farther away for a minute or so; they hung suspended over a plain of windswept darkness, cut hard into a bruised purple sky.

As we climbed the three-mile ramp that led up to the center of the bridge, a car broke from the wall of water on the other side of the highway, coming off the bridge with its watery headlights wavering in the dark and floating past us as they headed south. I looked in the rearview, saw only a single set of headlights pocking the dark about a mile behind us. Two in the morning, the rain a wall, the darkness puddling out on all sides as we

rose toward the colossal yellow fins, a night not fit
to banish the most recalcitrant of sinners into.

I yawned and my body groaned internally at the
thought of being cooped up in the small Celica for
another twenty-four hours. I fiddled with the radio,
got nothing but "yeah, buddy" classic rock stations, a
couple of dance music ones, and several "soft rock"
grotesqueries. Soft rock—not too hard, not too soft,
perfect for people with no sense of discrimination.

I shut the radio off as the tarmac grew steeper
and all but the closest of the dorsal fins rolled away
from us momentarily. Jay's taillights looked back at
me through the rain like red eyes and on our right
the bay kept widening, and a cement guardrail
streamed past in a current.

"This bridge is huge," I said.

"Jinxed, too," Angie said. "This is a replacement
bridge. The original Skyway—what's left of it anyway—is off to our left."

She lit a cigarette with the dashboard lighter as I
looked off to the left, found myself unable to dis-
cern anything in the shroud of falling water.

"In the early eighties," she said, "the original
bridge was hit by a barge. The main span dropped
into the sea and so did several cars."

"How do you know this?"

"When in Rome." She cracked her window just
enough to allow the cigarette smoke to snake out. "I
read a book on the area yesterday. There's one in
your suite, too. The day they opened this new bridge,
a guy driving to the inauguration had a heart attack
as he drove onto the ramp on the St. Pete side. His
car pitched into the water and he died."

I looked out my window as the bay dropped away from us like the floor of an elevator shaft.

"You lie," I said nervously.

She held up her right hand. "Scout's honor."

"Put both hands on the wheel," I said.

We approached the center span and the entire configuration of yellow fins enflamed the right side of the car, bathed the rubbery windows in artificial light.

The sound of tires slapping through the rain on our left suddenly hummed through the small open space in Angie's window. I looked left and Angie said, "What the hell?"

She jerked the wheel as a gold Lexus streaked past us, crowding into our lane, doing at least seventy. The wheels on the Celica's passenger side bit against the curb between the road and the guardrail, and the entire frame shuddered and bounced as Angie's arm went ramrod straight against the wheel.

The Lexus hurtled past us as we jerked back into the lane. Its taillights were off. It cut halfway in front of us, straddling both lanes, and I saw the stiff, thin head of the driver for a moment in a shaft of light from the fins.

"That's Cushing," I said.

"Shit." Angie honked the tinny horn of the Celica as I popped the glove compartment and pulled out my gun, then Angie's. I tucked hers on the console against the emergency brake, jacked a bullet into the chamber of my own.

Up ahead, Jay's head straightened as he looked in his rearview. Angie kept her hand on the horn, but the wimpy bleat it emitted was lost when the nose of

Mr. Cushing's Lexus swung into the rear quarter panel of Jay's 3000 GT.

The right wheels of the little sports car jumped up on the curb and sparks flew off the passenger side as it careened off the barrier to Jay's right. Jay swung his wheel hard to the left and jumped back off the curb. His sideview mirror was ripped off the car, and I turned my head to the side as it rocketed back through the rain and crashed into our windshield, ripped a spiderweb through the glass in front of my face.

Angie bumped the back of the Lexus as the nose of Jay's car slid to the left and his rear right wheel popped back up on the curb. Mr. Cushing kept the Lexus steady, grinding it into Jay's car. A silver hubcap snapped off and banged off our grille, disappeared under the wheel. The 3000 GT, small and light, was no match for the Lexus, and any second it would be propelled broadside, and the Lexus would be free to push it straight off the bridge.

I could see Jay's head as it bobbed back and forth and he fought the wheel as the Lexus ground harder against the driver's side.

"Keep this steady," I said to Angie and rolled down my window. I leaned my upper body out into the pelting rain and screaming wind and pointed my gun at the rear windshield of the Lexus. As the rain bit into my eyes, I fired three quick shots. The muzzle flashes exploded into the air like heat lightning, and the rear windshield of the Lexus collapsed all over the trunk. Mr. Cushing tapped his brakes and I jerked myself back inside as Angie rammed the Lexus and Jay's car shot out ahead of it.

Jay came off the curb too fast, though, and the right wheels of the 3000 GT bounced off the ground and then rose into the air. Angie screamed, and muzzle flashes erupted from inside the Lexus.

The Celica's windshield imploded.

The rain and wind launched a storm of glass through our hair and off our cheeks and necks. Angie swerved to the right and our tires ate curb again, the hubcaps crunching against the cement. The Toyota seemed to buckle into itself for a moment, then swerved back into the lane.

Ahead of us, Jay's car flipped.

It bounced on the driver's side, then rolled over onto its roof and the Lexus accelerated and hit it hard enough to send it spinning through the rain toward the bridge barrier.

"Screw these guys," I said and rose off my seat and extended my body over the dashboard.

I leaned so far forward my wrists passed through the shattered windshield and rested on the car hood. I steadied my hand as tiny specks of glass bit into my wrists and face and fired another three shots into the interior of the Lexus.

I must have hit someone, because the Lexus jerked away from Jay's car and swung back across the left lane. It hit the barrier under the last of the yellow fins so hard it bounced sideways and then backward, its heavy gold body jumping trunk first into both lanes ahead of us.

"Get back in," Angie yelled at me as she swung the Celica to the right, trying to clear the trunk of the Lexus as it jumped across our path.

The gold machine floated through the night

toward us. Angie turned the wheel with both hands, and I tried to get back into my seat.

I didn't make it, and neither did Angie.

When we smashed into the Lexus, my body shot airborne. I cleared the hood of the Celica and landed on the trunk of the Lexus like a porpoise, my chest slashing through the beads of water and pebbled glass Without slowing down much. I heard something crash on my right, a cement crashing that was so loud it sounded as if the night sky had been torn in half.

I hit the tarmac with my shoulder and something cracked by my collarbone. And I rolled. And flipped. And rolled some more. I held tight to the gun in my right hand, and it discharged twice as the sky spun and the bridge twirled and dipped.

I skidded to a stop on a bloody, howling hip. My left shoulder felt numb and flabby simultaneously, and my flesh was slick with blood.

But I could flex my right hand around the gun, and even though the hip I'd landed on felt as if it were filled with sharp stones, both legs felt solid. I looked back at the Lexus as the passenger door opened. It was about ten yards back, its trunk attached now to the crumpled hood of the Celica. A stream of hissing water shot from the Celica as I stood unsteadily, a tomato paste combination of rain and blood streaming down my face.

On my right, on the other side of the bridge, a black Jeep had skidded to a stop and the driver was shouting words at me that were lost in the wind and rain.

I ignored him and concentrated on the Lexus.

The Weeble fell to one knee as he climbed out of the Lexus, his white shirt saturated red, a meaty hole gouged across where his right eyebrow used to be. I limped toward him as he used the muzzle of his pistol to push himself off his knee. He gripped the open car door and watched me come, and I could tell by his bobbing Adam's apple that he was swallowing hard against nausea. He looked down at the gun in his hand uncertainly, then at me.

"Don't," I said.

He looked down at his chest, at the blood pumping from somewhere in there, and his fingers tightened around his pistol.

"Don't," I said again.

Please don't, I thought.

But he raised the gun anyway, blinking at me in the downpour, his small body wavering like a drunk's.

I shot him twice in the center of the chest before his gun hand cleared his hip, and he flopped back against the car, his mouth forming a confused oval, as if he were about to ask me a question. He grabbed for the open door, but his arm slid down between the doorframe and the windshield pillar. His body began a cascade to his right, but his elbow got pinned between the door and the car, and he died there— half-pointed to the ground, vise-gripped to the car, the beginnings of a question lying stillborn in his eyes.

I heard a ratcheting sound, and I looked up over the roof of the car to see Mr. Cushing leveling a shiny shotgun at me. He sighted down the bore, one eye squinting shut, a bony white finger curled around the trigger. He smiled.

Then a puffy red cloud punched through the center of his throat and spit over the collar of his shirt.

He frowned. He reached a hand up toward his throat, but before it got there, he pitched forward and his face hit the car roof. The shotgun slid down the windshield, came to rest on the hood. Mr. Cushing's tall thin body folded to its right and he disappeared on the other side of the hood, his body making a soft thump as it hit the ground.

Angie appeared in the darkness behind him, her gun still extended, the rain hissing off the hot barrel. Slivers of glass twinkled in her dark hair. Several razor-thin lacerations crisscrossed her forehead and the bridge of her nose, but otherwise she appeared to have survived the crash with a lot less damage than either the Weeble or I had.

I smiled at her, and she gave me a weary one in return.

Then she looked at something over my shoulder. "Jesus Christ, Patrick. Oh, Jesus."

I turned, and that's when I saw what had made the loud crashing noise when I was thrown from the Celica.

Jay's 3000 GT sat upside down fifty feet away. Most of the car had smashed through the barrier, and I was momentarily amazed that it hadn't dropped off the bridge entirely. The rear third of the car was perched on the bridge. The front two thirds hovered over nothing at all, the car held to the bridge by nothing more than crumbling cement and two mangled steel coils. As we watched, the front of the car dipped slightly into space, and the rear rose off the cement foundation. The steel coils creaked.

I ran over to the barrier, and got down on my knees, looked over it at Jay. He hung upside down in his seat, strapped in by the seat belt, his knees up by his chin, his head an inch from the car ceiling.

"Don't move," I said.

His eyes curled toward me. "Don't worry. I won't."

I looked at the barrier. Slick with beads of rain, it moaned again. On the other side of it was a small strip of cement foundation, not enough to be considered a good foothold for anyone over the age of four, but I wasn't in a position to sit back and wait for it to grow. Below the cement strip waited nothing but black space and water as hard as cliff face a hundred yards down.

Angie came up beside me as a breeze swept off the gulf. The car shifted to the right a bit, then jerked downward another inch.

"Oh, no," Jay said. He laughed weakly. "No, no, no."

"Jay," Angie said. "I'm coming out."

"*You're* coming out?" I said. "No. I got a longer reach."

She climbed over the barrier. "And bigger feet, and your arm looks fucked up. Can you even move it?"

She didn't wait for an answer. She gripped an intact section of the barrier and eased herself along it toward the car. I walked beside her, my right hand an inch from her arm.

Another gust of wind cut through the rain and the whole bridge seemed to sway.

Angie reached the car, and I held tight to her right arm with both hands as she lowered herself to a tenuous squatting position.

She leaned out from the barrier and extended her left arm as sirens rang in the distance.

"Jay," she said.

"Yeah?"

"I can't reach." She strained against my grip, the tendons in her arms pulsing under the skin, but her fingers fell just short of the upside-down door handle. "You're going to have to help out, Jay."

"How?"

"Can you open your door?"

His head craned as he tried to locate the door handle. "Never been upside down in a car before. You know?"

"I've never hung from the side of a bridge three hundred feet over the water," Angie said. "This makes us even."

"Got the door handle," he said.

"You're going to have to push the door open and reach for my hand," Angie said, and her body swayed slightly in the wind.

He blinked against the rain blowing into the window, puffed up his cheeks, and exhaled. "I feel like if I move an inch, this thing's going to tip."

"Chance we have to take, Jay." Her hand slipped down my arm. I squeezed, and her fingers dug into my flesh again.

"Yeah," Jay said. "I'll tell ya, though, I—"

The car lurched, and the whole bridge gave a loud creak, this one high-pitched and frantic like a scream, and the torn cement holding the car crumbled.

"No, no, no, no, no, no," Jay said.

And the car dropped off the bridge.

Angie screamed and jerked back from the car as the torn steel coil snapped into her arm. I gripped her hand tight, and pulled her over the barrier as her legs kicked at the open air.

With her face pressed against mine, and her arm wrapped tight around my neck, her heart hammering against my biceps, and my own pounding in my ear, we peered down at the place where Jay's car had plummeted through streams of rain and disappeared into black.

25

"He going to be okay?" Inspector Jefferson asked the EMT working on my shoulder.

"He's got a cracked scapula. Might be broken. I can't tell without an X ray."

"A what?" I said.

"Shoulder blade," the EMT said. "Definitely cracked."

Jefferson looked at him with sleepy eyes and shook his head slowly. "He'll be fine for a while. We'll get a doctor take a look at him soon enough."

"Shit," the EMT said and shook his own head. He wrapped the bandage tight, running it from under my armpit, up over my shoulder, down across my collarbone, around my back and chest, and up to my armpit again.

Inspector Carnell Jefferson watched me steadily with his sleepy eyes as the EMT did his work. Jefferson looked to be in his late thirties, a slim black guy of unremarkable height and build, with a soft, easygoing jaw and a perpetual smile playing lazily at the corners of his mouth. He wore a light blue raincoat over a tan suit and white shirt, a silk tie with a pink and blue floral print hanging slightly askew from an unbuttoned collar. His hair was cut so short and tight to his skull, I wondered why he bothered having any there at all, and he didn't even blink as rain dripped down the tight skin on his face.

He looked like a nice guy, the kind of guy you'd shoot the shit with at the gym, maybe have a few pitchers with after work. Kind of guy who loved his kids and had sexual fantasies only about his wife.

I'd met cops like him before, though, and he was the last guy you'd want to get too comfortable with. In the box, or testifying at a trial, or hammering away at a witness, this nice guy would turn into a shark in less time than it took to snap your fingers. He was a homicide inspector, a young one, and black in a southern state; he didn't get where he was by being any suspect's friend.

"So, Mr. Kenzie, is it?"

"Yup."

"You're a private dick up in Bahstan. Correct?"

"That's what I told you."

"Uh-huh. Nice town?"

"Boston?"

"Yes. Nice town?"

"I like it."

"I hear it's real pretty in the autumn." He pursed his lips and nodded. "Hear they don't like niggers much up there, though."

"There are assholes everywhere," I said.

"Oh, sure. Sure." He rubbed his head with the palm of his hand, looked up into the drizzle for a moment, then blinked the rain from his eyes. "Assholes everywhere," he repeated. "So since we're standing in the rain talking all friendly about race relations and assholes and the like, whyn't you tell me about that pair of dead assholes blocking all this here traffic on my bridge?"

Those lazy eyes found mine and I saw a glimpse of the shark in them for just a moment before it disappeared.

"I shot the little guy twice in the chest."

He raised his eyebrows. "I noticed. Yes."

"My partner shot the other guy as he drew down on me with a shotgun."

He looked behind him at Angie. She sat in an ambulance across from the one where I sat as an EMT wiped at the scratches on her face, legs, and neck with an alcohol swab and Jefferson's partner, Detective Lyle Vandemaker, interrogated her.

"Man," Jefferson said and whistled, "she's a first-class mega-babe *and* she can pump a round through the throat of an asshole from ten yards out in the pouring rain? That's one special woman."

"Yeah," I said, "she is."

He stroked his chin and nodded to himself. "I'll tell you what my problem is here, Mr. Kenzie. It's a matter of discerning who the real assholes are. You see what I'm saying? You say those two corpses over there—they're the assholes. And I'd like to believe you. I would. Hell, I'd love to just say, 'Okay,' and shake your hand and let you go on back to Beantown. I mean, really. But if, oh let's just say, you were lying to me, and you and your partner are the real assholes here, well, I'd look awful stupid just letting you go. And seeing how we don't have any witnesses as yet, well, all we got is your word against the words of two guys who can't really give us their words because you, well, shot them a few times and they died. You follow?"

"Just barely," I said.

Across the median divider of the bridge, traffic seemed heavier than it probably was normally at three in the morning because the police had turned the two lanes of normally southbound traffic into one southern and one northern lane. Every car that passed on that side of the bridge slowed to a crawl to get a glimpse of the commotion on this side.

In the breakdown lane, a black Jeep with two bright green surfboards strapped to its roof was stopped completely, its hazards flashing. The owner I recognized as the guy who'd shouted something at me just before I shot the Weeble.

He was a sunburnt rail of a guy with long, bleached-blond hair and no shirt. He stood at the rear of the Jeep and seemed in heated conversation with two cops. He pointed in my direction several times.

His companion, a young woman as skinny and blond as he was, leaned against the hood of the Jeep. When she caught my eye, she waved brightly, as if we were old friends.

I managed a half wave back at her, because it seemed the polite thing to do, then turned back to my immediate surroundings.

Our side of the bridge was blocked by the Lexus and the Celica, six or seven green and white patrol cars, several unmarked cars, two fire trucks, three ambulances, and a black van bearing the yellow words

PINELLAS COUNTY MARITIME INVESTIGATIONS. The van had dropped four divers at the St. Pete side of the bridge just a few minutes before, and they were somewhere in the water now, searching for Jay.

Jefferson looked at the hole Jay's car had left behind in the barrier. Bathed in the red of the fire engine's lights, it looked like an open wound.

"Fucked up my bridge pretty good, didn't you, Mr. Kenzie?"

"That wasn't me," I said. "It was those two dead assholes over there."

"So you say," he said. "So you say."

The EMT used a pair of tweezers to remove pebbles and slivers of glass from my face, and I winced as I stared off past the flashing lights and dark drizzle at the crowd forming on the other side of the barricade. They'd walked up the bridge in the rain at three in the morning, just so they could get a firsthand look at violence. TV, I guess, wasn't enough for them. Their own lives weren't enough for them. Nothing was enough.

The EMT pulled a good-sized chunk of something from the center of my forehead and blood immediately poured from the opening and split at the bridge of the nose and found my eyes. I blinked several times as he grabbed some gauze, and as my eyelids fluttered and the lights of the various sirens flickered like strobes, I saw a glimpse of rich honey hair and skin in the crowd.

I leaned forward into the drizzle and peered into the lights, and saw her again, just for a moment, and I decided my fall from the car must have given me a concussion, because it wasn't possible.

But maybe it was.

For one second, through the rain and lights and blood in my eyes, I locked eyes with Desiree Stone.

And then she was gone.

26

The skyway bridged two counties. Manatee County, on the southern side, consisted of Bradenton, Palmetto, Longboat Key, and Anna Maria Island. Pinellas County, on the northern side, was made up of St. Petersburg, St. Petersburg Beach, Gulfport, and Pinellas Park. St. Petersburg police had been the first on the scene, as had their divers and their fire trucks, so after some arguing with the Bradenton PD, we were transported off the bridge by the St. Pete cops, and driven north.

As we came off the bottom of the bridge— Angie locked up in the backseat of one cruiser, and me in the back of another—the four divers, dressed in black rubber from head to toe, carried Jay's body from Tampa Bay, up onto a grassy embankment.

As we passed, I looked out the window. They laid his wet corpse down in the grass, and his flesh was the white of a fish's underbelly. His dark hair plastered his face, and his eyes were closed tight, his forehead dented.

If you didn't notice the dent in his forehead, he looked like he was sleeping. He looked at peace. He looked about fourteen years old.

"Well," Jefferson said as he came back into the interrogation room, "we have some bad news for you, Mr. Kenzie."

My head was throbbing so hard I was sure a band of majorettes had taken up residence in my skull and the inside of my mouth felt like sunbaked leather. I couldn't move my left arm, wouldn't have been able to even if the bandages had permitted it, and the cuts on my face and head had caked and swelled.

"How's that?" I managed.

Jefferson dropped a manila folder on the table between us and removed his suit jacket and placed it over the back of his chair before he took a seat.

"This Mr. Graham Clifton—what'd you call him back on the bridge—the Weeble?"

I nodded.

He smiled. "I like that. Well, the Weeble had three bullets in him. All from your gun. The first entered his back and came out through his right breast."

I said, "I told you I fired into the car while it was moving. I thought I hit something."

"And you did," he said. "Then you shot him twice as he came out of the car, yeah, yeah. Anyway, that's not the bad news. The bad news is you told me this Weeble guy, he worked for a Trevor Stone of Marblehead, Massachusetts?"

I nodded.

He looked at me and shook his head slowly.

"Wait a minute," I said.

"Mr. Clifton was employed by Bullock Industries, a research and development consulting firm located in Buckhead."

"Buckhead?" I said.

He nodded. "Atlanta. Georgia. Mr. Clifton, as far as we know, never set foot in Boston."

"Bullshit," I said.

"'Fraid not. I spoke to his landlord, his boss in Atlanta, his neighbors."

"His neighbors," I said.

"Yeah. You know what neighbors are, don't you? The people who live beside you. See you every day, nod hello. Well there's a whole bunch of these neighbor types in Buckhead, who swear they saw Mr. Clifton just about every day for the last ten years in Atlanta."

"And Mr. Cushing?" I said as the majorettes in my head started banging their cymbals together.

"Also employed by Bullock Industries. Also lived in Atlanta. Hence the Georgia license plates on the Lexus. Now your Mr. Stone, he was mighty confused when I called him. Seems he's a retired businessman, dying of cancer, who hired you to find his daughter. He has no idea what the hell you're doing down in Florida. Says the last time he talked with you was five days ago. He thought, frankly, that you'd skipped town with the money he paid you. As for Mr. Clifton, or Mr. Cushing, Mr. Stone says he never heard of them."

"Inspector Jefferson," I said, "did you check out the owner of record of Bullock Industries?"

"What do you think, Mr. Kenzie?"

"Of course you did."

He nodded and looked down at his folder. "Of course I did. The owner of Bullock Industries is Moore and Wessner Limited, a British holding company."

"And the owner of the holding company?"

He looked at his notes. "Sir Alfred Llewyn, a British earl, supposedly hangs out with the Windsor family, shoots pool with Prince Charles, plays poker with the queen, what have you."

"Not Trevor Stone," I said.

He shook his head. "Unless he's also a British earl. He's not, is he? To the best of your knowledge?"

"And Jay Becker," I said. "What did Mr. Stone have to say about him?"

"Same thing he said about you. Mr. Becker skipped town with Mr. Stone's money."

I closed my eyes against the burning white fluorescent overhead, tried to quell the banging in my head with sheer willpower. It didn't work.

"Inspector," I said.

"Hmm?"

"What do you think happened on that bridge last night?"

He leaned back in his chair. "Glad you asked me, Mr. Kenzie. Glad you asked me." He pulled a pack of gum from his shirt pocket, proffered it to me. When I shook my head, he shrugged and unwrapped a piece, popped it in his mouth, and chewed for about thirty seconds.

"You and your partner found Jay Becker somehow and didn't tell anyone. You decided to steal

Trevor Stone's money and skip town, but the two hundred thousand he gave you wasn't enough."

"The two hundred thousand," I said. "That's what he told you he paid us?"

He nodded. "So you find Jay Becker, but he gets suspicious and tries to get away from you. You chase him on the Skyway, and you're both jockeying back and forth when this innocent pair of businessmen get in your way. It's raining, it's dark, the plan goes awry. All three of you crash. Becker's car goes off the bridge. No problem there, but now you've got the matter of two bystanders to take care of. So you shoot them, plant guns on them, shoot out their back window so it looks like they fired from the car, and that's it. You're done."

"You don't believe that theory," I said.

"Why not?"

"Because it's the stupidest theory I ever heard. And you're not stupid."

"Oh, flatter me some more, Mr. Kenzie. Please."

"We want Jay Becker's money, right?"

"The hundred grand we found in the trunk of the Celica with his fingerprints all over it, yeah, that's the money I'm talking about."

"But the hundred grand we used to bail him out of jail," I said. "Why'd we do that? So we could trade one stack of hundred thousand dollar bills for another?"

He watched me with his shark's eyes, didn't say anything.

"If we planted the guns on Cushing and Clifton, why did Clifton have powder burns on his hands? I mean, he did, didn't he?"

No response. He watched me, waiting.

"If we drove Jay Becker off the bridge, how come all the collision damage to his car was done by the Lexus?"

"Go on," he said.

"You know what I charge for a missing persons case?"

He shook his head.

I told him. "Now that's dramatically less than two hundred grand, wouldn't you say?"

"I would."

"Why would Trevor Stone shell out a combined four hundred thousand dollars, at least, to two separate private investigators to find his daughter?"

"Man's desperate. He's dying. He wants his daughter home."

"Almost half a million dollars, though? That's a lot."

He turned his right hand, palm up, in my direction. "Please," he said, "continue."

"Fuck that," I said.

His front chair legs came back to the floor. "Excuse me?"

"You heard me. Fuck that, and fuck you. Your theory's a crock a shit. We both know it. And we both know it'll never stand up in court. A grand jury would laugh it out."

"That so?"

"That's so." I looked at him, then back at the two-way mirror over his shoulder, let his superiors or whoever was back there see my eyes, too. "You have three dead bodies and a wounded bridge and front-page headlines, I'm assuming. And the only story that makes sense is the one me and my partner have been telling you for the last twelve hours. But you can't corroborate it." I locked his eyes with mine. "Or so you say."

"So I say? What's that mean, Mr. Kenzie? Now, don't be coy."

"There was a guy on the other side of the bridge. Looked like a surfer dude. I saw cops interviewing him after you got there. He saw what happened. At least some of it."

He smiled. A broad one. Full of teeth.

"The gentleman in question," he said, looking at his notes, "has seven priors for, among other things, driving under the influence, possession of marijuana, possession of cocaine, possession of pharmaceutical Ecstasy, possession—"

"What you're telling me is he's a possessor of things, Inspector. I get it. What does that have to do with what he saw on the bridge?"

"Your mama ever tell you it's impolite to interrupt?" He wagged his finger at me. "The gentleman in question was driving with a suspended license, failed a Breathalyzer, and was found with cannabis on his person. Your 'witness,' if that's what you think he was, Mr. Kenzie, was under the influence of at least two mind-altering substances. He was arrested a few minutes after we left the bridge." He leaned forward. "So, tell me what happened on that bridge."

I leaned forward. Into the twin beams of his studied glare. And it wasn't easy, believe me. "You got nothing but me and my partner holding smoking guns, and a witness you refuse to believe. So you're not letting us walk. Are you, Inspector?"

"You got that right," he said. "So run the story by me again."

"Nope."

He folded his arms across his chest and smiled. "'Nope'? Did you just say 'nope'?"

"That's what I said."

He stood up and lifted his chair, brought it around the table beside my own. He sat down and his lips touched my ear as he whispered into it, "You're all I got, Kenzie. Get it? And you're a cocky, white, Irish motherfucker, which means I hated you on sight. So, tell me what you're going to do."

"Send in my lawyer," I said.

"I didn't hear you," he whispered.

I ignored him and slapped the tabletop. "Send in my lawyer," I called to the people behind the mirror.

27

My lawyer, Cheswick Hartman, had caught a flight from Boston an hour after my phone call at six in the morning.

When he arrived at St. Petersburg Police Head-quarters on First Avenue North at noon, they played dumb. Because the entire incident on the bridge had happened in a no-man's-land between Pinellas County and Manatee County, they sent him to Manatee County and the Bradenton PD, feigning ignorance over our whereabouts.

In Bradenton, they took one look at Cheswick's two-thousand-dollar suit and the Louis of Boston garment bag in his hand, and dicked around with him some more. By the time he got back to St. Pete, it was three. It was also boiling hot, and so was Cheswick.

There are three people I know who should never, and I mean never, be messed with. One is Bubba, for obvious reasons. The other is Devin Amronklin, a Boston homicide cop. The third, however, is Cheswick Hartman, and he may be more dangerous than either Bubba or Devin, because he has so many more weapons in his arsenal.

One of the top criminal lawyers not only in Boston but in the country, he charges something in the neighborhood of eight hundred dollars an hour for his services, and he's always in demand. He has homes on Beacon Hill and the Outer Banks of North Carolina, and a summer villa on the island of Majorca. He also has a sister, Elise, whom I extricated from a dangerous situation a few years back. Since then, Cheswick refuses to accept money from me, and he'll fly fourteen hundred miles for me on an hour's notice.

But it screws up his life to do so, and when his time gets wasted even further by yokel cops with bad attitudes, his briefcase and Montblanc pen turn into a nuclear weapon and an ignition switch.

Through the grimy window in the interrogation room, I could see the squad room through even grimier venetian blinds, and twenty minutes after Jefferson left me alone, a commotion erupted as Cheswick burst through the scattered desks with a legion of police brass in tow.

The cops were shouting at Cheswick and each other and calling Jefferson's name and the name of a Lieutenant Grimes, and by the time Cheswick threw open the door of the interrogation room, Jefferson was in the crowd, too.

Cheswick took one look at me and said, "Get my client some water. Now."

One of the brass went back out into the squad room as Cheswick and the rest filed in. Cheswick leaned over me and looked at my face.

"This is good." He looked over his shoulder at a sweaty white-haired man with captain's bars on his uniform. "At least three of these facial cuts are infected. I understand his shoulder blade might be broken, but all I see is a bandage."

The captain said, "Well—"

"How long have you been here?" he asked me.

"Since three-forty-six in the morning," I said.

He looked at his watch. "It's four o'clock in the afternoon." He looked at the sweaty captain. "Your department is guilty of violating my client's civil rights, and that's a federal crime."

"Bullshit," Jefferson said.

Cheswick pulled a handkerchief from his breast pocket as a pitcher of water and a glass were placed on the interrogation table. Cheswick lifted the pitcher and turned to the group. He poured some water onto his handkerchief, and the spillage splashed on Jefferson's shoes.

"Heard of Rodney King, Patrolman Jefferson?"

"It's Inspector Jefferson." He looked at his wet shoes.

"Not once I get through with you." Cheswick turned back to me and dabbed the handkerchief against several of my cuts. "Let me make this clear," he said to the group, "you gentlemen are fucked. I don't know how you do things down here and I don't care, but you kept my client in an unventilated box for over twelve hours, which makes anything he said inadmissible in court. Anything."

"It's ventilated," a cop said, his eyes on fire.

"Turn on the air conditioner, then," Cheswick said.

The cop half turned toward the door, and then stopped, shook his head at his own stupidity. When he turned back, Cheswick was smiling at him.

"So the air conditioner in this room was turned off by choice. In a cinder block room on an eighty-six-degree day. Keep it up, gentlemen, because I already have a lawsuit in the mid six figures. And climbing." He took the handkerchief from my face, handed me a glass of water. "Any other complaints, Patrick?"

I inhaled the entire glass of water in about three seconds. "They spoke to me in a rude fashion."

He gave me a tight smile and clapped my shoulder just hard enough to make it scream. "Let me do the talking," he said.

Jefferson stepped up beside Cheswick. "Your client shot a guy three times. His partner blew out the throat of another guy. A third guy was rammed off a bridge in his car and died upon impact with Tampa Bay."

"I know," Cheswick said. "I've seen the tape."

"The tape?" Jefferson said.

"The tape?" The sweaty captain said.

"The tape?" I said.

Cheswick reached into his briefcase and tossed a videotape onto the table. "That's a copy," he said. "The original is with the offices of Meegan, Feibel, and Ellenburg in Clearwater. The tape was sent to them at nine this morning by private courier."

Jefferson picked up the tape and a thin drop of sweat slid from his hairline.

"Help yourselves," Cheswick said. "The tape was

recorded by someone heading south on the Skyway at the time of the incident."

"Who?" Jefferson said.

"A woman named Elizabeth Waterman. I believe you arrested her boyfriend, Peter Moore, on the bridge last night for DUI and a bunch of other things. I believe he gave a statement to your officers corroborating the events on the tape, which you chose to discount because he'd failed a Breathalyzer."

"This is bullshit," Jefferson said and looked for support from the rest of his colleagues. When he didn't get it, he gripped the tape so hard in his hand, I was sure it would shatter.

"The tape is a little blurry because of the rain and the videotaper's excitement," Cheswick said, "but most of the incident is on there."

"You've got to be kidding me," I said and laughed.

"Am I the coolest, or what?" Cheswick said.

28

At nine that night, we were released.

In the interim, a doctor had examined me at Bayshore Hospital, a pair of patrolmen standing ten feet away the whole time. He cleaned up my wounds and gave me antiseptic to ward off any further infections. His X ray revealed a clear fissure in my shoulder blade, but not a full break. He applied a fresh set of bandages, gave me a sling, and told me not to play football for at least three months.

When I asked him about the combination of the cracked scapula with the wounds my left hand had received from my battle with Gerry Glynn last year, he looked at the hand.

"Numb?"

"Completely," I said.

"There's nerve damage to the hand."

"Yes," I said.

He nodded. "Well, we don't have to amputate the arm."

"Nice to hear."

He looked at me through small, icy glasses.

"You're taking a lot of years off the back end of your life, Mr. Kenzie."

"I'm beginning to realize that."

"You plan on having kids someday?"

"Yeah," I said.

"Start now," he told me. "You might live to see them graduate college."

As we walked down the steps of the police station, Cheswick said, "You messed with the wrong guy this time."

"No kidding," Angie said.

"Not only is there no record of Cushing or Clifton working for him, but that jet you told me you took? The only private jet to leave Logan Airport between nine in the morning and noon on the day in question was a Cessna, not a Gulfstream, and it was bound for Dayton, Ohio."

"How do you silence an entire airport?" Angie said.

"Not just any airport, either," Cheswick said. "Logan has the tightest, most admired security system in the country. And Trevor Stone has enough pull to bypass it."

"Shit," I said.

We stopped at the limousine Cheswick had hired. The chauffeur opened the door, but Cheswick shook his head and turned back to us.

"Come back with me?"

I shook my head and instantly regretted it. The majorettes were still practicing in there.

"We have a few loose ends down here to tie up," Angie said. "We also have to figure out what to do about Trevor before we return."

"Want my advice?" Cheswick tossed his briefcase into the back of the limo.

"Sure."

"Stay away from him. Stay down here until he dies. Maybe he'll leave you alone."

"Can't do it," Angie said.

"I didn't think so." Cheswick sighed. "I heard a story once about Trevor Stone. Just a rumor. Gossip. Anyway, supposedly this union organizer was causing trouble down in El Salvador back in the early seventies, threatening Trevor Stone's banana, pineapple, and coffee interests. So Trevor, according to legend, made a few phone calls. And one day the workers at one of his coffee bean processing plants are sifting through a vat of beans and they find a foot. And then an arm. And then a head."

"The union organizer," Angie said.

"No," Cheswick said. "The union organizer's six-year-old daughter."

"Christ," I said.

Cheswick patted the roof of the limo absently, looked out at the yellow street. "The union organizer and his wife, they never found them. They became part of 'the disappeared' down there. And nobody ever talked again about striking at one of Trevor Stone's plants."

We shook hands and he climbed into the limo.

"One last thing," he said before the driver could shut the door.

We leaned in.

"Someone broke into the offices of Hamlyn and Kohl the night before last. They stole all the office equipment. I hear there's a lot of money in hot fax machines and copiers."

"Supposedly," Angie agreed.

"I hope so. Because these thieves had to shoot Everett Hamlyn dead to get what they wanted."

We stood silently as he climbed into the limo and it snaked up the street and turned right and headed for the expressway.

Angie's hand found mine. "I'm sorry," she whispered. "About Everett, about Jay."

I blinked at something in my eyes.

Angie tightened her grip on my hand.

I looked up at the sky, such a rich dark shade of blue it seemed artificial. That was something else I'd been noticing down here: This state—so ripe and lush and colorful—seemed fake in comparison with its uglier counterparts up north.

There's something ugly about the flawless.

"They were good men," Angie said softly.

I nodded. "They were beautiful."

29

We walked over to Central Avenue and headed north toward a cabstand the duty officer had grudgingly told us about.

"Cheswick said they're going to come back on us with gun charges, discharging firearms within city limits, shit like that."

"But nothing that'll stick," she said.

"Probably not."

We reached the cabstand, but it was empty. Central Avenue, or at least the section we were on, didn't look like a real friendly place. Three winos fought over a bottle or a pipe in the garbage-strewn parking lot of a torched liquor store, and across the street, several mangy-looking teenagers eyed potential prey from a bench in front of a Burger King, passed a joint, and gave Angie a once-over. I was sure the bandage around my shoulder and the sling under my arm made me look a bit vulnerable, but then they took a closer look, and I locked one of them in a weary stare until he turned his head and concentrated on something else.

The cabstand was a Plexiglas lean-to and we sagged against the wall in the liquid heat for a moment.

"You look like shit," Angie told me.

I raised an eyebrow at the cuts on her face, the half shiner beside her right eye, the gouge in her left calf. "You, on the other hand . . ."

She gave me a weary smile and we leaned against the wall for a full minute of silence.

"Patrick."

"Yeah?" I said, my eyes closed.

"When I got out of the ambulance on the bridge, and they walked me to the cruiser, I, ahm . . ."

I opened my eyes and looked at her. "What?"

"I think I saw something strange. And I don't want you to laugh."

"You saw Desiree Stone."

She came off the wall and slapped me in the abdomen with the back of her hand. "Get out of town! You saw her, too?"

I rubbed my stomach. "I saw her, too."

"You think she's a ghost?"

"She's no ghost," I said.

Our hotel suites had been trashed while we were gone. At first I thought it had been Trevor's men, maybe the Weeble and Cushing before they came after us, but then I found a business card on my pillow.

INSPECTOR CARNELL JEFFERSON, it read.

I refolded my clothes and placed them back in my suitcase, pushed the bed back into the wall, and closed all the drawers.

"I'm starting to hate this town." Angie came into

the room with two bottles of Dos Equis and we took them out to the balcony and left the glass doors open behind us. If the room was bugged by Trevor, we were already high on his shit list anyway; nothing we said was going to change his mind about dealing with us the way he'd dealt with Jay and Everett Hamlyn and was trying to deal with his daughter, who didn't have the decency to die easily. And if the cops had bugged the room, nothing we said would change what we'd told them at the station because we didn't have anything to hide.

"Why does Trevor want his daughter dead so badly?" Angie said.

"And why does she keep popping up alive?"

"One thing at a time."

"Okay." I propped my ankles up on the balcony rail and sipped my beer. "Trevor wants his daughter dead because somehow she found out he killed Lisardo."

"And why did he kill Lisardo in the first place?"

I looked at her. "Because . . ."

"Yes?" She lit a cigarette.

"I don't have a clue." I took a hit off her cigarette to quell the adrenaline that had been chewing through my blood since I'd shot from the car twenty hours ago.

She took her cigarette back and looked at it. "And even if he did kill Lisardo and she found out—even *if*—why kill her? He'd be dead before a trial, and his lawyers would keep him free till then. So what's the big deal?"

"Right."

"This whole dying thing, too . . ."

"What?"

"Most people are dying, they're trying to make their peace—with God, with family, with the earth in general."

"But not Trevor."

"Exactly. If he really is dying, then his hate for Desiree has to run so deep it can't even be measured by most human minds."

"*If* he's dying," I said.

She nodded and stubbed out her cigarette. "Let's consider that for a second. How do we know for sure he's dying?"

"One good look at him."

She opened her mouth as if to argue, then closed it and lowered her head to her knees for a moment. When she raised her head, she flipped the hair back off her face and leaned back in her chair. "You're right," she said. "Dumb idea. The guy's definitely got one foot in the grave."

"So," I said. "Back to square one. What makes a guy hate anyone, but particularly his own flesh and blood, so much that he's determined to spend his last days hunting her down?"

"Jay suggested a history of incest," Angie said.

"Okay. Daddy loves his little girl way too much. They have a conjugal relationship, and something gets in the way."

"Anthony Lisardo. Back to him again."

I nodded. "So, Daddy has him whacked."

"Not long after her mother died to boot. So Desiree goes into her depression, meets Price, who manipulates her grief and enlists her in the theft of the two million."

I turned my head, looked at her. "Why?"

"Why what?"

"Why would Price enlist her? I'm not saying he wouldn't want her along for the ride for a bit, but why would he let her in on the plan?"

She tapped her thigh with her beer bottle. "You're right. He wouldn't." She raised her beer and drank. "God, I'm confused."

We sat there in silence and chewed on it as the moon bathed Tampa Bay in pearl and the fingers of rose in the purple sky faded and eventually disappeared. I went back in and got us two more beers and came back out onto the patio.

"Black is white," I said.

"Huh?"

"You said it yourself. Black is white. Up is down on this case."

"True. Definitely true."

"You ever see *Rashomon*?"

"Sounds like a movie about a guy's athlete's foot." I looked at her from under hooded eyes.

"Sorry," she said lightly. "No, Patrick, I never saw *Rash-o-whatever*."

"Japanese film," I said. "The whole movie shows the same event told four different times."

"Why?"

"Well, it's a rape and murder trial. And the four people who were there tell four completely different accounts of what happened. And you watch each version and have to decide who's telling the truth."

"I saw a *Star Trek* like that once."

"You need to watch less *Star Trek*," I said.

"Hey, at least it's easy to pronounce. Not like *Rashaweed*."

"*Rashomon.*" I squeezed the top of my nose between my index finger and thumb, closed my eyes. "My point, anyway."

"Yes?"

"Is that we might be looking at this all wrong. Maybe," I said, "we accepted too many things as truth at the beginning and were wrong."

"Like thinking Trevor was an okay guy and not a homicidal, incestuous nutbag?"

"Like that," I said.

"So what else have we accepted as truth that we might be looking at from the wrong angle?"

"Desiree," I said.

"What about her?"

"Everything about her." I leaned forward, elbows on my knees, and looked through the bars of the railing at the bay below, at the three bridges cut across the placid water, each one fracturing and distorting the shafts of moonlight. "What do we know about Desiree?"

"She's beautiful."

"Right. How do we know that?"

"Oh, jeez," she said. "You're turning Jesuit on me again, aren't you?"

"Humor me. How do we know Desiree is beautiful?"

"From pictures. From even a short glimpse on the bridge last night."

"Right. Our knowledge, seen by our own eyes, based on *our* personal experience and contact with the subject and that one aspect of her. And that's it."

"Come again?"

"She's a beautiful woman. That's all we know

about her, because that's the only thing we ourselves can testify to about her. Everything else we know about her is hearsay. Her father tells us one thing, but he feels completely different. Doesn't he?"

"Yes."

"So is what he originally told us true?"

"About the depression, you mean?"

"About everything. Lurch says she's a beautiful, wonderful creature. But Lurch works for Trevor, so we can pretty much figure he was full of shit."

Her eyes were lighting up now. She sat forward.

"And Jay, Jay was obviously wrong when he told us she was dead."

"Exactly."

"So all his perceptions about her could have been wrong."

"Or blinded by love or infatuation."

"Hey," she said.

"What?"

"If Desiree didn't die, whose body was that with Jay's sweatshirt and a shotgun blast to the face?"

I grabbed the phone from the room, brought it out to the balcony, and called Devin Amronklin.

"You know any cops in Clearwater?" I asked him.

"I might know someone who knows someone."

"Can you see if they've ID'd a female shooting victim found in the Ambassador Hotel four days ago?"

"Give me your number."

I did, and Angie and I turned our seats until they were facing each other.

"Assume Desiree's not all sweetness and light," I said.

"Let's assume even worse," she said. "Let's assume she's her father's child and the acorn never falls far from the tree. What if she put Price up to the robbery?"

"How'd she know the money was even there?"

"I don't know. We'll deal with that one later. So she puts Price up to the robbery . . ."

"But Price figured after a while, 'Hey, she's a bad seed. She'll screw me over as soon as she gets the chance,' so he ditches her."

"And takes the money. But she wanted it back."

"But didn't know where he hid it."

"And Jay comes along."

"A perfect foil to put some pressure on Price," I said.

"Then Desiree figures out where the money is. But she's got a problem. If she just steals it, not only will her father be looking for her, but so will Price and Jay."

"So she has to get dead," I said.

"And she knows Jay will settle up with Price."

"And probably go to jail for it."

"Could she be that devious?" Angie said.

I shrugged. "Why not?"

"So she's dead," Angie said. "And so's Price. And then Jay. So, why show herself to us?"

I didn't have an answer to that.

Neither did Angie.

But Desiree did.

She stepped out onto the balcony with a gun in her hand and said, "Because I need your help."

30

"Nice gun," I said. "Did you pick it because it matches your outfit, or was it the other way around?"

She came out onto the patio, the gun shaking slightly in her hand, pointing somewhere into the space between Angie's nose and my mouth.

"Look," Desiree said, "in case you can't tell, I'm nervous, and I don't know who to trust, and I need your help, but I'm not sure about you."

"Like father like daughter," Angie said.

I slapped her knee. "Stole my line."

"What?" Desiree said.

Angie took a sip' of her beer, watched Desiree. "Your father, Miss Stone, had us kidnapped so he could talk to us. Now you're pointing a gun at us, ostensibly for the same reason."

"I'm sorry, but—"

"We don't like guns," I said. "The Weeble would tell you that if he was still alive."

"Who?" She stepped gingerly around the back of my chair.

274

"Graham Clifton," Angie said. "We called him the Weeble."

"Why?"

"Why not?" I turned my head as she edged along the balcony rail, finally came to a stop about six feet from our chairs, the gun still pointing at a space between us.

And good God, was she beautiful. I've dated some beautiful women in my time. Women who based their worth on their external perfection because the world judged them by pretty much the same standard. Lithe or lush, tall or petite, achingly attractive women around whom men forgot how to speak.

But none of them could come within a country mile of Desiree's radiance. Her physical perfection was palpable. Her skin seemed to have been lathered onto bones that were both delicate and pronounced. Her breasts, unencumbered by a bra, swelled against the thin material of her dress with every shallow breath she took, and the dress itself, a simple, unstructured peach cotton affair designed to be functional and loose, couldn't do much to hide the tight cords of her abdomen, or the gracefully hard cut of muscle in her thighs.

Her jade eyes sparkled, and seemed twice as bright because they were sheened with a dewy nervousness and set back against the sunset glow of her skin.

She wasn't unaware of her effect, either. During our entire conversation, she'd glance back and forth at Angie when speaking to her, her eyes skipping across her face. But when she spoke to me, she'd bore into me with those eyes, lean forward almost imperceptibly.

"Miss Stone," I said, "put the gun down."

"I can't. I don't . . . I mean, I'm not sure—"

"Put it down or shoot us," Angie said. "You have five seconds."

"I—"

"One," Angie said.

Her eyes welled up. "I just want to be sure—"

"Two."

Desiree looked at me, but I gave her nothing back.

"Three."

"Look—"

"Four." Angie turned her chair to her right and the metal made a short screech against the concrete.

"Just stay there," Desiree said, and the wavering gun turned toward Angie.

"Five." Angie stood up.

Desiree pointed the quivering gun at her, and I reached up and slapped her hand.

The gun bounced off the railing, and I snatched it from the air before it could drop to the garden six stories below. Lucky, too, because when I peered over the side, I saw a couple of kids, grade school age, playing on their ground-floor patio by the garden.

Look what I found, Ma. Boom.

Desiree's face dropped into her hands for a moment, and Angie looked at me.

I shrugged. The gun was a Ruger .22 automatic. Stainless steel. It felt light in my hand, but that's deceptive when you're holding a pistol. Guns are never light.

She'd left the safety on, and I ejected the clip into my sling, pulled it back out, and placed the gun in my left pocket, the clip in my right.

Desiree raised her head, her eyes red. "I can't do this anymore."

"Do what?" Angie pulled another chair over. "Sit down."

Desiree sat. "This. Guns and death and . . . Jesus Christ, I can't do it."

"Did you rip off the Church of Truth and Revelation?"

She nodded.

"It was your idea," Angie said. "Not Price's."

A half nod. "His idea. But I pushed him toward it after he told me."

"Why?"

"Why?" she said as two tears coursed her face, dropped off her cheekbones and landed on her knees just below the hem of her dress. "Why? You have to . . ." She sucked up air through her mouth and looked up at the sky, wiped at her eyes. "My father killed my mother."

I never saw that one coming. I looked at Angie. She hadn't either.

"In the car accident that nearly killed him?" Angie said. "Are you serious?"

Desiree nodded several times.

"Let me get this straight," I said. "Your father sets up a fake carjacking. Is that what you're saying?"

"Yes."

"And pays these men to shoot him three times?"

"That wasn't part of the plan," she said.

"Well, I'd hope not," Angie said.

Desiree looked at her and blinked. Then she looked at me, her eyes wide. "He'd already paid the men. When everything went wrong and the car flipped—that wasn't part of the plan—they panicked and shot him after they killed my mother."

"Bullshit," Angie said.

Desiree's eyes widened even further and she turned her head to a neutral point between the two of us and looked down at the concrete for a moment.

"Desiree," I said, "there's enough holes in that story to drive a couple of Humvees through."

"For instance," Angie said, "why wouldn't these guys, once they were arrested and tried, tell the police everything?"

"Because they didn't know my father hired them," she said. "One day, someone contacts someone and asks that a woman be killed. Her husband will be with her, this someone says, but he isn't a target. Just her."

We thought about that for a minute.

Desiree watched us, then added, "It's all chains of command. By the time it got down to the actual killers, they had no idea where the order came from."

"So, again, why shoot your father?"

"I can only tell you what I said before—they panicked. Did you read up on the case?"

"No," I said.

"Well, if you did, you'd see that the three killers weren't exactly rocket scientists. They were dumb kids, and they weren't hired for their brains. They were hired because they could kill someone without losing any sleep over it."

I looked over at Angie again. It was coming out of left field, and it definitely had an outlandish quality to it, but in a twisted way, it made some sense.

"Why did your father want to kill your mother?"

"She was planning to divorce him. And she wanted half his fortune. He could fight her in court, and she'd drag out all the sordid details of their life together. Her being sold to him, his raping me when I was fourteen, his continuing to assault me over the years, plus a thousand other secrets she knew about him." She looked at her hands, turned them palm up, then down again. "His other option was to kill her. And he'd exercised that option with people before."

"And he wants to kill you because you know that," Angie said.

"Yes," she said and it came out as a hiss.

"How do you know?" I said.

"After she died, when he got back from the hospital, I heard him talking with Julian and Graham. He was enraged that the three killers had been arrested by the police, instead of dealt with. The best thing that ever happened to those three kids was that they got caught with the gun on them and confessed. Otherwise, my father would have hired a top lawyer to get them off, bought a judge or two, and then had them tortured and killed as soon as they hit the street." She chewed her lower lip for a moment. "My father is the most dangerous man alive."

"We're starting to hold that opinion ourselves," I said.

"Who got shot in the Ambassador Hotel?" Angie said.

"I don't want to talk about that." She shook her head, then brought her knees up to her chin, placed her feet on the edge of the chair, and hugged her legs.

"You don't have a choice," Angie said.

"Oh, God." She laid her head sideways on her knees for a moment, her eyes closed.

After a minute or so, I said, "Try it another way. What made you go to the hotel? Why did you suddenly think you knew where the money was?"

"Something Jay said." Her eyes were still closed, her voice a whisper.

"What did Jay say?"

"He said Price's room was filled with buckets of water."

"Water."

She raised her head. "Ice buckets, half filled with ice that had melted. And I remembered the same thing at one of the motels we stayed in on our way down here. Price and me. He kept making trips to the ice machine. Just a little ice each time, never filling the bucket. He said something about liking the ice in his drinks to be as cold as possible. Fresh from the machine. And how the ice at the top was best because hotels never replace the dirty ice and water at the bottom of the machine. They just kept chugging ice in on top of it. I remember knowing he was full of shit, but couldn't think why, and at the time I was too exhausted to care. I was also starting to get frightened of him. He'd taken the money from me our second night on the road, and wouldn't tell me where it was. Anyway, when Jay said that thing about the buckets, I started thinking about Price in South Carolina." She looked at me, gave me her sparkling jade eyes. "It was under the ice."

"The money?" Angie said.

She nodded. "In a trash bag, laid flat under the ice in the machine on the fifth floor, just outside his room."

"Ballsy," I said.

"Not easy to get to, though," Desiree said. "You have to move all that ice; your arms are pinned in through the small door of the machine. That's how Price found me when he came back from his friends' house."

"Was he alone?"

She shook her head. "There was a girl with him. She looked like a prostitute. I'd seen her with him before."

"Your height, your build, same color hair?" I said.

She nodded. "She was an inch or two shorter, but not so you'd notice unless we were standing side by side. She was Cuban, I think, and her face was very different from mine. But . . ." She shrugged.

"Go on," Angie said.

"They took me in the room. Price was stoned on something. Flying and paranoid and raging. They"—she turned in her chair, looked out at the water, and her voice dropped to a whisper again—"did things to me."

"Both of them?"

She kept her eyes on the water. "What do you think?" Her voice was ragged and thick now. "After, the woman put on my clothes. Sort of to mock me,

I guess? They put a bathrobe around me and drove me to the College Hill section of Tampa. You know it?"

We shook our heads.

"It's like Tampa's version of the South Bronx. They stripped the bathrobe off me and pushed me out of the car, drove off laughing." She raised a quaking hand to her lips for a moment. "I . . . managed to get back. Stole some clothes off a line, hitched a ride back to the Ambassador, but the police were everywhere. And a corpse with the sweatshirt Jay had given me was lying in Price's room."

"Why'd Price kill her?" I said.

She shrugged, her eye wet and red again. "I think because she must have wondered why I was going through the ice machine. She put two and two together, and Price didn't trust her. I don't know for sure. He was a sick man."

"Why didn't you contact Jay?" I said.

"He was gone. After Price. I sat in the shack we had on the beach and waited for him, and the next thing I know he's in jail, and then I betrayed him." She clenched her jaw and the tears came in streams.

"Betrayed him?" I said. "How?"

"I didn't go to the jail. I thought, Jesus, people have probably seen me with Price, maybe even with the dead girl. What good would it do if I went to visit Jay in jail? All it would do is implicate me. I flipped. I lost my mind for a day or two. And then, I thought, the hell with it, I'm going to go get him out of there, have him tell me where his money is so I can post bail."

"But?"

"But he'd left with you two by that point. By the time I caught up with all of you . . ." She pulled a pack of Dunhills from her purse, lit one with a slim gold lighter, sucked the air back into her lungs, and exhaled with her head tilted toward the sky. "By the time I reached you, Jay and Mr. Cushing and Graham Clifton were dead. And I couldn't do anything but stand around and watch." She shook her head bitterly. "Like a brainless asshole."

"Even if you had caught up with us in time," Angie said, "there wouldn't have been anything you could have done to change what happened."

"Well, we'll never know now, will we?" Desiree said with a sad smile.

Angie gave her a sad smile in return. "No, I guess we won't."

She had no place to go and no money. Whatever Price had done with the two million after he'd killed the other woman and blown out of the Ambassador may have died with him.

Our interrogation seemed to have worn her out and Angie offered Desiree her suite for the night.

Desiree said, "Just a quick nap, I'll be fine," but when we passed through Angie's suite five minutes later, Desiree was flopped on her stomach, still dressed, atop the bedcovers, as deep in sleep as anyone I've ever seen.

We went back into my room, shut the door on Desiree, and the phone rang. It was Devin.

"You still want to know the name of the dead girl?"

"Yeah."

284   DENNIS LEHANE

"Illiana Carmen Rios. A working girl. Last known
residence, One-twelve Seventeenth Street Northeast, St. Petersburg."

"She took ten or so falls for hooking. On the plus
side, she probably won't have to worry about doing
any jail time in the near future."

"I don't know," Angie said as we stood in the
bathroom with the shower running. If the room was
bugged, now we had to worry about what we said
again.

"Don't know what?" I said as the steam rose in
clouds from the tub.

She leaned against the sink. "About her. I mean,
every story she told had a fantastic quality to it,
didn't you think?"

I nodded. "But none any less so than most of the
stories we've heard in this case."

"Which is what bothers me. Story upon story,
layer upon layer, and all of it either complete or par-
tial bullshit since this thing began. And why does
she need us?"

She sighed. "I don't know. Do you trust her?"

"Because I don't trust anyone except you."

"Yeah." I smiled. "Sorry."

She waved her hand at me. "Go ahead. Take it.
What's mine is yours."

"Really?"

"Yeah," she said and turned her face up toward mine. "Really," she said softly.

"Feeling's mutual," I said.

Her hand disappeared in the steam for a moment, and then I felt it on my neck.

"How's your shoulder?" she said.

"Tender. My hip, too."

"I'll keep that in mind," she said. And then she bent to one knee and tugged up my shirt. When she kissed the skin around the bandage over my hip, her tongue felt electric.

I bent and wrapped my good arm around her waist. I lifted her off the floor, sat her on the sink, and kissed her as her legs curled around the back of mine and her sandals dropped to the floor. For at least five minutes, we barely came up for air. These last few months, I hadn't just been hungry for her tongue, her lips, her taste—I'd been weak and light-headed from wanting.

"No matter how tired we are," she said as my tongue found her neck, "we don't stop this time until we both pass out."

"Agreed," I murmured.

Somewhere around four in the morning, we finally did pass out.

She fell asleep curled on my chest as my own eyelids fluttered. And I found myself wondering, just before I lost consciousness, how I could have thought—even for a second—that Desiree was the most beautiful woman I'd ever seen.

I looked down at Angie sleeping naked on my chest, at the scratches and swollen flesh on her face, and I knew that only now, at this exact moment and for the first time in my life, did I understand anything about beauty.

31

"Hi."

I opened one eye and looked into the face of Desiree Stone.

"Hi," she said again, her voice a whisper.

"Hi," I said.

"You want coffee?" she said.

"Sure."

"Sssh." She put a finger to her lips.

I turned, saw Angie sleeping deeply beside me.

"It's in the next room," Desiree said and left.

I sat up in bed and took my watch off the dresser. Ten in the morning. I'd had six hours' sleep, but it felt like about six minutes. The last time I'd slept before last night had been at least forty hours previous. But I guess I couldn't sleep through the day.

Angie seemed to be giving it a good bid, though.

She was curled into the tight fetal ball I'd become accustomed to during her months on my living room floor. The sheet had risen up to her waist, and I reached over and pulled it back over her legs, tucked it in at the corner of the mattress.

She didn't stir or so much as groan when I got off the bed. I put on jeans and a long-sleeved T-shirt as quietly as possible and headed toward the door adjoining the suites, then stopped. I came back around to her side of the bed and knelt by her, touched her warm face with the palm of my hand, and kissed her lips lightly, breathed in her smell.

In the last thirty-two hours, I'd been shot at, been thrown from a speeding vehicle, had cracked my shoulder blade, had taken innumerable shards of glass into my flesh, had shot a man dead, had lost about a pint of blood, and had been subjected to twelve hours of hostile questioning in a sweltering cinder block box. Somehow, though, with Angie's face warming my palm, I'd never felt better.

I found my sling on the floor by the bathroom, slipped my dead arm into it, and went next door.

The heavy dark curtains were drawn against the sun and only a small light on the nightstand provided any illumination. Desiree sat in an armchair by the nightstand, sipping coffee, and appeared to be naked.

"Miss Stone?"

"Come in. Call me Desiree."

I squinted into the near darkness as she stood up, and that's when I saw that she wore a French-cut bikini the color of roasted honeycomb, about a shade lighter than her flesh. Her hair was slicked back off her head as she came to me and placed a cup of coffee in my hand.

"I don't know how you like it," she said. "There's cream and sugar on the counter."

I flicked on another light, went to the kitchenette

counter, found the cream and sugar beside the coffee maker.

"Went for a swim?" I came back over by her.

"Just to clear my head. It's better than coffee really."

It might have cleared her head, but it was making mine awful fuzzy.

She sat back in the chair, which, I noticed now, was protected from the dampness of her skin and bikini by the bathrobe she'd removed at some point while sitting in it.

She said, "Should I put this back on?"

"Whatever makes you most comfortable." I sat on the side of the bed. "So, what's up?"

"Hmm?" She glanced at her robe, but didn't put it back on. She bent her knees, placed the soles of her feet on the edge of the bed.

"What's up? You woke me for a reason, I assume."

"I'm leaving in two hours."

"For where?" I said.

"Boston."

"I don't think that makes a whole lot of sense."

"I know." She wiped at some perspiration on her upper lip. "But tomorrow night my father will be out of the house, and I have to get in there."

"Why?"

She leaned forward, her breasts pressing against her knees. "I have things in that house."

"Things worth dying over?" I sipped my coffee, if only so the inside of the cup would give me something to look at.

"Things my mother gave me. Sentimental things."

"And when he dies," I said, "I'm sure they'll still be there. Get them then."

She shook her head. "By the time he dies, what I'm going to get might not be there anymore. One quick trip into the house on a night I know he'll be away, and I'm free."

"How do you know he'll be away?"

"Tomorrow is the night of the annual stockholders' meeting of his biggest company, Consolidated Petroleum. They hold it every year at the Harvard Club Room at One Federal. Same date, same time, rain or shine."

"Why would he go? He's not going to be able to make it next year."

She leaned back, placed her coffee cup on the nightstand. "You don't understand my father yet, do you?"

"No, Miss Stone, I guess I don't."

She nodded, used an index finger to absently wipe at a bead of water sliding down her left calf. "My father doesn't honestly think he's going to die. And if he does, he's going to use every resource he has left to buy himself immortality. He's the chief stockholder in over twenty corporations. The hard copy of his diversified portfolio for his United States interests alone is thicker than the phone book for Mexico City."

"That's some serious thick," I said.

Something flashed through her jade eyes for a moment, something incensed. Then it was gone.

"Yes," she said with a soft smile. "It is. His final months will be spent making sure each and every corporation allocates funds for something in his name—a library, a research lab, a public park, what have you."

"And if he dies, how's he going to make sure all this immortality-making gets done?"

"Danny," she said.

"Danny?" I said.

Her lips parted slightly and she reached for her coffee cup. "Daniel Griffin, my father's personal attorney."

"Ah," I said. "Even I've heard of him."

"About the only attorney more powerful than your own, Patrick."

It was the first time I'd heard my name pass from her lips. It had a disconcertingly sweet effect, like a warm hand pressed to my heart.

"How do you know who my attorney is?"

"Jay talked about you once."

"Really?"

"For almost an hour one night. He looked on you like you were a little brother he'd never had. He said you were the only person in the world he truly trusted. He said if anything ever happened to him, I was to come to you."

I had a flash of Jay sitting across from me at Ambrosia on Huntington, the last time we'd seen each other socially, and he was laughing, a heavy Scotch glass half filled with gin held up in his manicured hand, his perfectly coiffed hair darkening one side of the glass, exuding the confidence of a man who couldn't remember the last time he'd second-guessed himself. Then I had another flash of him being carried from Tampa Bay, his skin puffy and bleached white, his eyes closed, looking no older than fourteen.

"I loved Jay," I said, and the moment the words left my mouth, I didn't know why I'd said them. Maybe it was true. Or maybe, I was trying to see what Desiree's reaction would be.

"So did I," she said and closed her eyes. When she opened them, they were wet. "And he loved you. He said you were worthy of trust. That all sorts of people, from every walk of life, trusted you completely. That's when he told me Cheswick Hartman worked pro bono for you."

"So what do you want from me, Miss Stone?"

"Desiree," she said. "Please."

"Desiree," I said.

"I want you to, I guess, watch my back tomorrow night. Julian should be with my father when he goes to One Federal, but just in case anything goes wrong."

"You know how to bypass the alarm system?"

"Unless he's changed it, and I doubt that. He's not expecting me to try something this suicidal."

"And these . . . heirlooms," I said for lack of a better word, "they're worth the risk?"

She leaned forward again, grasped her ankles in her hands. "My mother wrote a memoir shortly before she died. A memoir of her girlhood in Guatemala, stories about her mother and father, her brothers and sisters, a whole part of my family I never met and never heard about. The memoir ends the day my father came to town. There's nothing in it of any great importance, but she gave it to me not long before she died. I hid it, and it's become unbearable to think of it still lying in that house, waiting to be found. And if my father finds it, he'll destroy it. And then the last piece of my mother that I have left will die, too." She met my eyes. "Will you help me, Patrick?"

I thought of the mother. Inez. Bought at fourteen by a man who thought anything was for sale. And unfortunately, he was usually proven right. What kind of life had she had in that big house with that crazed megalomaniac?

One in which, I guess, her only refuge was in taking pen to paper and writing about the life she'd led before that man had come and taken her away. And who to share her most precious inner world with? Her daughter, of course, as trapped and soiled by Trevor as she was.

"Please," Desiree said. "Will you help me?"

"Sure," I said.

She reached across and took my hand. "Thank you."

"Don't mention it."

Her thumb ran up the inside of my palm. "No," she said. "Really. I mean it."

"I do, too," I said. "Don't mention it. Really."

"Are you and Miss Gennaro . . . ?" she said. "I mean, have you been . . . for very long?"

I let the question hang in the ten inches of space between us.

Her hand dropped away from mine, and she smiled. "All the good ones are taken," she said. "Of course."

She leaned back in her chair and I held her gaze

and she didn't look away. For a full minute, we looked at each other in silence, and then her left eyebrow arched ever so slightly.

"Or are they?" she said.

"They are," I said. "In fact, one of the last good ones, Desiree—"

"Yes?"

"Dropped off a bridge the other night."

I stood up.

She crossed her legs at the ankles.

"Thanks for the coffee. How're you getting to the airport?"

"I still have a car Jay rented for me. It's due back at the downtown Budget tonight."

"You want me to drive you and drop it off?"

"If you don't mind," she said, her eyes on her coffee cup.

"Get dressed. I'll be back in a few minutes."

Angie was still sleeping so deeply I knew the only alarm clock that could wake her would be a hand grenade. I left her a note, and Desiree and I went out to her rented Grand Am and she drove toward the airport.

It was another hot, sunny day. Same as every other one I'd seen since arriving. At around three, I'd learned from experience, it would rain for half an hour, and things would cool for a bit, then the humidity would steam off the earth to follow the rain, and it would be brutal until sundown.

"About what happened back in the room," Desiree said.

"Forget it," I said.

"No. I loved Jay. I did. And I barely know you."

"Right," I said.

"But, maybe, I dunno . . . Are you aware of the pathology of many incest and sex abuse victims, Patrick?"

"Yeah, Desiree, I am. Which is why I said to forget it."

We pulled onto the airport roadway and followed the red signs for the Delta terminal.

"Where'd you get your plane ticket?" I said.

"Jay. He bought two."

"Jay was going along with this?"

She nodded. "He bought two," she repeated.

"I heard you the first time, Desiree."

She turned her head. "You could be back here in two days. Meanwhile, Miss Gennaro could get some sun, see the sights, relax."

She pulled up at the Delta gate.

"Where do you want to meet us in Boston?" I said.

She stared out the window for a moment, her hands on the wheel, fingers tapping lightly, her breathing shallow. Then she rummaged through her purse, distracted, and reached in the back for a mid-sized black leather gym bag. She wore a baseball cap over her hair, turned backward, a pair of khaki shorts, and a man's denim shirt, sleeves rolled up to her elbows. Nothing special, and she'd still put cricks in the necks of most men she passed on the way to her plane. As I sat there, the car seemed to shrink around us.

"Ahm, what did you ask me?" she said.

"Where and when tomorrow?"

"When are you arriving?"

"Probably tomorrow afternoon," I said.

"Why don't we meet in front of Jay's condo building?" She got out of the car.

I climbed out, too, as she took another small bag from the trunk and closed it, gave me the keys.

"Jay's building?"

"That's where I'll be lying low. He gave me a key, the password, the alarm code."

"Okay," I said. "What time?"

"Six."

"Six it is."

"Great. It's a date." She turned toward the doors. "Oh, I almost forgot, we have another date."

"We do?"

She smiled, hoisted her bag onto her shoulder. "Yeah. Jay made me promise. April first. *Fail-Safe*."

"*Fail-Safe*," I said as the temperature of my body dropped twenty degrees in the sweltering heat.

She nodded, her eyes crinkling against the sun. "He said if anything happened to him, I was supposed to keep you company this year. Hot dogs and Budweiser and Henry Fonda. Isn't that the tradition?"

"That's the tradition," I said.

"Well, then it's set. A done deal."

"If Jay said so," I said.

"He made me promise." She smiled and gave me a little wave as the electronic doors opened behind her. "So it's a date?"

"It's a date," I said, giving her my own little wave in return, beaming my best smile.

"See you tomorrow." She walked into the airport,

and I watched through the glass as her ass swayed
gently as she passed through a crowd of frat boys,
and then turned down a corridor and disappeared.

The frat boys were still watching the space she'd
occupied for all of three seconds as if it were blessed
by God, and I was doing the same.

Get a good look, guys, I thought. That's as close
to flawless as some of you will ever encounter. Never,
probably, was there a creature created who could
match her spirit of relentless near-perfection.

Desiree. Even her name stirred the heart.

I stood by the car, smiling from ear to ear, probably looking like a complete idiot, when a baggage
porter stopped in front of me and said, "You okay,
man?"

"Fine," I said.

"You lose something?"

I shook my head. "Found something."

"Well, good for you," he said and walked off.

Good for me. Yes. Bad for Desiree.

You were so, so close, lady. And then you blew it.
Blew it big time.

PART THREE

FAIL-SAFE

32

About a year after I finished my apprenticeship with Jay Becker, he got kicked out of his own apartment by a Cuban flamenco dancer named Esmeralda Vasquez. Esmeralda had been traveling with the road company of *The Threepenny Opera* when she met Jay her second night in town. Three weeks into the run of the show, she was pretty much living with him, though Jay didn't think of it that way. Unfortunately for him, Esmeralda did, which is why she was probably so irate when she caught Jay in bed with another dancer from the same show. Esmeralda got her hands on a knife, and Jay got his hand on his doorknob and he and the other dancer got the hell out of Dodge for the night.

The dancer went back to the apartment she shared with her boyfriend, and Jay came knocking on my door.

"You pissed off a Cuban flamenco dancer?" I said.

"It would appear so," he said, placing a case of

Beck's in my fridge and a bottle of Chivas on my counter.

"Was this wise?"

"It would appear not."

"Was this, perhaps, even stupid?"

"Are you going to rag on me all night or are you going to be a good lad and show me where you keep your chips?"

So we ended up sitting on my couch in the living room, drinking his Beck's and Chivas and talking about near castrations at the hands of women scorned, bad breakups, jealous boyfriends and husbands, and several similar topics that wouldn't have seemed half so funny if it weren't for the booze and the company.

And then, just as the conversation was running dry, we looked up and noticed the beginning credits to *Fail-Safe* on my TV.

"Shit," Jay said. "Turn it up."

I did.

"Who directed this?" Jay said.

"Lumet."

"You sure?"

"Positive."

"I thought it was Frankenheimer."

"Frankenheimer did *Seven Days in May*," I said.

"You're right. God, I love this movie."

So for the next two hours we sat, rapt, as President of the United States Henry Fonda clenched his jaw against a coldly crisp black-and-white world gone mad, and a computer foul-up caused the U.S. attack squadron to pass the fail-safe point and bomb Moscow, and then poor Hank Fonda had to clench his jaw some more and order the bombing of New York City to placate the Russians and avoid a full-scale nuclear war.

After it was over, we argued about which was better—*Fail-Safe* or *Dr. Strangelove*. I said it was no contest; *Strangelove* was a masterpiece and Stanley Kubrick was a genius. Jay said I was too artsy. I said he was too literal. He said Henry Fonda was the greatest actor in the history of cinema. I assured him he was drunk.

"If only they'd had some sort of supersecret code word to call those bombers back." He settled back into the couch, eyelids at half-mast, beer in one hand, glass of Chivas in the other.

"'Supersecret code word'?" I laughed.

He turned his head. "No, really. Say ol' President Fonda had just spoken to each squadron pilot privately, gave them each a secret word only he and they knew. Then he could have called them back after they crossed the fail-safe line."

"But, Jay," I said, "that's the point—he couldn't call anyone back. They'd been trained to think any communication was a Russian trick after they passed fail-safe."

"Still . . ."

We sat there watching *Out of the Past*, which had followed on the heels of *Fail-Safe*. Another terrific black-and-white movie on Channel 38, back when 38 was cool. At some point Jay went and used the bathroom, then came back from the kitchen with two more beers.

"If I ever want to send you a message," he said, his tongue thick with liquor, "that's our code."

"What?" I said.

"Fail-safe," he said.

"I'm watching *Out of the Past* now, Jay. *Fail-Safe* was a half hour ago. New York is blown to smithereens. Get over it."

"No, I'm serious." He struggled against the couch cushion, sat up. "I ever want to send you a message from beyond the grave, say, it'll be 'fail-safe.'"

"A message from beyond the friggin' grave?" I laughed. "You're serious."

"As a coronary. No, no, lookit." He leaned forward, widened his eyes to clear his head. "This is a rough business, man. I mean, it's not as rough as the Bureau, but it's no cakewalk. Something ever happens to me . . ." He rubbed his eyes, shook his head again. "See, I got two brains, Patrick."

"You mean two heads. And Esmeralda would say, you used the wrong one tonight, which is why she wants to cut it off."

He snorted. "No. Okay, yeah, I got two heads, sure. But I'm talking about brains. I got two brains. I do." He tapped his head with his index finger, squinted at me. "One of them, the normal one, is no problem. But the other one, that's my cop brain, and it never shuts off. It wakes my other brain up at night, forces me to get out of bed and think about something that was bugging me and I didn't even know it was. I mean, I've solved half of my cases at three o'clock in the morning, all because of this second brain."

"It must be tough getting dressed every day."

"Huh?"

"With those two brains," I said. "I mean, do they have different tastes in clothes and whatnot? Food?"

He shot me the bird. "I'm serious."

I held up a hand. "Seriously," I said, "I sorta know what you're talking about."

"Nah." He waved his hand. "You're still too green. But you will know. Someday. This second brain, man, it's a pisser. Say, you meet this person—a potential friend, a lover, what have you—and you want this relationship to work, but your second brain starts working. Even if you don't want it to. And it sets off alarm bells, instinctual ones, and you know deep in your heart that you can't trust this person. Your second brain's picked up on something your regular brain can't or won't. Might take you years before you figure out what that something was—maybe it was the way the friend stuttered over a certain word or the way the lover's eyes lit up when she saw diamonds even though she said she couldn't care less about money. Maybe it was—Who knows? But it'll be something. And it'll be true."

"You're drunk."

"I am, but that doesn't mean I'm not speaking God's truth. Look, I'm just saying, I ever get whacked?"

"Yeah?"

"It's not going to be by some mob ice-man or scumbag drug dealer or somebody I'd smell a mile off. It's going to be by someone I trust, someone I love. And maybe I'll go to my grave trusting them. Most of me." He winked. "But my second brain, I swear it's a bullshit detector, and it'll tell me to set up some sort of safeguard against this person, whether the rest of me wants to do it or not. So, that's it." He nodded to himself, sat back.

"That's what?"

"That's the plan."

"What plan? You haven't said a thing that's made sense in at least twenty minutes."

"If I ever die, and someone who was close to me comes up to you and says some bullshit about having a message about *Fail-Safe*, then you know you got to take them out or take them down or generally fuck up their shit in a big way." He held up his beer. "Drink on it."

"This doesn't involve slicing our thumbs with razors and mingling the blood or anything, does it?"

He frowned. "Don't need that with you. Drink."

We drank.

"But what if it's me who sets you up for a hit. Jay?"

He looked at me, one eye squinted shut. "Then I'm screwed, I guess." And he laughed.

He refined the "message from the grave," as I called it, over the years and beers in between. April Fools' Day was added as a second joke on the person or persons who might hurt him and then try to befriend me.

It's such a long shot, I used to tell him. It's like placing a single land mine in the Sahara Desert and expecting a particular guy to step on it. One guy, one land mine, a desert three and a half million square miles.

"I'll take the odds," he said. "Might be a long shot, but that land mine goes off, people are going to be able to see it for miles. Just remember that second brain of mine, buddy. When the rest of me's in the ground, that second brain might just send you a message. You make sure you're there to hear it."

And I was.

"Take them out or take them down or generally fuck up their shit in a big way," he'd asked me all those years ago.

Okay, Jay. No problem. My pleasure.

33

"Get up. Come on. Get up." I threw back the curtains and the hard sunlight poured into the room, filled the bed.

Angie had somehow managed to turn herself completely sideways on the bed while I'd been gone. She'd kicked the covers off her legs, and just a slim triangle of white sheet covered her bottom as she looked up at me through bleary eyes, her hair hanging in her face like a tangle of black moss.

"Ain't you just the Romeo in the morning?" she said.

"Come on," I said. "Let's go." I grabbed my gym bag, started stuffing it with my clothes.

"Let me guess," she said. "There's money on the dresser, it was swell, but don't let the door hit my butt on the way out."

I dropped to my knees and kissed her. "Something like that. Come on. We're in a rush."

She rose to her knees and the covers dropped away and her arms slid over my shoulders. Her body, soft and warm with sleep, crushed against my own.

"We sleep together for the first time in seventeen years, and you wake me up like this?"

"Unfortunately," I said, "yes."

"This better be good."

"It's better than good. Come on. I'll tell you on the way to the airport."

"The airport."

"The airport."

"The airport," she said with a yawn and stumbled out of bed and went into the bathroom.

The forest greens and coral whites, pale blues and burnt yellows dropped away and turned to square quilted patches as we rose into the clouds and headed north.

"Run this by me again," Angie said. "The half-naked part."

"She was wearing a bikini," I said.

"In a dark room. With you in it," she said.

"Yes."

"And you felt how?"

"Nervous," I said.

"Whoo," she said. "Wrong, wrong answer."

"Wait," I said, but I knew I'd signed my death warrant.

"We made love for six hours, and you still felt tempted by this little bimbo in a bikini?" She leaned forward in her seat, turned, and looked at me.

"I didn't say tempted," I said. "I said 'nervous.'"

"Same thing." She smiled, shook her head. "Guys, I swear."

"Right," I said. "Guys. Don't you get it?"

"No," she said. She raised her fist to her chin,

squinted so I'd know she was concentrating. "Please. Elucidate."

"All right. Desiree is a siren. She sucks men in. She has an aura, and it's half innocence, half pure carnality."

"An aura."

"Right. Guys love auras."

"Okeydoke."

"Any guy gets around her, she turns this aura on. Or maybe it's on all the time, I don't know. But in either case, it's pretty strong. And a guy looks at her face, her body, he hears her voice and smells her scent, he's a goner."

"All guys?"

"Most, I'd bet."

"You?"

"No," I said. "Not me."

"Why?"

"Because I love you."

That stopped her. The smile left her face and her skin paled to eggshell, and her mouth lay open as if it had forgotten how to use words.

"What did you just say?" she managed eventually.

"You heard me."

"Yeah, but . . ." She turned in her seat, looked straight ahead for a moment. Then she turned to the middle-aged black woman sitting in the seat beside her who'd been following our conversation since we got on the plane without any pretense to be doing otherwise.

"I heard him, honey," the woman said, knitting what appeared to be a small beaver with lethal-looking needles. "Loud and clear. Don't know about all this aura bullshit, but I heard that part just fine, thank you."

"Wow," Angie said to her. "You know?"

"Aww, he ain't that good-looking," the woman said. "He maybe rate a 'gee' but he don't rate no 'wow,' seem to me."

Angie turned back to me. "Gee," she said.

"Go on," the woman said to me, "get back to telling us about this slut made you coffee."

"Anyway," I said to Angie.

She blinked, closed her mouth by placing the heel of her hand to her jaw and pushing up. "Yeah, yeah, yeah. Back to that."

"If I wasn't, you know—"

"In *love*," the lady said.

I glared at her. "—with you, Ange, yeah, I would've been a dead man in there. She's a viper. She picks guys—almost any guy—and she gets them to do her bidding, whatever that may be."

"I want to meet this girl," the woman said. "See if she can get my Leroy to mow the lawn."

"But that's what I don't get," Angie said. "Guys are that stupid?"

"Yes."

"What he said," the woman said, concentrating on her knitting.

"Women and men are different," I said. "Most of them anyway. Particularly when it comes to their reactions to the opposite sex." I took her hand in mine. "Desiree passes a hundred guys in the street, at least half of them will think about her for days. And when she passes, they won't just, go, 'Nice face, nice ass, pretty smile,' whatever. They'll ache. They'll want to possess her on the spot, melt into her, inhale her."

"Inhale her?" she said.

"Yes. Men have a completely different reaction to beautiful women than women do to beautiful men."

"So Desiree again is . . . ?" She ran the backs of her fingers up the inside of my arm.

"The flame, and we're the moths."

"You ain't half bad," the woman said, leaning forward and looking past Angie at me. "If my Leroy could talk that sort of sweet bullshit you talk, he'd have gotten away with a lot more than he did these last twenty years."

Poor Leroy, I thought.

Somewhere over Pennsylvania, Angie said, "Jesus."

My head came off her shoulder. "What?"

"The possibilities," she said.

"What possibilities?"

"Don't you see? If we invert everything we thought, if we look at things from the perspective of Desiree being not just a little screwed up or slightly corrupt, but a black widow, a machine of relentless self-interest—then, my God."

I sat forward. "Run with it," I said.

She nodded. "Okay. We know she put Price up to the robbery. Right? Right. And then she gets Jay thinking about getting that money back from Price. She plays the opposite. You know, 'Oh, Jay, can't we be happy without the money?' but of course, inside, she's thinking, 'Take the bait, take the bait, you fool.'

And Jay does. But he can't find the money. And then she realizes where it is. And she goes there, but she doesn't get caught like she said. She gets the money. But now she's got a problem."

"Jay."

"Exactly. She knows he'll never stop trying to find her if she disappears. And he's good at his job. And she has to get Price out of the way, too. She can't just disappear. She has to get dead. So . . ."

"She killed Illiana Rios," I said.

We looked at each other, my eyes as wide as hers, I'm sure.

"Shot her point-blank in the face with a shotgun," Angie said.

"Could she have?" I said.

"Why not?"

I sat there thinking about it, letting it sink in. Why not, indeed?

"If we accept this premise," I said, "then we're accepting that she's—"

"Totally without conscience or morality or empathy or anything which makes us humane." She nodded.

"And if she is," I said, "then she didn't just become that way overnight. She's *been* that way for a long time."

"Like father, like daughter," Angie said.

And that's when it hit me. Like a building had fallen on me. The oxygen in my chest swirled into a vortex created by a single instant of horrifying clarity.

"What's the best type of lie in the world?" I asked Angie.

"The type that's mostly true."

I nodded. "Why does Trevor want Desiree dead so badly?"

"You tell me."

"Because he didn't set up that murder attempt on the Tobin Bridge."

"She did," Angie said in a near whisper.

"Desiree killed her mother," I said.

"And tried to kill her father."

"No wonder he's pissed at her," the woman beside Angie said.

"No wonder," I repeated.

34

It was all there to see in black-and-white for anyone who had the right information and the right perspective. With headlines such as THREE MEN CHARGED IN BRUTAL SLAYING OF MARBLEHEAD SOCIALITE, or ALLEGED THRILL-KILL TRIO ARRAIGNED FOR CARJACK KILL, the stories quickly fell off the front page when the three killers—Harold Madsen of Lynn, Colum Devereaux of South Boston, and Joseph Brodine of Revere—entered guilty pleas the day after the grand jury's decision to indict.

Angie and I went straight from the airport to the Boston Public Library in Copley Square. We sat in the periodical room and scrolled through microfilm of the *Trib* and the *News* until we found the stories, then read each one until we found what we were looking for.

It didn't take long. In fact, it took less than half an hour.

The day before the grand jury met, Harold Madsen's attorney had contacted the District Attorney's Office with a proposed deal for his client.

Madsen would enter a plea of guilty to first-degree manslaughter for a sentence of fourteen to twenty years. In exchange, he would finger the man who had hired him and his friends to kill Trevor and Inez Stone.

It had all the makings of a bombshell, because up to this point, no mention had ever been made of the murder resulting from anything but a botched car theft.

CARJACK KILLER CLAIMS: IT WAS A HIT, the *News* screamed.

But when the man Madsen claimed had hired them turned out to have died two days after Madsen's arrest, the DA laughed them out of his office.

"Anthony Lisardo?" Assistant District Attorney Keith Simon said to a *Trib* reporter. "Are you kidding me? He was a high school buddy of two of the defendants who died of a drug overdose. It's a pathetic ploy by the defense to give this sordid crime a grandeur it never had. Anthony Lisardo had absolutely no connection to this case."

No one on the defense team could prove he did, either. If Madsen, Devereaux, and Brodine had been contacted by Lisardo, that fact died with him. And since their story hinged on contact with Lisardo and no one else, they took the fall for Inez Stone's murder all by themselves.

A defendant who pleads guilty before a potentially costly trial for the state usually gets some time taken off his sentence. Madsen, Devereaux, and Brodine, however, were each convicted of first-degree murder, both the judge and the DA having rejected a reduction to second degree with depraved indifference. Under recent Massachusetts sentencing guidelines, there is only one possible prison term for first-degree murder—life without possibility of parole.

And personally, I wouldn't lose any sleep over three scumbags who shot a woman to death and obviously had abscesses where their hearts should have been. Nice knowing you, boys. Careful in the shower.

But the real criminal, the person who'd put them up to this, planned it, paid for it, and left them to suffer for it alone—that person deserved as much agony as, if not more than, those boys would be subjected to for the rest of their lives.

"Case file," I said to Angie as we left the microfilm room.

She handed it to me and I leafed through it until I found our notes on our meeting with Captain Emmett T. Groning of the Stoneham Police Department. Lisardo's companion the night he drowned was a kid named Donald Yeager of Stoneham.

"Phone books?" Angie asked the clerk at the information desk.

There were two Yeagers in Stoneham.

Two quarters later, we'd narrowed it down to one. Helene Yeager was ninety-three years old and had never known a Donald Yeager. She'd known a few Michaels, some Eds, even a Chuck, but not that Chuck.

Donald Yeager of 123 Montvale Avenue answered his phone with a hesitant "Yeah?"

"Donald Yeager?" Angie said.

"Yeah?"

"This is Candy Swan, program director of WAAF in Worcester."

"AAF," Donald said. "Cool. You guys kick ass."

"We're the only station that really rocks," Angie said and flipped me the bird as I gave her a thumbs-up. "Donald, the reason I'm calling is we're starting a new segment on our seven-to-midnight show tonight called, ahm, Headbangers from Hell."

"Cool."

"Yeah, and what we do is interview fans such as yourself, local interest stuff, just so you can speak to our other listeners about why you love AAF, who your favorite bands are, that sort of thing."

"I'm going to be on the air?"

"Unless you got other plans for the night."

"No. No way. Shit. Can I call my friends?"

"Absolutely. I just need your verbal consent, and—"

"My what?"

"You need to tell me it's okay for us to call you back later. Say around seven."

"Okay? Shit, it's the balls, man."

"Good. Now you'll be there when we call back?"

"I'm not going anywhere. Hey, do I like win a prize or something?"

She closed her eyes for a moment. "How's two black Metallica T-shirts, a Beavis and Butthead video, and four tickets to Wrestlemania Seventeen at the Worcester Centrum sound?"

"Awesome, man! Awesome. But, hey?"

"Yeah?"

"I thought Wrestlemania was only up to number sixteen."

"My mistake, Donald. We'll call you at seven. Make sure you're there."

"With bells on, babe."

"Where'd you come up with that?" I said as we took a cab back to Dorchester to drop off our luggage, clean up, replace the guns we'd lost in Florida, and get our car.

"I don't know. Stoneham. AAF. They seem to go together."

"The only station that *really* rocks," I said. "Dude."

I took a fast shower after Angie's and came back into the living room to find her rummaging through piles of her clothes. She wore a pair of black boots, black jeans, and no shirt over her black bra as she went through a stack of T-shirts.

"Mistress Gennaro," I said. "My, my. Whip me, beat me, make me write bad checks."

She smiled at me. "Oh, you like this look?"

I let my tongue fall over my lip and panted.

She came over to me, a black T-shirt hanging from her index finger. "When we get back here later, feel free to take it all off."

I panted some more and she gave me a beautiful, wide grin, mussed my hair with her hand.

"Sometimes you're sorta cute, Kenzie."

She turned to walk back to the couch and I reached out and caught her around the waist, pulled her back to me. Our kiss was as long and deep as the first one we'd had in the bathroom the night before. Maybe longer. Maybe deeper.

When we broke from it, her hands on my face,

mine on her lower back, I said, "I've been meaning to do that all day."

"Don't control your impulses next time."

"You're fine with last night?"

"Fine? I'm great."

"Yes," I said, "you are."

Her hands came down my cheeks, rested on my chest. "When this is over, we're going away."

"We are?" I said.

"Yes. I don't care if it's to Maui or just down the street to the Suisse Chalet, but we're putting a Do Not Disturb sign on the door and ordering room service, and we're staying in bed for a week."

"Whatever you say, Mistress Gennaro. You're the boss."

Donald Yeager took one look at Angie in her black leather jacket, jeans, boots, and Fury in the Slaughterhouse concert T-shirt with the rip over her right rib cage, and I'm quite sure he started composing his letter to the *Penthouse* Forum on the spot.

"Holy shit," he said.

"Mr. Yeager?" she said. "I'm Candy Swan from WAAF."

"No shit?"

"No shit," she said.

He opened his apartment door wide. "Come in. Come in."

"This is my assistant, Wild Willy."

Wild Willy?

"Yeah, yeah," Donald said, hustling her in and barely glancing at me. "Nice to meet you and shit."

He turned his back to me and I came in behind

him and shut the door. His apartment complex was a pale, pink brick building on Montvale Avenue, Stoneham's main strip. The building was squat and ugly, two stories high, and probably housed about sixteen units. Donald's studio apartment, I assumed, was representative. A living room with a foldout couch that spilled dirty sheets from under the cushions. A kitchen too small to cook an egg in. From the bathroom off to the left, I could hear the steady drip of water. A scraggly roach ran along a baseboard by the couch, probably not looking for food so much as lost and disoriented from the mushroom cloud of pot smoke that hung over the living room.

Donald tossed some newspapers off the couch so Angie could take a seat under a six-foot-tall, four-foot-wide poster of Keith Richards. It was a photo I'd seen before, taken back in the early seventies. Keith looked to be very stoned—surprise—and leaned against a wall with a bottle of Jack Daniel's in one hand, the omnipresent cigarette in the other, wearing a T-shirt that bore the words JAGGER SUCKS.

Angie sat down and Donald looked up at me as I threw the bolt lock on his door and removed my gun from its holster.

"Hey!" he said.

"Donald," Angie said, "we don't have a lot of time here, so we'll be brief."

"What's this got to do with AAF, dude?" He looked at my gun and even though I hadn't raised it from its place down by my knee, he recoiled as if he'd been slapped.

"The AAF story was bullshit," Angie said. "Sit down, Donald. Now."

He sat. He was a pale kid, emaciated, with bushy yellow hair cut short and sticking straight up off his apple-shaped head. He looked at the bong on the coffee table in front of him and said, "You guys narcs?"

"Stupid people annoy me," I said to Angie.

"Donald, we're not narcs. We're people with guns and not a lot of time. So, what happened the night Anthony Lisardo died?"

He clapped his hands over his face so hard I was sure it would leave welts. "Oh, man! This is about Tony? Oh man, oh man!"

"This is about Tony," I said.

"Oh, dude!"

"Tell us about Tony," I said. "Right now."

"But then you'll kill me."

"No we won't." Angie patted his leg. "I promise."

"Who put the coke in his cigarettes?" I said.

"I don't know. I. Do. Not. Know."

"You're lying."

"I am not."

I cocked the pistol.

"Okay, I am," he said. "I am. Put that thing away. Please?"

"Say her name," I said.

It was the "her" that got him. He looked at me like I was death itself and cringed on the couch. His legs rose off the floor. His elbows tightened against his sparrow's chest.

"Say it."

"Desiree Stone, man. It was her."

"Why?" Angie said.

"I don't know." He held out his hands. "Really. I

don't. Tony'd done some shit for her, something il-legal, but he wouldn't tell me what it was. He just said stay away from the chick because she was bad fucking news, buddy."

"But you didn't stay away."

"I did," he said. "*I* did. But she, man, she came over here, like, supposedly to buy some weed, you know? And, man, she, I gotta tell ya, she, well, wow, is all I can say."

"She screwed you so hard your eyes spun," Angie said.

"My *toes* spun, man. And, like, all's I can say is, well, she should have a ride named after her at Epcot. You know?"

"The cigarettes," I reminded him.

"Yeah, right." He looked down at his lap. "I didn't know," he said softly. "What was in them. I swear to God. I mean, Tony was my best friend." He looked at me. "My best friend, man."

"She told you to give him the cigarettes?" Angie said.

He nodded. "They were his brand. I was just sup-posed to leave them in his car. You know? But then we went driving and ended up down at the reservoir, and he lights one up and goes out into the water, and then he gets this funny look on his face. Like he's stepping on something and he don't like the way it feels? Anyway, that was it. Just that funny look on his face and he sorta touched his chest with his finger-tips, and then he went under water."

"You pull him out?"

"I tried. But it was dark. I couldn't find him out there. So after like five minutes, I got scared. I left."

"Desiree knew he had an allergic reaction to coke, didn't she?" I said.

"Yeah." He nodded. "Tony only did pot and booze, though as a Messenger and all, he wasn't supposed to—"

"Lisardo belonged to the Church of Truth and Revelation?"

He looked up at me. "Yeah. Since he was, like, a kid."

I sat on the arm of the couch for a moment, took a deep breath, got a mouthful of Donald Yeager's pot fumes for my trouble.

"Everything," Angie said.

I looked over at her. "What?"

"Everything this woman's done since day one has been calculated. The 'depression,' Grief Release, everything."

"How'd Lisardo become a Messenger?" I asked Donald.

"His mother, man, she's kinda nutty 'cause her husband's a loan shark and shit; she joined, forced Tony into it, about ten years ago. He was a kid."

"How'd Tony feel about it?" Angie said.

He waved his hand dismissively. "Thought it was a pile of shit. But he respected it, too, kinda, 'cause he said they were like his dad—always scamming. He said they had lots of money—boatloads of the shit— they couldn't report to no IRS."

"Desiree knew all this, didn't she?"

He shrugged. "Not so's she told me or nothing."

"Come on, Donald."

He looked up at me. "I don't know. Tony was a talker. Okay? So, yeah, he probably told Desiree everything about himself from the womb on. I mean, not long before he died, Tony told me he'd met this dude was going to take off the Church for some serious cash, and I'm like, 'Tony, don't be telling me these kinda things.' You know? But Tony was a talker. He was a talker."

Angie and I locked eyes. She'd been right a minute ago. Desiree had calculated every single move she'd made. She'd targeted Grief Release and the Church of Truth and Revelation. Not the other way around. She'd zeroed in on Price. And Jay. And everyone else, probably, who'd ever thought they were zeroing in on her.

I whistled softly under my breath. You almost had to hand it to the woman. She was a piece of work, unlike any other.

"So, Donald, you didn't know the cigarettes were laced?" I said.

"No," he said. "No way."

I nodded. "You just thought she was being nice, giving her ex-boyfriend a free pack of smokes."

"No, look, it's like, I didn't *know* know. I just, see, Desiree, she's, well, she gets what she wants. Always."

"And she wanted your best friend dead," Angie said.

"And you made sure she got it," I said.

"No, man, no. I loved Tony. I did. But Desiree—"

"Was a great fuck," Angie said.

He closed his mouth, looked at his bare feet.

"I hope she was the greatest of all time," I said. "Because you helped her kill your best friend. And you gotta live with that for the rest of your life. Take it easy."

We walked to his door, opened it.

"She'll kill you, too," he said.

We looked back at him. He leaned forward, packed weed into the bong with trembling fingers. "You get in her way—*anything* gets in her way—she'll wipe it out. She knows I won't say anything to any real cops, because I'm . . . nothing. You know?" He looked up at us. "See, Desiree? I don't think she cares about screwing. Good as she is at it, I get the feeling she could take it or leave it. But destroying people? Man, I bet that gets her off like a bottle rocket on the Fourth of July."

35

"What's she gain by coming back here?" Angie said, adjusting the focus on her binoculars and peering through them at the lighted windows of Jay's condo in Whittier Place.

"Probably not her mother's memoirs," I said.

"I think we can safely rule that out."

We were parked in a lot under an expressway off-ramp, on an island between the new Nashua Street Jail and Whittier Place. We'd sunk as low as possible in our seats so we could get a clear view of the bedroom and living room windows of Jay's place, and in the time we'd been here, we'd seen two figures—one male, one female—pass the windows. We didn't even know if the female was Desiree for sure because Jay's thin curtains were drawn and all we could see were silhouettes. The identity of the male was anyone's guess. Still, given Jay's security system, we thought it was a safe bet that that was Desiree up there.

"So what could it be?" Angie said. "I mean, she's got the two mil probably, she's safely hidden in Florida with enough money to get as far away as she wants. Why come back?"

"I don't know. Maybe to finish the job she started almost a year ago."

"Kill Trevor?"

I shrugged. "Why not?"

"To what end, though?"

"Huh?"

"To what end? This girl, Patrick, she always has an angle. She doesn't do anything for just emotional reasons. When she killed her mother and tried to kill her father, what do you think her primary motivation was?"

"Emancipation?" I said.

She shook her head. "That's not a good enough reason."

"A good enough reason?" I put my binoculars down and looked at her. "I don't think she needs much of a reason. Remember what she did to Illiana Rios. Hell, remember what she did to Lisardo."

"Right, but there was logic there. There was reason, twisted as it may have been. She killed Lisardo because he was the only link between her and the three guys who killed her mother. She killed Illiana Rios because it helped cover her tracks when she stole the two million back from Price. In both cases she achieved a notable gain. What's her gain now if she kills Trevor? And what was her original gain when she tried to kill him eight months ago?"

"Well, originally, we can assume it was money."

"Why?"

"Because she was probably the primary beneficiary

of his will. Her parents die, she inherits a few hundred million."

"Yeah. Exactly."

"Okay," I said. "But now that makes no sense. No way Trevor's still got her in the will anymore."

"Right. So why's she coming back?"

"That's what I've been saying."

She lowered her own binoculars, rubbed her eyes. "It's a mystery, isn't it?"

I leaned back against the car seat for a moment, cracked my neck and back muscles against the seat, and instantly regretted it. Once again, I'd forgotten about my damaged shoulder and the pain exploded across my collarbone, drove straight up the left side of my neck, and stabbed its way into my brain. I took a few shallow breaths and swallowed against the bile surging in my chest.

"Illiana Rios had enough in common with Desiree physically," I said eventually, "to make Jay think her corpse was Desiree's."

"Yeah. So?"

"You think that was by accident?" I turned on the car seat. "Whatever their relationship was, Desiree picked Illiana Rios to die in that motel room precisely because of their physical similarities. She was thinking that far ahead."

Angie shuddered. "That woman is *intense*."

"Exactly. Which is why the mother's death makes no sense."

"Excuse me?" She turned on the car seat.

"The mother's car broke down that night. Right?"

"Right." She nodded. "And then the mother called

Trevor, which ensured she'd be in the car with him when Lisardo's friends—"

"What're the odds, though? I mean, given Trevor's schedule and work habits and relationship with his wife to boot—what are the odds Inez would call him for a ride? And what're the odds he'd be there to receive that call? And what's to say he'd even agree to pick her up, not just tell her to hop a cab?"

"It is leaving a lot to chance," she said.

"Right. And Desiree never leaves anything to chance, as you said."

"You're saying the mother's death wasn't part of the plan?"

"I don't know." I looked up at the window and shook my head. "With Desiree, I don't know a lot. Tomorrow, she wants us to accompany her to the house: Ostensibly for protection."

"As if she ever needed protection in her entire life."

"Right. So why does she want us there? What is she setting us up for?"

We sat there for quite a while, binoculars pointed up at Jay's windows, waiting for an answer to my question.

At seven-thirty the next morning, Desiree showed herself.

And I almost walked into her field of vision.

I was coming back from a coffee shop on Causeway Street, Angie and I both having decided our need for caffeine after a night in a car made the risk worthwhile.

I was about ten feet from our car, across from

Jay's building when the front door opened. I pulled up short and froze by a support beam to the expressway ramp.

A well-dressed man in his late forties or early fifties came out of Whittier Place first, a briefcase in hand. He placed the briefcase on the ground, went to shrug into his topcoat, then sniffed and leaned back into the bright sunlight, got a taste of uncommonly warm March air. He put the topcoat back over his arm and picked up his briefcase, looked back over his shoulder as a small group of morning commuters came out behind him. He smiled at someone in the group.

She didn't smile back and at first the bun in her hair and the glasses over her eyes threw me. She wore a charcoal woman's business suit, the hem of the skirt stopping just at her knees, a stiff white blouse underneath, a dove-gray scarf around her neck. She paused to work at the collar of her black topcoat, and the rest of the crowd broke for their cars or walked toward North Station and Government Center, a few heading for the overpass that led toward the Museum of Science or Lechmere Station.

Desiree watched them go with flat contempt and an air of rigid hatred in the set of her slim legs. Or maybe I was reading too much into it.

Then the well-dressed man leaned in and kissed her cheek and she ran the backs of her fingers lightly across his crotch and stepped away.

She said something to him, smiling as she did, and he shook his head, a bemused grin on his powerful face. She walked into the parking lot, and I saw that she was heading for Jay's midnight-blue 1967 Ford Falcon convertible, which had been sitting in the parking lot since he'd left for Florida.

I felt a deep, uncompromising hatred for her as I watched her place her key in the door lock, because I knew the time and money Jay had spent restoring that car, rebuilding the engine, searching nationwide for specific parts. It was just a car, and appropriation of it was the least of her crimes, but it seemed like it was a part of Jay still alive out there in the lot and she was closing in for one last kick.

The man walked out onto the sidewalk almost directly across from me and I stepped back farther behind the support beam. He changed his mind about the topcoat as he got a hit of the biting wind coming down off Causeway Street. He put it on as Desiree started the Falcon, and then he began to walk up the street.

I stepped around the support beam and behind the car, and Angie's eyes met mine in the sideview mirror.

She pointed at Desiree, then herself.

I nodded, pointed at the man.

She smiled and blew me a kiss.

She started the car and I cut across the street to the sidewalk, followed the man up Lomasney Way.

A minute later, Desiree passed me in Jay's car, followed by a white Mercedes, which was followed by Angie. I watched all three cars wind up to Staniford Street and go right, heading toward Cambridge Street and an infinite number of possible destinations beyond.

By the way the man ahead of me tucked his

briefcase under his arm and dug his hands into his pockets at the next corner, I could tell we were in for a walk. I let fifty yards get between us and followed him up Merrimac Street. Merrimac emptied onto Congress Street at Haymarket Square and another blast of wind found us as we crossed New Sudbury and continued in the direction of the financial district, where more architectural styles mixed together than in just about any city in which I'd ever been. Shimmering glass and slabs of granite towered over sudden four-story bursts of Ruskinian Gothic and Florentine pseudopalaces; modernism met German Renaissance met postmodernism met pop met Ionic columns and French cornices and Corinthian pilasters and good old New England granite and limestone. I've spent entire days in the financial district, doing nothing but looking at buildings and feeling, on more optimistic days, that it could stand as metaphor for how to live in the world—all these different perspectives piling in on each other and still managing to make it work.

Though, if I had my druthers, I'd still nuke City Hall.

Just before we would have entered the heart of the financial district, the man turned left, cutting across the nexus of State, Congress, and Court streets, stepping on the stones that commemorate the site of the Boston Massacre, and walked another twenty yards and turned into the Exchange Place Building.

I broke into a trot because Exchange Place is huge with at least sixteen elevator banks. When I walked onto the marble floors under ceilings that stretched four stories above me, I didn't see him. I took a right into the express elevator corridor and saw two doors sliding to a close.

"Hold, please!" I jogged to the doors and just managed to get my good shoulder in between them. They receded but not before giving my shoulder a hard squeeze. Tough week for shoulders.

The man leaned against the wall, watching me as I came in, an annoyed look on his face, as if I'd interrupted his private time.

"Thanks for holding the door," I said.

He stared straight ahead. "There are plenty of other elevators at this time of morning."

"Ah," I said, "a Christian."

As the doors closed, I noticed he'd pressed floor 38, and I nodded at the button, and leaned back.

He looked at my bruised and pocked face, the sling around my arm, the clothes I'd wrinkled almost beyond recognition by sitting in a car for eleven hours.

"You have business on thirty-eight?" he said.

"I do."

I closed my eyes, leaned against the wall.

"What sort of business?" he said.

"What sort do you think?" I said.

"Well, I don't know."

"Then maybe you're going to the wrong floor," I said.

"I *work* there."

"And you don't know what sort of business they do? Jeez. First day?"

He sighed as the elevator raced past floors 1 through 20 so fast I thought my cheeks would slide off my chin.

"Young man," he said, "I think you've made a mistake."

"Young man?" I said, but when I got a closer look at him I realized my original estimate of his age had been off by at least a decade. His tan, tight skin and rich dark hair had thrown me off, as had the energy in his step, but he was at least a young-looking sixty.

"Yes, I really think you have the wrong place."

"Why?"

"Because I know all the firm's clients, and I don't know you."

"I'm new," I said.

"I doubt it," he said.

"No, really," I said.

"No way in hell," he said and gave me a paternal grin of perfectly capped white teeth.

He'd said "firm," and I took a guess that it wasn't an accounting firm.

"I was injured," I said, indicating my arm. "I'm a drummer for Guns N' Roses, the rock band. You heard of them?"

He nodded.

"So we had a show last night at the Fleet and somebody set off some pyrotechnics in the wrong place, and now I need a lawyer."

"Is that right?"

"Yes."

"The drummer for Guns N' Roses is named Matt Sorum, and you don't look anything like him."

A sixty-year-old Guns N' Roses fan? How could this be? And why was it happening to me?

"Was Matt Sorum," I said. "*Was*. He and Axl had a falling-out, and I was called in."

"To play at the Fleet Center?" he said as the elevator reached 38.

"Yeah, buddy."

The doors opened and he blocked them into the return panel by placing his hand against it. "Last night at the Fleet Center, the Celtics played the Bulls. I know. I'm a season ticket holder." He gave me that great smile again. "Whoever you are, pray this elevator gets back down to the lobby before security does."

He stepped out and stared at me as the doors began to close. Behind him, I saw the words GRIFFIN, MYLES, KENNEALLY AND BERGMAN in gold leaf.

I smiled. "Desiree," I whispered.

He reached forward and slapped his hand between the doors and they jumped back.

"What did you just say?"

"You heard me, Mr. Griffin. Or should I call you Danny?"

36

His office had everything the prosperous man needs, save a jet hangar. And he could have fit one if he chose.

The outside offices were empty except for a single male secretary, filling coffee filters at intervals of every fourth cubicle and inside each office. Somewhere, far on the other end, someone ran a vacuum cleaner.

Daniel Griffin hung his topcoat and suit jacket in his closet and walked around a desk so big I was sure it was measured in yard lines. He took a seat and motioned for me to sit across from him.

I stood.

"Who are you?" he said.

"Patrick Kenzie. I'm a private investigator. Call Cheswick Hartman if you want my life story."

"You know Cheswick?"

I nodded.

"You're not the one who extricated his sister from that . . . situation in Connecticut several years back?"

I lifted a heavy bronze statuette off the corner

of his desk, looked at it. It was a representation of some Eastern god or mythological figure, a woman wearing a crown on her head, but her face marred by the trunk of an elephant in place of a nose. She sat cross-legged as fish jumped from the sea toward her feet, her four hands holding a battle ax, a diamond, an ointment bottle, and a coiled serpent respectively.

"Sri Lankan?" I said.

He raised his eyebrows and nodded. "Ceylon back then, of course."

"Duh," I said.

"What do you want from me?" he said.

I glanced at a photo of a smiling beautiful wife, then at another of several grown children and a multitude of perfect grandchildren.

"Vote Republican?" I said.

"What?"

"Family values," I said.

"I don't understand."

"What did Desiree want?" I said.

"I'm not sure that's any of your business."

He was recovering from the shock out by the elevator, his voice deepening, and his eyes growing righteous again. It wouldn't be long before he was threatening to call security again, so I had to cut him off at the knees.

I came around the desk and moved a small reading lamp, sat on the desktop, my leg an inch from his. "Danny," I said, "if you were just having a tryst with her, you never would have let me out of the elevator. You have something huge to hide. Something unethical and illegal and capable of sending you to jail for the rest of your life. Now I don't know what that is yet, but I know how Desiree works, and she wouldn't waste five minutes on your flaccid genitalia if you weren't giving her something big in exchange." I leaned forward and loosened the knot on his tie, unbuttoned his collar. "So, tell me what it is."

His upper lip was speckled with sweat and his tight jowls had begun to sag. He said, "You're trespassing."

I raised an eyebrow. "That's the best you can come up with? Okay, Danny."

I got off the desk. He leaned back in his chair, pushing its wheels back from me, but I turned away from him and headed for the door. I looked back at him. "In five minutes when I call Trevor Stone to tell him that his lawyer is fucking his daughter, should I give him a message on your behalf?"

"You wouldn't."

"Wouldn't? I got pictures, Danny."

You gotta love the bluffs that work.

Daniel Griffin held up a hand and swallowed several times. He stood up so quickly the chair spun away from him, and then he placed his hands on his desk for a moment, sucked oxygen from the air.

"You work for Trevor?" he said.

"Used to," I said. "Not anymore. But I still have his number."

"Are you," he said, his voice rising, "loyal to him?"

"You're not," I said with a chuckle.

"Are you?"

I shook my head. "I don't like him and I don't like his daughter, and as far as I know both of them might want me dead by six o'clock tonight."

He nodded. "They're dangerous people."

"Yeah, Danny? Tell me something I don't know. What are you supposed to do for Desiree?"

"I . . ." He shook his head and walked to a small fridge in the corner. He bent by it, and I drew my gun, released the safety.

But all he pulled out was a bottle of Evian. He guzzled half of it, then wiped his mouth with the back of his hand. His eyes widened when he saw the gun. I shrugged.

"He's a mean, evil man and he's going to die," he said. "I have to think of the future. I have to think of who's going to handle his money when he's gone. Who's going to control the purse, if you will."

"Big purse," I said.

"Yes. One billion, one hundred and seventy-five million dollars at last count."

The figure rocked me a bit. There's the kind of money you can envision filling a truck or a bank vault. And then there's the kind of money that is too big for either.

"That's not a purse," I said. "That's a gross national product."

He nodded. "And it has to go somewhere when he dies."

"Jesus," I said. "You're going to alter his will."

His eyes dropped from mine and he stared out the window.

"Or you've altered it already," I said. "He changed his will after the attempt on his life, didn't he?"

He stared out at State Street and the back of City Hall Plaza and nodded.

"He cut Desiree out of it?"

Another nod.

"Who's the money go to now?"

Nothing.

"Daniel," I said. "Who's the money go to now?"

He waved his hand. "A variety of interests—
university endowments, libraries, medical research,
things like that."

"Bullshit. He's not that nice."

"Ninety-two percent of it goes into a private
trust in his name. I have power of attorney to release from that trust a certain percentage of interest
earned each year to the aforementioned medical research companies. The rest remains in the trust and
accrues."

"What medical research companies?"

He turned from the window. "Those specializing
in cryogenic research."

I almost laughed. "The crazy bastard is going to
freeze himself?"

He nodded. "Until there's a cure for his cancer.
And when he wakes, he'll still be one of the richest
men in the world because the interest on his money
alone will keep him current with inflation into the
year 3000."

"Wait a minute," I said. "If he's dead or frozen or
whatever, how's he keep an eye on his money?"

"How does he keep me or my successors from
stealing it?"

"Yes."

"Private accounting firm."

I leaned against the wall for a moment, took it all
in. "But, that private accounting firm only kicks
into action once he's dead or frozen. Right?"

He closed his eyes and nodded.

"And when does he intend to deep-freeze?"

"Tomorrow."

I laughed. It was so blatantly absurd.

"Don't laugh. He's crazy. He's not to be taken lightly, though. I don't believe in cryogenics. But what if I'm wrong and he's right, Mr. Kenzie? He'll dance on our graves."

"Not if you change the will," I said. "That's the one loophole in his plan, isn't it? Even if he checks the will before he climbs in his cooler or whatever the hell it is, you can still change or replace it with another, can't you?"

He sucked from the Evian bottle. "It's delicate, but possible."

"Brilliant. Where's Desiree now?"

"I have no idea."

"Okay. Grab your coat."

"What?"

"You're coming with me, Daniel."

"I'm doing no such thing. I have meetings. I have—"

"I have several bullets in my gun and they're calling their own meeting. Know what I mean?"

37

We hailed a cab on State Street and rode against the morning rush hour traffic down into Dorchester.

"How long have you worked for Trevor?" I said.

"Since 1970."

"More than a quarter of a century," I said.

He nodded.

"But you sold that out in a few hours last night for a touch of his daughter's flesh."

He reached down and straightened the crease in his trousers until the cuff of his pants settled just so on his gleaming shoes.

"Trevor Stone," he said and cleared his throat, "is a monster. He treats people like commodities. Worse than commodities. He buys, sells, and trades them, dumps them in the garbage when they're no longer of use to him. His daughter, I admit, I long thought to be his opposite. The first time we made love—"

"When was this?"

He straightened his tie. "Seven years ago."

"When she was sixteen."

He looked out at the gridlocked traffic on the other side of the expressway. "I thought she was a gift from heaven. A flawless, kind, caring beauty who would become everything her father wasn't. But as time wore on, I saw that she was acting. That's what she is, a better actor than her father. But no different. So, being an old man, and having lost my innocence a long time ago, I realigned my perspective on the situation and took what I could from it. She uses me, and I use her, and both of us pray for the demise of Trevor Stone." He smiled at me. "She may be no better than her father, but she's prettier and much more fun in bed."

Nelson Ferrare looked at me through bleary eyes and scratched himself through his Fruit of the Looms. Behind him, I could smell the stale sweat and spoiled-food aroma permeating his apartment like a fever.

"You want me to sit on this guy?"

Daniel Griffin looked terrified, but I don't think it was Nelson he feared yet, though he should have. It was Nelson's apartment.

"Yeah. Till midnight. Three hundred bucks."

He held out his hand and I put the bills in them.

He stepped back from the doorway and said, "Come on in, old man."

I pushed Daniel Griffin over the threshold and he stumbled into the living room.

"Handcuff him to something if you have to, Nelson. But don't hurt him, Even a little bit."

He yawned. "For three bills, I'll make him breakfast. Too bad I can't cook."

"This is outrageous!" Griffin said.

"At midnight, kick him loose," I said to Nelson. "I'll see you."

Nelson turned and shut the door.

As I walked down the hallway of his building, I heard his voice through the thin walls: "One simple rule of the house, old guy: You touch the remote control, I cut your hand off with an old saw."

I took the subway back downtown and picked up my personal car from the garage on Cambridge Street where I keep it stored. It's a 1963 Porsche I restored much in the same way Jay restored his Falcon—piece by piece over many years before it was even roadworthy. And after a time, it was the work, and not the result, that I felt a fondness for. As my father once said when he pointed out a building he'd helped construct before he'd become a fireman, "The building don't mean shit to me, but that brick there, Patrick? And that whole row on the third floor there? I put them there. The first fingers to ever touch them were mine. And they'll outlive me."

And they did. Work and its results always outlived those who labored at it as any Egyptian slave-ghost will tell you.

And maybe, I thought as I pulled the cover off my car, that's what Trevor can't accept. Because the little I knew of his businesses (and I could have been very wrong; they were so diversified), his stake in immortality was very slim. He didn't seem to have been much of a builder. He was a buyer and a seller and an exploiter, but El Salvadoran coffee beans and the profits they yielded weren't tangible once the coffee was drunk and the money spent.

What buildings bear your fingerprints, Trevor?

What lovers retain your face in their memory with joy or fondness?

What marks your time on this earth?

And who mourns your passing?

No one.

I kept a cell phone in the glove compartment and I used it to call Angie on the cell phone in the Crown Victoria. But she didn't answer.

I parked in front of my house and engaged the alarm, went upstairs, and sat around waiting.

I called her cell phone ten times in the next two hours, even checked my own phone to make sure the ringer button was in the "On" position. It was.

The battery could have died, I told myself.

Then she would have used the adapter and plugged it into the cigarette lighter.

Not if she was out of the car.

Then she would have called here.

Not if she didn't have time or wasn't near a phone.

I watched a few minutes of *Monkey Business* to get my mind off it, but even Harpo chasing women around the ocean liner and the prospect of the four Marx Brothers doing their Maurice Chevalier imitations to get off the boat with the singer's stolen passport wasn't enough to hold my concentration.

I turned off the TV and VCR, dialed the cell phone number again.

No answer.

That's what I got the rest of the afternoon. No

answer. Nothing but the ringing on the other end and the ringing in my head.

And the silence that followed. Loud, mocking silence.

38

The silence followed me as I drove back to Whittier Place for my six o'clock meeting with Desiree.

Angie wasn't just my partner. She wasn't just my best friend. And she wasn't just my lover. She was all those things, sure, but she was far more. Ever since we'd made love the other night, it had begun to dawn on me that what lay between us—what, in all probability had lain between us since we were children—wasn't just special; it was sacred.

Angie was where most of me began and all of me ended.

Without her—without knowing where she was or *how* she was—I wasn't merely half my usual self; I was a cipher.

Desiree. Desiree was behind the silence. I was sure of it. And as soon as I saw her, I was going to put a bullet in her kneecap and ask my questions.

But Desiree, a voice whispered, is smart. Remember what Angie said—Desiree always has an angle. If she was behind Angie's disappearance, if she had her tied up somewhere, she'd use her as a bargaining chip. She wouldn't have just killed her. There's no profit there. No gain.

I came down the expressway off-ramp for Storrow Drive and then swung right so I could loop around Leverett Circle and pull into Whittier Place. But before I reached the circle, I pulled over, engine idling, and put my hazards on for a minute, forced myself to take some breaths, to cool the broiling blood in my veins, to think.

The Celts, the voice whispered, remember the Celts, Patrick. They were crazy. They were hot-blooded. Your people, and they terrorized Europe in the century before Christ. No one would mess with them. Because they were insane and bloodthirsty and ran into battle painted blue with hard-ons. Everyone feared the Celts.

Until Caesar. Julius Caesar asked his men what was all this nonsense about these fearsome savages in Gaul and in Germany, in Spain and Ireland? Rome feared no one.

Neither do the Celts, his men answered.

Blind courage, Caesar said, is no match for intelligence.

And he sent fifty-five thousand men to meet over a quarter million Celts at Alesia.

And they came with blood in their eyes. They came naked and screaming with fury and hard-ons and complete and utter disregard for their own well-being.

And Caesar's battalions wiped them out.

By implementing precise tactical maneuvers, without any emotion whatsoever, Caesar's garrisons conquered the passionate, determined, fearless Celts.

As Caesar rode in his victory parade through the streets of Rome, he commented that he'd never met a braver leader than Vercingetorix, the commander of the Gallic Celts. And, maybe to show what he truly thought of simple bravery, Caesar underscored his point by brandishing the severed head of Vercingetorix throughout the course of the parade.

Brain, once again, conquered brawn. Minds subdued hearts.

To rush in like a Celt, shoot Desiree in the knee, and expect to get results, was stupid. Desiree was a tactician. Desiree was a Roman.

My raging blood chilled to ice as I sat in my idling car, the dark waters of the Charles rolling along on my right. My heartbeat slowed. The tremors in my hands disappeared.

This wasn't a fistfight, I told myself. Win a fistfight, all you are is bloody, your opponent slightly more so, but he's usually ready for another fight if the mood hits him.

This was war. Win at war, chop your opponent's head off. End of story.

"How are you?" Desiree said as she came out of Whittier Place, ten minutes late.

"Fine." I smiled.

She stopped by the car, appraised it with a whistle. "This is gorgeous. I wish it were warm enough to put the roof down."

"Me, too."

She ran her hands along the door before she opened it and got in, gave me a quick peck on the cheek.

"Where's Miss Gennaro?" She reached across and ran her fingers along the wood-finish steering wheel.

"She decided to stay in the sun a few more days."

"See? I told you. You wasted a free plane ticket."

We shot across to the expressway on-ramp, cut into the lane for Route 1 with several blaring horns going off behind us.

"I like the way you drive, Patrick. Very Bostonian."

"That's me," I said. "Beantown to the core."

"My God," she said. "Just listen to this engine! It sounds like a leopard's purr."

"That's why I bought it. I'm a sucker for leopard purrs."

She gave me a deep, throaty laugh. "I bet." She crossed her legs, leaned back in the seat. She wore a navy-blue cowl-neck cashmere over painted-on blue jeans and brown soft leather loafers. Her perfume smelled like jasmine. Her hair smelled like crisp apples.

"So," I said, "you been having fun since you've been back?"

"Fun?" She shook her head. "I've been holed up in that apartment since I landed. I was too afraid to stick my head out until you came." She pulled a pack of Dunhills from her purse. "Mind if I smoke?"

"No. I like the smell."

"An ex-smoker?" She pushed the dashboard lighter in.

"I prefer the term recovering nicotine addict."

We pulled through the Charlestown Tunnel and rode up toward the lights of the Tobin Bridge.

"I think indulging addictions has been given a bad rap," she said.

"Is that so?"

She lit her cigarette and sucked back on the tobacco with an audible hiss. "Absolutely. Everyone dies. Am I right?"

"As far as I know."

"So why not embrace the things that'll kill you anyway? Why single out certain things—heroin, alcohol, sex, nicotine, bungee jumping, whatever your predilection—for demonization when we hypocritically embrace cities which spew toxins and smog, eat rich food, hell, live in the late twentieth century in the most industrialized country on the planet?"

"You got a point."

"If I die from this," she held up the cigarette, "at least it was my choice. No excuses. And I had a hand—I had control—in my own demise. Beats getting hit by a truck while jogging to a vegetarians' seminar."

I smiled in spite of myself. "Never heard it put quite that way before."

We cruised up on the Tobin Bridge, and the span reminded me of Florida, the way the water seemed to physically drop from underneath us in a rush. But not just Florida, no. This was where Inez Stone had died, screaming as bullets entered her flesh and vital organs, as she looked into the face of madness and matricide, whether she was aware of the latter or not.

Inez. Had her death been part of the plan or hadn't it?

"So," Desiree said, "is my philosophy nihilistic?"

I shook my head. "Fatalistic. Marinated in skepticism."

She smiled. "I like that."

"Glad I could oblige."

"I mean, we all die," Desiree said and leaned forward in her seat. "Whether we want to or not. Just a simple fact of life."

And she reached over and dropped something soft into my lap.

I had to wait until I passed under a streetlight until I saw what it was because the fabric was so dark.

It was a T-shirt. It bore the words FURY IN THE SLAUGHTERHOUSE in white letters. It was ripped at the point where it would fall over the wearer's right rib cage.

Desiree dug a pistol into my testicles and leaned in to me until her tongue flicked along the outer edge of my ear.

"She's not in Florida," she said. "She's in a hole somewhere. She's not dead yet, but she will be if you don't do exactly what I say."

"I'll kill you," I whispered as the bridge peaked and began its curve toward the other side of the river.

"That's what all the boys say."

As we looped around Marblehead Neck, the ocean boiling and belting against the rocks below, I cleared images of Angie from my head for a moment, quelled the black clouds of worry that threatened to suffocate me.

"Desiree."

"That's my name." She smiled.

"You want your father dead," I said. "Fine. Makes a certain amount of sense."

"Thank you."

"For a sociopath."

"Such a sweet tongue."

"But your mother," I said. "Why'd she have to die?"

Her voice was thin and light. "You know how it is between mothers and daughters. All that pent-up jealousy. All the missed school plays and arguments over wire hangers."

"But really," I said.

She drummed her fingers on the barrel of the gun for a moment.

"My mother," she said, "was a beautiful woman."

"I know. I've seen pictures."

She snorted. "Pictures are bullshit. Pictures are isolated moments. My mother wasn't just physically beautiful, you dick. She was elegance incarnate. She was grace. She loved without reservation." She sucked in a breath.

"So, why'd she have to die?"

"When I was little, my mother took me downtown. A day for just the girls, she called it. We had a picnic in the Common, went to museums, had tea at the Ritz, rode the swan boats in the Public Garden. It was a perfect day." She looked out the window. "Around three o'clock, we came upon this child. He was my age—probably ten or eleven at the time. He was Chinese and crying because someone had thrown a rock from a passing school bus and hit him in the eye. And my mother, I'll never forget this, held him to her chest and wept with him. Silently.

The tears rolling off her cheekbones and the boy's blood staining her blouse. That was my mother, Patrick." She turned from the window. "She wept for strangers."

"And you killed her because of that?"

"I didn't kill her," she hissed.

"No?"

"Her car broke down, you fuck! Get it? That wasn't part of the plan. She wasn't supposed to be with Trevor. She wasn't supposed to die."

She coughed loudly into her fist, sucked a harsh, liquid breath back into her body.

"It was a mistake," I said.

"Yes."

"You loved her."

"*Yes.*"

"So her death hurt you," I said.

"More than you could possibly imagine."

"Good," I said.

"Good that she died, or good that her dying hurt me?"

"Both," I said.

The great cast-iron gates parted before us as we turned into Trevor Stone's driveway. I drove through the opening, and the gates closed behind me and my lights arced up ahead of us through the carefully manicured bushes and shrubs, curled left as the white gravel driveway snaked around an oval lawn with an enormous birdbath in its center, then broke gracefully to the right onto the main drive. The house lay a hundred yards up, and we passed through a row of white oak on either side, the towering trees standing proud and unyielding like sentries spaced at five-yard intervals.

When we reached the cul-de-sac at the end of the road, Desiree said, "Keep going. There," and pointed. I drove around the fountain and it lit up at the same time, yellow streams of light coursing through sudden eruptions of frothy water. A bronze nymph floated above it all, twisting in slow revolutions, dead eyes on a cherub's face watching me as I passed.

The road doglegged at the corner of the house and I followed it back through a stretch of pine to a converted barn.

"Park it there," Desiree said, and pointed at a clearing to the left of the barn.

I pulled over and shut off the engine.

She took the keys and got out of the car, pointing the gun at me through the windshield as I opened my door and stepped out into the night, the air twice as frigid as it had been in the city due to the wind screaming off the ocean.

I heard the unmistakable sound of a round ratcheting into a shotgun chamber, and turned my head, looked down the black barrel at Julian Archerson standing at the other end.

"Evening, Mr. Kenzie."

"Lurch," I said. "A pleasure as always."

In the dim light I could see a chrome cylinder sticking out of the left pocket of his topcoat. I got a closer look as my eyes adjusted to the darkness and realized it was an oxygen tank of some kind.

Desiree came around beside Julian and lifted a tube that hung off the tank, straightened the kinks in the tube until she extended a translucent yellow mask through the darkness.

She handed the mask to me and twisted the knob on the tank, and it hissed.

"Suck on this," she said.

"Don't be ridiculous."

Julian dug the shotgun muzzle into my jaw. "You don't have a choice, Mr. Kenzie."

"For Miss Gennaro," Desiree said in a sweet voice. "The love of your life."

"Slowly," I said as I took the mask.

"What's that?" Desiree said.

"That's how you're going to die, Desiree. Slowly."

I put the mask to my face and took a breath, immediately felt numbness tingle through my cheeks and fingertips. I took another one, felt a cloudiness invade my chest. I took a third, and everything went green, then black.

39

My first thought, as I swam back to consciousness, was that I was paralyzed.

My arms wouldn't move. My legs wouldn't
move. And not just the limbs themselves, but the
muscles.

I opened my eyes, blinked several times at a
dry crust that seemed to have formed over the
corneas. Desiree's face floated past, smiling. Then
Julian's chest. Then a lamp. Then Julian's chest
again. Then Desiree's face, still smiling.

"Hi," she said.

The room behind them began to take on
shapes, as if everything suddenly flew out of the
darkness toward me and stopped abruptly at their
backs.

I was in Trevor's study, in a chair by the front
left corner of the desk. I could hear the roar of
the sea behind me. And as the effects of my sleep
wore off, I could hear a clock ticking on my right.
I turned my head and looked at it. Nine o'clock.
I'd been out for two hours.

I looked down at my chest and saw nothing but

white. My arms were pinned against the side of the chair, my legs against the inside of the chair legs. I'd been bound with an entire sheet strapped over my chest and thighs and another over my lower legs. I couldn't feel any knots, and I realized both sheets were probably knotted at the back of the chair. And they were knotted tight. I was mummified, essentially, from the neck down, and no ligature marks or rope burns or handcuff abrasions would show on my body when it came time for the autopsy I was sure Desiree intended.

"No marks," I said. "Very good."

Julian tipped an imaginary hat to me. "Something I learned in Algeria," he said. "A long time ago."

"Well traveled," I said. "I like that in a Lurch."

Desiree came over and sat up on the desk, her hands under her thighs, legs swaying forward like a schoolgirl's.

"Hi," she said again, all sweetness and light.

"Hi."

"We're just waiting for my dad."

"Ah." I looked at Julian. "With Lurch here and the Weeble dead, who's your father's servant while he's out on the town?"

"Poor Julian," she said, "came down with the flu today."

"Sorry to hear that, Lurch."

Julian's lips twitched.

"So, Daddy had to call a private limousine service to take him into the city."

"Perish the thought," I said. "What will the neighbors say? My gosh."

She removed her hands from under her legs,

pulled the pack of Dunhills from her pocket and lit one. "You figured it out yet, Patrick?"

I tilted my head and looked up at her. "You shoot Trevor, shoot me, make it look like we shot each other."

"Something like that." She brought her left foot up onto the desk, tucked the right under her, watched me through the smoke rings she blew in my direction.

"The cops in Florida will vouch that I had some sort of personal vendetta or weird obsession with your father, paint me as a paranoid or worse."

"Probably." She tapped her ash on the floor.

"Jeez, Desiree, it's all working out for you."

She gave me a small bow. "It usually does, Patrick. Sooner or later. Price was supposed to be sitting where you are, but then he screwed up and I had to improvise. Then it was supposed to be Jay in that chair, but another couple of screwups and I had to improvise again." She sighed and ground her cigarette out on the desktop. "That's okay, though. Improvisation's one of my specialties."

She leaned back on the desk and gave me a broad smile.

"I'd clap," I said, "but I'm sort of incapacitated."

"It's the thought that counts," she said.

"Since we're sitting here without much to do before you murder your father and me, let me ask you something."

"Shoot, babe."

"Price took the money you two stole and hid it. Right?"

"Yes."

"But why'd you let him do that, Desiree? Why didn't you just torture the information out of him and kill him?"

"He was a pretty dangerous guy," she said, her eyebrows arched.

"Yeah, but come on. In the danger department, I bet you made him look like a sissy."

She leaned forward and looked at me with mild approval. She shifted again and crossed her legs up on the desk, held the ankles with her hands. "Yeah, in the end, I could have got the two million back within an hour if I felt like it. It would have been bloody, though. And Price's drug deal wasn't half bad, Patrick. If that ship hadn't sunk, he would have had a ten-million-dollar payday coming."

"And you would've killed him and taken the money the moment he collected."

She nodded. "Not bad, eh?"

"But then heroin started floating up on the beaches in Florida . . ."

"So the whole scam was null and void, yes." She lit another cigarette. "Then Daddy sent you and Clifton and Cushing down there, and Cushing and Clifton took Jay out of the equation, and I had to improvise once again."

"But you're so good at it, Desiree."

She smiled, her mouth open, the tip of her tongue running lightly under her upper teeth. She lowered her legs to the floor and came off the desk, walked around my chair several times, smoking, and looking down at me with a radiant sheen in her eyes.

She stopped and leaned against the desk again, her jade eyes holding my own.

I'm not sure how long we remained that way, staring into each other's eyes, waiting for the other to blink. I'd like to say that as I looked long and deep into Desiree's shimmering green eyes, I understood her. I'd like to say I recognized the nature of her soul, found the common link between the two of us, and therefore, among all human beings. I'd like to say all that, but I can't.

The longer I looked, the less I saw. Porcelain jade gave way to hints of nothing. And hints of nothing gave way to an essence of nothing. Except, maybe, naked greed, brazen wanting, the polished soul of a machine that knew only how to covet, and very little about anything else.

Desiree stabbed her cigarette out on the desk beside the other one, and dropped to her haunches in front of me. "Patrick, you know what sucks?"

"Besides your heart?" I said.

She smiled. "Besides that. What sucks is I kind of liked you. No man has ever rejected my advances before. Ever. And it turned me on actually. If we'd had the time, I would have gotten to you."

I shook my head. "Not a chance."

"Oh, no?" She came forward on her knees and laid her head on my lap. She turned her head onto her left cheek, looked up at me with her right eye. "I get to everyone. Just ask Jay."

"You got to Jay?" I said.

She nuzzled her cheek against my thighs. "I'd say so."

"So why were you stupid enough to say 'Fail-Safe' to me at the airport?"

She brought her head off my lap. "That's what tipped you off?"

"I was sitting on the fence about you since we met, Desiree, but that's what knocked me off it."

She clucked her tongue. "Well, good for Jay. Good for him. He set me up from the grave, didn't he?"

"Yes."

She leaned back on her haunches again. "Oh, well. Lot of good it did him. Or you." She stretched her torso and ran both hands through her hair. "I'm always prepared for contingencies, Patrick. Always. Something my father taught me. As much as I hate the prick, he taught me that. Always have a backup plan. Three, if necessary."

"My father taught me the same thing. Much as I hated the prick, as well."

She cocked her head to the right. "Really?"

"Oh, yeah, Desiree. Really."

"Is he bluffing, Julian?" She looked back over her shoulder.

Julian's impassive face twitched. "He's bluffing, dear."

"You're bluffing," she said to me.

"'Fraid not," I said. "Dear. Heard from your father's attorney today?"

Headlights arced through the house as tires crunched the gravel outside.

"That would be your father," Julian said.

"I know who it would be, Julian." She was staring at me, her jaw muscles moving almost imperceptibly.

I looked as deeply into her eyes as I'd look into the eyes of a lover. "You kill Trevor and me and make it look like we killed each other, it won't do you any good without an altered will, Desiree."

The front door opened.

"Julian!" Trevor Stone bellowed. "Julian! Where are you?"

Tires pulled away on the gravel outside and headed back down the drive toward the front gate.

"Where is he?" Desiree said.

"Who?" I said.

"Julian!" Trevor called

Julian moved toward the door.

"Stay," Desiree said.

Julian froze.

"Does he roll over and fetch bones and shit?" I said.

"Julian! Jesus Christ, man!" Trevor's decrepit footfalls drew closer on the marble floor outside.

"Where is Danny Griffin?" Desiree said.

"Not answering your calls, I take it."

She pulled her gun from underneath her sweater.

"Julian! In the name of God!" The heavy doors burst open and Trevor Stone stood there leaning on his walking stick, dressed in a tuxedo with a white silk scarf, his body trembling against the cane.

Desiree pointed her gun at him, her arm rock-steady as she knelt on the floor.

"Hi, Daddy," she said. "Long time, no see."

40

Trevor Stone carried himself with as much composure as I've ever seen in any man who had a gun pointed at him.

He glanced at his daughter as if he'd seen her just yesterday, glanced at the gun as if it were a gift he didn't much care for but wouldn't refuse, and walked into the room and headed for his desk.

"Hello, Desiree. The suntan becomes you."

She flipped her hair and tilted her head toward him. "You think?"

Trevor's green eyes flicked across Julian's face, then glanced my way. "And Mr. Kenzie," he said. "I see you returned from Florida no worse for wear."

"These sheets binding me to a chair notwithstanding," I said, "I'm peachy, Trevor."

He rested his hand on the desk as he came around behind it, then reached for the wheelchair by the windows and sat in it. Desiree pivoted on her knees, following him with the gun.

"So, Julian," Trevor said, his rich baritone

filling the large room, "you've chosen to side with youth, I see."

Julian crossed his hands in front of his waist, tilted his head toward the floor. "It was the most pragmatic option, sir. I'm sure you understand."

Trevor opened the ebony humidor on his desk and Desiree cocked the pistol.

"Just a cigar, my dear." He withdrew a Cuban the length of my calf, snipped the end off, and lit it. Small circles of smoke puffed from the fat coal as he sucked in his ruined cheeks repeatedly and got it going, and then a rich, almost oak-leaf smell permeated my nostrils.

"Hands where I can see them, Daddy."

"I wouldn't dream of doing otherwise," he said and leaned back in the chair, puffed a ring into the air above his head. "So, you've come to finish the job those three Bulgarians couldn't manage on the bridge last year."

"Something like that," she said.

He tilted his head and looked at her out of the corner of his eye. "No, it's exactly like that, Desiree. If your speech is nebulous, remember, your mind will appear to be so as well."

"Trevor Stone's Rules of Engagement," she said to me.

"Mr. Kenzie," he said, back to staring at the rings he exhaled, "have you sampled my daughter?"

"Daddy," Desiree said. "Really."

"No," I said. "Haven't had the pleasure. Which makes me unique in this room, I think."

His ruined lips formed their imitation of a smile.

"Ah, so Desiree's fantasy of our having a sexual history persists."

"You told me yourself, Daddy: If something works, stick with it."

Trevor winked at me. "I'm not without sin, but I do draw the line at incest." He turned his head. "And Julian, how did you find my daughter's technique in the bedroom? Was it satisfactory?"

"Quite," Julian said, and his face twitched.

"Better than her mother's?"

Desiree's head jerked around to look at Julian, then jerked back to Trevor.

"I wouldn't know about her mother's, sir."

"Come now." Trevor chuckled. "Don't be modest, Julian. For all we know, you're this child's father, not me."

Julian's hands tightened, and his feet parted slightly. "You're imagining things, sir."

"Am I?" Trevor turned his head and winked at me.

I felt like I was locked in a Noël Coward play that had been rewritten by Sam Shepard.

"You think this is going to work?" Desiree said. She rose off her knees. "Daddy, I am so beyond normal concepts of proper and improper sexual behavior, it's not even quantifiable." She stepped past me and came around the desk behind him. She leaned over his shoulders. She placed the muzzle of her gun against the left side of his forehead then drew it across to the right so hard the target sight left a thin line of blood. "If Julian were my biological father, so what?"

Trevor watched as a drop of blood fell from his forehead and landed on his cigar.

"Now, Dad," she said and nipped his left earlobe, "let's push you out into the center of the room where we can all be together."

Trevor puffed on his cigar as she pushed, trying to appear as casual as he had when he entered the room, but I could see that it was beginning to wear on him. Fear had found its way into his proud chest, into the cast of his eyes and the set of his ruined jaw.

Desiree pushed him around to the front of the desk until he was facing me, the two of us sitting in our chairs, wondering if we'd ever stand up again.

"How's it feel, Mr. Kenzie?" Trevor said. "Bound there, helpless, wondering which breath will be your last?"

"You tell me, Trevor."

Desiree left us and walked over to Julian and they whispered for a moment, her gun pointed straight at the back of her father's head.

"You're the wily type," Trevor said, leaning forward, his voice lowered. "Any suggestions?"

"Far as I can see, Trevor, you're fucked."

He gestured with his cigar. "As are you, boy."

"A little less so, though."

He raised his eyebrows at my mummified body. "Really? I think you're mistaken. But if the two of us put our heads together, why we might—"

"I knew a guy once," I said, "he molested his son, had his wife killed, caused a gang war in Roxbury and Dorchester which killed sixteen children at least."

"And?" Trevor said.

"And I liked him more than I like you," I said. "Not by much, mind you. I mean, he was a scumbag, you're a scumbag, it's sort of like having to choose between two types of crotch rot. But still, he was poor, no education, society had shown him in a million different ways how little a fuck it gave about him. But you, Trevor, you've had everything a man could want. And it wasn't enough. You still bought your wife like she was a sow at the county fair. You still took a baby you brought into the world and turned it into a monster. This guy I was talking about? He was responsible for the death of at least twenty people, that I know of. Probably a lot more. And I put him down like a dog. Because that's what he deserved. But you? With a calculator, I bet you couldn't add up all the people whose deaths you've been responsible for, whose lives you've destroyed or made unbearable over the years."

"So you'd put me down like a dog, Mr. Kenzie?" He smiled.

I shook my head. "No. More like a sand shark you catch when you're deep-sea fishing. I'd haul you onto the boat, club you until you were stunned. Then I'd open up your belly and toss you back into the water, watch as the bigger sharks came and ate you alive."

"My, my," he said. "Wouldn't that be a sight?"

Desiree crossed back to us. "Having fun, gentlemen?"

"Mr. Kenzie was just explaining to me the subtleties of Bach's Brandenburg Concerto Number Two in F major. He truly revolutionized my perception of it, darling."

She slapped his temple. "That's nice, Daddy."

"So, what are you planning to do with us?" he said.

"You mean after I kill you?"

"Well, I was wondering about that. I don't see why you would need to confer with my beloved servant, Mr. Archerson, if all was going according to plan. You're meticulous, Desiree, because I trained you to be so. If you needed to confer with Mr. Archerson, there must be a proverbial fly in the ointment." He looked at me. "Would it have something to do with the wily Mr. Kenzie?"

"Wily," I said. "That's twice now."

"It'll grow on you," he assured me.

"Patrick," Desiree said, "you and I do have some things to discuss, don't we?" She turned her head. "Julian, will you take Mr. Stone to the pantry and lock him in?"

"The pantry!" Trevor cried. "I love the pantry. All those canned goods."

Julian placed his hands on Trevor's shoulders. "You know my strength, sir. Don't make me use it."

"Wouldn't think of it," Trevor said. "To the canned goods, Julian. Posthaste."

Julian wheeled him out of the room and I heard the wheels squeak on the marble as they made their way past the grand staircase toward the kitchen.

"All those hams!" Trevor cried. "All those leeks!"

Desiree straddled me and placed the gun against my left ear. "Here we are."

"Isn't it romantic?"

"About Danny," she said.

"Yes?"

"Where is he?"

"Where's my partner?"

She smiled. "In the garden."

"The garden?" I said.

She nodded. "Buried up to her neck." She looked out the window. "Gosh, I hope it doesn't snow tonight."

"Dig her out," I said.

"No."

"Then kiss Danny good-bye."

Knives danced in her irises. "Let me guess—unless you make a phone call by a certain time, he's dead, blah, blah, blah."

I looked at the clock over her shoulder as she shifted her weight on my thighs. "Actually, no. He'll be getting a bullet in his head in about thirty minutes regardless."

Her face sagged along the jawline for just a moment and then her hand tightened in my hair and the gun dug into my ear so hard I half expected it to pop out the other side. "Unless you make a phone call," she said.

"No. A phone call won't cut it because the guy holding him doesn't have a phone. I either show up at his door in thirty—no, twenty-nine—minutes, or we have one less lawyer in the world. All in all, who's going to miss a lawyer?"

"And where's that leave you if he dies?"

"Dead," I said. "Which is where I'm going to be anyway."

"Have you forgotten your partner?" She cocked her head toward the windows.

"Oh, come on, Desiree. You've already killed her."

I looked in her eyes as she answered.

"No, I haven't."

"Prove it."

She laughed and leaned back on my thighs. "Fuck you, buddy." She wagged a finger in my face. "Your desperation's showing, Patrick."

"So's yours, Desiree. You lose that lawyer, you lose it all. Kill your father, kill me, you've still got only two million. And we both know that's not enough for you." I tilted my head so the gun slipped from my ear, then nuzzled the slide with my cheekbone. "Twenty-eight minutes," I said. "After that, you'll go through the rest of your life knowing how close you were to over one billion dollars. And watching as other people spend it."

The butt of the gun hit the top of my head so hard the air in the room turned scarlet for a moment and everything spun.

Desiree came off my thighs and slapped me across the face with her open hand. "You think I don't know you?" she screamed. "Huh? You think I don't—"

"I think you're short a lawyer, Desiree. That's what I think."

Another slap, this one with nails trailing after it that tore through the flesh over my left cheekbone.

She drew back on the hammer of the gun and placed the muzzle between my eyebrows and screamed in my face, her mouth a gaping hole of furious, disrupted insolence. Spittle boiled at the corners of her mouth, and she screamed again, her index finger turning deep pink as it curled around the trigger. The shock of her screams, the violent residue of them, eddied around my skull and burned my ears.

"You will fucking die," she said in a wet, ragged voice.

"Twenty-seven minutes," I said.

Julian came bursting through the doors and she pointed the gun at him.

He held up his hands. "A problem, miss?"

"How fast can you drive to Dorchester?" she said.

"Thirty minutes," he said.

"You have twenty. We're going to show Mr. Kenzie his partner in the garden." She looked down at me. "Then you, Patrick, are going to give us your friend's address."

"Julian'll never get through the door alive."

She raised the gun over my head, then paused halfway through her strike. "Let Julian worry about that," she hissed. "The address for a look at your partner. Deal?"

I nodded.

"Untie him."

"Dear?"

"Don't 'dear' me, Julian." She bent by the back of my chair. "Untie him."

Julian said, "This isn't wise."

"Julian, by all means tell me what my options are."

Julian didn't have an answer for that.

I felt the pressure leave my chest first. Then my legs. The sheets fell away and spread across the floor in front of me.

Desiree knocked me out of the chair by pistol-whipping the back of my skull. She crammed the muzzle into the side of my neck. "Let's go."

Julian took a flashlight off the top of a bookcase

and pushed the French doors open onto the back lawn. We followed him out as he turned left, the light dancing across the grass ahead of him in a halo.

With Desiree gripping the back of my head and her gun against my neck, I was forced to bend to her height as we stepped off the lawn and followed a short pathway that led around the corner of a shed and an overturned wheelbarrow, broke through a thicket of trees and out into the garden.

It was, in keeping with the rest of the place, enormous—at least the size of a baseball diamond, fringed on three sides by frosted hedges four feet high. We stepped over a plastic tarp rolled up in front of the entrance, and Julian's flashlight bounced over furrows of iced dirt and the pikes of grass hardy enough to survive the winter. A sudden movement, low and to our right, caught our eyes, and Desiree stopped me with a yank to my head. The halo light jerked right then back to the left and an emaciated hare, its fur spiked by the cold, jumped through the circle of light and then vaulted off into the hedges.

"Shoot it," I said to Desiree. "It might have some money."

"Shut up." She said, "Julian, hurry up."

"Dear."

"Don't call me 'dear.' "

"We have a problem, dear."

He stepped back and we looked past him at the circle of light shining into an empty hole about five and a half feet deep and a foot and a half square.

The hole might have been tight and neat once, but someone had made an awful mess coming back out of it. Trails of dirt deeper than rake marks were ripped through the earth, and soil had been spewed in a wide radius around the hole. Someone hadn't just been desperate pulling herself out of that hole. She'd been angry.

Desiree looked left, then right. "Julian."

"Yes?" He peered down at the hole.

"How long since you last checked on her?"

Julian consulted his watch. "At least an hour."

"An hour."

Julian said, "She could have reached a phone by now."

Desiree grimaced. "Where? The nearest house is four hundred yards away, and the owners are in Nice for the winter. She's covered in dirt. She's—"

"In this house," Julian hissed, looking back over his shoulder at the mansion. "She could be inside *this* house."

Desiree shook her head. "She's still out here. I know it. She's waiting for her boyfriend. Aren't you?" She called to the darkness, "Aren't you?"

Something rustled to our left. The sound might have come from the hedges but it was hard to be sure with the surf raging just twenty yards away on the other side of the garden.

Julian bent by a row of tall hedges. "I don't know," he said slowly.

Desiree pointed her gun to her left and let go of my hair. "The floodlights. We can turn on the floodlights, Julian."

"I really don't know about this," Julian said.

A whisper of wind or surf noise curled against my ear.

"Goddammit," Desiree said. "How could she have—?"

And something made the sort of squishing sound a shoe makes when it steps in a puddle of icy slush.

"Oh, my," Julian said and shone the flashlight down on his own chest at the two shiny blades of garden shears that protruded from his sternum.

"Oh, my," he said again and stared at the wooden handles of the shears as if waiting for them to explain themselves.

Then the flashlight dropped and he pitched forward. The blade points popped out through his back and he blinked once, his chin in the dirt, then sighed. Then nothing.

Desiree turned the gun toward me but it popped out of her hand as the handle of a hoe smashed into her wrist.

She said, "What?" and turned her head to her left as Angie stepped out of the darkness covered in dirt from head to toe and punched Desiree Stone so hard in the center of her face that I'm sure she was well into dreamland before her body hit the ground.

41

I stood by the shower in the downstairs guest bathroom as the water sprayed across Angie's body and
the last of the dirt sluiced down her ankles and
swirled into the drain. She ran a bath sponge along
her left arm, and the soap dripped down along her
elbow and hung there for a moment in long tear-
drops before falling to the marble basin. Then she
went to work on the other arm.

She must have washed each part of her body
four times since we'd come in here, but somehow
I was still entranced.

"You broke her nose," I said.

"Yeah? You see any shampoo in here?"

I used a facecloth to open the medicine cabinet.
I wrapped the cloth around a small vial of shampoo and squirted some into my palm, walked back
to the shower.

"Turn your back to me."

She did, and I leaned in and rubbed the shampoo into her hair, felt the wet tangles envelop my
fingers, the soap churn up through the roots as
my fingers massaged her scalp.

"Feels very nice," she said.

"No kidding."

"How bad's it look?" She leaned forward and I pulled my hands from her hair as she raised her arms and scrubbed her hair with more force than I'd ever use on my own hair if I intended to reach my forties with it still attached to my head.

I rinsed the shampoo off my hands in the sink. "What?"

"Her nose."

"Bad," I said. "Like there's three of them all of a sudden."

I came back to the shower as she tilted her head back under the water and the white foamy mixture of soap and water poured between her shoulder blades and cascaded down her back.

"I love you," she said, her eyes closed, head tilted back to the spray, her hands wiping the water away from her temples.

"Yeah?"

"Yeah." She threw her head forward and reached for the towel as I put it in her hand.

I leaned in and shut off the water and she wiped her face, blinked her eyes open and found mine. She sniffed at water in her nose and wiped her neck with the towel.

"When Lurch dug the hole, he dug it too deep. So when he threw me in there, my foot hit a rock sticking out of the wall of dirt on the way down. About six inches above the bottom. And I had to tense every muscle in my body and keep my foot on this little ledge. And it was hard. Because I was looking up at this prick shoveling dirt on me with absolutely no emotion in his face." She lowered the towel from her breasts toward her waist. "Turn around."

I turned around, faced the wall as she dried some more of herself.

"Twenty minutes. That's how long it took him to fill the hole. And he made sure I was packed in tight. At least at the shoulders. Didn't even blink when I spit in his face. Do my back?"

"Sure."

I turned around and she handed me the towel as she stepped out of the shower. I ran the thick terry cloth over her shoulders and then down along the muscles of her back as she twisted her hair in both hands and pulled it up against the back of her head.

"So, even though I was on this little shelf, there was still a good bit of dirt below me. And at first I couldn't move, and I got terrified, but then I remembered what allowed me to stand on that rock with one foot for twenty minutes while Mr. Walking Dead buried me alive."

"What was that?"

She turned in my arms. "You." She slid her tongue over mine for a moment. "Us. You know. This." She patted my chest and reached behind me, took the towel back. "And I moved around and twisted and more dirt fell below my feet and I kept squirming and, oh, three hours later, I started making some progress."

She smiled and I kissed her, my lips meeting teeth, but I didn't care.

"I was scared," she said, draping her arms across my shoulders.

"I'm sorry."

She shrugged. "Wasn't your fault. My fault for not picking up Lurch on my tail this morning while I tailed Desiree."

We kissed and my hand planed through some beads of water I'd missed on her back and I wanted to pull her body so tight it would either disappear into mine or I'd disappear into hers.

"Where's the bag?" she said when we finally broke the embrace.

I lifted it from the floor of the bathroom. Inside were her dirty clothes and the handkerchief we'd used to wipe her prints from the handles of the hoe and the garden shears. She tossed the towel in and I added the facecloth, and then she took a sweatshirt from the small pile of Desiree's clothes I'd placed on the toilet seat and put it on. She followed that with a pair of jeans and socks and tennis shoes.

"Sneakers are a half size too big, but everything else fits fine," she said. "Now let's go deal with these mutants."

I followed her out of the bathroom, trash bag in hand.

I pushed Trevor into the study as Angie went upstairs to check on Desiree.

We stopped by the front of the desk and he watched as I used another handkerchief to wipe down the sides of the chair where I'd been bound.

"Removing any trace of yourself from the house tonight," he said. "Very interesting. Now why would you do that? And the dead valet—I assume he's dead?"

"He's dead."

"How will he be explained?"

"I really don't care. They won't link us to it, though."

"Wily," he said. "That's you all over, my young man."

"Relentless, too," I said. "Don't forget why you hired us."

"Oh, sure. But 'wily' has such a ring to it. Don't you think?"

I leaned against the desk, hands crossed over my lap and looked down at him. "You do the wacky old coot imitation very well when it serves you, Trevor."

He waved at the air with the third of his cigar that still remained. "We all need our bits of shtick to fall back on every now and then."

I nodded. "It's almost endearing."

He smiled.

"But it's not really."

"No?"

I shook my head. "You have far too much blood on your hands for that."

"We all have blood on our hands," he said. "Do you remember some time back when it became fashionable to throw away Krugerrands and boycott all the products coming out of South Africa?"

"Of course."

"People wanted to feel good about themselves. What's a Krugerrand after all in the face of such an injustice as apartheid? Yes?"

I yawned into my fist.

"Yet at the same time that the beautiful, righteous American public boycotts South Africa or fur or whatever they'll boycott or protest tomorrow, they turn a blind eye to the processes which provide them coffee from Central or South America, clothing from Indonesia or Manila, fruit from the Far East, just about any product imported from China." He drew back on his cigar and stared through the smoke at me. "We know how these governments work, how they deal with dissent, how many employ slave labor, what they do to anyone who threatens their profitable arrangements with American companies. And we don't just turn a blind eye, we actively encourage it. Because you want your soft shirts, you want your coffee, and your high-top sneakers and your canned fruit, and your sugar. And people like me get it for you. We prop up these governments and keep our labor costs low and pass the savings on to you." He smiled. "And isn't that good of us?"

I raised my good hand and brought it down on my thigh several times, made the exact noise I'd make clapping both hands together.

He held his smile and puffed his cigar.

But I kept clapping. I clapped until my thigh began to sting and the heel of my palm grew numb. I clapped and clapped, filling the big room with the sound of flesh hitting flesh until Trevor's eyes lost their gaiety and his cigar hung from his hand and he said, "All right. You can stop now."

But I kept clapping, my dead gaze fastened on his dead face.

"I said enough, young man."

Clap, clap, clap, clap, clap, clap, clap.

"Will you stop that annoying noise?"

Clap, clap, clap, clap, clap, clap.

He rose from his chair and I used my foot to push him back into it. I leaned in and increased the tempo and the force of my hand against my flesh. He closed his eyes tight. I clenched my fist and hammered it on the arm of his wheelchair, up and down, up and down, up and down, up and down, five beats per second, over and over. And Trevor's eyelids clenched tighter.

"Bravo," I said eventually. "You're the Cicero of the robber barons, Trevor. Congratulations."

He opened his eyes.

I leaned back on the desk. "I don't care right now about the labor organizer's daughter you chopped into pieces. I don't care how many missionaries and nuns lay in shallow graves with bullets in the backs of their heads because of your orders or the politics you entrenched in your banana republics. I don't even care that you bought your wife and probably made every moment of her life a living hell."

"Then what do you care about, Mr. Kenzie?"

He raised the cigar to his lips and I slapped it off his face, let it smolder in the rug at my feet.

"I care about Jay Becker and Everett Hamlyn, you useless piece of shit."

He blinked at the drops of sweat forming on his eyelashes. "Mr. Becker betrayed me."

"Because to do otherwise would have been a mortal sin."

"Mr. Hamlyn had decided to call several authorities and report my dealings with Mr. Kohl."

"Because you destroyed a business it took him his entire life to build."

He removed a handkerchief from the inside

pocket of his dinner jacket and coughed heavily into it for a minute.

"I'm dying," he said.

"No you're not," I said. "If you truly thought you were going to die, you wouldn't have killed Jay. You wouldn't have killed Everett. But if either of them hauled you into court, you couldn't climb into your cryogenic chamber, could you? And by the time you were able, your brain would be gone, your organs completely shot, and freezing you would have been a waste of time."

"I'm dying," he repeated.

"Yeah," I said, "now you are. And so what, Mr. Stone?"

"I have money. You name your price."

I stood up and ground my heel on his cigar.

"My price is two billion dollars."

"I only have one."

"Oh, well," I said and pushed him out of the study toward the stairs.

"What are you going to do?" he said.

"Less than you deserve," I said. "But more than you're ready for."

42

We climbed the grand staircase slowly, Trevor leaning on the railing and taking halting steps, his breathing labored.

"I heard you come in tonight and watched you walk across your study," I said. "Your steps were a lot surer then."

He gave me the tortured face of a martyr. "It comes in spurts," he said. "The pain."

"You and your daughter," I said, "you never give up, do you?" I smiled and shook my head.

"To yield is to die, Mr. Kenzie. To bend is to break."

"To err is human, to forgive is divine. We could keep going with this for hours. Come on. Your turn."

He struggled up to the landing.

"Left," I said and handed him back his walking stick.

"In the name of God," he said. "What are you going to do with me?"

"At the end of the hall, take a right."

* * *

The mansion was built so that its back faced east. Trevor's study and his recreation room on the first floor looked out at the sea. On the second floor, the master bedroom and Desiree's room did the same.

On the third floor, however, only one room faced the water. Its windows and walls could be removed, and in the summer a rail would be placed around the edges of the parquet floor, the slats in the ceiling removed to open up to the sky overhead, and hardwood squares fitted across the floor to protect the parquet. I'm quite sure it was no easy task to break this room down every sunny summer day, nor to put it back together and protect it from inclement weather at whatever time of night Trevor Stone chose to retire, but then, he didn't have to worry about that. Lurch and the Weeble had to, I assumed, or whatever servants had been their servants.

In the winter, the room was laid out like a French drawing room with gilded Louis XIV chairs and chaises; delicate, embroidered settees and divans; fragile gold-encrusted tea tables; and paintings of bewigged noblemen and noblewomen discussing opera or the guillotine or whatever the French discussed in the numbered days of their doomed aristocracy.

"Vanity," I said, looking at Desiree's pulpy, broken nose and Trevor's ruined lower face, "destroyed the French upper class. It triggered the revolution and sent Napoleon into Russia. Or so the Jesuits told me." I glanced at Trevor. "Am I wrong?"

He shrugged. "A bit reductive, but it's not far off."

He and Desiree were tied to their chairs on either end of the room, each a good twenty-five yards from the other. Angie was off in the west wing of the first floor, gathering supplies.

Desiree said, "I'll need a doctor for my nose."

"We're a little short on plastic surgeons at the moment."

"Was it a bluff?" she said.

"Which?"

"About Danny Griffin."

"Yeah. Total bluff."

She blew at a strand of hair that had fallen in her face and nodded to herself.

Angie came back into the room and together we cleared all the furniture to the sides, left a wide-open swath of parquet between Desiree and her father.

"You measure the room?" I asked Angie.

"Absolutely. It's exactly twenty-eight yards long."

"I'm not sure I could throw a football twenty-eight yards. How far is Desiree's chair from the wall?"

"Six feet."

"Trevor's?"

"The same."

I looked at her hands. "Nice gloves."

She held them up. "You like 'em? They're Desiree's."

I held up my good hand, also gloved. "Trevor's. Calfskin, I think. Very soft and supple."

She reached into her purse and pulled out two pistols. One was an Austrian Glock 17 nine-millimeter. The other was a German Sig Sauer P226 nine-millimeter. The Glock was light and black. The Sig Sauer was silver aluminum alloy and slightly heavier.

"There were so many to choose from in the gun

cabinet," Angie said, "but these seemed the best for our purposes."

"Clips?"

"The Sig holds fifteen. The Glock holds seventeen."

"And one each in the chamber, of course."

"Of course. But the chambers are empty."

"What in God's name are you doing?" Trevor said.

We ignored him.

"Who's stronger, you think?" I said.

She looked at them both. "It's a toss-up. Desiree's young, but Trevor's got a lot of strength in those hands."

"You take the Glock."

"Pleasure." She handed me the Sig Sauer.

"Ready?" I said as I pressed the butt of the Sig Sauer in between my bad arm and my chest, worked the slide with my good hand, and jacked a round into the chamber.

She pointed the Glock at the floor and did the same. "Ready."

"Wait!" Trevor screamed as I crossed the floor, the gun extended and pointing directly at his head.

Outside, the surf roared, and the stars burned.

"No!" Desiree screamed as Angie crossed the floor toward her, gun extended.

Trevor bucked against the ropes that bound him to the chair. He jerked his head left, then right, then left.

And I kept coming.

I could hear the hammering of Desiree's chair on the parquet floor as she did the same, and the room seemed to shrink around Trevor as my footfalls grew closer. His face rose and expanded over the target sight; his eyes rocketed from side to side. Sweat poured from his hair and his ruined cheeks spasmed. His milky white lips curled back against his teeth and he howled.

I stepped up to his chair and put the gun against the tip of his nose.

"How's it feel?"

"No," he said. "Please."

"I said, 'How's it feel?'" Angie yelled at Desiree from the other side of the room.

"Don't!" Desiree screamed. "Don't!"

I said, "I asked you a question, Trevor."

"I—"

"How does it feel?"

His eyes darted on either side of the barrel as red veins erupted across the corneas.

"Answer me."

His lips blubbered then clenched and the veins in his neck bulged.

"It feels," he screamed, "like shit!"

"Yes, it does," I said. "That's how Everett Hamlyn felt when he died. Like shit. That's how Jay Becker felt. That's how your wife and a six-year-old girl you had cut up and thrown into a vat of coffee beans felt. Like shit, Trevor. Like nothing."

"Don't shoot me," he said. "Please. Please." And tears rolled from his vacant eyes.

I removed the gun. "I'm not going to shoot you, Trevor."

As he watched in amazement, I dropped the magazine from the butt into my sling. I pressed the gun in against my injured wrist and worked the slide, ejected the live shell from the chamber. I bent and picked it up and placed it in my pocket.

Then as Trevor's confusion grew, I pushed down on the slide lock and removed the slide from the top of the frame and dropped that into my sling. I reached into the frame and removed the spring above the barrel. I held it up for Trevor to see, then dropped it too into my sling. Lastly, I removed the barrel itself, added it to the other pieces.

"Five pieces," I said to Trevor. "Total. The clip, the slide, the spring, the barrel, and the gun frame. I'm assuming you're adept at field-stripping your weapons?"

He nodded.

I turned my head, called to Angie, "How's Desiree with the field-stripping concept?"

"I believe Daddy taught her well."

"Wonderful." I turned back to Trevor. "As I'm sure you know, the Glock and the Sig Sauer are identical weapons in terms of field stripping."

He nodded. "I'm aware of that."

"Bitchin'." I smiled and turned away from him. I counted off fifteen paces as I walked, stopped and removed the gun pieces from my sling. I placed them neatly on the floor, spaced out in a straight line.

Then I crossed the floor to Angie and Desiree. I stood at Desiree's chair and turned back, counted off another fifteen paces from her chair. Angie came up beside me, and placed all five pieces of the disassembled Glock on the floor in a straight line.

We walked back to Desiree, and Angie untied

her hands from the back of the chair, then bent and tightened the knots around her ankles.

Desiree looked up at me, choosing to breathe heavily through her mouth instead of her ruined nose.

"You're crazy," she said.

I nodded. "You want your father dead. Correct?"

She turned her face away from me, looked at the floor.

"Hey, Trevor," I called. "You still want your daughter dead?"

"With every breath I have left," he called.

I looked down at Desiree and she tilted her head, looked up at me through hooded lids and the honey hair that had fallen in her face.

"Here's the situation, Desiree," I said as Angie went and untied Trevor's arms and checked the knots on his ankles. "You're each bound at the ankles. Trevor a little less tightly than you, but not much. I figure he's a little slower on his feet so I gave him a hair of an edge." I pointed down the long, polished floor. "There are the guns. Get to them, assemble them, and do what you will with them."

"You can't do this," she said.

"Desiree, 'can't' is a conception of morality. You should know that. We *can* do whatever we put our minds to. You're living proof."

I walked to the center of the room, and Angie and I stood there, looking back at them as they flexed their hands and got ready.

"If either of you gets the bright idea to join forces and come after us," Angie said, "we'll be on our way to the *Boston Tribune* newsroom. So don't waste your time. Whichever one of you lives through this—if either of you does—would be best served getting on a plane." She nudged me. "Anything to add?"

I watched the two of them as they wiped their palms on their thighs, flexed their fingers some more, bent toward the ropes at their ankles. The genetic resemblance was obvious in their body movements, but it was deepest and most glaringly apparent in those jade eyes of theirs. What lived in there was greedy and recalcitrant and without shame. It was primordial and knew more about the stink of caves than the airy leisure of this room.

I shook my head.

"Have fun in hell," Angie said and we walked out of the room and locked the doors behind us.

We headed straight down the servants' stairwell and came out by a small door that led off one corner of the kitchen. Above us, something scratched the floor repeatedly. And then there was a thump, followed instantly by another from the other end.

We let ourselves out and followed the path along the back lawn as the sea grew still and quiet.

I took the keys I'd taken back from Desiree as we wound past the garden and the reconverted barn and stopped at my Porsche.

It was dark out, but there was a glow shining over the night from the stars above, and we stood by my car and looked up at it. Trevor Stone's massive home shimmered in the glow, and I looked out at the flat swell of dark water to the place where it met the horizon and the sky.

"Look," Angie said and pointed as a white asterisk of light shot across the dark sky, trailing embers, lunging toward a point beyond our view, but not making it. It shorted out two thirds of the way there and imploded into nothing as several stars around it seemed to watch without interest.

The wind that had been screaming off the ocean when I arrived had died. The night was impossibly still.

The first shot sounded like a firecracker.

The second sounded like communion.

We waited, but nothing replaced the gunshots but silence and the distant lapping of tired waves.

I opened Angie's door and she climbed in, reached across, and pushed mine open as I came around.

We backed out and turned around, drove past the lighted fountain and the oak sentries, around the short minilawn with the frozen birdbath.

As the white gravel sucked under my grille, Angie produced a boxy remote control she'd taken from the house and pressed a button, and the great cast-iron gates with the family crest and the letters TS in the center parted like arms bidding us welcome or farewell, both gestures often seeming the same, depending on your perspective.

EPILOGUE

We didn't hear what had happened until we got back from Maine.

The night we left Trevor's we drove straight up the coast to Cape Elizabeth and checked into a small bungalow overlooking the ocean at a hotel that was surprised to see just about anyone up there before the spring thaw.

We didn't read newspapers or watch TV or do much of anything except put up the Do Not Disturb sign and order room service and lie in bed in the morning and watch the late winter whitecaps churn in the Atlantic.

Desiree had shot her father in the stomach, and he'd fired a round through her chest. They lay there facing each other on the parquet floor as the blood leaked from their bodies and the surf lapped at the foundation of the home they'd shared for twenty-three years.

Police were said to be baffled by both the dead valet in the garden and evidence that both father and daughter had been bound to chairs before they killed each other. The limo driver who dropped Trevor back at the house that night was questioned and released, and police could find no evidence that anyone but the victims had been in the house that night.

Also during the week we were gone, Richie Colgan's series on Grief Release and the Church of Truth and Revelation began to appear. The Church immediately filed suit against the *Tribune* and Richie, but no judge would impose an injunction on the story, and by the end of the week, Grief Release had temporarily closed its doors in several locations across New England and the Midwest.

No matter how hard he tried, though, Richie never discovered who the faces and power behind P. F. Nicholson Kett were, and Kett himself could not be found.

But we didn't know any of that in Cape Elizabeth.

We knew only each other and the sounds of our voices and the taste of champagne and the warmth of our flesh.

We talked about nothing of any import, and it was the best conversation I'd had in a long time. We looked at each other for long periods of charged, erotic silence, and often broke out laughing at the same time.

In the trunk of my car one day, I found a book of Shakespeare's sonnets. The book had been a gift from an FBI agent with whom I'd worked last year on the Gerry Glynn case. Special Agent Bolton had given it to me while I was locked in the throes of depression. He told me it would provide comfort. I didn't believe him back then, and I tossed it in my trunk. In Maine, though, while Angie showered or slept, I read most of the poems, and though I'd never been a big fan of poetry, I took a liking to Shakespeare's words, the sensuous flow of his language. He certainly seemed to know an awful lot more than I did—about love, loss, human nature, everything really.

Sometimes at night, we'd bundle up in the clothes we'd bought in Portland the day after we arrived, and let ourselves out through the back door of our bungalow onto the lawn. We'd huddle together against the cold and work our way down to the beach, sit on a rock overlooking the dark sea, and take as full a measure as possible of the beauty laid out before us under a pitch-black sky.

The ornament of beauty, Shakespeare wrote, is suspect.

And he was right.

But beauty itself, unadorned and unaffected, is sacred, I think, worthy of our awe and our loyalty.

Those nights by the sea, I'd take Angie's hand in mine and raise it to my lips. I'd kiss it. And sometimes as the sea raged and the darkness in the sky deepened, I'd feel awe. I'd feel humbled.

I'd feel perfect.

Gaby Gerster / © Diogenes Verlag

About the Author

DENNIS LEHANE is the author of thirteen novels—including the *New York Times* bestsellers *Live by Night*; *Moonlight Mile*; *Gone, Baby, Gone*; *Mystic River*; *Shutter Island*; and *The Given Day*—as well as *Coronado*, a collection of short stories and a play. He grew up in Boston, Massachusetts, and now lives in California with his family.